POLITICS AND THE GARGERYS

POLITICS AND THE GARGERYS

HUGH SOCKETT

Waterside Productions

ISBN-13: 978-1-958848-95-1 print edition
ISBN-13: 978-1-958848-96-8 e-book edition

Waterside Productions

2055 Oxford Ave
Cardiff, CA 92007
www.waterside.com

For Justin and Jonathan

TABLE OF CONTENTS

INTRODUCTION

Life for human beings is the continuing challenge of how to match the resources of the planet with human needs and wants. Such a challenge requires governance, which begets politics in systems of government, sophisticated or not.

Politics attracts the talents of men of ambition, worthy or unworthy determined either by the desire to serve a community of by a lust for self-aggrandizement, and often an uncertain mixture of the two manifest in many an individual. In *Politics and the Gargerys*, it is the desire to serve that moves two wounded officers from campaigns on the North-West Frontier, borne of reflections on their part in warfare, that human phenomenon which represents at bottom a struggle for power and with it governance. War is, after all, the continuation of politics by other means.

In this era, as women are formally excluded from politics, they find other ways to realize their ambitions. Dickens writes in the first half of the century and includes few examples of powerful women. Miss Havisham is an eccentric: Joe Gargery's tyrannical first wife is given short shrift and even Betsy Trotwood seems more of a caricature. In this book, however every woman is, in the modern phrase, empowered. For although literature provided avenues for women of talent to display excellence, the quest for the franchise breaks open the question of women's status, not just in the polity, but more generally in human life. Indeed there was a mood among women that a drastic change was in the air, and their political ambition found different outlets. Hannah (née Gargery) supports her husband's work in Ireland. Clara, Malcolm Gargery's wife brings her children to South Africa where he meets Emily Hobhouse, a highly controversial campaigner for improved conditions in the British concentration camps. Angharad Llewellyn inherited a fortune from her Australian sheep-farmer husband but emerges as a munificent philanthropist for miners' families caught up in the regular catastrophes in the pits.

So politics is not merely the arts and crafts of elected officials, but also of men and women who serve their communities in what one would now call civil society. Sadly the political and military cataclysms of the twentieth century are just around the corner.

My gratitude to my friend John O'Connor is unbounded. I am in debt to his wisdom, cautions, and meticulous attention to the manu-script, indeed as he has done through both trilogies. As ever, I have had wonderful support from my wife, Ann.

Leesburg, 2022

1902

I

"They just made a mistake," whispered Mary.

"What do you mean?" Asked Hamish.

"The Choir should have waited for the King's arrival before playing that psalm."

"How do you know?"

"Look at the program, Hamish, 'I was glad when they said unto me,' comes after the King is in front of the Archbishop, but they have just sung it and the King is still not visible."

"I don't suppose the King will notice."

"Perhaps not, but I am sure Queen Alexandra will."

Sir Hamish and Mary MacDonald had been sitting for two hours in Westminster Abbey among the ranks of Appeal Court and High Court judges awaiting the arrival of Edward VII as King and Emperor of India for his Coronation. It was now August 9th, 1902, and the ceremony had been originally planned for June 25th. Unfortunately the King fell ill with perityphlitis three days before the event which necessitated the removal of the appendix to his stomach, hence the delay.

While that delay meant that several monarchs from across the Empire had to return home, the occasion was splendid and popular unlike the rough and ready coronation of the King's mother sixty-four years earlier. Apart from the blunder of Psalm 122 which Mary had pointed out, one other infelicity was felt by the elderly Archbishop of Canterbury who created some concern as he could not get up off his knees after pledging allegiance so that the King and several nearby bishops were obliged to help the Primate to his feet. Fortunately he had already done his duty and crowned His Imperial Majesty, so a mild constitutional crisis was avoided.

Mary and Hamish were given seats in the nave of the Abbey but in the middle of a row. They could just see the procession of the Choir, bishops and the archbishops, the King and Queen accompanied by pages as they walked toward the Chancel, but they could see nothing of the ceremony itself for that took place near the High Altar where the ancient Coronation Chair stood. This irritated Mary intensely: She was short of stature, the wooden chairs difficult with the coronation cushions were uncomfortable and, they had to be seated two hours before the Service began. The ceremony seemed endless, though they enjoyed listening to the Choir and the music. Hamish felt no real discomfort as the woolen bulk of his judge's robes did something to ameliorate the seat problem.

Four hours later the heard their names called for their brougham at the west door of the Abbey and through cheerful crowds they traveled west past the Houses of Parliament to their home in Cheyne Row, Chiswick.

"Well," said Mary, enjoying a cup of tea with her husband in the late afternoon, "we have a new monarch."

"I had not seen him before, he really is a big fellow, isn't he?"

"Indeed he is, and for his doctors the operation on his abdomen is a singular achievement."

"Now tell me, Mary, what are we to make of the stories about him and his women?"

"I am sure most of them are true, given Elizabeth's experience with him."

"Remind me, what was that?"

"He invited her to a soirée for his chosen women when she was receiving her husband Timothy's posthumous award, I find him quite disgusting, I'm afraid. Powerful men cannot resist the urge at every opportunity to flaunt their prowess as lovers."

"But why do women of station find him attractive, Mary, for he is no Adonis?"

"Oh, Hamish, the attraction of being a trophy, I suppose, though I must confess that I am really not able to judge, as I have never had the experience," she said with a smile, "but it is he, not any lady of his affections, who disposes. I mean that no woman in the position of a king's lover would ever take the initiative to leave him, rather he collects and disposes as he wishes, whatever they might want."

"Perhaps the age of Edward VII will mean more of that kind of behavior without the Queen as an example."

"True. After all the Empire has had a woman on the throne for this very long period, but there will be men as far into the future as the eye can see. The King already has two grandchildren, both boys, so we can assume that there will be men on the throne ad infinitum."

"Yet I was not impressed with the monarch as a woman in recent years," said Hamish reflectively, "though I grant you not every woman would lock herself away for an interminable period after the death of her husband as the Queen did. Look at Clara Gargery, for example. She married Malcolm a mere eleven months after Sam's death in that dreadful explosion."

"I still say a little prayer from time to time that you were not closer to the bomb and so did not suffer too badly from it."

"As do I."

"At first I thought that Gargery marriage was unseemly, but the bursting out of their romantic love made waiting intolerable for them. He was also off to fight the Pathan tribes in India and she told Pip and Harriet that the thought of a second lover dying would be impossible for her to bear. Hence the haste."

As Mary had arranged, they then took their dinner early, both now being in their seventieth decade. Their life together was unlike many of their rank and station where a husband might dine at his club two or three times a week, a very rare occurrence for Hamish. For it was a simple fact of their marriage that they were very close friends and they preferred each other's company to anyone else's.

"It is interesting, is it not," said Mary during dinner, "that a couple of women we know who have lost their husbands are not remarried."

"Who are you thinking of, darling?"

"There's that beauty Elizabeth Egerton I mentioned earlier. We know her only slightly, but her husband was the man murdered at his Foreign Office desk."

"That was six years ago now, was it not? And of course, there is Victoria Pirrip. My goodness, that was a strange affair. When I advised Albert what to do with his syphilis, I did not contemplate the possibility that he would kill himself, especially in such a dramatic way."

"We do know, of course, that in recent years Victoria has been developing a relationship with John Eustace as they both came to our dinner party, but it is possible that she is disinclined to marry a Vicar if she lacks a serious religious commitment. Perhaps they both welcome their independence."

"Hey ho, time for bed, my dear Mary, as it's been a long day for both of us. I am sure the King is still enjoying a gay old time at some banquet or other tonight. Whether that is true of the new Queen is another matter."

"Perhaps, but he is about our age you know, so his health and his responsibilities may dull his appetite for both food and women now that he is King. But then, being King, he will be able to issue commands to his women with increased authority."

That May all the members of the Gargery family had decided to find a spot to watch the Coronation procession and the postponed event did not lessen their enthusiasm. That was enhanced by an invitation from Sir Clarence and Lady Fotheringaye-Smythe to join them on a stand outside the Whitehall Banqueting House when the postponed date was announced. How Sir Clarence had managed to obtain enough places on the stand was a matter of grateful conjecture in the Gargery household.

"I suppose being a Member of Parliament carries certain privileges."

"But surely, Pip," said Harriet, "Emma and he would have a place in the Abbey."

"He is a canny fellow, so I expect he realized that sitting there would not be to his or her liking, even if he had been invited."

"I thought this was not a matter of invitation, but a royal command."

"One would think so as a formal matter, but then I don't think the Abbey could contain all those monarchs and others who had some kind of expectation for a place, let alone the country's bigwigs, so I don't think the Lord Chamberlain would mind if Sir Clarence asked privately for leave to avoid the command."

As Clarence's guests arrived, they had to pass through the Banqueting Hall, the only completed part of the colossal palace James I had wanted to build. First to arrive was Elizabeth Egerton and her three children.

"Oh, my goodness," she said to them, "I came here to a reception once with your father. That ceiling is magnificent," and as they passed on to the stand, she exclaimed, "and what a splendid position to view the goings-on."

"You do realize, don't you Mamma," said Henry the eldest, "that we have just stepped through the door that Charles I passed to a similar stand built especially for his execution."

"That is horrible," said his seventeen-year old sister, Charlotte, "it gives me the shivers."

"It was certainly a terrible event in the nation's history, though the door would need to be enlarged were our present King to meet the same fate," said Oliver the younger son, laughing. "An Eton history beak told us once that after the execution, the coffin with body and head inside was covered with a black cloth was taken to Windsor on a carriage for burial. It was late January and it began to snow on the way so that when it reached Windsor, the coffin was completely white. Many a follower of Saint Charles the Martyr thought this was a clear divine signal of his innocence."

"I have always thought of him as innocent, but it was the only way for Cromwell to get rid of him," said Elizabeth. "Your father told me years ago that he once dined with a man who showed him a bone which was said to be from King Charles' forearm. The man's ancestor was Constable of the Tower at Victoria's coronation."

"Good heavens," said Charlotte, "how disgraceful and insulting to the King's memory."

"Not really. The story was that several of the German princes staying at Windsor for the celebrations got very drunk and broke into St. George's Chapel and then into the vault where the coffin lay as they wanted to see the King's severed head. The Constable had to clear up the mess afterwards, but retained the forearm bone as a souvenir, though if he had Papist tendencies, he would have regarded it as a holy relic."

"That sounds like stuff and nonsense to me, a most unlikely tale," said Charlotte, now a young woman whom many regarded as rather prim.

Further discussion of that topic was stayed as Pip arrived with Harriet. Malcolm and Clara. Hannah and Tom followed, each couple with their children, and all of them found that they had been obliged to send their carriages away half a mile or so from the Abbey which meant a walk through Parliament Square along Whitehall to the Banqueting House.

"Gather round," said Clarence with his most authoritative voice as the remainder of the party continued to arrive, "I must say this is a delight to see you all, and some of you will now know each other, but very quickly, these friends are Pip and Harriet Gargery," said he, gesturing with a white gloved hand in the direction of the older Gargerys only to be interrupted by Pip who said:

"I am not sure whether you all know my son Malcolm and his wife Clara, and this is my daughter Hannah and her husband Tom, each with their children, and this is our son Joseph."

"I think everyone knows my wife Emma and our children," Clarence continued, mildly miffed by Pip's intervention, "but this is Elizabeth Egerton and her family," he said moving toward each family in turn, "and here are the Mastersons, the Levys, and our new young lawyer Simon Garthwaite and his wife, Isabella. Have I left anyone out?

At that moment, Simon and Margaret Brandram and their twenty-four year old son Jude came up the grand staircase and into the Banqueting Hall to join the Smythe party.

"What a pleasure," cried Clarence, loudly now as the hubbub of excitement in the Hall and outside grew, "here are Simon and Margaret Brandram, of course. Simon my friend, we are sorry indeed that your mother Honora cannot be with us, but I am sure a journey from Cornwall would be hard for her."

"Indeed, you are right, but she sends everyone her love and warmest regards."

"Well, now, everyone, it is ten o'clock and the procession is due from the Palace any moment, so let us take our seats, then we will have lunch while the King is being crowned and watch the returning procession after that."

Clarence was clearly in an expansive mood, especially as Courtisone and Jaggers was thriving under his direction with legal briefs coming in thick and fast. This, and the fact that the Conservative Party won the 1900 election precipitated his decision not to stand again. His mood that day was exemplified by the magnificent lunch he had paid for as the host of his friends.

Henry Egerton had recovered from the emotional upheavals of his father's murder six years earlier and he had followed him into work at the Foreign Office, more as a sign of his respect for his father than any long-held desire to be a diplomat. Sitting next to Joseph, a contemporary of his at Cambridge, they soon fell into conversation.

"So you are among the academic elite then, Joseph? What is your expertise?"

"I am especially interested in the problems of succession as they affected the Tudors and the plots and arguments which surrounded each succession. Henry VII seized the crown in battle, his son Arthur died before becoming king, and the younger son Henry VIII succeeded, but his life seemed one long struggle to produce a satisfactory succession. Then his young son died, no doubt worn out by the political maelstrom in which he lived, and there followed the chaos of the reign of Mary, which was in some ways an interruption,

8

especially with her early death. Then Elizabeth I who never married but reigned for a long time such that her succession was a permanent problem throughout. The problem of succession raises all kinds of interesting problems like primogeniture and creates a multitude of struggles and enmities."

"How fascinating. The late Queen's succession was unusual too."

"Indeed, an almost Tudor situation. If I can put it like this, the Tudor problem was with women. If you consider the matter, the Tudor Century had so many notable women, although there were several important women in the Lancaster and York families before that. Catherine of Aragon was a thorn in the Tudors' side and Henry VIII's behavior with women needs no further explanation. Then Mary Queen of Scots, let alone Queens Mary and Elizabeth and such lesser notables as Bess of Hardwick."

"How interesting, and if we then include Shakespeare's women, there are plenty of women of great variety, many of them very strong personalities, and central to his plots."

Sitting in front of them on the stand and overhearing this conversation, Elizabeth Egerton turned round to say:

"Now gentlemen, in this last century we have witnessed many other famous and powerful women, the Queen apart, Jane Austen, the Brontes, Mary Woolstencraft, George Eliot, among them and, of course Florence Nightingale. These women have strongly influenced how we see ourselves."

"Here they come," shouted Clarence and all eyes turned right toward Trafalgar Square where the Household Cavalry with their plumed helmets were coming into view, though the horses' hooves could not be heard over the cheering crowds.

Horatio and Beth Fletcher and the alphabet children decided to join all the villagers on the Green at All Hallows. Vicar John and Victoria also stayed there rather than travel to London. This was a typical country fair celebration especially as it was near Harvest Festival, with its bunting and flags, although this was not a part of the county that had the abundance of orchards or hop fields to be found in other parts of Kent.

It was almost two years since the loss of Charlie and Frank. The fall of the elm tree at Numquam House had left a continuing shadow over their parents' lives, though the birth of Ivor that year proved a delight. He had bright red hair, quite unlike the rest of the family, and Horatio teased his wife by saying he was on the lookout for a fellow with red hair so he could pick a fight with him. On the way to the Village Green, he said:

"All the men of the Village will be here, so I'll be on the lookout," he said with a grin at his wife.

"Now see here, Harry. I am right fed up with your instipuations or whatever they are, here am I, a good wife to you, bearing your children, feeding the lot of you, trying to get over the bleeding loss of our two kids," and she began to weep, "when would I get time to bed some red-haired fellow, come on now tell me, when am I not in your sight, it makes me sick, it does, and I won't put up with it no longer."

"It's only a joke, Beth, I loves young Ivor, but I'll stop if it hurts you."

"You don't have any idea of what it's like to bear a child, do you, you just stand by and make silly noises when they're born, but I have to go through the labor and the pain only to 'ave you go on at me. It's not funny, Harry, it's not funny anymore. Besides the kiddies hear you and the baby is going to be teased enough about it as he grows and you'll make it as if he's not really part of the family."

"I'd not thought of that," said Horatio, "and I am sorry, love. I'll give over teasin' you and I'm really sorry, 'cos I loves you to bits, you know."

"Well, nuff said then," said Beth, "Let's enjoy the celebrations."

The seven children left after the Elm Tree accident were mixed in character with Arthur the eldest proving a sensible and careful leader of the younger ones. On this occasion he was in his element at fifteen years old, shepherding the three younger children around the fair, while young Beth his sister helped her parents with the younger two, Horatio and Ivor the baby.

"What a good boy that is, Harry," said his mother, "weren't we lucky for him to have that scholarship? Quite unlike our family, really. And he were only twelve!"

"I don't think he wanted to go to that fancy King's School at first," was the reply, "but he's riding to Rochester with Philip every day, so he has company."

"Look, there's our Victor with the Vicar."

Approaching them was the Reverend John Eustace and Mrs. Victoria Pirrip, Horatio's sister. Her son Philip was sixteen and was also a pupil at the King's School in Rochester, as his dead father Albert had also wanted. The Pirrip family was very fashionably dressed as usual, and the Vicar's frock coat and dog collar signified his status, so it seemed to the local folk that here was to be a new family of class in the Village.

10

"Allo, Victor," said Horatio, wrapping his arms around his sister much to her embarrassment but she recovered, saying,

"I have some news for both of you, John and I are getting married, first we thought October on All Hallows Eve, but now we think the Spring, April perhaps."

"I am so thrilled that your sister has consented to marry me, Fletchers both, as I suppose we have been courting for far too long."

"Well, I dunno, what would Mum have said, you marrying a vicar?"

"I never knew her," said John, "but the tales I have heard suggest that she would have been thrilled."

"Oh yes," said Horatio suddenly, "we both wish you every happiness and a long life together and what does it matter what Mum would have said?"

"Oh, I do think it matters," replied Victoria, "and I think she'd be really delighted for me."

"Don't get me wrong, Sis, I am sure she would," said her brother, anxious to keep in her good books.

"And I think our Dad would be delighted too," she added just to make sure Harry understood that she did not want her future husband to have any sense of family discord at their marriage.

"You're lucky," said Beth, "we've got a supply of pages and bridesmaids ready."

"Thank you, Beth," said John, "but we have in mind a quiet wedding at the moment. In my position as Vicar, we'd have to invite the whole village. We are also widower and widow, so it is not as if we are young people. But nothing has been decided yet, only that we intend to marry."

"Will you move into the Vicarage, Victor?" Asked Horatio.

"As John said, nothing is yet decided."

Celebrations continued into the evening and many families went to the Rose and Crown in the village or the Three Jolly Bargemen along the road as the sun went down but John and Victoria were not anxious to share their news yet beyond the family, though Victoria thought Beth would not be able to keep it quiet.

"I'd like you to stay with me tonight," said Victoria as John stopped the trap outside Numquam, "but I suppose we must wait."

"I fear so, my dear, we do not want any gossip in the Village, do we?"

"No indeed: Let us discuss our wedding tomorrow. Perhaps we can ask Pip to marry us?"

"Oh my," said John, "that will require some thought and planning. Talk about it tomorrow?"

"Good night, my dear John," and they kissed fervently in the twilight before Victoria went into the house with a wave of her hand.

Back in Chelsea, all the Gargerys were assembled for dinner with Pip and Harriet as hosts and Elizabeth Egerton and her three children had also been invited to join them.

"This is such a strange day," said Clara, "it feels like the beginning of a new century once again, though we went through that two and a half years ago."

"What worries me from time to time," said Pip, "is that we English are becoming so much like the Romans. One way or another we control about a quarter of the world's surface, and are clearly the most important empire since, but our hubris will in all likelihood bring us down. Maybe not this century, but it will happen as night follows day."

"There is the obvious danger of that," said Tom, "but I think we can weather it. I am so glad now not to be in the Army. Without sounding sentimental, I hope, Hannah and I value our family so much that the thought of losing any of us would damage the ever-deepening love we have for each other and which we share with our children. I look back on my soldiering and feel enormous guilt at having killed other men who were probably like me, deeply committed to my wife and children."

"Oh Tom," said Malcolm, "we had this discussion on the Dundalk coming home from India. As we have discussed several times, our moral sentiments are now such that we should engage in politics. As you know, Clara and I have been working with the South Africa Reconciliation Committee now that dreadful war with the Boers is over."

"In that respect," said Clara, "I have begun to understand how extraordinarily privileged I have been in my life, notwithstanding Sam's death. That Reconciliation Committee has been learning so much about the plight of Boer women and children in the aftermath of war, without homes, with disease, poverty and hunger."

"But what do people expect?" cried Hannah. "If we build an empire, we must have soldiers to hold it, and politicians committed to it, most of whom could not care a button about the damage done to the innocent from the family that loses the husband which Tom thinks about right down to the starving women and children in those dreadful camps. It makes me so angry."

"Father and I had a long discussion about war some months ago now," said Joseph, "and he told me of his feelings as a young man, and how his pacifist perspective was undermined by being a spectator of war, even though he was a farrier."

"What do you mean?" asked Tom.

"Please explain Father," said Joseph, "you can set it out much more clearly than I can."

"Well," said Pip, rising from his chair and walking around the room, "a pacifist must inevitably be neutral in any conflict, but the very fact of being on or near a battlefield makes that impossible, even if you were to be a pacifist working as a medical orderly or, like me, a farrier not directly involved in combat. The situation demands that you take sides. In my case I was more than energetic in my support for those men in the Light Brigade at Balaclava and my hatred for the Russians was unbounded.

"In that context, I simply could not be a Christian and love my neighbor. I hated my enemy with passion even though frankly I still have only a little idea what that war was about. I returned home not merely with this damned leg, but with a more severe loss, the loss of my innocence and the loss of my pacifism."

"That is so sad, Father," said Hannah, "like Tom, being in combat or close to it makes one realize what an enormous sin it is before God. Moreover, it is greed, sheer greed at root. Empires are built on greed. I won't bore you with the account Karl Marx and the communists give, but tell me, who here really wants the nation to have an empire?"

"That is so provoking," said Elizabeth, "I suppose I want all the luxuries having an empire provides, though I don't care deep down whether Britain has an empire or not."

"I think all this stuff about civilizing the natives is a lot of tommy rot," said Oliver, emerging into the conversation, "what we really mean is forcing people who are unlike us to become like us, rather than respecting them. It's like Eton where you have to become like an Etonian with airs and graces, traditions and customs, attitudes and emotions," at which everyone laughed and Oliver blushed a little.

"There is truth in that, darling," said Elizabeth, anxious to support her son but then with loving sarcasm continued, "I noticed so many ways in which you changed when Eton civilized you," at which the laughter doubled and redoubled.

"Malcolm and I are both entering politics with Clarence's help," said Tom, "and we must begin to stake our claims for parliamentary seats. We can then have some influence on how our empire develops."

"Tom," said Malcolm abruptly changing the conversation, "I have just had an idea as a way for us to enter Liberal politics. There have been five by-elections this month alone, Sevenoaks, Belfast South, East Worcestershire, Tiverton and Clitheroe, where a Labor fellow won. In 1902 two Liberals overcame conservatives, not uncommon in the course of a Parliament."

"Are you suggesting that we should work at by-elections for the Liberals to get ourselves known? Already this year, Newmarket has been captured by Liberals."

"I am."

"A capital idea," said Clara and Hannah joined in the enthusiasm, "let us plan this with precision."

"I have been hearing talk in my club recently about something called National Efficiency. It appears that the ideas come from America and it seeks to avoid sentimentalism of all kinds and examine everything rationally, in terms of how money, especially public money can be spent more effectively. In the newspapers I have read that this has been the primary thrust behind the Education Bill now going through Parliament."

"As we go forward," said Malcolm, "we need to study this notion in detail. I must say I have neglected the political detail of the Education Bill, the creature of Mr. Balfour, I believe. However, I am very cautious about any notion that does not value the individual first and foremost."

"Now I must now thank you all so much for coming here after our long day on the stand," said Harriet, "and what a wonderful conversation with which to begin a new reign. I suppose we are all Edwardians now."

II

A very well-dressed lady in deep mourning alighted from a cab outside 11, Old Square in Lincoln's Inn. She trod the four steps up to the door, knocked on the door and was immediately ushered into the library on the left of the hallway, serving as a waiting-room..

"How can I help you?" asked Robert Gillingham, the senior clerk at Courtisone and Jaggers, and a man very proud of his career from his times as a junior clerk under Mr. Jaggers. As senior clerk Robert ran the office, but also played an important role in decisions about which briefs would be accepted, judging the strength of a case, the income generated and so on. He judged which briefs were worth taking and balanced the work between the lawyers. Thus his primary responsibility was to tender advice on these matters to Sir Clarence as Head of Chambers, advice which was invariably accepted.

Robert soon realized that this formidable lady was Mrs. Angharad Unworthy whose widowhood had created such a variety of problems for young Mr. Hamish almost thirty years ago.

"Mrs. Unworthy, what a pleasure to welcome you to Old Square," he said with a nonchalance which left her mildly flabbergasted.

"What's your name? I think I saw you here all that time ago."

"Indeed, Madam, I have risen from a lowly clerk copying out letters to be the Senior Clerk in Courtisone and Jaggers."

"Well, bless my soul, how wonderful is that. My name is Mrs. Llewellyn now, but I am a widow again, and I would like to meet Mr. MacDonald."

"Ah, that will not be possible, I am afraid. He is now Sir Hamish MacDonald and a judge in the High Court, so he no longer acts as a lawyer. It is Sir Clarence Smythe who is responsible for his former clients."

"I think I met him, a tall shy man with a funny surname."

"Yes, that is he. Please to wait and I will see whether he is able to see you."

Robert hurried into Clarence's office and said:

"Sir Clarence, did you ever meet a young Welsh widow many years ago, one of Sir Hamish's client then? She is the waiting room."

"I vaguely remember the stories, Gillingham, but I can't say I met her. What does she want?"

"She didn't say, but you perhaps did not know that her husband was an Australian sheep farmer who died after an altercation with the natives and left her very wealthy indeed."

"Then I must see her. Kindly ask her to come now. A rich Welsh lady indeed, what on earth could she want?"

"She's a widow for the second time so you will see."

A few minutes later, Mrs. Angharad Llewellyn came in and Clarence was pleased to see a woman, seemingly nearer fifty than forty, very handsome and beautifully dressed, although she was in mourning.

"Please come in and sit down, Mrs. Llewellyn. How good of you to come. How can I help you?"

"It is a long story, so I hope you don't have any immediate appointments, Sir Clarence."

"No, I am at your disposal."

"I was a client of Mr. MacDonald long ago, and, to be honest, I decided a bit later that I needed to have a solicitor nearer my home in South Wales but Mr. Zachary Jones died last month and for a number of reasons, I thought I'd come back to Mr. MacDonald, and Robert told me he is a judge now, so I think I will make you my lawyer, and perhaps you will be my advisor too."

As he noticed Mrs. Llewellyn' nervous manner and speech at meeting him, Clarence said: "Tell me about yourself since you saw Mr. MacDonald."

"That must have been 1874 or 1875. I was married to Ezekiel Unworthy then and we were in Queensland, you know, in Australia. He was not a good man, indeed he were a bastard if you follow me, but he was very rich. He had a terrible row with the Abbos and was so badly wounded that he eventually died. I came back to Wales with my children, though my older son Gareth stayed there as he had been given two thousand acres. So Mr. MacDonald helped me; he got me a bank account and a proper will. He told me to buy a nice house in a nice area and leave my father's farm west of Cardiff."

"But how did you come to the Jaggers office, rather than anywhere else?"

"Ah, there's story. Ezekiel my husband was the bastard son of a convict, name of Magwitch as I recall, whose lawyer was Jaggers. He had come to London looking for Jaggers before we met, but Jaggers was dead, so he had a Mr. Pip see to his investments. A few years later we came to London with our children as Ezekiel was looking for more investors."

"And was that satisfactory?"

"No, there was a terrible row as Mr. Pip and a lady called Estella found out Ezekiel was using slaves, so Mr. Pip showed him the door. But Estella was so friendly to me and when I came back after Ezekiel was injured, I needed a lawyer, so I came to find Mr. Pip, but he was dead so I had Mr. MacDonald."

"That is indeed a long story. So Mr. MacDonald, as he then was, gave you advice which I assume was satisfactory?"

"Oh yes, it has been wonderful until this last year. I bought a nice house at Radyr north of Cardiff, more in the country like, and I was still a young woman when I came back from Australia, so I went to the nearest big church, Llandaff Cathedral to become part of a community. I was a farm girl, see, so what with my money I inherited from Ezekiel, I had to become a lady. After I gave the Cathedral five hundred pounds, Canon Thomas advised me for five years with my language and lady-like behavior. That must have been 1882 or so, for I then met Dai Llewellyn in the Cathedral congregation."

"I see," said Clarence, "so you were establishing yourself for several years after your first husband died."

"That's right and Dai and me, we got on very well. He had not married. He seemed a very nice man, older than me and a bachelor, so I persuaded him to marry me, well, I shouldn't say that, but you need to know everything about me. Now Dai was a pit manager, but it was a small pit and he was also a director, so we bought a bigger house closer to the center of Cardiff and married in 1884, but we kept the Radyr house."

"Was Mr. Llewellyn a wealthy man?"

"He was forty-five and he liked it that I was so rich. You see, I was always worried after what Mr. MacDonald said, that I might marry someone who was just after my money. Yet he was as sober as a judge, my Dai. I loved him and he was a good influence on me, unlike my first husband. So what with my clergy friend from Llandaff and my Dai, I've been a different person than what I was in 1875."

"Did Dai pass away then?" said Clarence consciously managing not to ask, 'did Dai die?'

17

"Yes, he'd been sick for some time and died this June. He was so disappointed to miss the Coronation, last thing he said to me, now I'll miss the Coronation and he just croaked. He taught me about the mines and the dreadful tragedies that happen, the accidents, you know. Would you believe over 600 men have died in pits since 1890 and that does not include the numerous accidents, men getting burnt, hurt in a rock fall? There's real calamities every year, it seems."

"So where does this leave you?'

"My will at present says that my money will be divided among my children, none of whom really need it. I'd like to give a large proportion of it to some charitable cause, probably for Welsh miners and their families, but how do I arrange that?"

At that moment, Hamish walked in, his cases being completed for the day.

"So sorry, Clarence, I did not know you were with a client."

"No, please stay, this is Mrs. Angharad Llewellyn, previously Mrs. Unworthy."

"Great Scot," cried Hamish, as Angharad got up and they shook hands. "How marvelous to see you again. Let me see, it must be thirty years or so. How are you? How's the family?"

"I am very well, but a widow again and so I am looking for help with you and your colleagues."

"Of course, of course, you finish your discussion with Sir Clarence and he can then ask Robert to show you to my rooms upstairs as I would love to know how you have got on since we last met," and with that, Hamish gave a broad smile and excused himself, amazed at how Angharad had retained some of that earthy beauty with which she was so well endowed when they last met.

"Are you staying in London?" Asked Clarence.

"Yes. Dai and I used to come to London regular to shop and sometimes see a show and stay at Claridge's Hotel which is very comfortable, though a bit expensive. So I am staying there for a week or so, as I need to do some shopping."

"Why don't we meet again then, and I will draw up some possibilities for you and I'll talk with Sir Hamish too. Let me call Robert and you can go upstairs to see him."

Sir Hamish was sitting at the large partners desk that had been used by Mr. Jaggers as Mrs. Angharad Llewellyn was shown in by Robert. He got up, taking

18

Angharad by the arm and showing her to one of the two large brown leather chairs while he sat in the other.

"It is a very long time ago when we met in Cardiff."

"Oh yes, Sir Hamish, and I still blush from time to time when I remember that occasion."

"I must confess I have not before or since had such an opportunity as you presented to me, Angharad. You don't mind if I call you Angharad?"

"No and I'll call you Hamish which is a bit intimate," and they both smiled broadly. "Well, we was young then, wasn't we?

"Ah yes indeed. But tell me has everything worked out for you? I gather you married again and that your husband died."

"To be honest, I came here with two problems, and because of our past dealings I wanted to share one of them with you only, though I didn't know you'd become a judge and a Sir."

"I do remember our relationship with admiration for your courage, especially with your father."

"Oh yes, he went on for years badgering me about my money, you know, but I ignored him, though I made sure they didn't want for anything. Enough of him, I have a very serious problem, and I only want to discuss it with you."

"Tell me."

"About two years after you and I met, I formed a relationship with a man, I'll call him Barry. I met him at a Pontypool Rugby dance. I'd moved to Radyr by then and I'd met a neighbor whose husband was a director or something at the Club. This Barry was a rugby player and we was dancing and one thing led to another, and I was pregnant."

"How unfortunate," said Hamish thinking about how attractive this woman was all those years ago and she had not lost her rather blunt charm.

"I thought about marrying him if he had asked me, but when I told him about the baby, he told me he wasn't interested. I think he was already married but he didn't say. Now, and this is confidential, isn't it?"

"Indeed."

"I decided I could not keep the baby what with my having had four children, but I had the money, see, to get myself a good doctor to get me seen too, if you know what I mean."

"Oh dear, you knew that was illegal both for him and for you, didn't you."

"Yes, but at least I was having it done properly not in the back streets of Cardiff. But I met this Barry by accident in Pontypridd Market when I should have been six months gone, and he asked me what had happened. I told him I had miscarried the baby but he didn't believe me. He said he'd tell the police and then I'd have to tell them about the doctor, wouldn't I, and he wanted money to keep quiet."

"Ah, blackmail, what a despicable man."

"At first I refused, but then I saw him from my bedroom window in Radyr one day walking along the street. I tried not to let him in, but he came in the next day when my kiddies were at school. I told him to sod off but he started to beat me, just like my first husband, but then he raped me. Of course I was pregnant again."

"What a terrible dilemma, how long ago was this?"

"Fifteen years maybe, no more like twenty."

"You could not report him to the police for fear he would tell of your situation. So what did you do this time?"

"I decided to pay him and I went to the doctor again. But this Barry wanted more and more money each month and, while I could afford it, over the past twenty odd years, I must have given him ten thousand pounds altogether."

"Good heavens, did your husband know about this?"

"No, of course not. He was too gentle and sweet a man to get mixed up in my troubles and I kept all my money dealings to myself. So you see now why you are the only person I can trust with this information."

"So this man is guilty of blackmail and rape, what a dreadful predicament for you."

"As you know, I can afford these payments to him, so it is not like I am poor. But this has gone on for so long, I need to find a way to stop it and I can't tell all this to my Cardiff lawyer or it will soon be the talk of the town. People in Wales love gossip, you know."

"I don't think that's a Welsh problem only, believe me."

"Can you help me?"

"I would have to bring one of these lawyers here into our confidence. What did you discuss with Sir Clarence?"

"I want to change my will and leave a lot to help miners. My husband was a pit manager and he was always telling me stories about the poverty and the hard work. Sir Clarence is going to think of some ideas as to how my money might be spent."

"I think with your permission I will share your story with Sir Clarence. My immediate reaction is for us to write to this man you call Barry and threaten him with a charge of rape and blackmail and that you should stop paying him immediately he receives our letter. But I will talk with Sir Clarence about that. There is another alternative which I will not share with you yet."

"This is such a relief. But tell me what the alternative is."

"In my position as a judge I cannot. But tell me, are you staying in London?"

"Yes, as I told Sir Clarence, I am staying at Claridge's."

"I assume you have this Barry's address."

"Yes, I found that out not long ago. He works down the pit too."

"Leave it with me. By the way, we are hosting a small dinner party tomorrow with friends and I am sure my wife Mary would be glad for you to come as you are alone in London. She gets quite angry about such experiences as yours, though you need not tell her if you do not wish to."

"That is so kind. I will get a carriage from the hotel. Your wife had a funny left arm, right?

"That is right: What a good memory you have."

When Angharad left, Hamish was somewhat nonplussed by his reaction to Angharad and he knew he would have to present his dinner invitation carefully to Mary as she would certainly remember the Cardiff incident.

"Do you remember that client I had in Cardiff?" Asked Hamish soon after he got home.

"The deshabilée woman who sought your favor?"

"Indeed, that was 1874 or 5, I cannot remember which. But today she came into the office and met with Clarence and then with me."

"But you don't take clients, do you?"

"Good heavens no, But she specifically wanted to seek my advice and, of course, as I did not know what kind of advice it would be, I could hardly refuse to see her."

"Has she changed much?"

"She has indeed. Considerable wealth and age have made a very sensible and nice woman and after she had burdened me with her problems, I felt so sorry for her that I invited her to join us tomorrow evening with the Gargerys."

"Good heavens, Hamish, that is so unlike you. She will certainly make an interesting dinner guest. Are you willing to share her problems with me?"

"Of course but you must give no intimation at all to her that you know. You'll remember that her first husband was that Australian who was killed and it left her extremely wealthy once she had sold the vast sheep farms he had in

Queensland. I then advised her to remove herself from her family, especially her father and buy a suitable house in Cardiff."

"Advice which I am sure she followed."

"Yes, indeed but she met a blaggard and soon became pregnant, though he was married. He wanted nothing more to do with her. Six months later, they met accidentally and he bullied her on the street into saying why she was not carrying his child which he had already disowned and then proceeded to blackmail her for ridding herself of the child."

"Was this a miscarriage or something else?"

"She tried to bluff him with a tale about a miscarriage but she had found a friendly doctor and the man extracted that information from her by force. She could afford to pay him what he demanded. Two years later, he knew where she lived as he went there regularly to collect his money. She was remarried by then to an apparently nice gentleman who worked as a pit manager. One day this Mr. Blaggard came round one morning to collect his money and she refused, telling him she had paid him enough. So he beat her and he raped which caused another pregnancy.

"Good gracious me, what a terrible story," said Mary, "why did she not go to the police?"

"That would expose him, true, but the police would want to know the doctor's name to verify her story, would they not? Remember she has children from her first marriage."

"So what does she want you to do?"

"I told her I would have to share her distress with Clarence and we will need to find some way to confront this man with charges of blackmail and rape and cease these payments."

"I can see why you would feel sorry for her, though it is beyond our duty, I think, to have her to dinner."

"She is staying at Claridge's which gives one an idea of her wealth, and I was wondering whether Harriet might take her up as a cause."

"She might, and I will make a judgment about all this when we meet her."

"Thank you my dear for your understanding: I just blurted out the invitation without thinking, but I know you will forgive me."

"Nothing to forgive, Hamish. You are in no way an impetuous man and I am sure that compassion was your motive, though perhaps you found her attractive too," she said with a broad smile.

"She must be in her fifties I would say, but yes, she is still an attractive woman."

It was only a week before the Coronation that Clarence and Emma Smythe had returned from their chateau in Provence after a splendid August of sun, excellent food and wine, and relaxation with their children. Malcolm, Clara and the children had visited them for a fortnight too and the experience warmed their hearts such that toward the end of their stay they began to search for a suitable villa for themselves.

Just outside the pretty village of Vence, they stumbled on a house which seemed to be in some disrepair, but its charm was that it was built on a slope with the main rooms being immediately accessible from the track which ran along the hill and the bedrooms were on two lower levels. It was what Clara thought of as upside-down and it had a spectacular view of the Mediterranean Sea from every room in the house with garden running down in terraces down the hill. Negotiations took ages as the sellers took a long time making up their minds, but finally by November 1902 the deal was completed and Malcolm and Clara were celebrating their acquisition.

Outside their Down Street house, the November rain had been coming down in bursts most of the day but relaxing after breakfast with Malcolm in the warmth of her drawing room chair with her new baby son, also called Malcolm, Clara expressed her delight at the news of the purchase.

"It is so thrilling and I hope we can spend two months there in the summer, though we could also go there in the Spring. I think we should sell the house in Port Elizabeth, as it is very unlikely that we will ever go there."

"It is a good investment though, so perhaps we do not need to decide on that yet. We will definitely have summers in the villa and as it only twenty or so miles from the Smythes with their small chateau, we will be invited to their large parties I'm sure."

"Probably, but I want the villa to be just for us and the children, but I suppose we might make an exception in the case of Pip and Harriet."

"And the Heskeths too, I do not doubt. I am glad to say that I trust the men who are restoring the house. Monsieur Lombardo seemed very anxious to please us. I suppose that as Vence is near Italy, it attracts skilled Italian artisans and he told me his grandfather had moved there from Ventimiglia years ago."

"I liked him enormously," said Clara. "I am sure he will not let us down."

"He certainly seemed pleased by the advance I gave him."

"On another matter, I am going this morning to meet Emily Hobhouse again," said Malcolm, "she has been in France recovering from her exertions but is now back in London."

"Where does she live?"

"Rossetti Gardens Mansions so I will call there."

"There was this terrible rumpus when she was denied entry to South Africa and the authorities sent her back, as I recall, such a tragedy."

"Yes, I met her briefly after that but she was totally exhausted and on her way to France, so we were not able to meet for any length of time. She was at Annecy when the Treaty was signed. I am quite astonished at the virulence with which some quarters of the press have attacked her as I saw some of those concentration camp conditions as you know and they were a thorough disgrace to the Empire."

"I would like to meet her at some point: perhaps we could have her to dinner with our friends and hear more firsthand about her trials and tribulations, as well as her successes. Do invite her and allow her to choose a time."

Malcolm arrived at Rossetti Gardens at eleven o'clock.

"How are you, Miss Hobhouse?" Asked Malcolm as her maid showed him into her drawing room."

"I am better for my time in France, Major Gargery, and I must say I wept tears of joy when I heard the Treaty with the Boers had been signed. Nevertheless I am convinced there will still be camps with scarcely unaltered conditions and I do plan to return and dare the authorities to send me back home again."

"I read the Fawcett Commission report and I must say it seemed to support everything you had been saying for years. I am also reading your book *The Brunt of the War and Where it Fell*, and in Hatchards, the man who sold it to me looked at me suspiciously as if I were an undesirable."

"I am glad it is finally in print as I think that even a person with a closed mind will find it distressing."

"I hope so too, but you know, Major, these men, Brodrick at the Foreign Office and General Kitchener too, seem to think it unpatriotic to raise concern about the way the women and children have been treated, always arguing about the mortality figures but seemingly unconcerned about what those figures mean for individual families."

"Miss Hobhouse, can I change the subject and ask for your advice?

"Of course, Major."

"First, I am no longer a soldier, so I am a major no more."

"I will still think of you as Major."

"That apart, I am strongly considering entering politics on the Liberal side, of course. I believe women should be enfranchised but I suspect it can only be a gradual process. I am deeply concerned for the tragedies one hears about in the mines and they are a constituency which would still need to be won, notwithstanding the importance of the trades unions. My stance to imperial foreign policy has been hugely influenced by your work at the concentration camps. Such matters now seem to me worth trying to fight for in the political arena and, as my wife and I are comfortable in financial terms, I think I could have a shot at a parliamentary constituency. What do you think?"

"I do not know you that well, of course, but I think your military career and your stance as you call it would be most attractive not merely to the party but on the hustings. As I grow older I find myself becoming more radical in all matters, driven I suppose by the extraordinary callousness which I have come across in high places. At the same time, I think I have friends such as Lord Ripon who might assist you and we can discuss that as you develop your Liberal Party affiliations."

"Thank you very much indeed for that signal of support. I know that you have a controversial reputation, but I am on the side of the angels."

Discussion continued for over an hour on such topics when Miss Hobhouse indicated that she was promised forth for lunch. As she got up to prepare to leave, Malcolm invited her to dinner in Down Street and they agreed that early January would be suitable, two weeks hence.

Mary was fascinated at the thought of dinner with the young widow who offered Hamish her favors when he went to her hotel room to discuss her will. She remembered her as pretty with blue eyes, fair hair and inviting lips, but very brash and uncouth in her manner and her style then.

"Hamish, you said this Welsh woman was now a lady. What do you mean?"

"Clarence told me she said she was counselled by a clergyman who taught her the ways of lady, language and so on, as she felt he wealth demanded it."

"How interesting. It has never occurred to me that one could change one's class by having lessons," she said with a mild sarcasm.

"Nor me, but I admire her for it."

Pip and Harriet arrived early as they were bidden to do, and Hamish spoke of his former professional relationship with their guest. In a complimentary fashion he said that he had noticed how her Welsh intonations and style of speech had been ameliorated. Harriet wondered why she had been invited, but as she was about to ask when the lady arrived.

"Mrs. Llewellyn," said Mary as she was shown into the drawing room, "you are welcome indeed. I think our paths crossed very briefly in Cardiff a long time ago."

"Yes, you had a baby boy with you as I recall."

"Yes, that was our son James, who is now married."

"Time flies as they say, and I was amazed at how you coped with a baby, what with your arm and all. It was a lovely sight."

"Thank you, bringing up children has not been without its difficulties, but let me introduce Mr. and Mrs. Gargery who are dining with us, and my husband will be with us shortly," at which Hamish entered the room and welcomed the visitor with a broad smile.

"Angharad, how good to see you again and Mary and I are so delighted you could come."

"Are you in London long?" Asked Harriet.

"I am going to stay until my two legal matters are settled."

"Are they serious?" Asked Pip.

"I don't know how much you know about me. When I was last here seeing my lawyers, I had a wonderful conversation with Estella, I think her name was, and she was such a comfort as I was all over the place at that time, and she had a very nice friend with her, Charlotte was it?"

"Ah yes, Estella was a great friend to all of us too."

"I have been so grateful to Canon Thomas at Llandaff Cathedral in recent years, starting before I married my second husband. When you are suddenly very rich like me, you can either go out and spend it all on stupid things, or you can try to better yourself and others, as I have with my children."

"How wise that is," said Pip, "and does this imply you are a religious person?"

"Oh Mr. Gargery, I wish I knew. I liked going to the Cathedral which is quite near my house in Radyr. I loved the music and I understood what the clergy were saying, but it all seemed too uncertain. Of course I'd been sent to chapel as a young girl so I do believe in a God."

"I wondered whether your attitude to your wealth comes from a religious belief."

"Perhaps. I don't know. It seems to me to be inhuman to have a lot of money and not share it. I mean, what do I want with all this money when I could help poor people, especially miners, but I don't know how to do it? See, my second husband Dai worked as a pit manager, he told me a lot about mining and the people, especially the families of the miners."

The maid came into announce that dinner was to be served, and Hamish squired Angharad into the dining room.

Harriet, Pip and Mary hung behind.

"What an extraordinary woman," said Harriet.

"Yes," said Pip, "how interesting is her perspective on herself, something that must have grown gradually over the years, but she is also mysterious in some way. Fascinating to me is that our lives as children were not that different, she on a farm in Wales, and me at a Forge in Kent."

As they took their places and the maid was serving soup, Angharad said, "I've been talking too much about myself and I must say I have never felt more welcome to such a splendid house. But Mr. Gargery, tell me about yourself."

When Pip had finished telling his story, Angharad said:

"You see what your wife did, using her money to help poor people, though they were Africans. I think that's wonderful. Of course, I'm honored to be at a table with a judge but I just think of him as that attractive young man who spent a night at our farm when my father made a fool of himself and my mother gave him enough breakfast to feed an army."

"Indeed," said Hamish, "after I had finished three or four sausages, I found four more on my plate."

"We've not heard about this, have we Harriet?" said Pip.

"Nothing to it, really, was there, Angharad, but your mother did insist on my having more sausages than I could digest," and everyone laughed.

"And look at you now," said Angharad, "sending people to prisons or the gallows."

"I suppose that is one way to describe the work of a judge," said Hamish tactfully, "but I see my job as one of ensuring that justice is done, usually in accordance with the law but there are occasions when law and justice conflict."

"Tell me, Mrs. Gargery," said Angharad, not feeling rebuffed but turning to Harriet, "what is it like to be the second wife of a man? I don't mean to be rude, but my two marriages were completely different."

"Well, it is no secret around this table that Pip and I were lovers when we were young and parted because I did not want to be married and he wanted to have children."

"So you got back together after his first wife died, and what was that like?"

"Oh dear," said Harriet, "we love each other, don't we Pip, but we are very aware of our faults and I believe that one has to love someone not merely for their virtues but also for their faults."

"I suppose that's true, though that was impossible with my first brute of a husband."

"Angharad," said Hamish changing the subject, "tell us now about your conversation with Sir Clarence."

"I want to find some way in which I can best give away my money to help the poor, especially miners. My children have their own lives and their Trust funds or whatever you call them, and my grandchildren will be fine too. I'd like to make a will, quite different from that I made with Hamish's help all those years ago. I'd like to arrange to spend seventy per cent of it or so now."

"Perhaps you do not know," said Mary, "that we are all are directors of a philanthropic enterprise, the Jaggers Trust for the Relief and Education of the Poor. We dispense probably five to ten thousand pounds annually. We have run homes for male and female prostitutes, we gave money to agricultural laborers, and we have worked extensively in Ireland."

"Really? I did not know that, and to be honest, I'd never thought of giving money to an organization that was already doing good work, though Sir Clarence did talk in general terms about that, perhaps me joining the Trust. I don't know what he will suggest eventually. We will see."

"Do you want to share your other predicament?" Asked Hamish. "I assure you this is a very sympathetic audience and together we have had to confront some very harsh situations in the past, which I believe our common wisdom was able to resolve?"

"Thank you, Hamish, I know you will keep that problem confident, I mean confidential, but I am not ready to share that experience yet, though

I do hope I can become a friend to all of you, as I am thinking I might move to London."

"You would be most welcome, my dear," said Mary.

Conversation then moved to rather more trivial topics, but when Hamish and Pip retired for port, Angharad decided she should tell her new women friends of this predicament from which she garnered what she felt was loving support from both Mary and Harriet.

1903

III

Clara had asked the Smythes, the MacDonalds, the Gargerys and the Heskeths, to meet Emily Hobhouse, and she added Elizabeth Egerton to make twelve. Rufus greeted Miss Hobhouse with delight, as indeed he did with most guests, especially those he remembered, but whether she had the smells of Africa in her clothes or not, his greetings were effusive and difficult for Malcolm to rein in, though Miss Hobhouse was not averse to being spoilt by a dog, especially one that reminded her so much of Africa.

However, her character was immediately apparent as the company gathered in the drawing-room. She interrogated Hamish about the Law, particularly on the exercise of executive power in the Colonies in time of war. Mary told her of a judge's struggles with the differences between law and justice. She was especially fascinated by Pip and his African mission, a conversation in which Malcolm and Clara both joined with their different experiences in Port Elizabeth.

Then she turned to Tom and Hannah and examined the similarities between their Irish experiences and imperial behavior in Africa. Finally, once Emily found out that Elizabeth's husband had been in the Foreign Office, she let loose a blast at the attitudes of politicians and generals.

Abdul came in to announce that dinner was ready.

"Excuse me," said Emily addressing Abdul, "did you come from Africa?"

"Yes, Ma'am, I am Abdul Ibrahim and I came with Mrs. Gargery as I worked for her in Port Elizabeth."

"You and I must talk at some point if your mistress will allow as I would like to hear about your life in Port Elizabeth as you are a Malay and a Muslim, am I right?"

"Yes, Ma'am, if Mrs. Gargery will allow, I would be glad to speak with you."

Clara was stunned that her visitor should talk directly to a servant without regard for the etiquette of permission, but then this was an unusual woman whose style and intellect had already been revealed.

Pip was impressed with this daunting woman whom he had only read about in the newspapers unable to fathom how a woman who was trying to help destitute women and children could be so reviled.

"How do you see the Boer situation now that the war is done?" He asked.

"I think I may very well return there this year. I was fortunate enough to meet three Boer generals when they were over here in August just after the Coronation."

"Who were they?"

"De Wet, De la Rey and Botha. They had come to get more financial support for re-establishing their lands after the devastation wreaked by the war, and by British soldiers in particular. They seemed to me to be very determined indeed to resurrect their country."

"Will they get help?" Asked Mary.

"They met the King and the Foreign Secretary and I think the politicians are satisfied to conclude the war, but they have reaped the whirlwind for the memories of British treatment will fester in the minds of the Boer families for years to come."

"Forgive my innocence," said Elizabeth, "some newspapers say that the Government are right in arguing that conditions in those camps was not as bad as you made out."

"Malcolm saw some of the camps, but I do not need to explain from my own experience." Emily Hobhouse said testily, "Millicent Fawcett and her Commission reported in February and they ignored my reports when they were there, and then came to the same conclusion as I."

"But why were the camps there in the first place?"

"Ah, you indeed are an innocent, my dear. In brief, the Boer army was defeated in the field with four hundred thousand British troops under Kitchener by the end of 1901. The country is so vast that the Boers began attacking British soldiers and disappearing into the night. So Kitchener, as Roberts had before him, gave troops permission to burn houses and crops, kill animals and in some case just shoot civilians for harboring the enemy."

"The camps, Elizabeth," Malcolm added, "were intended as a way to limit support for the Boer armies, but also because thousands of women and child

34

had suffered the destruction Emily described. Families from towns far away from the battle fields were put in the camps too as they supported their men."

"Then of course," Emily continued, "it became difficult to feed those interned, not least because so many crops had been destroyed, and conditions in the camps were so dreadful: No clean water, little milk for the children, hardly any wood for them to cook and keep warm, indeed most of the camps were utterly insanitary. I was also interested in the mortality rates. The Government here has constantly under-estimated those numbers but I estimate that over twenty-six thousand Boer woman and children have died in the camps of disease or malnutrition, and goodness know what the figures are for the Xhosa and other native Africans groups who were also put in camps: The mortality figure there is certainly not less than forty thousand."

"Does this mean that over sixty thousand women and children have died in this war as a result of British policies?" Asked Clara, clearly appalled at the figures, "manifestly civilians are always affected by war but is there anything to compare with this in our history?"

"I have been reviled in the newspapers and in some quarters of public life as my support for these women and children brands me as a traitor. Yet if any English woman had accompanied me and seen what I have seen, they would have been not merely disgusted but ashamed of what was being done in their name. I try to navigate the politics but am often defeated. On one journey I was not allowed to land, but I lost the struggle of wits and was forced onto another boat which was no more than a troopship for the wounded, and I was returned to England, like a package."

"Why on earth did that happen?" Asked Harriet.

"Kitchener regarded me as a threat. As Field-Marshal, he needed complete public support and any criticism of the management of the camps was not to be tolerated. He knew I would write a report about the conditions, and he wanted to prevent it. I wrote various letters to him accusing the Army of brutality and other sins, but to no avail. High Commissioner Milner was no better."

"I suppose," said Pip, "there are several levels of disappointment here. We tried in Africa to help poor people with the message of Christ. Our politicians just want to support the Imperial mission which seems simply about controlling a country to extract as much wealth as we can from it. But this Empire talk also fosters unbridled patriotism. Now I am as fond of my country as any man, but I hope I have enough moral sense to think it is my duty to condemn actions my country takes which are wrong."

"Very well put, Father," said Malcolm, "and hysterical patriotic responses are magnified in the newspapers where accurate information is at a premium."

"That's right," said Tom who had listened to Emily with a grave countenance, "I hope to stand for Parliament, as does Malcolm, and I know we will have to be trimmers, to trim our real views to be able to get public support, but hopefully, only on matters which have little moral import."

"Of course," said Mary, "if women have the vote and could enter Parliament, Emily would obviously have far more influence on policy."

"I do not know what influence I might have in present circumstances, but I hope that making a noise will stir some consciences here, but then the main task really is not to spend one's time fighting in the political arena but getting there with money to ameliorate shocking conditions."

"I so admire what you are doing," said Hannah, "and as almost a doctor myself, I find the camp conditions repulsive and our behavior totally un-Christian. At the same time, I still think that we must not avoid Karl Marx's analysis which is like a gauntlet lying their waiting to be picked up."

"How do you mean? I know of Marx but have not read him, " said Emily. "Anyone who preaches revolution is beyond the pale as far as I am concerned."

"I agree with you on rejecting revolution, just as I reject Marx's views on religion as the opium of the people, but we should come to grips with his claims that it is the economic structure which creates the power of capital, obvious in the struggles for colonies."

"Indeed," added Pip, "when Harriet and I encountered him and his friends in Manchester all those years ago he clearly thought that merely trying to better the conditions of the industrial poor as a policy simply supported the existing structure, whereas he wanted to smash that structure as the only way to effect the betterment of the people and for them to be in control."

The men did not retire for port. Miss Hobhouse prepared to take her leave.

"What a marvelous evening," said Emily, "and I am sure we could talk far into the night about such matters. I need as much rest as I can get, but before I have to leave we have not heard from our sober judge here. Sir Hamish, what are your views on all this?"

"Quite simple really. Marx is focused on the economic structure but it is not clear that in a revolution we would find a system of law that sought justice for every man and every woman. Events in France in 1780 and 1870 provide sufficient warning. As I hear about the camps, I am struck by the injustice of it all and it matters not a jot whether such injustices are carried out by generals, politicians, soldiers or paupers, it strikes right at the heart of any moral code that I can think of."

"Is that not interesting?" said Emily. "I am a woman and it is my compassionate nature that stirs me to action. Whereas, Judge, you see that the lens of justice is the vehicle we should use to assess these wrongs."

"True, but that does not mean I have no compassion and that you are not interested in justice, does it?"

Victoria was now feeling more at peace than she done for years. Albert's death had badly affected her and her children, especially Philip who seemed difficult and distracted sometimes as a pupil at King's School in Rochester where Victoria hoped that he would enjoy a good education in a morally healthy environment. His cousin Arthur was a scholarship boy too and as both were now eighteen, if young for their age, both were able to ride the eight miles from Numquam each day, mostly together, sometimes not.

Unlike Beatrice and young Nellie, her daughters, her son Philip seemed to welcome John Eustace as a friend of his mother's but as time went on it became apparent to him that the relationship was more than one of just friendship, Philip's attitudes changed. He became rude and actively hostile to John, leaving the room when he appeared and telling his sister's stories about the Vicar which were untrue.

Victoria discovered this when Nellie asked her mother why the Vicar whipped his dog so often.

"Where did you get that story?" asked Victoria in alarm.

"Philip told us."

"But he does not have a dog, Philip is making this up and it is a lie. What else has he told you?"

"He said the Vicar is only after your money, Mum," and she began to cry.

"That is wicked; is he back from school yet?"

"Not yet."

"He should be back by now."

An hour later, Philip appeared, bruised and somewhat disheveled, his satchel of books in disarray, almost falling off his horse in front of the house, rather than going straight to the stables."

"What on earth have you been doing?" asked Victoria, "I need to have words with you, young man," at which gave her a very surly look such that she would have spontaneously slapped him but refrained as she could see he had been hurt.

"We'll talk later, meantime let's get you patched up and into bed and you can tell me what happened."

As she was tending to his wounds, he began to cry, saying:

"When I was coming out of school, Balderstone was waiting for me, and he just started punching me and teasing me about my father and saying awful things about him. I went outside and tried to run away but he followed me and he was still punching me, but then I got really angry and we began to fight. I gave him one good punch and he fell back against the classroom wall, so I ran to the stables as fast as I could for the horse to come home."

"Was he unconscious?"

"I didn't wait to find out, I got up on Prinny and rode home."

"Oh, Philip, I knew you're really sorry about your father and you miss him, I know, and that boy is very nasty to hurt you like that."

"But how did Father die? You've never told me. I am almost eighteen, Mother, and I need to know."

"I will, I will, but not now."

"You will not go to school tomorrow as you need your bruises to heal. I'll write to the Headmaster and complain about this boy. We need soon to talk with John about your going to University in the autumn. What this boy's last name again?"

"Balderstone, Eric Balderstone."

"Just rest now."

John came to see her that evening and was very sympathetic and understood the problems Philip had about his father. He was not surprised about the boy's reaction to him, and he comforted Victoria by saying that it did not matter and that Philip would soon change when they were married and all living together. After all he was now a young man about to go to university.

Early the following morning Victoria finished her letter and gave it to the postman to deliver. As he left, a rider came up the Numquam drive and asked if she was Mrs. Pirrip.

"I am she, but who are you?

"I am Detective Splinting from Rochester and I want to talk to you about your son."

"Please come in. My son is in bed as he was beaten up in school yesterday by a boy called Eric Balderstone."

"I will need to talk with him now, in bed or not."

"What is the matter?"

"I am afraid that Eric Balderstone has died. He hit his head on a wall: The doctor said he had a skull like an eggshell. We think Philip killed him and I need to ask him some questions."

Victoria was thunderstruck. Philip a killer? But she composed herself, realizing that Philip was in great danger.

"Please come up to his room: I am sure he will be awake now."

"Philip," she said as they came into his bedroom, "this policeman wants to ask you about what happened with Eric Balderstone yesterday."

"Alright, but my head aches."

As Splinting looked at this eighteen-year old, realizing that he looked younger than he was and he could not help thinking about his own son of the same age, so he was sympathetic.

"Tell me about your fight with Eric," said Splinting.

"He started to punch me when I came out of school and was saying very nasty things about my father who is dead. I wanted to get home and was trying to get to the stables for my horse, and I got very angry and gave him a really good punch and he fell against the wall and I ran away to my horse and came home and my mother patched me up."

"We have a problem, Philip. Eric is dead."

"What? Dead? How can he be?" said Philip bursting into tears.

"The doctor says his skull was thin and when you hit him and he hit the wall, his skull broke and he died quickly. Did you see that he was dead?"

"No, once I gave him a good punch, I ran away."

"Has he insulted you before?"

"Yes, several times, but he'd never followed me like that. He is supposed to behave like an adult now we are in the senior form."

"As he has died, the Coroner must find out why he died and there is a good possibility he will call it manslaughter which means we would then have to charge you. If that happens we must put you before a magistrate on a charge of manslaughter immediately," at which Victoria shrieked in anguish.

"No, no, no, he did not intend to kill the boy did he?"

"That's why the charge is manslaughter, not murder. Please bring him to the Coroner's court in Rochester Guildhall at 10 o'clock tomorrow. I am not going to take him into custody, as I should, as he needs to continue to recover. I am, however, relying on you, Mrs. Pirrip, to ensure his attendance or there will be serious trouble."

"I will, I will," she said. Philip was weeping and turned over when she tried to comfort him as Splinting left.

"We are going to fight this, my dear. I will send for John and ask his advice."

Mid-morning John cantered up to the house after the Numquam gardener had delivered a message. He did not go up to the bedroom to see Philip but sat with Victoria in her drawing room to hear of the event.

"There is no option but to find a lawyer,"

"But I know several lawyers, John. Perhaps if I send a wire someone will come for tomorrow's hearing."

It was just before lunch at Courtisone and Jaggers when Robert received the wire. He hurried in to see Sir Clarence who was about to meet with Lord Bakersfield again.

"H'mm," said Clarence, reading the wire, "ask Mr. Garthwaite to come in."

Simon Garthwaite was the lawyer who had approached Mr. Justice MacDonald after the Infanticide Case in 1894 and asked about joining Courtisone and Jaggers. After talking with Clarence as the senior partner, he joined on a temporary arrangement which was then made permanent as Simon proved to be an outstanding advocate in Court.

"Simon," said Clarence, "I need you to go down to Kent as soon as you can this afternoon to meet a Mrs. Victoria Pirrip. Her son has to attend the Coroner's court tomorrow morning as I understand he killed a boy and there could be a charge of manslaughter. Mrs. Pirrip is an old friend of ours. He will be kept in custody so try to prevent that."

"I will obtain the address from Robert and go immediately."

Robert suggested the Blue Boar which lawyers from Courtisone and Jaggers had used before, and Simon told him to book him a room there before hastening down to Victoria Station. At half past six exactly he rang the Numquam House doorbell. The maid showed him into the drawing room where John and Victoria were sitting, and on the sofa wrapped in a blanket was Philip.

"How marvelous of you to come, Mr. Garthwaite," said Victoria after she read his card.

"Sir Clarence Smythe asked me to come to assist in what I understand to be a possible prosecution of your son on a charge of manslaughter."

"How helpful of Clarence. This is the Vicar of All Hallows, John Eustace who is also my fiancé, and this is my son Philip who has been urged by the police to make himself available at the Coroner's Court tomorrow."

At this, Philip moaned quietly as Simon took hold of an occasional chair and sat himself very close to Philip:

"Now young man, tell me exactly what happened and do not neglect any small detail."

After he had told his story, Simon said: "Now can we now get the whole story. First, where were you standing when Balderstone first punched you?"

"I was coming out from the door near the changing-room."

"Was he waiting for you outside or inside?"

"Inside where he started punching me. I think he was waiting for me."

"What was he saying, was he threatening you?"

"Not exactly."

"What do you mean, not exactly, was he or was he not threatening you?"

"Please," interrupted Victoria, "don't upset him."

"Mrs. Pirrip, not only do I need to know these details, but if this were to go to trial as is a possibility, he will undergo much more rigorous examination than I am giving him, so if you wish me to represent him tomorrow, you must just listen."

"He was making very nasty remarks about my father who is dead," said Philip.

"What did he actually say?"

"He said my father spent time with whores and that he jumped off a ferry 'because he could not stand to live with me and my mother."

At this, John and Victoria sat wide-eyed and in an aghast silence.

"Did your father commit suicide, then?"

"I don't know, my mother has never told me. She just said he had died."

At this, Victoria interrupted, saying: "I have tried to shield my children from the truth, and he did commit suicide as he had a terrible disease."

"Thank you, Mrs. Pirrip, so Balderstone knew this, but Philip didn't?"

"Quite so as the news did get around, I'm afraid."

Turning to Philip, Simon asked, "Did Balderstone mention anything about a disease?"

"No, I don't think so."

"What was it what he said that made you so angry?"

"I don't want to tell you."

"I'm afraid you must."

"I am sorry, Mum and John, I am sorry."

"Why?" Said Victoria and John in unison.

"He said, 'your mother's whoring it with the Vicar.'"

Victoria clapped her hands to her mouth and began to weep. John's face turned red and he spluttered out:

"How dare he, the little villain!"

"Right," said Simon, "I now have a very clear picture of what upset you such that you punched him and he fell against the wall. I am deeply sorry and I will do my level best tomorrow but the main goal tomorrow will be to ensure that you are not taken into custody. If that arises I will certainly ask both of you, Vicar Eustace and you Mrs. Pirrip, to vouch for Philip. Frankly I doubt whether the police will want him in custody, Philip, but the fact is that a boy died as a result of your actions and the Law cannot forgive that, I am afraid."

"What will happen to me?"

"We will attend the Coroner's enquiry tomorrow and he will decide whether a charge of manslaughter should be brought. I would certainly act as your counsel, but Sir Clarence may also want to add his weight to your case if a trial were to be the outcome. To be frank I think you should entertain the possibility that you will be sent to prison for a time, even though killing him was not your intention. By then there will be a prison for juveniles like yourself which has recently opened in a village near here, Borstal, I believe.

"But let us take one step at a time. I will leave now and will go to the school early tomorrow before meeting you at the Court. If I am allowed I will subject you to the questions I have been asking you this evening."

"Goodness gracious me," said Victoria in consternation, "prison, really?"

"Well, you see darling," said John, "that is the law: As I understand it, it is virtually impossible for anyone bringing about the death of another not to suffer imprisonment, for a long or short sentence."

"I will be staying at the Blue Boar," said Simon, "I hope the whole matter will be dealt with in half an hour as country magistrates and coroners like to dispose of cases quickly as they have other occupations."

As John left, Victoria asked him to rode over to the Cottage and tell Horatio and Beth what had happened and what the future was likely to be.

When he had left, Victoria said: "I am so grateful that Sir Clarence asked Mr. Garthwaite to help us. It makes such a difference to have a good lawyer."

"I will have to thank Sir Clarence, but I like Mr. Garthwaite very much, don't you?"

"Yes indeed, a splendid fellow."

Harriet was delighted when Elizabeth called on Valentine's Day and in a much earlier life, she would have been tempted to send her a valentine card. Like Clara Gargery, Elizabeth was a woman of outstanding natural beauty and as Harriet's secret desires merely dimmed with age, she was her effervescent self in Elizabeth's company.

"Harriet, my dear," said Elizabeth, kissing her on both cheeks as was becoming the fashion and which made Harriet's nerves tingle, "I want to talk to you about something very serious."

"You have found a lover?" Asked Harriet with a giggle.

"No such luck, I am afraid, but I have been to a meeting in Marylebone where a woman seemed to get in touch with the spirits of the dead and I would like to get in touch with Timothy's spirit if I could."

"Goodness me, I don't know what to say to that. I don't know anything about it but I recall a discussion with Mary MacDonald once when she said that Oscar Wilde's wife Constance was interested in the subject. I have read too that the Queen tried to get in touch with Albert. Annie Horniman is also interested in the occult."

"Who is she? I don't know the name."

"She plans to open the Abbey Theatre in Dublin if my information is correct, and she is a real radical, wearing trousers and smoking cigarettes in public. I think it was Katherine Bradley who told me about her."

"My goodness. Mine was a very sober and serious occasion and there were no radicals apparent there, and the spirit raised was singularly uninteresting."

"Now tell me," said Harriet, "What do these people in Marylebone believe?"

"I am not sure, and I don't really care if I could somehow communicate with Timothy. You see," and she began to weep silently, "we never had the chance to say goodbye. He went off to the Foreign Office as usual and was murdered there."

"I know, my dear, it must have been agony for you."

"I would love to be able to part from his spirit as I could not part from him in real life, so when I saw a notice of this meeting, I thought it worth examination," said Elizabeth, now pulling herself together. "They gave me various pamphlets afterwards and in answer to your question, I think these spiritualists think that all sentient forms of life survive our physical death and indeed retain a sense of who we are, our personal identity they call it."

"Good heavens, they take life after death literally."

"Indeed. In that after-life there is eternal progress, that we are all spiritually linked and of course as with some forms of Christianity, we must justify our actions on earth, though I am not clear yet whether we do that before God."

"But do you really think you might commune with Timothy in some way?"

"I don't know, but one pamphlet confirmed your remark that the late Queen and her husband had been interested in the occult, and that she held what are called seances after his death, for a child in the North somewhere at a seance said he had encountered Albert and that he used his private name for the Queen which no one could have known. That was conveyed to Windsor which led to several attempts for her to contact her husband."

"That is so interesting, though I confess I have no wish to talk to anyone I can think of who had died, well, Estella maybe. It would be good to know how she is dispensing her wisdom in the hereafter," and she laughed gaily, though Elizabeth did not find that possibility amusing.

The maid came into the drawing room at that point with a letter. Harriet took her letter knife and opened the envelope, saying, "How delightful, it is from Antonia," then, "Oh how tragic, her husband Aubrey seems to be dying. I have only been to the house twice and he always seemed a sickly fellow, but they have six children so that will be a great loss. Please forgive me, Elizabeth. I so enjoy your company and I will be thrilled to experience a séance with you if you will permit me. But I must go to Antonia, poor woman, she will be so distressed."

"I know, losing one's husband is like losing a part of your body, so please give her my sympathies, and I would be delighted for you to come with me to Marylebone at some point, and I will let you know when might be convenient."

IV

For some years it had become a fashionable mode of exercise for families, in-dividuals and married couples to take their constitutional, as it was called, in the two main green areas of central London, St James Park and Hyde Park. Magnificent horses walked amidst couples in all their finery, men outdoing each other with the latest style in silk hats and women too, sometimes with hats which looked as though they had just been plucked from a herbaceous border. It was also a place where casual meetings turned into friendships, where gossip was exchanged and political understandings created, especially when clement weather brought out the best and the finest of London society.

Both the Gargerys and the Heskeths had often taken the air in Hyde Park, but rarely met there, not that it mattered as they met so frequently as friends. That February morning, however, their unusual meeting in the Park was immediately consumed with conversation about the announcement of a by-election in Rye.

"Such a fine morning," said Tom after the usual greetings, "for making decisions about our ambitions. I want to be a protagonist for the Liberal cause by giving my strong support for the Liberal candidate in Rye. I have had an encouraging reply from the candidate."

"This is one of many occasions," said Clara with a smile, "when the future of a husband's career is of great importance to his wife. I am not sure about you, Hannah, with your medical commitments, but I am determined not to stay at home, but be a vociferous supporter."

"I am of the same mind, Clara, as they will enjoy themselves too much without us."

"Wait, wait. As I have only one eye, I rely on my darling wife to see all that is going on around me."

"And I need my wife to tend to those I have knocked down in my haste to achieve glory."

After the laughter died down, Tom read the other three the reply, "there is a real chance here for a victory," and Hutchinson writes that he would be "delighted to have as much support and help as we can afford."

It was rapidly agreed that the four of them should go to Rye to support Hutchinson. Clara sent Oliver down to Rye on the train on February 12th to select the most appropriate inn where they could hold two rooms until after the election, due on March 17th. Meantime the two couples continued their morning saunter.

Oliver returned in great excitement reporting that they had obtained the last two rooms available which were the most expensive and the cost seemed to him to be double the usual rate of two pounds per night. The town was already in election fever with bunting in contrasting colors of blue for the Conservatives and yellow for the Liberals.

By Valentine's Day, the Gargerys and the Heskeths were installed in the Mermaid Inn. Pip and Harriet stayed in London looking after Hector and Susanna, and Matilda was given responsibility for the Gargery children. At breakfast the first morning in Rye, Clara and Hannah were both missing their little ones and so they all agreed to return home each Thursday, returning on a Monday morning. Malcolm and Tom were like greyhounds straining at the leash, anxious to start their run for what they hoped would eventually end at a seat in the House of Commons.

They met with Hutchinson that morning and he first introduced two other men, both seated at what seemed makeshift desks. Sidney Hampton was identified as the agent and indicated that he had worked for the party for many a year. The younger man, Matthew Johnson was set on a political career after the university or so he said, but both Tom and Malcolm thought such a career unlikely as Johnson was small with a quiet voice and a shy manner.

"My opponent will be a Mr. Edward Boyle, a barrister and local worthy, whose platform is based primarily on agricultural issues especially in the hop industry, and he is against Home Rule. I assume, gentlemen, that you are Home Rulers."

"Indeed," said Tom, "my wife and I have spent time in Ireland working on behalf of the Jaggers Trust for the Relief and Education of the Poor at their estate near Londonderry. The only solution is Home Rule. But Hutchinson, we describe it as the Irish problem, but of course the problem is in fact the property of the British, especially the English."

"With your experience then, Hesketh, would you take on speaking for Home Rule on my behalf? There are various meetings planned and I hope we can arrange each one around a central topic, say education, foreign entanglements, Ireland to serve as the focus at each meeting."

"I'd be glad to."

"Gargery, I am taking on the education issue full bore which I think is more important than anything else. I was badly defeated in 1900 but I have reason to think that I have the advantage this time. My opponent, while known in East Sussex, is not the sitting member. Popular sentiment here seems to be for Home Rule and the Education Act last year has the nonconformists up in arms."

"I will be glad to support you on education and on the plight of the poor nationally."

"You should not think this in any way a request for you not to use this by-election as a way of getting yourselves known in Liberal Party circles, but some will see you as outsiders in this constituency which is proud of its Sussex identity. You will visit towns like Burwash, Hastings and Winchelsea, formerly a famous port but now the river has dried up, but it still has a Mayor and Aldermen but with a mere two hundred souls living there."

"I take it you mean that we should therefore speak with admiration of everything of Sussex when and if we speak publicly?" said Tom.

"Yes," said Hutchinson, "you know, sentences like 'it is such an honor to be in this noble town of Winchelsea with its magnificent etc., etc.' Get to know the history of the town where you speak."

"Thank you for this advice, Hutchinson," said Malcolm, "we will come to listen to your speech in Hastings next week on the Education Act, something we need to learn about and that will give us a good feel of such meetings."

Dinner in the Mermaid their second evening was excellent.

"Did you like Dr. Hutchinson?" Asked Clara as the soup was being served.

"Very much, darling, a thoroughly honest individual seeking to serve his country in the best possible way."

"I agree," said Tom, "and we will stay the course and see him into Parliament. Now we must begin to visit the towns, go to public places and find out what is moving the electorate, about twelve thousand men altogether, though I doubt whether more than a half will cast their vote."

"I hope we can generate enthusiasm for the man. I am convinced that Liberals will need to be aroused and maybe we can get three-quarters of them to vote."

"Did Hutchinson discuss votes for women?" Asked Hannah.

"That was not a topic, no," Tom replied.

"What a travesty. I hope you will find time to raise it."

On the morning of February 16, 1903, Philip Gargery's name was called in the Court of Mr. Lamberton Gooding, the Rochester Coroner, held at the Rochester Guildhall to explain the death of Eric Slapton Balderstone of Slapton House, Rochester. The case was quite a simple one, Gooding thought. The two boys had been engaged in a fight in which Balderstone had been knocked down and fell against a wall and received injuries to his skull as a result of which he died.

"You are Philip Pirrip?" Asked Gooding, "now please state your full name and address," which Philip then did in such a quiet voice that he was asked to speak up.

"And you are the son of Victoria and the late Albert Pirrip?"

"Yes, sir."

"And you are eighteen years old?"

"Almost, sir."

Gooding then asked: "Do you understand the seriousness of my enquiry into the cause of death of Eric Balderstone?"

"Yes I do."

"This seems straightforward to me as I read the police report. Detective, remind me of the detail so that it is in the Court record," at which Splinting set out the basic facts of the case, including a report from a doctor in the hospital where Balderstone was taken that he had an eggshell skull.

"Now, Master Pirrip, I am told this gentleman with you is a lawyer. Do you wish him to speak on your behalf?"

"Yes I do."

"Thank you, your Honor, I am Simon Garthwaite of Courtisone and Jaggers of Lincolns Inn," said Simon who was quite unused to the relative informality of a country Coroner's Court as compared to the Old Bailey.

"If your Honor pleases, I would like to question Master Pirrip here under oath."

"Really? I suppose so, but I do not approve of time-wasting lawyers," said Gooding with a smile although he was quite flattered to be addressed as 'Your Honor,' as he was not a magistrate.

"I respect your wishes, Your Honor, and I am sure you will wish to know Master Pirrip's perspective on this terrible accident for which he feels genuine remorse."

"Go ahead, then," said Gooding with a degree of impatience.

After Philip took the oath he swayed on this feet and it was obvious that he had injuries to his head, on which Simon remarked as he began.

"Now, Master Philip, I am going to ask you in detail about the events that led to Balderstone's death. I am sure that His Honor will appreciate any fact that will lead him to a wise decision, so please be sure to be completely accurate."

"I will," said Philip, scarcely able to control his nerves, his voice breaking.

"You have heard Detective Splinting's account which was derived from your conversation with him when he interviewed you yesterday."

"Yes, sir,"

"Your Honor, there are some critical details here to be considered over and above the detective's account. Master Pirrip, how did you first encounter Balderstone on this occasion?"

"He was standing inside the door to the yard when I finished my class and I was going to stables to get my horse to go home. As I passed him, he punched me on the shoulder, but I tried to ignore him, but he followed me outside, punching me all the time on my back and on my arm and head."

"I see, and what was he saying to you?"

"He was saying very nasty things about my father."

"What exactly?"

Philip's discomfort was obvious, "he said my father went with whores and that he had killed himself by jumping off the ferry into the Channel, sir." The few people in the audience gasped including a young reporter from the Rochester Gazette who made a hurried note.

"Did this make you angry?"

"No sir, not really angry at that point; I was very upset and wanted to get away from him. I just wanted to get to my horse."

"Was he punching you all this time?"

"Yes, sir, he was much bigger and stronger than me."

"At what point did you get angry and get into a brawl with him?"

Philip had to be told to speak up when he replied: "He said my mother was the Vicar's whore, sir, and I got very angry. We struggled a bit and he hit me on the head, so I just punched him as hard as I could and ran way for my horse."

"I see; then he fell back against the wall and hit his head? Now tell me, exactly, what did you then do?"

"I saw he had fallen over after I hit him and he fell, but I just ran away as quickly as I could to get away from him and as I was in great pain from his punching me on my back and on my head that I wanted to get home as soon as I could."

"So you hurried away and finally, when you got to your horse, you did not have to pass by the place where Balderstone was lying, so you did not know that he was seriously injured."

"No, sir, the stables open onto a track at the back of the school, so I did not pass him."

"That you, Master Pirrip. You may resume your seat.

"Your Honor, if it pleases you I would like to ask you to hear about the character of these two boys from the representative of King's School."

"That would be most helpful, Mr. Garthwaite," said Gooding, "I must confess Master Pirrip's testimony does put a different gloss on these events."

"Mr. Ambrose Combleton, would you step forward," said Simon. "There is no need for you to swear an oath for, as the Senior Tutor at Kings School, your veracity will not be in question."

"I wish that were generally true," said Gooding with a wry smile.

"If you would, Mr. Combleton, please give the School's assessment of these two boys."

"Certainly. Philip is a quiet reserved boy, physically somewhat immature, whose work has not been as promising as we hoped since the tragic and untimely death of his father, a catastrophe which we well understand can make a boy feel rootless and out of sorts. He has no record at all of any disciplinary infringements, and the school regards him as a model pupil, always punctual and thorough with his work. He is a credit to his family, who have borne various tragedies."

"Just a moment," said the Coroner. "Pirrip, of course. I dealt with the case of the two Fletcher boys killed by a falling tree. Did that happen in your presence, Master Pirrip?"

"Yes, sir, they were my cousins."

"Bless my soul, how unfortunate. Please continue, Mr. Combleton."

"We anticipate he will eventually go to the University if he can surmount this particularly horrendous family tragedy to which he has been subject."

"Thank you, now what of Eric Balderstone?"

"We have been disappointed in Balderstone, I'm afraid. He was not a good scholar, being lazy and slapdash, but also he had a tendency to be rude to other boys and indeed to the masters who teach him, especially if they were new to the school. He was like a man physically, even with a moustache at sixteen years of age. He has a record of several disciplinary infringements, one of which includes his assault on another junior boy, not a colleague in Philip's class. We did not know, and from my conversation with them yesterday, nor did his parents know that his skull had this congenital weakness."

"Mr. Combleton, I assume that you have experience of other scholars who tumble about and hit their heads on stones?" Asked Simon.

"Oh indeed, one of the older boys who rides to school daily fell off his horse last year. He was coming into the stables and the horse reared at something that frightened him. He fell and cracked his head against the stone wall of the stable and was unconscious for half an hour but came round before we could get him to the hospital."

"Thank you Mr. Combleton, that will be all.

"Your Honor, you have heard from Master Pirrip and just now from the Senior Tutor on the different characters of these two boys and the incident that has led to the unfortunate, indeed tragic death of Balderstone. It seems to me, and I am sure your Honor will agree, that while your verdict might be manslaughter, that would be inappropriate for what is manifestly an accidental death. Indeed if we are to assign blame, it falls, I suggest, more on the victim than young Pirrip.

"For there is no sign that Pirrip had any malice aforethought except as a response to a battery of continuous insults. We have heard of the case of an eggshell skull and it is very rare condition indeed, but I am sure Your Honor will know that boys do not merely fall off horses and bang their heads from time to time, but they do so in playing such games such as Rugby Football which has become the staple of school games in recent years.

"May I frame my conclusion to your Honor like this. Here is a boy, almost a young man, who is studious and scholarly with no blemish on his record, suffering a grievous loss in the death of his father, as well as the death of his cousins to which you kindly referred, for whom any sort of custodial sentence would be most damaging to him, not as a matter of his liberty but to the whole of his promising future."

He sat down to murmurs of approval.

"Thank you, Mr. Garthwaite. You have put the whole situation in the appropriate context. My judgment is that Balderstone's demise is to be regarded as one of accidental death. I see no reason for the police to carry the matter further.

"Master Pirrip," Gooding continued, "I am most sorry for the distress this accident has caused you and I offer you my condolences on the death of your father whom I met from time to time. He was a good man."

"Thank you, sir."

"Also Mr. Combleton, while I am grateful for your testimony, I hope that the School will seek to ensure that bullying is eliminated from the life of the boys in your care. I am not a member of the school of hard knocks. Whereas some of my contemporaries regard their school lives nostalgically, I found my education to be a long saga of trying to avoid the predatory and sometime brutal behavior of older boys, for which there is no excuse. Such acts are common assault and punishable by the Law. Indeed such assaults that occur within a school does not make them immune from prosecution, and that also applies to sexual misdemeanors. The Court is now closed."

Victoria and John stood outside the Guildhall waiting for Simon and Philip to appear after they had signed various documents for the Court. A woman approached them in mourning clothes and asked: "Are you, Mrs. Pirrip?"

"I am."

"I am Eric's mother, and I wish you and your son no ill, though I grieve for mine. I just want Philip to know that I do not blame him. Eric had gone astray recently, and ... " starting to weep, she hurried away to a carriage.

"Mr Garthwaite, we cannot thank you enough," said Victoria as he came over to them with Philip, "I do expect an invoice for your services."

"That will be a matter for Sir Clarence, but a very pleasing outcome. I must catch the London in ten minutes, so forgive me. Cheer up, Philip, it was not your fault."

As they rode home in the carriage, Victoria put her arms around Philip for whom the events of the last three days had been daunting, while John sat quietly on the other side.

"My lovely boy," said Victoria, "as I sat there listening, I realized just how hard your life has been which I have not paid attention to, as your father and

I fell out some time ago. I became depressed and anxious, even more so when he came down with that disease, I neglected you."

"What was this disease, Mother, surely you can tell me now?"

"It is called syphilis and it leads to physical and mental deterioration, and he clearly could not cope with it, so he killed himself."

"But how did he get it? Could I inherit it?"

"No, no, it is passed from women to men when they are intimate, do you know what I mean?"

"You mean when a man goes to a whore."

"Yes."

"So Father actually did consort with a whore."

"Oh dear, how dreadful, that must have been so hurtful to you, Mother."

"It was, it was. But you know for some reason he had changed from when I first knew him. I don't know why, but now let's think about you. For you, my poor boy, you had that business where you and Arthur fell out of the tree, again, not your fault. Then we had the tree falling down and you saw it fall when you were running back from the stables. Then your father died, and now this business with Eric Balderstone. What a catalogue of happenings to one so young."

"I do feel sometimes that I am marked for sorrow somehow. Nothing good seems to happen to me, but I don't want to go back to that school."

"Certainly not. You are almost finished with schooling anyway but I think you should go to a university, as Mr. Combleton suggested. I think we have to find you a tutor."

"I'd certainly need one."

"I wonder, John, would you be my tutor for the next few months?"

John had been quite silent as the woman he loved conversed about these most serious matters with her son, but he was listening carefully amid the rocking of the carriage, and he sat up with a start when he heard what Philip had just said.

"Well, Philip, that is such a pleasure to be asked and I would be delighted. Together we will prepare you for your entry to university this next year Where I am deficient, we can call in someone else, for example in mathematics. But I am gratified by your invitation too as I have been under the impression that you did not think much of me, and your mother told me of the things you had said about me to your sisters."

"I hated you taking the place of my father. Now I know about him, there is no reason to dislike you. You are a scholar too, and I think you'd be a good teacher."

"Are you happy that we will be getting married," Asked Victoria.

"Yes, Mother, you deserve some comfort and happiness now, and," he said with a slight giggle, "I need a tutor."

"I have thought of numerous ways to satisfy your interests, Mrs. Llewellyn," said Clarence as Angharad sat in his office one morning in late February, barely able to resist a private smirk when he realized how his statement might be interpreted.

"That sounds very exciting, Sir Clarence, but why don't you call me Angharad as I am not used to formalities?"

"I have investigated a number of possibilities, Angharad. You could spend capital on a building for the entertainment of miners and wives in a town of your choice on the coalfield or spend money renewing or bringing up to date existing facilities, such as stands for customers to watch sports, like Rugby. You could set up a charity for supporting families of miners killed or maimed in accidents. Given the amount of money you indicated to me that you would wish to spend, all of these are possibilities."

"I am spoilt for choice, Sir Clarence, but do you have a favorite?"

"I do: Charitable support. I am Chairman of the Jaggers Trust for the Relief and Education of the Poor. We can set up a Llewellyn Trust with a similar constitution and work in tandem. You will be chair of your Trust but will also be a director of the Jaggers Trust. Similarly one or two of the Jaggers directors will be on your Governing Board."

"That all sounds very complicated, Sir Clarence. Why don't I just give the money to your Trust?"

"Would you not like to be involved in the work yourself? We have Board members who have run our estate in Ireland and it gives them great satisfaction. Of course," he said contemplating the legal framework for her suggestion, "we could easily incorporate your money into the day-to-day operations of the Jaggers Trust with you on the board and your money earmarked for projects in Wales. I will put that proposal to the members informally if you agree but I am sure they will be delighted."

"That sounds better to me."

"I marvel at your achievement, Angharad, but you don't seem to have much contact with your children."

"No, I don't. They think me strange, I think. Anyway they're all married and while I'd like to be good friends with them and see my grandchildren, they have really cut me off."

"That's such a pity."

"One last matter, Angharad. Have you heard from your blackmailer recently?"

"Hamish told you about that, then?"

"Yes."

"No, I haven't. That's strange. I've been in London all this year and I had my maid in Radyr send my letters to Claridge's, but nothing from him. Why is that?"

"Let me just say this. In this practice, Courtisone and Jaggers, we have a long tradition reaching back to Mr. Jaggers and his clerk Mr. Wemmick…"

"Oh, I met them twice," she replied with a sniff.

"As I was saying, this tradition is one of taking steps outside the law to avoid lengthy proceedings which would be likely to end in some distress for those with whom we are concerned."

"I'm not sure what you mean."

"Well, we sent two reliable friends of ours down to Cardiff to meet with this Barry and he agreed not to continue to pursue you for money and expressed his sorrow for what had happened."

"Oh my, you put the frighteners on him, didn't you!" she exclaimed laughing, "Why didn't I think of that, I could have found some boys from the docks to do that."

"I suppose that is a way to describe it, but our two friends reasoned with him and neglecting other modes of persuasion, they told him that Courtisone and Jaggers would inform the police of the rape, if he did not desist. No physical force was needed, but then our friends are sturdy gentlemen of military background."

"Oh my god. Thank you so much, that is such a weight off my shoulders."

"You should really thank Robert, as he inherited from Mr. Wemmick the knowledge and foresight in such matters."

"Oh my gawd, I must thank him, but to be honest, I thought I'd never get rid of Barry but I could never stand up in a court and say what had happened to me."

"We understood that, but this extra-legal process produces the desired result. Justice is done, if not through the process of Law."

"I cannot thank you enough, Sir Clarence. Now I am going to move to London properly and help with your charity work, if my friend Hamish agrees," and she smiled broadly.

"I think we will be delighted to work with you."

When Clarence got home, he told Emma that he had suggested she join the Board.

"You know, Clarence, that is a very deft move. Do you remember all those discussions about widening the membership of the League and how Nellie was the only woman not of our class? This Welsh woman will bring a very valuable perspective to the Board, and with Albert gone, we should be of one mind and without the acrimony he introduced to our efforts."

"That is very nice of you, darling. I think you will find her, how do we say it these days, something of a rough diamond, an expression which I am sure was introduced by Cecil Rhodes or someone like him."

V

Simon Garthwaite proudly told his colleagues at Courtisone and Jaggers of his success in Rochester, and the news then spread rapidly to all the friends and acquaintances who knew Victoria and her family history. The sentiment was one of great relief for her, especially after the problems she had suffered with her philandering husband.

Pip thought he might go down to Kent to share in the relief that the grandson of his old army friend Fletch was quite blameless. Harriet was delighted that Victoria's trouble had been relieved, but she was most dismayed as she had just heard of Aubrey's death and felt a consoling visit to Antonia was of much greater importance and she insisted that Pip come with her to Putney to console Antonia.

"I did not know her husband, and I scarcely know her," Pip grumbled as their brougham made its way out along the river side to Putney.

"I know, my dear, but I think she would appreciate a man expressing condolences. Besides you'll be surprised at her ménage, I am sure."

Antonia opened the door to greet them but to their surprise she was not in mourning clothes.

"How good of you to call," said Antonia, "there is really no need."

"Who is it?" A child's voice called from the interior of the house somewhere.

"Just some friends, come and meet them."

There was a rumble like an approaching storm, and six children between fifteen and seven came from various corners of the house and were abruptly standing there and each introduced themselves politely.

"Now, my dears," said Antonia, "I want to go into the library and talk privately with our friends, so now you have been introduced, you can go about your business."

The children scattered, and Pip and Harriet went with her into the library.

"How are you handling Aubrey's passing with your children?"

"We have always tried to tell them the truth, however difficult. The girls are younger than the three boys and were matter of fact but outstandingly compassionate. They were constantly asking him what they could do for him and they'd read to him in his final days, stroking his head and arms, lying with him in bed, it was actually very moving," and a tear trickled down her cheek.

"How wonderful," said Pip, "and what about the boys?"

"Quite different, angry, trying to find someone to blame, but as we are not religious, God was fortunate to avoid their wrath. Once my eldest son, also Aubrey, saw clearly that there was little hope, he got very annoyed with everyone, especially me, though he knew I was not to blame. Our early discussions with the children helped so that it was not a shock. Earlier, it had just became hey-ho, that another interesting fact about life, but as they could not prevent it, the difference in attitudes between my girls and boys became clear. We talked about it constantly, very anxious to help them, the boys especially."

"What about the youngest?" Asked Harriet.

"Clung to me like a limpet, as if I had the power to change the situation."

"And now it is over, have they returned to their earlier selves?"

"Perhaps, but the turbulence of our loss is so overwhelming."

"But what about you, my dear, how are you coping?"

"As I said earlier, I was so accustomed to him becoming ill that I still do say to myself 'I must tell that to Aubrey' though I know perfectly well he is not there. It is the strangest experience, bereavement."

"Pip, darling, would you like to take a turn in the beautiful garden and look at the daffodils as I'd like to talk with Antonia."

"Do pick some to take home if you have none, we have so many."

"I will," said Pip rather disgruntled about being banished.

"Do you remember Elizabeth Egerton?"

"Yes, of course, that extraordinarily beautiful woman? "

"Yes, did you know her husband was murdered at his desk in the Foreign Office? It turned out that his assassin was a man called George Fortescue, one of his colleagues."

"Great Heavens! Really? Aubrey and I knew George Fortescue quite well. He and his family disappeared, must be well over a year ago now. I remember Aubrey managed to take a cab to his house, but it was shuttered."

"I don't quite know how to say this," said Harriet, "but he was hung for treason as he was the culprit. The proceedings were all in camera, and I assume he was able to make arrangements for his family to go elsewhere."

"How shocking and how terrible for Jemima, his wife. What on earth could have possessed him to kill someone? What happened to her, I wonder? Goodness me, I must seek her out, as she was obviously blameless, but then women are often damaged by their husband's bad behavior, aren't they?"

"Indeed, the sins of the husbands are visited upon their wives, it is true, but to return to Elizabeth: Soon after she was widowed, there was almost a stampede of men offering her themselves, in one case an earlier lover before she married who literally threw himself at her. It seems that widows are a target for lecherous men. Of course the King was notorious when he was Prince of Wales, and I doubt that anointment and coronation will have changed him, although I think he preferred his women married, not widowed."

"I doubt whether I will ever be in his company," said Antonia with a smile, "but you know, Harriet, Aubrey told me I should not cleave to his memory. At least we had such a discussion many years ago when an old friend of his died suddenly. We both agreed that celibacy would suit neither of us, unlike our dear departed Queen."

They wandered out into the garden to find Pip, deep in what seemed a serious conversation with young Aubrey.

"Mother," cried Aubrey as they approached, "Mr. Gargery has suggested that I come and visit him. He has been so helpful with me about Aubrey dying."

"That would be marvelous, my dear."

"Why not bring your brothers," said Harriet, "and perhaps we can take a trip along the river? Would that be a good idea, Antonia? I'll ask Elizabeth as well."

"Of course."

On the way home, Pip asked Harriet what she had talked about with Antonia which required his being sent out to grass. Harriet declined to answer, aware that, as he grew older, her husband was becoming increasingly strict and conventional about the relationships between men and women.

Clara had left Malcolm in Rye in the middle of the first week of March as she was missing her children. On Friday morning her sister-in-law Hannah called and they walked across Piccadilly from her Down Street home into the Park and encountered Emma Smythe who had left her carriage nearby as she wanted fresh air before shopping in Kensington. In the distance they noticed the unmistakable figure of Sir Clarence going in the opposite direction.

"Is Clarence not with you?" asked Clara as they approached.

"No, we had a long walk this morning and he had work to do. As it is such a nice Spring morning, I thought I would stay longer and, by Jove, here are you two, how pleasing!"

"Since we got back from South Africa," said Clara, "I feel I have not quite got back into a proper rhythm of life. Malcolm and I talk about nothing but this by-election, and the ambitions of our two men in their bid for Parliament. A general election is still three years away, but it is all hands to the pump, as they say, and I am having to get used to what a husband in politics might mean for me.

"Might we develop some ideas together on how we can help Tom and Malcolm in their individual pursuit of political glory after all wives are supposed to be stalwart supporters, even if they are silent?"

"Clarence's constituency will prove an excellent seat for Tom as he works on foreign policy," said Emma.

"Tom certainly believes citizens there are exactly the people who will want to be well informed and supportive of government foreign policy after the experience with the Boer War where public opinion was quite unbalanced."

"I am pleased for you, Hannah," said Clara, "while we don't know yet where Malcolm might be the Liberal candidate, he is getting his teeth into our domestic agendas. We must also get our presence known at the top of the Liberal Party starting at as senior level as we can. Malcolm was at a mess dinner with Winston Churchill in India and you have entertained him too, Emma."

"Yes, as my dear Clarence is an MP, he will certainly be able to invite a leader or two, even that Welshman David George, is it, no, David Lloyd George I think, and he is already a rising star in the Liberal Party."

"Isn't his weather wonderful?" said Hannah, changing the subject, "and I am so thrilled that you and my brother are so happy, Clara. Of course I have always admired and loved him with a passion, so I am biased in his favor."

"Thank you Hannah, while I still cherish my dear Sam's memory, my good fortune in meeting Malcolm is my true miracle."

"Sam was a treasure indeed," said Emma, and they all laughed quietly. "Let me see, you have George and Alice from your marriage to Sam, and now Andrew, Susanna and Charles with Malcolm. Is that it?"

"Goodness me no, my dear, babies just seem to pop out of me. I find neither pregnancy nor labor difficult. We can afford a large family and, between ourselves, I suspect I am pregnant at the moment."

"Not for me, I'm afraid," said Hannah, "I find it a great trial and though I love Tom and my two children enormously, I am in no hurry to have a third. My father went mad with fright when I was pregnant last time, imagining I was going to die and he would then have another woman he loved dying unnecessarily."

"That is very sad. But back to action, we are The Three Musketeers, perhaps?"

"How delightful! Emma as Athos, you as Porthos and me as Aramis."

"And Elizabeth as D'Artagnan?"

"It is not enough just to hold dinner parties, is it?" Said Emma. "While I am getting increasingly frustrated at not being able to vote, the other issues facing the country are so important. How do we handle these trade unions? Should we think about what happens to the poor worker when he gets old? I think about my maids and wonder what their old age is going to be like. And then there's Ireland."

"I agree," said Hannah, "for my part, as a doctor, I think we must have laws about health, so far generally restricted to venereal disease. I am impatient to have government insist that all children are vaccinated whether their parents like it or not. We now know, unlike the days of the plague, that most of the diseases we encounter are transmitted from one person to another. Medical research enquiries are so small and all over the place and, as the Government can't organize it, the profession must do so itself: But doctors are such Tories."

"Disease apart," said Emma, "the real blessing for the Irish peasant is this Land Purchase Act which has given the tenant farmers rights including rights to buy their land, though Clarence thinks it is just a way of heading off Home Rule."

They had stood together talking, but then wandered slowly back in the direction of Piccadilly.

"That is such an anomaly, you know," said Emma, "men who become doctors seem often more interested in feathering their own nests than in curing their patients, but tell me, my dear friends, what does our conversation mean for helping our husbands become MPs?"

"Important, I think, to press them to develop policies that will help the poor in as many ways as possible."

"I agree," said Clara, "and then there's education."

"If people are educated, then they should be more conscious of their health conditions," said Hannah. "My goodness, these ideas are taking shape as a mission, my friends."

"Perhaps we can have the League meet without discussing the suffrage and work out a women's Liberal platform."

"Yet," Emma continued, "we always talk about having people who are outside our circle, who are much poorer than we are, but we never do anything about it. It is as if our principles are false."

"Emma, our problem is that we simply do not know anyone. Years ago, Victoria's mother Nellie was the one example, I am told. If we attend meetings, I am sure there will be inspired women from the lower classes whom we might invite."

"Let us be very serious about this. Let us make it our task to go to meetings and find recruits to the League."

"A good idea" said Clara grimly, "but at bottom, class will out."

"Tell me again, how are your babies?" Asked Hannah as they started to go their separate ways.

"Beautiful and lovely, and I am now going to fetch them all for a walk to look at the changing of the guard in front of Buckingham Palace."

The election campaign was proving frenetic for Tom and Malcolm in their vociferous support for Hutchinson in the Rye by-election. People in the constituency quickly became accustomed to the man with the eye-patch and his companion with a wooden leg touting the virtues of the Liberal candidate. Both got opportunities to address meetings, events which they valued as neither was accustomed to public speaking.

Tom and Malcolm were on the Hutchinson platform at a mildly raucous meeting in Hastings Town Hall just after Valentine's Day. David Lloyd George has come down from Westminster to support Hutchinson's candidate so the hall was packed and the meeting gave the two an idea of their future. Sitting up there on a most uncomfortable wooden chair, Malcolm thought audiences look rather different when you face them from this height.

Lloyd George had long blond hair, flashing eyes, and was a formidable presence. He had been a solicitor and spoke with his usual Welsh vigor and humor for twenty minutes about domestic issues and the iniquities of the Conservative Government. So easily did he win the attention of the audience that Tom thought he must have delivered it a thousand times, but in his peroration he turned to Ireland with only the fury that a Celt could deliver.

"So my friends," he concluded, "Ireland gives us the opportunity to think about our great nation and Empire. We should repeal the Acts of Union which have made up Great Britain. I am sure that there are Welshmen and Scotsmen who see themselves laboring under the English yoke," which raised roars of dissent from the Conservative element in the audience which Tom immediately noted as a deliberate attempt to flush out hecklers and raise the excitement.

"Some will say that it is good for them. But no, gentlemen," he said his voice rising to a crescendo that made the rafters ring, "Home Rule for England, Home Rule for Scotland, Home Rule for Wales and Home Rule for Ireland," at which a voice from the back of the hall shouted:

"Home Rule for Hell!"

"Quite right," said Lloyd George with a lowered voice, "every man for his own country!" At which the crowd burst out into laughter, jeers and cheers and it took time for the chair of the Hastings Liberal Party to restore order.

It was left to the candidate to sum up. He was not the most energetic speaker but he was serious.

"Let me put before you some facts, gentlemen. Ours is an unhealthy nation. Forty percent of military recruits for the Boer War were declared unfit by virtue of their physical condition. One-third of the population live below the poverty line. The Government's Education Act is a confounded mess, as nonconformists must pay taxes to support schools run by the Church of England. But you know this. We are Liberals and within two years we will once again be the party of Government," at which there was loud and prolonged applause all round and a verse or two of "For he's a jolly good fellow!"

Later that evening, Tom and Malcolm sat with Charles Hutchinson and Lloyd George, David as they were now privileged to call him. They ordered beer which was brought to them by an attractive young woman, quite unusual for a good English hotel where such positions as waiters were held by men.

"Come here, my dear," said Lloyd George as she walked around the table to serve him, 'what's your name?"

"Sally, sir."

"Tell me, Sally, would you like to be able to vote for me?"

"I don't rightly know, sir, but I think I'd like to."

As Malcolm was seated next to him, he noticed Sally beginning to blush as Lloyd George's hand stroked her back and her posterior.

"Well, my dear," he said, "I'll talk to you in person about that later."

"Yes sir," said Sally smiling.

"Meantime I must confer with these gentlemen," he said, seemingly quite unembarrassed by his lecherous behavior, as Sally flounced off back to the bar.

After they had told Lloyd George of their backgrounds, he turned to Malcolm,

"You seem a couple of eager men devoted to the Liberal cause. Mr. Gargery, you were in South Africa then?"

"Yes, my family and I were in Port Elizabeth, but I had the privilege of working with Miss Hobhouse and I have met her recently in London."

"What did the bloody Government think they were doing? Henry Campbell-Bannerman and I were enraged when we read her reports, just a policy of extermination, quite unjustified."

"I agree wholeheartedly. The generals seemed able to persuade the Cabinet of the propriety of their strategy."

"Such a waste of men, on our side as well as the Boers. I foresee great difficulty in asserting the political will over the military arm of the nation. They deceived us, but as we were losing men, it became difficult for Government to control the generals, especially Kitchener."

"In combat," said Tom, "events on the battlefield take over and, certainly in the case of the North-West Frontier where we both were serving, political control was difficult and when it was exerted, it was often disastrous, though I must admit timid generals are worse."

"Important and sensible comment, Hesketh. You must have studied the Afghan War and the tragedy of the Khyber Pass."

"Indeed. Now David, while I know volunteer soldiers will die for their country, recruits often believe they are immortal, so it is up to the generals not to be cavalier about their losses of men. Throwing men after men into a situation is madness and I do speak with military experience."

"The Khyber was a disaster indeed," said Malcolm, "but in my experience of India, generals like Bindon Blood were very conscious of the price being paid in men and he sought to diminish the dangers while seeking ways to conquer the enemy."

"Now I meet many a Welshman who has fought for his country, and I am not surprised that many of them who have fought in India or South Africa have only the most rudimentary grasp of what they are fighting for. King and Country seems an abstract ideal."

"I could not agree more, David," said Tom. "In India we were fighting the Afghan tribes because the Company had tried to take over their ancestral lands. Building an Empire is a suspect notion."

"Don't ever say that to an audience, Mr. Gargery. Let me tell you from my experience what is required in a speech.

"First, you must train your voices to be able to carry your ideas forcibly. This is not shouting, mind you, just throwing your voice at the rear of that hall, like taking a shy at a coconut, but knowing when and where to emphasize and to lower or rise your voice. Then you must be oratorical, but only in brief bursts. Use metaphor and historical examples too. But mainly, don't look at the ceiling, but with each phrase search the eyes of men in audience, and, of course, especially focus on women," he said with a smile.

"Finally you must be sure of your ground otherwise you will be caught out by some fellow or other when questions are allowed. But now gentlemen, I must bid you good evening, as I must engage young Sally in the possibility of her voting," and with that he rose and walked behind the bar.

Later he could be seen escorting the young woman up the stairs of the Inn. Hutchinson shook his head slowly as they watched that scene.

"It will be his downfall one day, soon rather than later, I suspect."

"I have never seen anything like that, have you?" said Tom.

"No, and I hope not to see it again," Malcolm replied.

At other meetings early in March, Malcolm spoke, gradually getting into his stride with repartee from hecklers, but the task was to promote the candidate, Charles Frederick Hutchinson, not himself. However brief his contribution, it regularly provided him with the opportunity to talk about the health of the nation, and to praise Hutchinson as a doctor of whom the nation needed more.

It was at the aptly named town of Battle that what was a rowdy meeting turned to combat. After introductions, Hutchinson had to leave to go to St. Leonards' to address another meeting. Four members of the local Liberal committee were on the platform, but this time, Tom and Malcolm were in the audience, standing at the back. The Chairman had begun to defend the Liberal platform but then veered off into harsh criticism of Edward Boyle, the Conservative candidate.

"Why would you vote for such a man? What does he know of anything but agriculture? On Ireland he is wrong. On Education he defends the indefensible."

"Rubbish!" shouted a man at the back.

"Liberal scum," shouted another.

"If you gentlemen cannot wait until question time, please leave as you are disrupting the meeting," said the Chairman, at which there were whistles and catcalls and several men began to push and shove members of the audience and knock over their chairs.

"What are these foreigners doing here? "shouted the first man, pointing at Tom and Malcolm, "Where do you come from, Eyepatch?"

"These men are up for a fight," said Tom quietly, and with military precision, he slammed his fist into the midriff of a bull of a man wielding a chair. Most of the audience scattered to the side of the Hall as Tom, Malcolm and two Liberal Stewards faced a group of seven or eight men who, not merely content with disrupting a meeting verbally, were ready for a fight, driven no doubt by the amount of beer they had consumed beforehand in the bar of the George Hotel.

"Get these men into the street," shouted Malcolm, handling a smaller man by the scruff of the neck and hurling him through the door, as Tom sat in a chair wielding his crutch with great effect.

One of the stewards swung a chair at a man just as Tom was about to grab him, but narrowly missing Malcolm, though it left the man virtually unconscious on the floor, so Malcolm unceremoniously threw him out to join his fellows in the street.

The whole event lasted only a few minutes and once the villains were all out on the street, there were cheers from the remains of the cowed audience for Tom, Malcolm and the stewards.

"So this is politics," said Malcolm with a smile as they left for the hotel.

VI

Harriet called on Elizabeth to elicit her interest in the election campaign but also to let her know of the various plans inspired by the League to address the concerns of women more widely than the vote.

"Thank you, Harriet, it sounds a fascinating and worthwhile endeavor but I will not be able to be a part of it."

"Oh dear, why? Are you a hidden Tory?" Asked an astounded Harriet.

"Of course not. I have decided to spend a year in America and I will book passages for June or July."

"Great Heavens, why?"

"Timothy and I were in Washington for three years and we met some very interesting men and women. I am not yet fifty years old and I find my life here mildly satisfying but widowhood simply does not provide for me much of a thrilling existence. I am not interested in remarrying. My two boys are now beginning their own lives properly and neither have any interest in coming with me. Oliver is interested in politics and he will no doubt help the Liberal cause."

"And Charlotte, your daughter?"

"She is very enthusiastic to accompany me. She was too young to remember much of our time there, but she has been reading the work of Mark Twain voraciously."

"I don't know the gentleman."

"Oh Harriet, that is a serious blot on your escutcheon. You must go immediately and purchase Tom Sawyer and Huckleberry Finn which are not only wonderful stories but explain a great about slavery to the English mind in novel form. Charlotte came running into my bedroom the other day, saying the Mark Twain had spoken in favor of votes for women."

"I suppose I have been so engulfed in English literature that it has never occurred to me to read anything outside books which come from these islands."

"That is such a pity, my dear, but Charlotte's fascination will lead us goodness knows where in our travels in America. She speaks of travelling up the Mississippi River from New Orleans."

"Oh dear, this gets worse for me, where is New Orleans? Is that north or south in the United States?"

"You astonish me, Harriet. Do you think our friends know as little of America as you?

"I really do not know. I cannot remember any conversation with them about the country."

"Do you recall anything about my mother or whether Estella mentioned her?"

"No, I don't think so, or I have forgotten. At sixty-five, I find my memory trifles with me."

"My mother was an American. I have not heard from her since we parted in Paris sometime in the mid-seventies. She abandoned my father when the war broke out in 1870 and went off to Monaco. Sometime after his death, we met at a reception held by John Sargent's parents in Paris and there she had a Romanian count in tow, and she expressed little interest in me or my future children, saying I was always my father's child."

"How did you cope with that, abandoned by your mother? That must have been quite awful."

"I did not care a jot. I had such a strong relationship with my father and I nursed him for a few years in Athens before he died. My mother apart, we had friends in the Diplomatic Corps from several countries when we were posted to Washington, people we constantly met at receptions. In Washington, the climate was awful in the summer as the whole city was built on a marsh. I knew a couple of women who were musical enthusiasts, so it was a splendid social life, typical I suppose of a diplomatic family. We travelled too, primarily on the East Coast. Timothy hated New York, but when we journeyed up Long Island by train for a weekend, that was lovely. Boston was very special too.

"So you have much to revisit," said Harriet as Charlotte came into the room.

"Indeed and we are also going to search out our family, aren't we, Mamma? I don't know whether my American grandmother is still alive, but she must have relatives we could call upon."

"Goodness me, Charlotte, I can see you are excited by your visit to America."

"Indeed I am, but I am seeing myself not as a visitor, but an explorer. I am sure Mamma won't let me go off on my own and I won't have a brother to escort me, so I will have to persuade her to come."

"What sort of explorations, apart from your family?"

"There are some natural features I want to see, Niagara Falls and the Grand Canyon for example, but there are some wonderful places quite near Washington, the Blue Ridge Mountains and the Chesapeake Bay."

"How about your studies, though?"

"I love Mark Twain as Mamma has probably told you. I have led a very sheltered life so far and my father's murder contributed to that as we bound together tightly as a family thereafter, thanks to my darling mother. I do want to explore American literature more thoroughly than one author, and the poets like Longfellow."

"Dear me, I am so ignorant. Who is he?"

"Don't you know The Song of Hiawatha, Harriet?" Asked Charlotte, her voice rising, "I am surprised, especially as you are a poet, aren't you? It has the most enchanting rhythm. Let me read you a verse," and she got up and took down a book from the bookcase.

"Here, listen to this. I won't read it all as it is very long, but so evocative of the American Indians, and I will exaggerate the rhythm:

'Then the generous Hiawatha
Led the strangers to his wigwam,
Seated them on skins of bison,
Seated them on skins of ermine,
And the careful old Nokomis
Brought them food in bowls of basswood,
Water brought in birchen dippers,
And the calumet, the peace-pipe,
Filled and lighted for their smoking.
All the old men of the village,
All the warriors of the nation,
All the Jossakeeds, the Prophets,
The magicians, the Wabenos,
And the Medicine-men, the Medas,

Came to bid the strangers welcome;
"It is well", they said, "O brothers,
That you come so far to see us!"'

"Goodness me," said Harriet, "where have I been all these years. When was this written?"

"Fifty years ago, or so."

Elizabeth had been listening with admiration to her daughter whose fascination with literature matched her own with music.

"We will certainly do plenty of exploring but I remember from our time there that the educational opportunities in colleges are much greater for women so perhaps you can study there."

"Perhaps, Mamma, but one ambition is to go to a talk by Mark Twain as I gather he tours the world and America giving talks."

Afterwards, on her way home, Harriet called into see Mary as she often did.

"Have you heard?" Asked Mary as Harriet walked into her drawing-room.

"Heard what?"

"Honora is close to death."

"Oh, how sad and such a life," and she sat down heavily on the settee.

"Simon came to tell me and revealed all manner of things about her which I will keep to myself for now."

"I have news of another departure to tell you. Elizabeth is going to America for a year."

"Why on earth would she do that?"

"She will go with Charlotte, meet old friends, family and explore, her mother was American of course."

"H'mm, I suspect we won't see her again unless she returns with a rich American husband."

"Oh, Mary, you know you can be quite cruel sometimes."

"Caustic, maybe, even cynical, but cruel never."

Rye is a quiet town not used to excitement. Fishermen come and go. The main street winds up the hill on what was a track first made by Saxons starting a small community near the sea. Across the marsh up on the hill its people could see the town of Winchelsea, once the center of southern England's wine trade. Rye became more important as a port and Winchelsea struggled to retain its glory, except in the capacious wine merchant's houses with their huge cellars, now empty except for the wine that a gentleman's household might need for its daily consumption.

The early days of March 1903, however, were raucous and enthusiastic, though in several quarters nervous and overwrought. Rival bands of supporters regularly roamed the streets. There were clashes and mock fights, sometimes at night becoming real, fueled by beer, cider and strong drink. Songs, too:

'Vote, Vote for Charley Hutchy,

Kick old Boyley out of door,

For Charley is our man,

And we'll have him if we can,

And we won't vote for Boyley any-more.'

Throughout the campaign, Tom and Malcolm had become completely immersed in the struggle of an election. For men of a military bent, it was understood as a game of strategy and tactics, and they admired the framework within which Hutchinson had developed his plans, realizing just how important this was to convey to supporters.

Once votes were cast on the 17th, two weary men sat in the bar at the Mermaid Inn rehearsing the best moments of the campaign and what they had learned.

"Interesting to compare politics to war, isn't it?

"I suppose we have to view what happens through that lens, though we do not have problems of ammunition supply," replied Malcolm grimly.

"No, I mean the strategy first: How to create the balance between attacking one's opponent and putting forward one's message."

"That certainly. That night of the battle in Battle, I thought the Chairman's attack on Boyle was really uncalled for. It became too personal, not enough about the issues. I do hope to avoid that, Tom."

"But what would you do if you were the target?"

"There are some well-tried responses, like 'I will not deign to descend to the level of my opponent,' and such dismissive comments."

"That is a good line, but it depends. I suppose if it is clear one is losing, then lashing out on the rival's personality becomes very tempting."

"Certainly. Tactics are another matter. Clearly the Chairman's attack were a blunder, and Hutchinson was furious with him afterwards, 'not the words of a gentleman' and so on, but the fight merely served to encourage the lower elements to look for opportunities for fisticuffs, either at meetings or on the street."

"I must say I had not heard of such behavior at an election thus far. I remember reading The Pickwick Papers by that fellow Dickens and there the election seems mainly about bribery."

"Not much of that with a secret ballot. One other matter is the balance between the local and the national. By that, I mean, should the focus be dominantly one or the other?"

"This is a matter of tempering the wind to the shorn lamb, isn't it, Malcolm? Throughout a campaign and beforehand in whatever manifesto one writes, one must know enough about the voters, different of course from the larger populace, to judge how much local issues matter against national issues, and how far the latter influence the former."

"For my part, I now need to find myself a constituency, hopefully within six months so that I can immerse myself in its local politics and meet both the voters and the institutions, the churches for example."

"Now that's an important insight which I should not have missed with my Irish experience, Malcolm: The churches, of course, community institutions with many members, and one would have to court the non-conformists as well, of course."

"Listen to that noise outside, it sounds as though there could be a rough night or two before the announcement."

"I'm to bed too, my friend."

"Good night, Tom. I can't wait to return to my wife's bed."

"Nor I."

After breakfast, two days later, they walked up toward the Town Hall steps where a large crowd had gathered. At noon, the Registrar of Elections appeared, flanked by the two candidates.

"In my official capacity, I am here to announce the results of the by-election for the constituency of Rye." Cheers from the crowd.

"For Mr. Edward Boyle, there have been cast 4,376 votes," which announcement was followed with much louder cheers.

"For Dr. Charles Fredrick Hutchinson, there have been cast 4,910 votes," at which the crowd interrupted with whoops and cheers which took a few minutes to subside before the Registrar was able to say, "and I declare the said Dr. Charles Frederick Hutchinson to be the member of Parliament for Rye. God save the King!"

The crowd cheered and cheered, and Hutchinson stepped forward to express his thanks to his supporters, the Registrar and sundry others. He also thanked without naming them men who had come from outside the constituency to work with him, except Mr. Lloyd George. The London Times later reported that the outsiders, politicians excepted, were a source of suspicion in the constituency, especially among the supporters of the defeated candidate, which of course was ignored by politicians,

Hutchinson saw Tom and Malcolm in the crowd and came to thank them.

Taking off his spectacles which had steamed over in his excitement, he said:

"I am so grateful for your work here," he said, "and I hope I am re-elected in a general election and we will work together in a new House of Commons."

The two men reciprocated their thanks and explained how much they had learned before hurrying off to the London train.

Horatio and Beth were thrilled that Victoria was to marry again, and he had insisted that they would organize everything as if they were her mother and father.

"Look, love," he said when she was over there in January, "is you sure you'd want to do it where you married Albert, same church and same house for the reception? You could use the Bargemen but it's not the place for John's people now, is it, and it's not close to the church like the Rose and Crown?"

"You can't have it here in the living room, Harry, now can you?" said Beth.

"Oh no, I thought we'd have a big tent, though it depends how many you'se having."

"I think you're ever so generous and I really appreciate it, but my John's got this Vicarage, you know, with two really big rooms. It has five bedrooms as well and the garden's lovely, with flower beds and an orchard. I was surprised when he said he had rights to plots of land nearby too, tithe land they call it, and he gets money from that."

"But will you let us be the host? You'se my flesh and blood, you know, and after all that happened, the least I can do is to send you off on your wedding day."

"I'll talk to John. He's very busy as it's Lent, but we are thinking about an April wedding."

After many a discussion, the reception was to be at the Vicarage, Horatio would be the host, and that they would limit the guest list to fifty.

As the Spring went on and the April date came closer, Victoria felt it was important to have the children of people she knew come to her wedding. She had three page boys and three bridesmaids, not because it was a fancy do but because they were her nephews and nieces. Beatrice was now twenty-two and very happy to be without a responsibility. John had eventually decided to ask his cousin Michael Eustace to be his best man, as Horatio would be giving his sister away.

One significant argument was who should conduct the service.

"Might we invite Pip to conduct the ceremony? I know he has been ordained, albeit as a Methodist, but he and Harriet are close to my family."

"I was thinking of inviting an old friend with whom I had studied at Cambridge. He is Sebastian Wittering, vicar of a church in Northamptonshire and recently returned from a mission in South America."

"But I don't know him."

"I know and he is a bit of an odd stick, but he is very nice, I assure you."

"But Pip would be so delighted."

"I would have to ask the Bishop for permission for Pip, my dear, and the Bishop is just not the sort to allow it. More than that, he would probably want to be asked to conduct the service too, trying to be everything to everybody. We can easily ask Pip to be part of the ceremony, say, by reading the Marriage at Cana story although I always feel that turning water into wine is inappropriate."

"That would satisfy him, I think. We must certainly avoid any altercation with the Bishop, but I hope I like Sebastian."

"I know you will, and Pip and he will have much to talk about."

"Might Pip give us a sermon?"

"That is very risky indeed, Victoria. He might get carried away as he did at times when he stayed with me. No, I think a short lesson will satisfy Pip."

"Then I will write to ask him."

"Thank you, darling."

"I am thinking of asking my brother if he will agree to sell Numquam House, difficult though that is in terms of family history. We don't need the bother of keeping it up, and I must attend completely being your wife."

"Oh dear, that would be a pity, as the house is so special."

"Well, I suppose we could lease it to a family and give Horatio half the proceeds."

"If you do that, it will still be available when your children are grown up and they might need it."

"Just a thought. Now about the Vicarage. I want to spend my money on a complete redecoration. I enjoyed using Albert's money at Numquam, and now I can do the same with the Vicarage. It's a bit draughty, isn't it, though very charming in its way. We will need new modern fittings and we need new gas lamps, though you are still using candles upstairs, aren't you?"

"Yes, not much was done to the house by my predecessor; as he was not married he must have been quite content with living in a couple of rooms with a maid, and a cook. But my dear, it will be your household. I need to keep my study as it is, but the rest of the house is yours to fashion as you wish."

"I will give the matter my deepest thought," she said smiling, "and we will go to London and examine every emporium in the city."

The parish of All Hallows was ancient and though the church was small and compact, much like the village of one hundred souls, it extended to include small farms to the west and south and north to the marshes on the Estuary. Visitors admired the church, as ten years earlier it had been substantially restored and, now bedecked with spring flowers, it was a very pretty sight.

Pip and Harriet stayed in the Blue Boar and they used the opportunity to walk through the Parish as Pip recalled details of his past, especially his journey home from the Crimea, wounded with a stick.

"I don't know much about it," she said, "but is it unusual that the Vicar of a parish is married in his own church?"

"I don't know," he replied, "but there seems to be a great deal of enthusiasm for it."

They were sitting in the Rose and Crown enjoying a local beverage after arriving an hour before the ceremony.

"As I think about it," he said, "we'd only come to this public house very rarely, perhaps on a market day, as the Bargemen is near St Mary Hoo, west of here and so nearer the Cottage."

At that moment, Malcolm and Clara came in, followed by Hamish and Mary, all of whom had come down by an early train and ridden by carriage from Rochester Station.

"What a crowd of people for a country wedding," said Clara.

"Victoria told me a month or so ago that it was seen as a very special occasion in the village and that they planned a reception in the Vicarage and then a later party in the garden for the villagers."

"It will be interesting to meet those on John's side of the aisle, friends and acquaintances from his London curacy and his relatives," said Mary, "I wonder whether any of his former wife's family will come."

"There is no doubt, It seems to me," said Harriet, "that John is thrilled to be marrying Victoria, and she easily come to see herself in an important position in the village where she grew up."

"Would it be difficult to have a honeymoon," Asked Clara; "he would need to find someone who could manage the parish while he was away."

"The marriage will be good for the village," said Pip. "I'm sure he will show off his bride while also indulging the village community anticipating he can improve attendance at church. Although this is an ancient church, there is no local squire or historic landowner to please. The wealthier of his parishioners are the farmers. Time to go over to the Church now," and the six of them got up. Hamish left a sovereign at the bar which delighted the landlord.

Thus it was that on the Saturday after St George's Day, in the year of our Lord 1903, Horatio Fletcher led his sister Victoria Pirrip down the aisle at the Church of All Saints, All Hallows to marry the Reverend John Eustace. Afterwards, as the Vicar and his bride came out from the church arm in arm, volumes of rice engulfed them as every villager in sight had armed themselves with baskets of the stuff. No doubt bemused by the going-ons, a cat jumped up onto the top of the wall near a small gate, where a small path gave privileged access to and from the Vicarage and the Church. John and Victoria chose not to use that gate, but to walk through the throng down to the street and then along to the main Vicarage gates. The guests from London were delighted by the cheers and good wishes which accompanied the pair and joined in with gusto.

Celebrations in the Village went on into the evening. One of the Friendly boys slept in a ditch on the way home. A seventeen-year old Butterworth daughter might have suffered the fate worse than death had she not run like the wind away from Matthew Comely when he got too fresh. Old Ma Strongham went fast asleep in the back room settle at the Rose and Crown where the landlord sat counting the proceeds of the evening and wishing the Vicar got married every year. So, as was said around the village for several days, a good time was had by all, especially the alphabet children and their cousins.

Mary had corresponded with Simon's mother Honora who had been living in Cornwall over the years since she left Chiswick. No letters had come for well over a month so she wrote to Simon and the reply indicated that his mother was failing.

"Honora is very unwell," said Hamish when he came home after visiting his Chambers following a day in court and enquiring with Simon about his mother. "It seems as though she has some kind of wasting disease and now has a full-time nurse. It has developed quite suddenly which will account for her not writing."

"I will make plans to visit her next week if you can manage without me for a few days. I have never been to Cornwall."

"Of course, my dear, and you should take your maid with you."

"Ede? Yes, I suppose so, but I rather wish you were coming."

"So do I."

The journey was unnecessary, however, as Simon called on Mary the following morning to say that he had a message to say that Honora has passed away.

"I am so sorry not to have seen her of late," said Mary, "I admired her so much for her courage and the way she handled all the travails that beset her."

"For me and for Jude, she was like a gift from God," said Simon. "While we were happy enough as orphans in North Wales, our move to live with her and my step-father was such a tumultuous change in our lives. After she told us about our origins, I lost all interest in discovering who my father was, and as I have grown older and understand the darkest ways of the world, my admiration for her has known no bounds."

"I don't really know how she managed to cope with your twin brother Jude's death."

"It is so long ago now, Mary. I felt I had to protect my mother immediately after Jude drowned. I have not told anyone this, so please respect my confidence. Truth to tell, my brother and I were quite aware of the danger of Lake Garda but we were both inebriated. We had even seen the notice about the dangers of swimming, but whereas I became cautious and frightened, Jude was exhilarated. So while it was indeed an accident, and my brother courted danger and drowned, I just could not bring myself to tell my mother that, so I made up the story about our not seeing the sign and never mentioned our drunkenness to her."

"Oh dear me, oh dear, what a dilemma for you. You have never told anyone of this?"

"No, not Margaret certainly. I did not want there to be any risk that my mother would hear of it. Now she is gone, it is no matter. It would have hurt my father Frederick very deeply too."

"You acted wisely and thoughtfully, Simon. Did she ever raise the possibility of another explanation for his death?"

"Some years ago she and I were talking about him and it did cross her mind, so she said, that he had been more than foolish, but she put that thought behind her."

"In that respect only it must be a relief that she has died."

"My brother Jude's drowning had a brutal effect on my life and then the heinous murder of my daughter Frederica. I so remember the thrills and delight my brother and I had in everything we did in those halcyon days between our arrival in London and his death in Lake Garda. My marriage too has been complicated and difficult."

"Why, though please do not tell me if you are reluctant?"

"No, it is helpful to confide in someone. I have been loyal to Margaret and understand her faults. She was engaged to marry Jude, as you know, and I felt I should step into the breach. I was very attracted to her but I soon began to see it more as an act of pity than love."

"Oh my dear, how frightful."

"I cannot tell you, Mary, how good it is to talk with you in this open and frank way. I was never able to do this with my mother, as I think that after she was raped she never quite surmounted that sense of dread about the world that she had. In many ways, my daughter's murder meant as much to her if not more than Jude's."

"Are you sure?"

"Yes, not because her love for Jude was not paramount in her life, but because she knew Frederica's murder could have been avoided, had Margaret brought her up sensibly."

"What do you mean?" Asked Mary, now completely astonished by these revelations.

"This was another conversation with my mother in which we never told each other properly about the murder. Margaret had confessed to me soon afterwards that she herself had such a restricted background growing up with a confused mother and an autocratic father that she rebelled through

Frederica. She encouraged her with ideas about free love and a woman's independence which she had encountered at the meeting of your League, different from her own upbringing."

"But her daughter was just a child?"

"Yes, but there is more. I surmised from conversation with Detective Sampson that the maid Ethel was a very bad influence on Frederica too. They wished they had been able to track her down but she had disappeared, although the police did not need the evidence. Sampson just wanted the court to hear the extent of Charlesby's villainy.

"So, Mary, I am afraid I have never been able to forgive Margaret for not seeing how Ethel and Frederica were close, nor for her cavalier attitude in bringing her up. I also blame myself. I was far too deeply involved in establishing myself as a lawyer to pay close attention to my children's upbringing."

"Goodness me, no wonder that you are such a sober man, reluctant to engage in the social world, though I must tell you that Hamish holds your work as a lawyer in the highest esteem."

"Thank you for that and I think Clarence shares that opinion which is of great comfort. I am forty-one years old, Mary, and as I look down the path of life I feel in some ways that my life is trivial. Of course I enjoy my work as a lawyer, but far too much of it is cleaning up other people's problems, even in my criminal work."

"Do you know Tom Hesketh?"

"Not really, apart from Board meetings."

"Yes, but he is not a soldier now, and he is proposing to run for Parliament. Perhaps political work would interest you."

"It would, provided I do not have to run for a seat. I am not brash enough to flaunt my qualifications before any sort of public," and they both smiled.

"My guess is that he is about your age. He has a very strong conscience and as you know he has worked recently in Ireland on the estate that the Jaggers Trust bought from Clara Gargery."

"I have heard his reports at Board meetings but have not come to know him."

"He has a purpose and now you must start to see life with a purpose and care for your son Jude, your brother's namesake."

"Jude is twenty-four now. He finished his degree and wanted to do the Grand Tour but that has become the Really Grand Tour and he has been away for two years now. He writes regularly and is presently in Austria. He suffered greatly when Frederica died. He will be very saddened by his grandmother's death, I know. Indeed that might be the jolt that will bring him home."

"My son James has travelled far and wide too and has returned with a wife."

"I'd be in ecstasy if my son returned with a wife as I trust his judgment about women. I believe he takes after me and he has only seen me as a very sober quiet man which he emulates."

"I find this contrast so interesting. Here are you and I whose sons have gone off exploring the world, yet Emma's son Henry Smythe has stayed at home, showing no interest in seeing the world, but moving straight into lawyering. His brother Oliver was sent to South Africa but from what I gather of him, he would have been off like a cannon anyway. Just different choices, I suppose."

"Perhaps the choice lies in the matter of being comfortable at home. At times, I think my son Jude understands quite well how unintelligent and wayward his mother is and can't stand being near her after his sister's death. He must realize how she carries some responsibility for that tragedy in his life."

"How do you cope with that thought? It seems despairing to me."

"I suppose it is, but I am glad for him to build his own life, although that leaves me a loneliness that overwhelms me at times."

"Then you shall come every week and talk to me. I am sure we can be firm friends."

"Thank you, Mary: That will be a singular comfort. Let me say more. If it were legally and financially possible, I think Margaret and I should divorce and go our separate ways."

"Goodness me, that is a radical step. Have you talked about this? Is she as unhappy as you?"

"Probably but we barely talk these days."

VII

The June meeting of the Board took place at 11 Old Square and several members were agog at the possibility of Mrs. Angharad Llewellyn attending. Clarence first introduced Mrs. Elizabeth Egerton as an observer, saying that she would be in America for a year but that he hoped she would join the Board on her return. While Mrs. Egerton added an elegant presence to the Board, Hamish in particular wondered quite why Clarence had invited her, but then remembered Mary's story that he had thrown his cap at her, quite unseemly behavior.

Clarence then turned to Angharad and asked her to say a few words of introduction, but once she got going, the few words turned into the many.

"Thank you, Sir Clarence. I am the daughter of a Welsh farmer, but I married a very successful Australian sheep-farmer Ezekiel Unworthy when I was sixteen and I inherited a very large amount of money when he died after a fight. He was the illegitimate son of a man called Magwitch who was a half-brother of Mrs. Estella Pirrip," which caused ripples of interest among the younger members of the Board.

"Really?" interrupted Elizabeth, "the old convict was Estella's father?"

"Oh yes," said Harriet, "didn't you know? I would have thought your aunt Charlotte would have told you."

"No, but I interrupted, Mrs. Llewellyn, please forgive me."

"Not at all. Anyway I came back here from Australia with my four children, apart from the eldest and I lived near Cardiff. I married my Dai twenty-one years ago, but he died last year. For reasons I won't mention, I came to see the lawyer I had worked with when my first husband died, now Sir Hamish MacDonald and I met Sir Clarence as I wanted advice on what to do with my money.

"I've been taking cuttings of accidents in the mines," Angharad continued, "which I am sure you Londoners are not aware of. Just this year in January," and here she read from a notebook she had with her, "for instance, 'Thomas Morris was killed by the fall off a huge stone, leaving a wife and seven children.' Then there are reports of accidents to boys, children who work with their fathers at the pit-face hauling coal. I won't go on, but there is such a need for support."

Her lilting Welsh accent and her pleasant demeanor held the interest of all the members.

"I suppose," said Adam Masterson, "the question is whether you merge your interest with this Trust, or we establish your Trust and have overlapping memberships."

"That was the way I thought we could construct the relationship," said Clarence.

"But what is the best way to help?" asked Mary, "help with the families in general, or just help for those who have suffered?"

"I don't know. I'd like for you all to give me some ideas."

"Ruled out, I suspect," said Simon with rich sarcasm, "is help improving safety within the mines."

"Yes," said Angharad, "the owners are very conscious of the problems but ignore it. To be honest, working in the pits is a very dangerous business indeed and it requires hard men whose lives depend on the other men, so they are very aware of each other if you know what I mean."

"The owners won't then like any intrusion from people like us, but can't the Government impose safety regulations?" Asked Aaron.

"I've had a quick look at legislation," said Clarence, "and there are rules about inspections and the training of pit managers, but nothing about safety."

"That's right," said Angharad, "my Dai had to be trained as a manager, that I know."

"I am especially interested in this," said Malcolm. "As I think members of the Board know, both Tom and I each want to find a parliamentary seat for the Liberal Party. I have read of great discontent in the Welsh valleys and the unions are quite strong there. I am going to specialize in domestic matters and Tom in foreign policy. I would be delighted to work with Mrs. Llewellyn in whatever framework we finally decide is appropriate."

"Thank you, Mr. Gargery, and I'd be delighted to work with you."

"I think that my wife Clara would join us, too. She is unable to attend the meeting today."

"Let us return to the framework," said Clarence. "I suggest we incorporate an appropriate amount of Mrs. Llewellyn's wealth into a Llewellyn Trust. As I recall, Angharad, your proposed endowment is a quarter of a million pounds which will still leave the residue of the Unworthy bequest with you."

"Yes and I have Dai's legacy too, so I won't be short," she said giggling, as eyebrows were surreptitiously raised around the table at this enormous figure.

"Mrs. Llewellyn will chair the Trust and she will have two members of the Board also on her Board, and as Malcolm and Clara have expressed interest in the work, it makes sense for them to join. Courtisone and Jaggers will be that Trust's lawyers and we will draw up a formal constitution. Aaron, perhaps you would join that Board too to be its lawyer."

"I'd be delighted."

"We have not had a financial statement of the Jaggers Trust this half-year, have we?" asked Simon.

"While we have spent well and wisely, market conditions have been such that our capital is now over two hundred thousand pounds, a large increase from the original Jaggers bequest of eighty thousand. We have spent all our income but our capital has increased greatly in value, due I think to old Mr. Courtisone's wise investments. We have not been tempted to change that stock, though we did consider American railways for a time. So we are very healthy but do not match Mrs. Llewellyn's munificence."

"I think of the money Ezekiel left me and you know I don't really deserve it. My children already have trusts, and I'll have to work out with Clarence how I change my will. I'll leave enough for a slap-up dinner for the Board at Claridge's," and she laughed gaily which prompted others to join in.

Both Hamish and Elizabeth had been silent during this whole discussion, he no doubt preoccupied with a case due to come before him.

"Do you have views on this, Hamish?"

"Everything seems to me entirely satisfactory. Perhaps the Board might make an excursion and visit these mining areas to see for ourselves the conditions we are talking about. Few of us were able to go to Ireland to the Clumber Estate, but it will not require a sea journey for us to go to Cardiff by train and then on to the Welsh Valleys where the mines are."

"That would be exciting," said Angharad. "Perhaps my Board members can draw up a plan with me."

"We would be delighted," said Malcolm.

As usual, the Board then adjourned to the Cheshire Cheese for lunch. Once again, venison was on the menu, and conversation was very lively. Simon had been quiet during the discussion but he was seated next to Elizabeth, a woman he did not know.

"You are going to America, then?"

"Yes indeed, quite soon, primarily I now think to see my mother but I will be back within a year, I am sure."

"Then you will delay getting used to the vagaries of this Board. Its main feature is paralysis of decision," and they both laughed. "I have had a yen to go America at some point, as I have traveled only in Europe."

"Where in Europe?"

"Something of a grand vacation I took with my twin brother when we were at Cambridge, but nothing since as that was marked by my brother drowning in an Italian lake."

"Oh, how terrible, and a twin too," said Elizabeth, turning to look closely at Simon and thinking what a fine-featured and gentle man he seemed to be, soft-spoken and really quite handsome. As he turned to look at her, their eyes met and each held the gaze, each surprised by the encounter.

"But I know of your loss, Elizabeth, but I feel a marked man as my daughter was also murdered."

"Oh, my goodness, of course, that terrible case! You were her father? I did not put two and two together, so my profound apologies," she said putting her hand gently on his arm.

"We share grief then, don't we?' he said, responding to her looking at him as they continued to hold their glances for some while, both wondering what this meant.

Since Timothy's murder, Elizabeth had fended off suitors, but never met anyone she might think of as a future partner, but this Simon Brandram was seriously attractive, though she assumed he was much younger than her. For Simon, talking with this beautiful woman was unnerving, not least because she seemed to welcome his attention. The conversation he had with Mary about his misery and his thinking of divorce as liberating, he drew a bow at a venture.

"I would very much like to meet with you before you leave for America, not least because I don't know the country and would value advice about where to go."

So this is it, thought Elizabeth, as she said, "that would be delightful. Would you care to come to my house in Eaton Square, perhaps on Thursday?"

"That would indeed be delightful and I will call at noon."

As the lunch was concluding, he shook her hand, holding it just that brief time longer than was formally appropriate, and she smiled softly, looking directly into his eyes. As she rode home, thinking about him, she decided she did not care if he was married, as he probably was. She would need to discover what his marriage was like, but then again if she was frank with herself, she really did not care. Simon Brandram was a complete and delightful surprise.

For Angharad returning to Claridges, her sentiments were unlike Elizabeth's. She contemplated her good fortune that everyone had been so kind and helpful, but then loneliness swept over her. I must find myself a husband soon, she thought, or I will go mad.

With Simon in the offing, Elizabeth had decided that staying for six months, not a year would be adequate, and she booked first class cabins for June 30th. on the Cunard liner RMS Luciana for Charlotte and herself, just three weeks away. The starboard side was chosen so that they would look out to the south as the ship crossed the Atlantic, a six-day journey from Liverpool to New York. They planned to leave London on the morning train to Liverpool, as the ship was to leave at 6 p.m., allowing them plenty of time to settle on the ship before dinner.

Family discussions were quite intense as Oliver was particularly sorry not to be included in the visit, but his studies came first and Elizabeth promised him that if he got a good degree she would pay for his crossing.

"Who are the people you plan to visit, Mamma?" He asked that evening.

"I am currently constructing a list, but my singular dilemma will be to seek out your grandmother, although she may not be alive or be with that dreadful Romanian count I met in Paris all those years ago. I have told you, I am sure, why we broke off our relationship as she was so cavalier in her treatment of my dear father."

"Yes, you have, but what was her maiden name?" asked Charlotte.

"She was Mary-Lou Beauregard, a Southern family from South Carolina. Her family was able to escape the Civil War from their cotton plantation west of Charleston as my grandfather, Simeon Beauregard, had married a lady from northern New York, called Sophia Antonia Drew, as I recall."

"Were the Drews rich?"

"He was a manufacturer of some kind, I forget what his company made, and my grandparents met at a reception in New York and immediately fell in love, he a Yankee and she a Southern Belle."

"Beauregard," said Oliver, "that suggests the original migrant was from France."

"I think so, probably a few generations back, but my mother's head was so full of herself that I doubt whether she ever thought about anything but the present."

"That is surely a little harsh, Mother. I hope she is still alive as I would like to meet her. How did my grandparents come to marry?"

"Charlotte, I'd be fairly certain she is alive as I think I would have heard otherwise. As to their marriage, they were frightfully young. Mind you this was before the Civil War, 1853, and she was touring in London with her parents. She was a mere sixteen years old, and my father was just twenty-one and they met at an occasion in Mayfair. My aunt Charlotte always complained that they were far too young. She will be in her late sixties by now."

"But do you really want to meet her?" Asked Oliver.

"Oh I don't know, dear boy, but I would like you to recognize and treasure your American ancestry. I suppose I feel an obligation, too. She was an only child, so there will be none of her siblings to meet, but I am sure there will be Drew cousins.

"What about other friends?"

"I am fairly confident that there will be none of the diplomatic community we knew still there. We had Jewish friends in Paris, and I heard some time ago that two children from those families had emigrated, the Meyers and the Ashkenazys. Jonathan Ashkenazy moved on to California, but I am sure that Daniel Meyer will be in New York. I have written to Sarah for his address."

"There was also a charming couple, the Dennisons who lived in northern Virginia, George and Cecily. He was a congressman and we visited their estate once or twice, not a great distance from Washington. They originated as Yankees from Pennsylvania and Cecily's father bought a run-down plantation near the Potomac river in Virginia soon after the War ended. I have written to them as I kept their address. The other couple I liked were Pieter and Gudrun

Bach originally from somewhere in the state of Michigan, quite religious in attitude, no relation to the composer, I might add. He was a lawyer working for the Federal Government, and I expect they will still be there.

"Where will we live, Mamma?"

"We will start in a hotel in New York, though the summers are hot there, so rather than moving to Washington when we arrive in July, we will find a house near Boston and the sea. Newport, Rhode Island can be charming in the summer and your father and I went there once, but it is now a place where the very rich have built their houses overlooking the sea, so we cannot expect to find a house on the beach in that place."

"Do we still have Father's guide to America? I looked at it once when I was about ten."

"Like the map it may have got mislaid in the move from Paris, so Oliver, would you visit Hatchards tomorrow and purchase the new Baedeker Guide to the United States for us?"

"Of course, Mamma. I may get two copies so that I can be apprised of everything about where you are when you are away."

"Now my children, one matter. I am entertaining a charming man for lunch on Thursday. Do not jump to conclusions, he wants to visit America but knows nothing of it. He is on the Jaggers Trust Board."

"For my part," said Henry, "I very much hope you will find a suitable partner. It is a long time since Father died, we are growing up and will be leaving this house and you deserve and need company."

"Now then, as I said, don't over-estimate this lunch, but I must say I have been anticipating being alone with something like dread."

"Who is he?" Asked Charlotte.

"He is Simon Brandram, a lawyer in the Courtisone and Jaggers practice and we got talking over lunch after the meeting."

"That sounds exciting," said Oliver, "and I am sure Charlotte and I agree with Henry."

"But you won't put off our American visit, will you, Mamma?"

"Good gracious me no! I have talked to Simon for only twenty minutes!"

The following afternoon Elizabeth called on Harriet.

"We have been preparing ourselves for our time in America, Harriet."

"I can hardly believe it, Elizabeth, for I am uncertain whether you will return here."

"Those are my present plans."

"But what if you fall in love with a rich American, someone with a business or land that he cannot desert?"

"Who knows?" replied Elizabeth laughing, "I suppose I am not yet past the age at which I could give birth."

"You are not on the change of life then?"

"Not as I understand it, but I am fifty this year, so I do not anticipate motherhood in my life."

"I hope earnestly that you don't find America more attractive than London, husband or no husband for then what would we do?"

"How do you mean – what would we do? My dear, you will go along with your lives without me. I will miss you, of course, but this is something I must do."

"Ah, I see. You must discover what happened to your mother."

"Buried underneath my plans for such a visit was a daughter's need to find her mother. I now see that as the emotional explanation for my going. What if she is alone and dying with no one to care for her? Such things I must discover. Of course, I expect I will find her as flirtatious and frivolous as ever, with a husband in tow who might well still be that Romanian count. I will also seek out the Drew family, my grandmother's, don't you know, as I am sure they would be people of a fixed above."

"What if she is dead?"

"Then my chances of returning home quickly will be substantially increased and do remember I have two boys here to draw me back. I will need to be in a position to veto their choice of partners, will I not? Oliver is a student and he has the Malcolm Gargerys to look out for him. Henry is starting at Courtisone and Jaggers soon and Clarence was keen to have him. One thing is certain, I will not be seeking out a medium to find Timothy's spirit either in London or America."

"Did you go to a séance then?"

"Yes, and I have never ever encountered such silly antics before, so my interest was quickly stilled."

"Good, so I do not need to engage with it either. With regard to Henry, I am sure Clarence would do anything for you after his previous blunder trifling with your affections."

"I am going to interpret that kindly, Harriet, but you might be saying that Henry is being welcomed into his new position because Clarence wanted to begin an affair with me."

"How stupid of me and I do apologize. I meant no such thing."

"I understand and I am somehow so sensitive to manifestations of love or hatred these days. I suppose I am monumentally insecure without Timothy although he died several years ago. I should have moved house immediately, but I could not bear it. Now it seems too late. Perhaps my visit to America is also no more than an attempt to squelch my grief," and tears began to appear in her eyes.

"Perhaps so, my dear. Grief is nothing to be ashamed of, provided it does not engulf you. Strangely, I recently went into our bedroom and Pip did not hear me coming. I found him there in tears looking at an artist's drawing of his dead son, Lachlan, that child who was Malcolm's elder brother."

"I remember that you told me Pip was beside himself with fear when Hannah was expecting a child. I can see now exactly why. I look at my children when they are with me and indeed two of them are really adults, but the fear that any one of them might pre-decease me runs through my veins like a poison."

"I think all mothers and father feel that sense of utter dread. I do with Joseph, though he is such a studious young man that the only kind of death he might face would be a large bookcase toppling on top of him," and they both laughed.

"Although you are older than me, Harriet, you remind me so much of my Aunt Charlotte and the famous Estella too. I love the memories I have of them. I have another missed opportunity; my father was so close to his brother Frederick, but I have not seen him since Timothy's funeral. But then perhaps he cannot bear to meet me and my children as it would be too hard for him to recall his brother, especially as my boys look like different versions of my husband, much less so of me. I must be in touch with him before I leave."

"You should see him before you leave. I have noticed this, by the way. Pip is not my son's father, but Joseph looks not one jot like Aristide, his father. In some ways, he looks like Pip."

"Really? We would have to ask Mr. Darwin, if he were still alive, whether such physiognomies could be the result of nurture, not nature."

"As I think about from time to time, Joseph has adopted his step-father's mannerisms, the way he cocks his head when he is puzzled, the broadness of his smile, the tones of his laughter, and I am sure he would adopt his gait if Pip's leg were not knocked about."

"Incidentally Harriet, what will you do without a piano?"

89

"Ah, I have discovered through a visit to Steinways' office in Bond Street that I can hire one when I am settled there."

"How wonderful for you."

"I started asking about prices for their pianos and I hope I can afford what they call a studio grand piano. I will keep here the Bechstein Timothy bought for Charlotte when she is married as she is getting on well under his new piano tutor. I have no need to seek out a new Steinway for this house as Timothy gave me a splendid example."

"This has never occurred to me, I mean, do pianos have different tones?"

"Oh indeed. One of my favorite pieces is an impromptu of Schubert's, Opus 9, no 3. It can sound quite different on different pianos. For me it should sound like very gentle rippling water but a different piano can almost make it feel like a rushing stream or a brook."

"Oh my such distinctions! With such an instrument we shall expect you to play for us frequently when you come back."

"I will never be able to perform in a concert hall, only in a drawing room."

"That will be quite enough. However, we will arrange some kind of going-away party for you and your family. Such beauty as yours is a terrible loss to the country," she said smiling.

Throughout this long conversation, Elizabeth was on the verge of sharing with Harriet that fact that she was lunching with Simon Brandram, but wisely she held her counsel as she was not sure quite whether Harriet could be trusted with a confidence, especially as she must know Simon and his family well.

Harriet promptly went to her room afterwards wondering why her desire for this woman never seemed to abate. Elizabeth was simply exquisite, a woman whose gaze was like that of Helen of Troy, able to drive men to battle and women to weep at missing the opportunity to possess her. God knows what the Americans will make of her, she thought, and she was constantly amazed that she was still without a partner.

Sir Clarence had been concerned that the visit of the Board to Wales with Mrs. Llewellyn would become more of an outing and less of a serious enquiry. He asked his senior clerk, Robert Gillingham to do due diligence on an organization of which he knew little, the South Wales Miners' Federation. Robert discovered that its leader, William Abraham (known as Mabon) was well respected for his conciliatory attitude to relationships between miners and mine owners and was MP for the Rhondda West Constituency.

Robert also reported on the existence of two associations of owners, one the creature of Lord Merthyr, virulently opposed to unions and the other The South Wales Coal Owners Association, whose leader, a Mr. David Thomas seemed also more conciliatory as Robert judged by his public statements.

Sir Clarence was not embarrassed by his lack of knowledge of the organizations which produced the material that was the lifeblood of British industry, coal. Professional men in London rarely understood the work of the laboring classes though their lives were based on the comforts that ultimately derived from the substance.

"Perhaps, Robert, we should meet with this Mabon man one morning and then that Mr. Thomas from the Association in the afternoon."

"I have also done some work on the Association and Mr. David Thomas is an MP too, for a town with an unpronounceable Welsh name. It is two words, but only has one vowel in each word, though there are five consonants in each."

"I know Thomas only very slightly, and his constituency is Merthyr Tydfil, that's how you pronounce it."

"How can children learn English if they learn that language?"

"Don't worry, Robert, people the world over speak more than one language. I think I will ask Mr. Thomas to meet with the Board here in London and then we can meet Mr. Abraham when we go to Cardiff."

On his way home, Clarence called on Angharad at Claridge's. The concierge sent Buttons to her room with a message that Sir Clarence would be pleased to meet with her and that he was in the lobby.

She came down immediately and a waiter brought them tea in the salon.

"What brings you to my humble abode?" said Angharad with a broad smile.

"Your humble abode, Angharad, is a palace. I have not seen the hotel before."

"Now then, Clarence, why are you here?"

"I wanted to tell you that I have asked a Mr. Thomas, President of the Coal Mine Owners Association or whatever it is called to meet with the Board, before we go to Cardiff where I have arranged for us to meet with a Mr. Abraham who leads a miners' union."

"I wish you'd asked me first, but it doesn't matter. You should know them both as they are MPs. Dai used to call Mr. Thomas names which I cannot repeat, and he thought Abraham was an extinct volcano who did not properly understand where the miners' hearts and minds were."

"Oh dear, should I cancel in the invitations then?"

"No, no, I suppose it will do us good to meet them. I learnt such a lot from my Dai and I'll be ready with some questions for both. It's odd for me, you know, I grew up on a farm, not in a mining district, so mining is not built into my soul as it is for many a Welshman or woman. But it won't do just to meet with these big knobs, you know. We must watch men coming up from the pit and see where they live, and their wives and children too. I think the Board will be shocked into action."

The meeting that followed with Mr. Abraham at the end of June was held at the Courtisone and Jaggers Office. Present for the Board were the lawyers, Smythe, Masterson, Levy and Garthwaite together with Sir Hamish MacDonald and Lady MacDonald, Malcolm and Clara Gargery, Tom and Hannah Hesketh, Lady Emma Smythe, Mrs. Angharad Llewellyn of the Llewellyn Trust. Mrs. Egerton was preparing for her trip and Mr. Brandram was appearing at Oxford Assizes.

Emma button-holed her husband before the meeting and whispered in his ear, "darling, when you meet persons in trade or other occupations, you can sometimes sound very patronizing, so please watch yourself with this Welshman."

"I will, my dear, I will. Let us make a start."

"We have asked you to meet with Board, Mr. Thomas, as The Jaggers Trust is a philanthropic organization for the relief and education of the poor and we have recently created a relationship with the Llewellyn Trust of which Mrs. Llewellyn is the benefactor. We are proposing to begin charitable work with miners' families, so we would like to speak with mine owners first before speaking with the miners associations. Our interest lies not in taking sides in any dispute but trying to get a full picture of the situation which really comes to our notice because of the regularity of accidents and of course with the Coal Strike of five years ago which, as you know, lasted six months and left thousands destitute. Welcome, Mr. Thomas, please begin."

"Let me first say a little bit about myself before I come to the 1898 issue. I've been fortunate that my father was a pioneer in the coal industry and I have succeeded him in his business. My family was reasonably well-to-do and I've been to Cambridge University, but my health is not good, I spent my time studying mathematics, rowing and boxing. I'm a liberal by inclination and politics, but not a religious man."

"We are grateful for that introduction, Mr. Thomas," said Clarence, "I'm a Cambridge man myself. Tell the Board about the circumstances of the Strike in 1898."

"It is really quite simple. Coal is subject to both foreign and domestic consumption and output and demand vary. The owners wanted to introduce a sliding scale for miners pay whereby wages are tied to the price of coal on the market which obviously means fluctuations in miners' income. While I am anxious to keep my company as much in profit as any man, such a sliding scale seemed to me to be most unfair. No reason why hard-working men should pay for price fluctuation. So the men were on strike for six months, but no changes were made."

"That's right," said Angharad, "shocking it was, what with the poverty for the families, and I remember my Dai saying how much discontent there was among the men in the pit he managed. What did you do, Mr. Thomas?"

"I told the Association I would not accept it, and so during the Strike I kept my mines open …

"Which must have given you profit and a major advantage, I assume," said Malcolm.

"And the shareholders, of course."

"Let me understand this," said Mary, "you employ men to work in this highly dangerous occupation underground and young boys as well. Although you do not use the sliding scale you have described, I assume you pay individual miners in terms of what they produce from the mine."

"Yes, ma'am, and there are different types of coal and demand fluctuates for each type, but what a miner earns is determined by what he extracts from the ground."

"Tell us ignorant people about the process," said Aaron with a sneer.

"I will make it as straightforward as I can. My company rents land from landowners, like the Marquess of Bute or Lord Aberdare, for example. We sink a shaft down to the point where we find a seam of coal in the rock. Of course, the Welsh coalfield is large, so we are not explorers. We then widen the shaft and now are able to install machinery to take the miners down to the seam."

"These are local men?"

"Often, but men do come from other mining areas, like the Forest of Dean, or from the countryside."

"We then create what we call a pit, and miners dig along the seams underground, horizontal with the ground above, cutting out the coal and either filling carts with coal or having ponies to drag a cart along to the shaft for it to be hoisted to the surface."

"Did you say ponies? Animals underground? I never heard of such a thing," said Clara.

"Yes, ma'am. However, to get at the coal itself means a lot of material we call slag being hoisted from the pit as well, which is put in heaps around the pit. Coal is then taken by rail to various destinations, including ports to fire His Majesty's ships, locomotives, and to foreign countries."

"Mr. Thomas, we hear about mining safety and the absence of regulations," said Adam quietly.

"Mining is inherently dangerous," said Mr. Thomas; "as the miners work along the seams underground, they use wooden poles to prop up the roof. A pit-prop can give way, there can be an unexplained fall of rock, and there are problems of gas generated from the coal, so most mines will have birds, often canaries in cages. If the birds die, miners know the air is bad. That is often when there are explosions."

"One can see the dangers of being a miner, and presumably many of them are injured one way or another. What then happens?"

"When they are injured, they cannot work and have to be dismissed."

"Do you have any responsibility for a miner and his family if he is injured?"

"No. Of course I am sorry, and I am supportive of the idea in my party for some kind of national health insurance."

"But this is where philanthropy could help," said Clarence. "Tell me, at some point, a particular pit will cease to be profitable, will it not?"

"Yes, indeed. This may sometimes be because the seam gets so small, the effort is not worth it. Most often, the tunnels get so long and the time it takes a miner so long to get to the coal-face is so great that it is not worth continuing. In that case, we simply start another pit."

"What distance does a miner have to travel underground to get at the coalface, as with your pay system, he can earn no money until then?"

"It varies with the mine, but sometimes it can take an hour from arrival at the pit-head to the coalface."

"And an hour back, of course, so presumably most men work twelve or fourteen hour days, every day but Sunday."

"Yes, indeed."

"This is most helpful, Mr. Thomas," said Hamish, "do you regard the formation of miners unions as a hindrance and what do you see them trying to achieve?"

"They are a damn nuisance, always carping at safety, conditions and pay. But it's their choice: This is what I have to offer as a mine-owner and they are not obliged to take it up."

"Do we have any more questions?" Asked Clarence.

"Thank you, Mr. Thomas. Just in conclusion, we assume the owners would not oppose any philanthropic endeavor we might launch."

"Not at all, as long as it does not upset relations between miners and ourselves as owners, and I ask you to beware of union men you might talk to. Some of them are radical lunatics."

At this Clara started.

"I beg your pardon, Mr. Thomas, but do you regard free expression as lunacy?"

"No ma'am, just a figure of speech."

"What you have said all sounds very straightforward and simple, Mr. Thomas," she went on, "but what are we to make of an industry in which mining families are shockingly poor and living in very wretched conditions?"

"That is the way our great economy works, I'm afraid."

"Alright for the few, but not for much longer if followers of Karl Marx have their say," said Hannah ruefully.

"I think you misunderstand the Welsh miner, Mrs. Gargery. He is in general a fair-minded family man devoted to King and Country," at which there was a look of disbelief around the table and the meeting closed.

After Mr. Thomas had taken his leave, Clarence called Robert into the meeting.

"Robert, while everyone is here, I want you to note the names of those who will come with us to Cardiff and you will then arrange bookings for the train, for three nights in a Cardiff hotel, and whatever transport is available for us to visit the mines."

"I'd host you all in my house in Radyr," said Angharad, "but it is too small."

"Quite," said Clarence with a smile of dismissal, "which of you is unable to go?"

After discussion around the table, everyone would go except Hamish, whose court duties prevented it, and Adam would stay to hold the fort at Courtisone and Jaggers. Clara hummed and hawed, but Malcolm persuaded her to come.

VIII

S imon returned home after his conversation with Elizabeth with a shifting view of the world. He had developed the habit of spending long hours at work, but did not go to his club for dinner, so Margaret and he had dinner alone together each night as Jude was away.

Over dinner that evening, Margaret put down her knife and fork and asked without aggression:

"What are we going to do about our marriage, Simon?"

Managing to handle the shock of her question, Simon replied without thought or hesitation, "I don't know. We have come apart, I think. Let me be blunt, I don't love you any longer and we may have rushed into our marriage with Jude's death. Both of us assumed similarities of style and affection that weren't there, but they carried us through. Of course, Frederica's death was a body blow too."

"That is right and I am not surprised by what you say. I talked with Mary about it. Would you be very hurt, Simon, if we lived separate lives? Now that Jude is not with us, and I am on my own all day, and we share nothing over the weekend, I am bored and want to find a new way for my life. I am more than forty years old and frankly I don't want to spend the next twenty years or so cooped up like a chicken in this house."

"If we live separate lives, neither of us will want to be celibate. I can talk with Adam my colleague who is knowledgeable about divorce but mutual consent may well not be allowed."

"Oh I don't know, divorce is a very big step and I need financial security, Simon."

"I would be sure that you can easily find a partner, Margaret, as you are such an attractive and vivacious woman."

"Maybe, maybe. If I read the newspaper right, it seems that adultery is the only acceptable reason for divorce."

"I believe that is so, and it involves one of us providing evidence which seems ridiculous and sordid, but are we really at that stage? I would prefer to have a separate room after this conversation and perhaps you would too."

"Yes, I think so. I am sorry, Simon, but I do think this is for the best. All that time ago now, I heard women talking about their freedom and their independence at Estella's house meeting. I want to take advantage of that and I want to be an active suffragette."

"Well, Margaret, your life is yours to decide. Whether we divorce or live separately is a matter for the future and for consultation."

The following day, Simon went to Eaton Square to receive a very warm welcome from Elizabeth. After they had down at either end of a large settee, Simon said:

"I want to let you know at the outset of our friendship that I am married. Last night my wife and I discussed divorce or separation quite amicably and we made a mutual agreement to go our separate ways."

"Thank you for telling me, Simon. I have heard your name and knew of your mother's awful situation when I was living with my aunt Charlotte and it was she and Estella who helped her find her way back to you brothers. If I calculate aright, you must be some years younger than me, but in terms of a friendship or something more than friendship, we are both adults in the prime of our lives, so I discount the fact of age."

"I guessed you were older than me, and I too had no feelings one way or the other about that but let me begin. I married the woman who was engaged to my twin. It seemed simply inevitable after he was drowned and I suppose we simply shared the grief, and I some of the guilt. I wallowed in grief for some time, and my often ebullient nature seemed to be quietened. I was invited to join Courtisone and Jaggers and I enjoy every minute, but our marriage just drifted along, though I confess to irritation at several of my wife's mannerisms and behavior. Too much like her coarse mother."

"I can well see how your romance could not be as authentic as you hoped, am I right?"

"You are. But my wife also encouraged our sixteen year old daughter to seek independence which ended in a tragedy which, I think, completely smashed our marriage. Frederica was a beautiful young woman whom I adored and she was murdered by a vile predator who was sent to the gallows."

"Oh my dear Simon," said Elizabeth, moving along the settee to hold his hand, "I had heard the story but did not associate it with you."

Simon tried to hold back his tears as the memories of his daughter flooded into his mind.

"It is one thing to foster a young woman's independence, but quite another to encourage her to seek a sexual relationship before she is remotely ready to cope with its vicissitudes. But enough of my past. I confess I had seen you at meetings but not really looked at you. Yet you have rocked my emotions to their foundations, Elizabeth," he said, grasping her other hand and turning towards her such that they were face to face looking searchingly into each other's eyes.

"That is true for me too. I am sure you know my story, my husband was murdered in the Foreign Office by one of his so-called colleagues."

"I do."

"My marriage was so perfect, we loved each other so profoundly that these past years I have not been able to even consider another partner. Like you, I was aware of you, but at the recent meeting I looked at you, I admit, with a desire to have you in my life, though I did not know quite how."

"That exceeds my dreams of you, dear Elizabeth, but I need to be cautious. Sometimes I feel like an animal that is constantly getting wounded, indeed from my very birth. I do remember one thing about you, I know not where it comes from, but you are a great pianist, are you not?"

"Well, yes, I suppose so. I don't play often enough these days."

"Jude and I were brought up by a family in North Wales before my mother found us, and we were schooled in Welsh habits which included singing. In our youth we were always singing together, but after his death, I have rarely let my voice rip."

"Then we shall start now." Holding his hand, she led him into her music room.

"Goodness me, I have never seen such a beautiful piano."

"Yes it is lovely and its tone is exceptional, a gift from Timothy. Now let me see," she said, rustling through music in a cabinet, "ah, here we are. Let us sing a few songs before the maid calls us to lunch."

"Play something for me first. What do you know from memory?"

"I have been working on the third movement of the Moonlight Sonata, so here goes," she said as she sat down on the piano stool and raced into the galloping dreamy arpeggios and chords that Beethoven left for our enjoyment and with the speed of the scale that ends the movement, he could only burst into applause. That done, she pulled out the song book and they sang together Drink to Me Only, Men of Harlech, Hearts of Oak, the Ash Grove and several others before the bell rang for lunch.

"How will I cope with you going to America?" He asked.

"How will I cope with going, now that I know you?"

"Perhaps I will come for a while, once you have told me where I should go, which towns and cities, mountains and rivers I should visit."

"No, my dear Simon, if you come to America, we will visit such places together."

They hesitated in the hall in front of the dining room door and after searching each other's eyes, their faces came closer and they kissed briefly acknowledging a profound sense of reverence for each other.

A week after the meeting with the owners, Board members enjoyed the train and were excited by the journey through the Severn Tunnel which, as the ebullient Garthwaite proclaimed, was a good rehearsal for a visit to the mines, a remark that amused Malcolm, but few others. Robert had arranged for them to stay at the Angel Hotel, meeting first with Mr. Abraham and going on to visit the mines the following day, returning to London in the evening if a second night at the hotel was not needed.

The meeting with Mr. William Abraham, Mabon as he was known, was held in the Angel Hotel in Cardiff on a rainy day at the end of July. He was a big burly man with a very powerful voice who looked initially as thought he might take over the meeting. After introductions were made, he said:

"I want to tell you, ladies and gentlemen, that I am a proud man. I am an MP on the radical side of the Liberal Party, but my major interest is in trade unions. I have worked to bring miners together, and I am President of The Miners Federation."

"Tell us about this sliding scale for miners' pay, if you would be so kind," said Clarence.

"The terrible strike of five years ago was the responsibility of the owners in implementing such a system. The miners lost, except of course in Mr. Thomas' mines. But I am glad to say that we are about to reach an agreement this very month with the Owners Association to scrap the sliding scale and go back to the old system, but I am hopeful we will get to a situation where miners are paid wages. You see, my friends, I am by nature a conciliator. I was a reluctant supporter of the strike, but I could see its appalling effects on families in the Valleys."

"I am sure you have been informed of our purpose here, Mr. Abraham, and I don't suppose you remember my husband Dai Llewellyn."

"Ah," said Abraham, "you must be the rich woman he married, I mean, I could tell you was Welsh, couldn't I, not like these other folk here, well, well, now see here, Mrs. Llewellyn, your Dai was a good man, an excellent manager, liked by owners and miners alike, a model of a man, really. So why are you here with these English people?"

"I want you to be honest, now, Mr. Abraham. Our purpose is to find a way to help mining families in distress, so tell us about them."

"Where do I start? I'll tell you about things as I see them. First, while there are explosions from time to time which the newspapers like to talk about, loss of life and injury to the miner are much more widespread in their effect on families. So safety is a major consideration. Miners do not earn when they are hurt, so poverty in the family is terrible. I believe the second worst danger to miners is illness caused by the conditions underground: Eyesight, crawling in cramped conditions all day, and the chest diseases created by the dust and dirt. Of course when a man dies, his family is destitute. I am also opposed to young boys of twelve years old working underground."

"Is this still usual?" asked Mary.

"Yes, Lady MacDonald, the miner will use his son as his 'boy' who will work to support his father at the coalface, though not do any work on the seam.

"My work, as I have said, is one of conciliation, of trying to bridge the increasing gap between miners and owners. I fear that the men who have been treated badly in the name of profit will one day rise to break down the system, but I gather you intend to go up the Rhondda Valleys to see conditions for yourselves. I have an assistant, Gareth Pugh, who used to work underground until his lungs made it impossible, and I am sure he would be pleased to be your guide."

"I would like to be able to understand the conditions under which miners work," said Simon Brandram, "presumably there is some form of ventilation or how could men work underground like moles?"

"Fans are used with great power nowadays, though even so the air is very dense underground."

"Are explosives ever used? I recall there being an explosion several years ago now which killed many men."

"That would be at the Tylorstown pit, Lady MacDonald. Quite apart from the men killed, almost one hundred children were left fatherless."

"What a tragedy," Mary exclaimed.

"The Coroner's report was very thorough and he recommended changes which have been implemented. They are quite technical, but also indicative of the need for miners to undertake responsibilities below ground usually left to managers."

"My goodness, we have so much to learn. Thank you very much indeed," said Clarence. "Tell us where we might meet."

"I will ask Mr. Pugh to come with the carriages and meet you at Pontypridd Railway Station tomorrow at ten o'clock."

Two months after their marriage the redecoration of the Vicarage was complete and the Eustace household was proving delightful. Philip and John had settled into a growing regard for each other in the tutor-pupil relationship and both were beginning to see just how talented the other was. Philip had an acute questioning and subtle mind, and John was a patient and clever tutor, pushing his pupil into surprisingly difficult intellectual territory. Beatrice was now fifteen and Nellie eleven, and neither regretted leaving Numquam House as the memory of the elm tree accident was so fresh in their minds.

It did not take long for the house to be leased to a Mr. Charles Eggleton and his wife Maud. The couple had come from Peckham Rye in London and, as they seemed sensible and middle-aged and promptly provided a year's rent when the contract was established, there was no reason for John or Victoria to have any apprehensions about them. John was pleased that the lady of the house had immediately begun to attend his church regularly.

A week after their move, Victoria walked to Numquam calling without an invitation to welcome her new tenants. The maid, who was also new to the house, opened the door and showed Victoria into the drawing room, once graced with John Singer Sargent's portrait of Mrs. Estella Pirrip. It was a little while before Mrs. Eggleton arrived and she seemed in some distress, moving with difficulty to a chair.

"I am sorry to call without invitation and will gladly call again if it is inconvenient."

"No, no, Mrs. Eustace, I had a bad fall earlier and I am somewhat discomfited."

"Oh my dear, how awful."

"I slipped on the bottom stair and fell into the hall."

"I hope you recover soon."

"Oh I will. Tell me about this house and its history. I noticed a memorial in the garden to someone called Molly."

"The house was bought long before I was born by a woman called Estella Pirrip just after she had been reunited with her long-lost mother, Molly. I'm not sure of the circumstances but she was attacked in the garden at that spot early one morning and died."

"Did anyone know why?"

"My mother told me the story long ago, and it was a matter of revenge as I recall and was certainly not random."

"I must ask my sister to exorcise her spirit and put her to rest. My sister is the Marylebone Medium, you know. I am sure there will have been other tragedies in the house if her spirit has not been set free."

"That is true. Last year two of my brother's children were killed when an old elm tree out there by the gates fell down on them all playing in the wind."

"What a tragedy! She will need to talk with those children, too, so they can tell their parents they are at rest."

A somewhat baffled Victoria thought of spiritualism as utter nonsense after discussing it with her husband some months ago but she decided to let Mrs. Eggleton know the whole story.

"Then of course, my mother and father brought about the death of a recruiting sergeant who was intent on kidnapping and killing my mother."

"Goodness gracious me, where did that happen? I am not sure we should have taken the house with these tragedies."

"That was in the dining-room, a man called Whistler, but they were found not guilty by the magistrate as it was judged to be justifiable homicide."

"Two murders and a terrible accident, then. My sister must come at once. Can we get some people here who knew the dead men and the children?"

"I suppose I am nearest to Molly as she was my husband's step-grand-mother. She might have seen him once or twice before she died. The children's parents live nearby, that's my brother and his wife."

"I will arrange a séance just as soon as she can come down to Kent."

"That will be most interesting," said Victoria, "but tell me, I did not meet you when your husband signed the lease. How come you are both here?"

"Not a long story. We had a son who died as an infant, and a daughter who died quite young. We have never really found out why, but she was dead in her cot one morning. So Charles and I thought we should come away from Peckham Rye where we lived."

"What was your husband's occupation?"

"He was a butcher with his own abattoir next to the house, so we lived with the smell of the flesh of cows and pigs all the time. It was a successful business but he decided we should come here, though I feel it to be out of the way from my sister and, for that matter, from my brothers who work in the city of London."

"I see you have been at church, which has pleased my husband greatly."

"Yes, I enjoy it very much, especially as it is the only occupation that my husband allows me to pursue."

"Why is that?"

"I am sure you know too well just how domineering husbands can be."

"Not at all, neither my first nor my second husband would dare to try that on me."

"Really, I thought all married women obeyed their husbands to the letter."

"Oh no. Now I am a member of a League of Women, a group of ten or so of us who meet from time to time to discuss problems which we share or ambitions that we have."

"And your husbands allow this?"

"We don't ask permission, you know. Why should we? They know our interests."

"I have never had that kind of experience, I must say."

"I suppose he is violently opposed to women voting, too."

"I fear so. Sometimes I wonder why my life is like this."

"Let us talk regularly. I am sure he does not regard the Vicar's wife as a threat," at which both women heard a horse coming up the drive and Mrs. Eggleton's demeanor changed rapidly.

"It is Charles," she said, "do you mind leaving now?"

Victoria returned quietly to the Vicarage, hurrying down the drive while Mr. Eggleton stabled his horse. At home her husband was busy in his study talking with a young couple, presumably wanting to be married, so she had the maid prepare lunch and then they sat together for a while outside in the sunshine. The more she lived with John, the greater the bonds of affection between them.

"I have just had the most extraordinary experience with our new tenant."

After explaining the details of the conversation, John showed her his pocket-book in which he begun to write brief descriptions of his parishioners, at which he said:

"I am going to write 'Maud Eggleton, church goer, husband a retired butcher, sister a medium, two dead children, dominated' does that sum her up?"

"Very well, but I am perplexed about her safety and I am glad her sister the medium is coming to call."

"Now that will be an experience I have longed to see as I want to find out how they get away with it."

Angharad was very pleased to have met with those London people, all of whom were quite charming, a word she was now learning to use with precisely the tones which indicated approval or disapproval. Finding a husband was another matter. It was clearly no use going anywhere but Cardiff and even that might be a difficult furrow to plough. Perhaps Bath with its long history of entertaining the married and the unmarried might still be a possibility. She had visited a Music Hall in London, and the new Cardiff Empire Theatre seemed a good choice among the several such places the city could offer. If a husband did not emerge there, she would take a flat or a house in Chelsea, and perhaps Mrs. Pirrip or Mrs. Gargery would introduce her to single or widowed men.

She was quite proud that the members of the Board of the Jaggers Trust would be seeing the conditions in the Valleys, and she was quite pleased with herself that her unearned wealth had got her to a social position where she could hobnob with judges and titled men and women. She hoped that they would all be profoundly shocked by people and conditions and realize just how important her philanthropic plans were.

Through Dai, she had got to know a family from his pit. Owen Williams was Dai's age, and they attended school together for a while. Owen was a union man before they invented unions, and Angharad had written to him asking him to help her with the Board. She knew Owen would be reluctant to miss a day at the coalface so she offered him twenty pounds for the day, a large sum of money for a working miner. Owen had a wife, Ethel, and six children and they lived in a typical miner's cottage in a row of similar gimcrack houses thrown up by the mine owners for their labor force.

Owen Williams and a man he did not know, Gareth Pugh, stood nervously on the platform at Porth awaiting the train from Cardiff. Descending from the first class carriages was a large party of elegantly dressed men and women and it seemed to both men that it was Mrs. Llewellyn who was leading the party.

"Good morning, Owen," said Angharad, and turning to Gareth she said, "and you must be the Mr. Pugh whom Mr. Abraham or was it Mr. Thomas invited to join us. I am Mrs. Llewellyn, and I want you to meet members of the joint Boards of the Jaggers and the Llewellyn Trusts."

With that she introduced the members of the Board who, it must be said, looked somewhat out of place on Pontypridd Station with their silk hats and morning coats and the ladies, if not in the height of fashion, were clearly of more than modest incomes. Their presence invoked stares and whispers from station employees and bystanders alike.

"Who's they, then?" said a small man in a flat cap to his friend.

"Furrigners, I shouldn't wonder," was the reply.

"I have two carriages ready on Mr. Thomas's instructions," said Gareth Pugh, wheezing as though he was speaking through a sieve covered with rice paper.

"Thank you," said Angharad, "and I asked Owen Williams to accompany us too. Now I thought about this, and I thought Owen might take half of us to start with his family and the pit where he works, and Gareth to take us the rest of us up to Tylorstown to meet some of the families that lost their men in the explosion six years ago."

As they left the station it began to rain but the carriages were covered, as most were in South Wales, rain being a constant feature of the climate. They passed various pit heads with their great wheels turning to facilitate the cages descending into the ground and returning with what had been extricated from the rock below.

The Owen Williams party carriages stopped at a house in a row on Aberrondha Road which led up the Valley.

"It will be a bit of a squeeze, but with six of our visitors, I think there will be room for us to meet with my wife and children."

As they got down from the carriage, Clara turned to Malcolm,

"Have you ever been in such a dreary place? I wonder if the sun ever shines here, the hills are black, covered with the rubbish from the mine, I suppose."

Mrs. Williams was a slim woman with an apron covering what Mary thought was a shabby dress, but realizing it was her best.

"I'm making you a cup of tea before you go to the mine and meet some of the miners. I've borrowed enough cups and saucers from my neighbors."

"We are trying to understand the conditions under which miners and their families live," said Clarence, eager to ensure that Angharad was not in complete command. "We are anxious to provide help and support from mining families, especially those that have suffered from accidents or other difficulties."

"Well, sir, I don't know where to begin really. To be honest, life here is very hard indeed," and as she began to speak, her confidence grew so that all those watching listened to her soft quiet voice:

"My husband works all day except Sunday down the pit. He's been lucky not to suffer injuries. Next door is Mrs. Jones and her husband Dai lost his arm six months since, so they had no money, and so Mrs. Evans and I collected for them, but then she lost two of her young'uns to the pneumonia. We can't afford to put him under the doctor, though we have money put by when we can for a funeral. There's only one young doctor in the Valley. He's not like other doctors, isn't Dr. Grant, he won't take money."

"We would like to meet him," said Clarence.

"To be honest, there's hardly a family I know that hasn't had a loss or an accident. Those mines are hell-holes, but what can we do?"

"It is such hard work," said Owen, "and we get paid only by the amount we mine so I have to have my boy working with me. He's fourteen now and a strong lad, but in an ideal world he should be in school as he's a bright boy."

Conversation about the conditions of mining families proceeded for an hour before Angharad suggested they take a carriage to the mine nearby where Owen worked. The party left the Williams household and went back down the valley in the carriage to the pithead near Trehafod. Everywhere was filthy with coals and coal dusts. A shift ended and men emerged from the clanking shaft, their clothes, bodies and faces completely black.

"Excuse me," said Mary to a couple of miners, "is that lamp you are carrying safe?"

"We call them Davy lamps after him what invented them. Quite safe really, its falling rocks and explosion that are not safe. Last week, our friend Harry was at a coalface and it fell on him, buried him. We pulled him out, but his head was smashed and him a widower with three young'uns."

Clarence and Malcolm wandered around the pithead. The rain had stopped but the sky was threatening.

"Look at those heaps. I'd be surprised if they didn't collapse."

"Dreadful, covering a green hillside presumably."

"Presumably, Is this not such a paradox, Clarence? I mean we at home have coal on the fire and when we travel in locomotives or on liners, coal is providing the energy, and yet, what are the conditions, the prices in lives and families these people pay?"

"Seeing this and meeting the few people we have, I am not surprised that the miners get angry about the conditions. Here is coal, the lifeblood of the country and they are hardly paid a living wage."

"What can be done, politically?"

"I don't know, Malcolm. I hope that we win the election and that you become an MP. The owners are resistant to any legislation, but the Liberals must take on these issues. Otherwise we will lose voters to the Labour Party and that would mean Tory rule for eons."

Tom, Clara and others were in the Gareth Pugh party and alighted at the Ferndale mine, higher up the valley at Tylorstown and they were fortunate that the clouds broke up while they were there and they could see the beauty of the valleys.

"That explosion here was terrible indeed," wheezed Gareth, "not just because the men who died, but because of the ninety children were left fatherless."

"Yes, we heard about that."

"Funny thing, though. When the bodies were brought, and it was a long time because the explosion blew the top off the mineshaft, they didn't look like they were hit by rock from an explosion. Their faces were normal, like they was sleeping. Seems like they were gassed or something."

"Are the owners going to continue to leave all this dirt on the hillsides, Mr. Pugh?" Asked Clara looking at the hills around her, "is there really nowhere else for it go?"

Taking short breaths at short interval, Gareth replied:

"The slag destroys the hillsides, and the sensible place is for it to go back into mines no longer used," and he paused for breath, "it was suggested once but the owners, none of whom nearby, dismissed it as non-productive work, but of course they don't live here, and the landowners don't care either."

"How long were you working underground?" Asked Malcolm.

"Nigh on twenty-year man and boy but my lungs got so bad, I could scarcely lift a shovel."

"Do you work for the Federation then?"

Gareth paused before answering then began to cough, wheeze and apologize for his condition while the party looked on in dismay, for here was a strap of a man probably in his thirties laid low not by some terrible accident but by the conditions under which he had worked.

He recovered slowly and said slowly, carefully and quietly, grasping for breath with each phrase he spoke.

"I don't rightly know why you posh people have come here but if you can help mining families who have suffered, God bless you. But the time is coming when there will be a popular rising among miners, when their patience will run out and they will stop working. It will make the 1898 Strike like a picnic. It will be violent too, in my estimation. Machinery will be smashed, mines will be blown up. I hope the owners come to their senses."

"Are the feelings against the owners that bad?" said Tom.

"What would you feel, Mr. Hesketh, if you was a miner?" to which there was no answer.

"I want to thank you most sincerely for showing us what mining does to families," said Mary, "and I am puzzled for, if you will pardon this thought, there is something noble about the sense of being in a community that the miners seem to have."

"I can't pardon the thought, Ma'am. Bugger the bloody community, excuse my language, when there's men like me and worse, condemned to an early death. Nobility is alright for rich people like you."

"I apologize, Mr. Pugh, and I do understand."

"Well, in my estimation again, it cannot last for long. There's speakers in union meetings telling us about some German fellow called Karl Marx, and the speak of revolution."

"My father will be fascinated to hear about that," murmured Hannah, moved by these awful conditions and the sickness that seemed to prevail.

IX

The new tenants at Numquam were providing the Vicar and his wife with much food for thought and, indeed, gossip:

"I gave her communion on Sunday, and I swear that under her veil her face was bruised."

"And she had that fall when I went to see her. Do you think he is maltreating her?"

"Perhaps, but I will make a pastoral visit today."

The house seemed to be quiet as John approached on horse-back. His knock was answered by a young maid and she asked him to wait in the hall, and he could hear a man's raised voice somewhere in the house. The maid returned with an apology from Mrs. Eggleton, saying that she was indisposed and would the Vicar please call another day, so John rode back to the Vicarage now seriously concerned about the couple at Numquam.

The following afternoon, however, Mrs. Eggleton called at the Vicarage and was ushered into the drawing room.

"I apologize for not seeing you yesterday. I was resting and feeling unwell, though I could not sleep and my husband was arguing with a gardener he wanted to employ, a fool of a man whom he employed but the man was simple and incompetent, knowing nothing about plants."

"What is his name?"

"Oh, I don't know, he's someone from another village, I think."

Victoria offered tea and once that arrived, Mrs. Eggleton said:

"My sister, the Marylebone Medium, is coming to visit me later today and I am hoping she will stay for a while and that she can hold a séance. I feel Numquam is, well, haunted, and perhaps Hortense can raise that Molly's spirit and she can be able to rest. Then there are the boys killed by the tree. Would you both come?"

"As you might suppose," said John, "I am not someone who holds that access to the spirit world is possible, but I would be prepared to participate."

"How about you, Mrs. Eustace?"

"Indeed, though I don't think I have any interest in raising the spirit of my first husband."

"I am sure that all these spirits cannot be raised at one séance."

"Would you like to bring your sister here for a social call, say tomorrow afternoon?"

"I'd be delighted for you to meet her. In any case it will be a week or so before she would conduct a séance as she would need to absorb the Numquam atmosphere."

"And Mr. Eggleton, will he take part?"

"Goodness me, no. Unfortunately he detests my sister and he will try to be away for the whole of her visit, I am sure."

John and Victoria were quite nervous the following afternoon when Mrs. Eggleton arrived accompanied by the said sister, Miss Hortense Wigglesworth. Once again tea was provided, and both John and Victoria were astonished by their visitor. She was clearly quite beautiful with long black hair which she wore on her head as was the fashion. Her blue eyes were startling in color, but it was her demeanor that gave her presence an almost ethereal quality, especially from a woman whose commanding presence did not lie in her height and build, for she was quite slight and short. Her voice was also husky and very deep for a woman, and, as Victoria said later, one could not imagine her laughing.

"You are most welcome, Miss Wigglesworth, and we are looking forward to the séance your sister has promised us."

"Thank you, Mrs. Eustace. I cannot promise you a séance, I am afraid. I will need to live with my sister to see whether any contacts with the spirit world are possible there. I would never hold a séance in this house."

"Why?"

"Vicarages are hostile places to spirits. Whoever heard of a haunted vicarage? My sister is convinced her house is haunted she has told me of at least four people in living memory who have died there savagely, so I would expect their spirits to be in the house."

"How do you come to have this facility for encountering the spirit world?"

"I do not know. I seem to have become a medium after an other-wordly experience with my mother."

"What was that?"

"My mother and I were together in Oxford Street. I was nineteen. We were crossing the thoroughfare and she unwittingly dropped her purse but walked on. I stopped to pick it up and continued to cross when a carriage hurtled past me just brushing my coat."

"Oh my goodness," said Victoria, "what an escape."

"Indeed, but when I reached my mother after three or four paces, I looked around to look at my body in the road."

"I don't understand," said John.

"O ye of little faith is the expression, I believe Mr. Eustace. Do you not see that my spirit was independent of my body and it was my spirit that urged me to look at my body lying crushed in the road? At that moment, I knew I could communicate with the spirit world, though I had never imagined the possibility before that incident."

"That is a strange experience," said Victoria, fascinated by the story, "had that happened to me, I would have thrown myself weeping into my mother's arms, terrified that I had missed death by inches."

"I simply shook myself, took my mother's arm and we walked on. My life was changed. I am unmarried, as I simply could not allow my body to be possessed by a man."

"I expect you have heard about the four unusual deaths at Numquam House from Mr. Eggleton."

"When I have considered the situation there, I think we may start with trying to contact the two children."

"That seems to me the most appropriate," said Mrs. Eggleton, "as no one alive is interested in the spirit of the women whose memorial is there, or of the military man in the drawing-room."

Conversation drifted on for a half hour or so before the visitors got up to leave.

Mrs. Wigglesworth turned to Victoria as she was leaving and in that eerie voice said, "I am sure we could engage with Albert's spirit, you know. I feel him in the shadows here somewhere and I expect to find him at Numquam."

"I am not interested Mrs. Wigglesworth," said Victoria brusquely, "that man destroyed my life and those of my children by his own ghastly behavior and he can rot in hell as far as I am concerned."

"Even if he needs to apologize?"

"Don't be ridiculous, Miss Wigglesworth," said John. "Please do not continue to upset my wife."

At that, the visitors said their goodbyes and left.

"Spirit or no spirit," said John, "I have a very bad intuition about that woman."

"I do too," said Victoria, "and it is only curiosity that would make me go to that séance."

Neither Pip nor Harriet had been on the trip to South Wales so the conversation at a dinner with Malcolm and Clara later that evening passed it by and initially it was full of Malcolm's experiences in the South Africa mining communities.

"How rich is the Trust these days," Said Pip. I cannot quite understand where we are with expenditure and capital."

"I detect a concern in your voice," said Clara, "and I agree. The Trust needs a large capital project, preferably away from London."

"Pip and I got to know Salford and Manchester quite well, though it was some time ago, but a capital expenditure on funds for the poor would be well received there, I think."

"I'll be frank about this," said Malcolm. "If and when I find an industrial constituency, I would like to introduce the Trust with its wealth to my constituents."

"What a grand idea," exclaimed Pip, "you would bring largesse to a poor community and with the changes in the franchise for men, that would glean their support."

"Tom could do this too but Clarence's constituency is not one that would qualify, except in small areas, as a place where the poor might be relieved."

"The problem, then," said Pip, "is to find a constituency; but should that come before the Trust invests or afterwards?"

"You mean whether my arranging for Trust money would win me the nomination, or, indeed win the election?"

"This is a conundrum," said Clara, "but we need to be clear ourselves that any deployment of Trust funds is not for Malcolm's personal or political benefits but for the social benefits he would bring as a Liberal MP. I believe in my husband's goodness and selflessness but a newspaper could well criticize such a strategy as the use of a philanthropy for personal benefit."

"In that case," said Harriet, "the ideal would be for the Trust, led by Malcolm, to shower benefits on a constituency which he is not seeking to represent, but preferably adjoining so that such benefits are well known, although I know that sounds devious."

"Harriet and I need to do something to help you become an MP, my son: What can we do?"

"Let us consider that," said Malcolm, "I will value your guidance, especially if it were in your old stomping grounds."

"We are not near death's door, are we my dear? Life in the old dog yet!"

The following morning Malcolm felt it was time to make a move to find a constituency and sent a message to Old Square asking to meet with Sir Clarence.

Robert met him on his arrival in the hall, saying, "I gather you are hoping to enter the political fray."

"I hope so, but it will depend on finding a constituency."

"Well now, my younger brother works for Sir Humphrey Ewing and has done so for many years as his political manager, not that he is needed much. Sir Humphrey is a Conservative for a Norfolk constituency, but Dick wants a change, so he might well be prepared to come and help you."

"Now that would be wonderful, but first I must find somewhere," as Robert knocked and opened the door to Clarence's office.

"Welcome, Malcolm. Welcome. I have begun to survey the possibilities. Would you be averse to a Scottish seat? There's a possibility in Glasgow."

"I'm not averse to anything, actually as long as it primarily a poor working class district. Of course, the electorate will now include all men, and I will have a clear position on votes for women."

"That will be essential."

"I am hoping to speak to four men before the July recess, including Basil Carpenter, the Glasgow man. You know the important thing here is to get you into Parliament. Your philanthropic work can continue outside the constituency."

Discussion on the constituency issue continued for a half hour and Malcolm changed the subject.

"As you know, we live just off Piccadilly. Down Street is not badly affected by horse manure, but the main thoroughfares are in a terrible state."

"What do you mean?"

"There are now over eleven thousand hansom cabs in London, let alone private carriages, broughams and the like. Horse-drawn omnibuses need twelve horses a day. On any one day over fifty thousand horses are at work in London, let alone the carts and drays. God knows how many tons of manure litter the streets of the capital."

"Good Lord, I had never thought about that seriously, it never struck me it could be so bad. One must hope that these new machines, these automobiles actually work."

"Ah, that is my concern too. I gather that in some areas of the country there is rule that a man with a red flag must walk in front of the vehicle which, of course, negates the vehicle's purpose. But I heard from a man in my club that a much more sophisticated working automobile was produced in Germany in 1901."

"I still don't know how they work, Malcolm. I do see them occasionally, but do you think they have a future?"

"We cannot sustain horse traffic so the automobile comes at a propitious time. Might you both come with Clara and me to Stuttgart to inspect these automobiles where they are made? They are prodigiously expensive, a friend tells me, but the vehicles have been sold to the Rothschilds, Astors and other such rich Americans as viable means of transport."

"That could be most interesting. We will be leaving for our villa in France once the Law Term ends."

"And we too will be on our way south, so perhaps we can all go via Germany or even better call there on the way back in September."

"Excellent. I am going to a reception at the German Embassy and perhaps Paul Metternich, the present Ambassador can help us meet the automobile people."

"That would be valuable: name of Daimler-Benz as I recall."

"I am sure the Ambassador would provide one, but then these are trades-people who make automobiles, so he may not know them, unless of course he has bought one."

Mrs. Eggleton and Miss Wigglesworth found out from Victoria where the Fletchers lived and after a week went over to the Cottage to see whether

Horatio and Betty would be interested in a séance to engage with the spirits of Charlie and Ernest.

As the trap arrived on a magnificent July morning, Beth and the young children came out of the Cottage in the sunshine to greet them.

"Good morning, I am Mrs. Eggleton and this is my sister Miss Wigglesworth: My husband and I are the new tenants at Numquam House."

"Pleased to meet you, I am sure. I am Beth Fletcher and here are Dottie-do-da, Georgiana and Horatio, my younger children. Ivor's the baby."

Horatio came out from the Forge, and Beth introduced him and they all stood outside as the children darted to and fro between them.

"So new tenants at Numquam," he said, "that's nice. My sister Victoria and I own half of it each as it was my mother Nellie's property."

"Oh," said Mrs. Eggleton, "we did not know that, we thought it was Mrs. Eustace's home only."

"Well, she lived there with her family after my Mum died, so there was an understanding between us. Of course then her first husband died and now she's at the Vicarage."

At the news of a death, Miss Wigglesworth pricked up her ears and in her silky voice, said:

"Oh, we did not know that. Who was he?"

"He was Albert Pirrip and a well-known wood merchant in these parts," but he refrained from telling of Albert's suicide.

"Mrs. Eustace said you have had your own tragedy."

"Yes," said Beth, "that was at Numquam when the old elm tree fell in the wind when the children were playing in the garden, Victoria's and ours. Terrible it was, terrible. We lost our Charlie and our Frank."

"Are you religious people?" asked Miss Wigglesworth.

"Not really," said Beth, "we'se bin to the church once or twice, but not regular."

"I have a gift. I can use my gift to contact the spirits of those who have passed into the spirit world. I am a medium."

"What's that, when it's at home?"

"Let me describe what I can create," she said in her most beguiling manner.

"My guests sit around a large table holding hands in a darkened room and I go into a trance, seeking out spirits of those who have passed on and, often a spirit will come through me and make contact with a person in the room."

"Crikey, so what happens then?" asked Beth.

"A spirit from the other world will deliver a message through me as the medium, often one of comfort, but sometimes one of pain. Sitting around the table in this manner is called a séance."

"My sister is saying," said Mrs. Eggleton, "that perhaps in such a circumstance you might commune with the spirits of your dead children."

"Jesus Christ, no," exclaimed Horatio, "I've never heard such claptrap. My boys are dead and buried and we'll remember them as they were, not get some mumbo-jumbo from their spirits."

"Are you sure, darlin,'" said Beth plaintively, "it would be nice to hear them if they can talk to us."

"It won't bring them back to life. It will just be a terrible upset for us. We's not having to do it, Miss Wiggleworth or whatever your name is. Please to leave us now. It is difficult enough to bear our loss, let alone having someone coming and interfering."

"We will be on our way then," said Mrs. Eggleton, "and if you decide to take up the opportunity, you will know where to find us."

"I don't think we will," said Horatio firmly, as the women mounted the trap and went up the track.

"Never heard such Nonsense," he continued, "people with nothing to do can sit around a bleeding table trying to get in touch with Granny is not for the likes of us."

"I thought we might give it a try."

"But what would happen, Beth? We're not going to hear Charlie saying, 'Hallo Mum, Hallo Dad, God's given me a new horse,' or some such nonsense. It will just bring it all back to us, those terrible times. Best left alone."

"I suppose you're right."

Miss Wigglesworth was surprised by Mr. Fletcher's reaction, but then all that showed was that he was not a good candidate for her powers. Maud Eggleton, on the other hand, was quite shocked at his vehement attitude.

"Now Maud," said Hortense as the trap took them back to Numquam, "I know there is something else on your mind."

"I could give you a long list."

"I am your sister, you know."

"Alright, I swore to myself I'd never tell anyone as I am so ashamed."

"Why?"

"It's my husband, Charles. He now sleeps in his own bedroom and I am sure too that he is already having his way with our new maid April, a slut if ever there was one. She's quite a beauty in a coarse sort of way. I can tell the signs. I am sure he will be bedding her now while we are out if he hasn't left to avoid you. He's also got very nasty and brutal. I have bruises up and down my body. Since we took this house he has made it difficult for me to get any money to spend on anything I need. We have a slate for food but April does all the shopping."

"Oh dear, oh dear. I won't have you troubled, Maud," said Hortense in her most secretive voice, "I must do something about it, bring him down a peg, punish him for his sins."

"What do you mean?"

"My first thought is that we should kill him."

"What? Kill Him? That's preposterous."

"Why not? He is nasty, cruel and vindictive, not to mention disloyal and if he is planning to leave with young April, he's hurting her as well."

"Oh, but I couldn't. Nor could you, could you?"

"Maud," she said creepily, looking directly into her eyes, "I would not have suggested it if I was not sure we could do it."

"But how?"

"Tell me, do you hate him?" She said, purring like a cat.

"As you know, I married him to please my mother. She was dying, our father had died long since, and Mother wanted me settled. He was in a good trade as a butcher and he seemed nice enough, and we have not wanted for money."

"But he turned out to be a rotten egg, didn't he, so do you hate him?"

"I do. I hate him for all these years of my life when I have been bullied and knocked about, not to mention my dead children. I think he had a hand of some sort in both their deaths. He never really showed them any love or affection, just seeing them as a nuisance. Yes, I do really hate him. Perhaps it is his trade, cutting up the flesh of dead animals that makes him so."

"So he's a murderer as well. I knew it," she said, again in these cool tones, gazing at her sister with intensity, "so I'll work out how we can do it. I'll stay on for a while to get this accomplished."

Simon and Elizabeth met regularly before her departure date for America but their meetings were not replete with romantic conversations. It was just an intense and blossoming friendship but both regarded any further commitment with great caution, even though both of them were in continuous physical contact, holding hands and occasionally stroking cheeks and whiskers.

"I want you to meet my children before Charlotte and I leave."

"That would be a delight and I have today arranged to be away from my work for three months. A month or so traveling there and the same on my return. Then I will have a month in America and will stay with you if I may."

"Of course, of course you shall stay with us wherever we are, nothing could be more delightful and gives me something marvelous to look forward to. But you shall come to dinner tomorrow, just a week before we depart for Liverpool the day after, the last day of June."

"I am not sure that I can bear to let you go," he said, putting his arms around her, as they stood gazing out on the street.

"Do you think one can forget what to do?" she asked laughing.

"I doubt it, though it has been a year or so for me too."

"My desire for you is overwhelming, Simon darling, but it is necessary to defer that until my return and your situation is clearer. But let us go out of town for lunch in the country, spending the whole day together. There is an old Inn, the King's Arms at Amersham where we had lunch as a family once. I believe it goes back to the fifteenth century. Would tomorrow suit you?"

"Of course, I need you. I know it has been scarcely a month, but I know we are about to spend our lives together, healing each other from our griefs."

"That is probably the best few words I have heard for many years."

"Whether we will ever marry does not matter to me, and one day I will tell you about a three-year relationship I had when my father was a diplomat in Paris."

"Save that for a winter's evening when we can tell each other all kinds of bits of our histories and revel in our togetherness."

A cab from Amersham Station put them down in the courtyard of the Kings' Arms. They were greeted by a man so elderly that he might well have been there at the foundation of the Inn, but they indicated that they had merely come for lunch. As the waiters brought them their meal, they talked about each other about their growing passion for each other, their hands usually entwined.

"Great Scot," interrupted a loud male voice suddenly, "it's Simon Brandram."

Turning round abruptly, Simon replied, "Well, well, Teddy Piltcher, what brings you here?" and turning to Elizabeth, he said, "Teddy was in my year at

Cambridge, wonderful sportsman, got a blue in rowing and cricket as I recall. So Teddy, what brings you here?"

"Teaching of course, it allows me full rein for my passion for sports, allows me plenty of time. I get time off from school to play for Hertfordshire too or will do when they get themselves together. It is an old club, you know, founded twenty-five years go. But introduce me to your lovely companion."

With hesitation but realizing the truth was the best option, he said, "this is Elizabeth Egerton, a very dear friend."

"Well charmed, I am sure. Now I must be off to meet some of the team in the Bar. Bit of a celebration really."

"Well you enjoy yourself, Teddy, and it is so good to meet you again,"

"Likewise," said Teddy and he ambled off into the Bar.

"Well?" said Elizabeth, her eyes sparkling.

"He was a chum, but an innocent in the world, totally engrossed in sport. He'll make an excellent schoolmaster."

"But what of us? Will he put the word out?"

"He is an interesting man, I do not believe he would harbor any suspicion about any of his friends. He would not even be curious as to how I find myself here with you, he will just assume there is a very good reason and certainly never wonder to himself 'why is Simon with that lady?'"

"You know, darling, I really don't care if the word gets out."

"Nor me. Well, not yet."

After lunch, they walked along the High Street, turning into a country lane blessed with all the natural accoutrements of the English countryside. They stood together at a gate to a meadow where a couple of horses were grazing. They did not speak, but held hands, the comfort and warmth of each other's company being enough to them both to understand that they might well soon be lovers.

X

Mrs. Egerton and her daughter Charlotte arrived in America toward the end of July and stayed for a week at the new Algonquin Hotel on 44th Street in New York. They took an excursion to Philadelphia for two nights, a city they did not enjoy, but their primary task was to find out where Elizabeth's mother was living. After breakfast on the third morning of their arrival, Elizabeth said:

"We are going to hire a private investigator, Charlotte, if we are to find my mother, and the concierge tells me a firm called Pinkertons has the best reputation."

"What a funny name," said Charlotte with a giggle.

They walked into a dour office later three blocks away later in the morning, and a tall gaunt man behind a desk said:

"The Pinkertons Agency is at your service, Madam," with just that amount of unction that displays politeness without fawning on the customer.

"Thank you, I wish you to find my mother."

"The Pinkertons Agency can well accommodate your desires, for we have been in existence for fifty years and our customers have included Mr. Rockefeller, the Government of our fine United States, as well as tracking down villains in the Western States of the Union. Tell me about your mother," said he, as he took a large writing pad from under the desk in front of him.

"She is Mary-Lou, Countess Wassilko von Serecki. She is in her late sixties. I would guess she would be living in one of cities on this East Coast."

"I am sure with a name like that, our agents will have no difficulty in finding her, probably by the end of the first week in August, I'd say next week."

"I need her address only and I do not wish her to know that you have located her on my behalf. I am Mrs. Elizabeth Egerton, staying at the Algonquin."

"We do charge a fee at the outset of an investigation and then a final fee which depends on what we have needed to do. That will be twenty dollars."

Elizabeth paid and they left.

"Why did they not ask for a description?" said Charlotte.

"With that Romanian name, they had no need. If she were Jane Smith, I am sure much more detail would have been asked for."

The Pinkerton search for the lady with the Romanian surname was accomplished much earlier than promised once it had been circulated to Pinkerton offices nationwide.

"This is not going to be easy, Charlotte," said Elizabeth the following week as the carriage made its way up Beacon Hill to 28 Brimner Street. It was a rowhouse, rather narrower than its neighbors, but in beautiful brick, with iron railings on both sides of the steps leading to the main door, unusual because it was partly glass, installed no doubt as no one in the street could see into the house as the door was a good six feet above the sidewalk, but as the house faced east, sunlight would stream into the hall every morning.

A maid opened the door as mother and daughter stood waiting.

"Can I help you, Ma'am?" Said the maid.

"I am look for Countess Wasiki," said Elizabeth.

"I will see if she is at home," said the maid and shut the door, returning quite promptly to say that her mistress was not at home.

"Tell her that her daughter and grand-daughter wish to see her."

"Daughter?" said the maid, somewhat shocked, at which an elderly bent old lady appeared from the back of the hall walking with a stick shuffling toward the door.

"Is that you, Elizabeth? Oh my goodness, come in, come in. Mary, fetch some coffee and a cookie or two."

"Mother, how are you? This is Charlotte, my daughter and your grand-daughter," at which Mary-Lou stepped forward and grabbed Elizabeth and held her tight at which both of them burst into tears, while Charlotte looked on, moved but embarrassed at this old woman, her grand-mother.

"Now, who is this?" said Mary-Lou reaching out to hold Charlotte by the hand.

"I am Charlotte, my mother's only daughter."

"Come into the lounge, my dears," and though Elizabeth had never heard a drawing room called a lounge before, she held her mother's left hand while the old lady propelled herself on her walking stick and sat down in an elegant chair higher than normal, obviously built to cope with her infirmity.

"How is your husband, Mother?" Said Elizabeth once she was settled in a chair close by, while Charlotte made herself comfortable on the settee, focusing her gaze directly at this fascinating acquisition discovered as a close relative.

"He died suddenly six years ago. Something with his heart, the doctors said," and it was immediately noticeable to Elizabeth how her mother's voice had lost that sing-song voice of the Southern belle and was quieter, even more Yankee than she expected, though the twang of Southern Carolina was still apparent, if only slightly.

"How sad for you, Mother."

"We had a good life. When we came back from Paris after I last saw you, we said we would never take a ship again. We were tossed around on the Atlantic for what felt like years, but we made up for it by traveling across country. We lived in a small town out west, San Francisco, for a while and then up to Canada and back. It was too sad for me to go south to my Daddy's old plantation. He was only sixty when he died, broken-hearted by the war, I guess. My mammy lived a bit longer, but she too died before her time in my solemn estimation. With them both gone, I sold the house in New York near Albany and the plantation and the Count and I lived comfortably here. But enough about me, tell me about your children and this charming young lady here?"

The rest of the morning was spent explaining most of the family history: Henry now a lawyer, Oliver at Cambridge and his exploits at Eton and in South Africa, and of course, the Fitzroys, Charlotte Mudge's marriage to Percy Vere and their life in Pompeii."

"So how come you are here in America?" Asked Mary-Lou," and why is your husband not with you?"

The story of Timothy Egerton's murder in the Foreign Office reduced Mary-Lou to tears which lasted all the time Elizabeth unfolded the events up to the execution of George Fortescue.

"How did you manage, my dear? How terrible for you, and him such a senior person in the Government."

"I had no option but to accept it, though I was especially sad, and Charlotte dear, this is news to you. For two or three months before he was killed, he changed dramatically, drinking very heavily so that I scarcely knew him. After the event, of course, I was kept in the dark, being told he had committed suicide for reasons of state, but then when I was told he was murdered, it was like his dying was happening all over again. Told he had committed suicide, I was full of regret and saddened that he should do such a thing and hurt us all so much, but when I was told he was murdered, I was completely shattered as my emotions about his suicide had been completely false."

"For the life of me," said Mary-Lou, "I cannot understand why they deceived you. How much of an evil was that?"

"I agree and they apologized, saying that announcing it was suicide enabled them to flush out his killer more easily. So there was a good reason, but oh my, how painful it was."

"Mamma," said Charlotte, her face covered with tears, "why have you not explained this to me before?"

"I don't know. I suppose I wanted to protect you, but now you are old enough."

"And as my new grandchild," said Mary-Lou addressing Charlotte, "you must now help your Mamma."

"There was an aftermath which will amuse you," said Elizabeth, "and this you do know, Charlotte. I got a command from Buckingham Palace to say that Timothy would receive posthumously a Knighthood of the Royal Victorian Order."

"What on earth is that?"

"It is a medal given to someone whom the Queen is especially grateful for a man's service. I went to the Palace to be given it and the Queen was ill, so I received the medal from the Prince of Wales, now the King. Afterwards he invited me to join a soiree of his favorite ladies!"

"Oh my, was that an honor? Our newspapers are full of his amorous adventures."

"I declined of course, and he promptly left the room, offended perhaps."

"You have had some adventures, haven't you. Are you still playing the piano?"

"Yes indeed, do you have a piano here?"

"Yes, it is in the music room opposite. I call it the music room as it is really a study, a library, and an office rolled into one. You will stay for lunch, won't you?"

"We would love to, and perhaps we can take a walk this afternoon."

Mary-Lou called her carriage after lunch and they went out to Cambridge and on to Harvard, where Elizabeth noted the quite grand buildings, saying that she hoped Charlotte would go to one of the new women's colleges in Cambridge, England.

"Quite right, my dear," said Mary-Lou. "Of course I was very young when I married your father but I have wished I had more of an education, as the

Count was well educated and I felt sometimes I could not converse with him about anything sensible."

"Times have changed, Mother, not least here in America. There is so much more wealth than I recall when Timothy and I were posted here."

"I didn't know that," exclaimed Mary-Lou, "you mean you were here for a few years and made no effort to see me?"

"I was still very bruised at that time, Mother."

"Say no more then, but how long will you stay and what will you do?"

"An important decision to make," said Elizabeth as they stopped the carriage so that they could sit on the bank of the Charles River for a while as the old lady could not walk very far and they could watch the rowers."

"What do you think, Charlotte?" Asked her mother, "Should we find a house in Boston?"

"Why not stay in my house for a while? I am on my own you know, and there are three bedrooms for guests."

"That would be lovely, I think, let us stay a month and then see."

"My Drew cousins are expecting to visit in September for a week or so. I think you'll like them, though I haven't seen them for several months and I am too old to go up there now."

"Let us talk about that tomorrow. You look tired now."

The carriage took them back to Brimner Street, and as Elizabeth and Charlotte were leaving, Mary-Lou caught her daughter by the hand and embraced her.

"I am so sorry for being such a neglectful mother. I was just a child and got into some awful bad habits."

"Let us put that aside now, Mother. I am here to get to know you again. I have had you on my conscience since Timothy died."

"Really? I am not sure I am worth it." she said with a tear in her eye and when they were back at the house, she went to her bedroom to rest.

"I wonder what Simon will make of her if he comes, Charlotte." said Elizabeth.

Charles Eggleton had decided not to hire a permanent gardener. As a man used to strong physical exercise in carrying around animal carcasses before butchering them, he decided to tend the garden himself. He saw no reason to hire a man and accommodate him when the work was simple. He learnt from a book on growing fruit how to tend the orchard, he thought growing vegetables unnecessary as plenty were available in the local market, but his only concession was to hire a man to scythe the grass in the summer to keep it in trim. Gardening had the added attraction that he could be alone and away from his wife Maud whom he had come to detest for her fawning ways and general incompetence in running a large house.

If he disliked his wife, his feelings about his sister-in-law were very mixed. That he hated her as much as his wife was true, but she fascinated him with her deep silky voice, her short stature and her extraordinary eyes. Although he was careful not to be open about his secret lust, he would definitely take the opportunity if it presented itself. He was enjoying April the maid whenever he wanted, and he discovered she was a vigorous and enthusiastic young woman.

Hortense had not been at Numquam for three weeks as she had been busy in Marylebone with her seances. By the middle of August, demand had dropped and, as there was an open invitation she caught the train on the South-East and Chatham Railway to Chatham and then took a trap to Numquam House.

As the trap arrived and she dismounted, she saw her sister's husband in his shirtsleeves obviously digging in some kind of trench, so she walked across the garden to see what he was doing without announcing her arrival to Maud. That she hated the man with a passion was not in doubt, but she recognized that he held a perverse attraction for her.

"I thought you had a gardener," said Hortense as she approached, her husky voice immediately arousing her brother in-law.

"No, Hortense, I work the garden now," he said, hopping out of the trench and coming close to her. "It is good physical exercise and I am growing to like it. It is certainly more interesting than cutting meat all day but stay and watch me if you wish."

"It certainly builds up your physique. You look quite strong, but I must let Maud know of my arrival."

"Come, come, you don't need to do that just yet," he said, taking her by the hand, "I have a large horse in my stable and he probably wants to come out and see you," he said with a leer.

Hortense was puzzled by this strange approach but nevertheless interested to see what it was about. He led her into the stables and immediately put his arm around her tiny waist, drawing her to him and holding her tightly against him, as he lifted her small frame up on to a table.

"I have always found you most desirable, you know, Hortense. Now you can stroke my horse. Sometimes I think I should have married you, not Maud, and I see in your eyes that deep down you would like me to take you."

"Never, Charles, never, no man has ever touched me, so please desist!" she cried, but whether she did not push him away because she was not strong enough, or whether without thinking she had inadvertently given him that slight smile a woman gives indicating her readiness, she was caught between disgust and desire. He kissed her hard over her empty protests, and handling her skirts roughly, he said:

"Your first time, eh? Oh well, you naughty creature, let me show you what you have been missing. After this, you'll always be coming begging my horse for more."

She was surprised by how easily she took him to her and after her groans of satisfaction had died down, he restored her dress, but then kissed her violently, gripping her body in a vice with his hands which aroused both her lust and her hatred.

"You blaggard, Charles, you will suffer for this."

"Why, my dear, you obviously enjoyed it, didn't you, and you will want to seize the opportunity whenever you are here, I am sure. Next time, I will come to you at night."

They walked out of the stable as Maud approached from the house.

"I thought I heard your voices," said Maud innocently.

"I was showing Hortense my new horse," he said and went on to detail his plans for the trench, and then said brusquely,

"Off you go now, both of you, and let me get on with this work."

So the sisters left and walked back to the house, Hortense gripped by mixed feelings about this encounter with her brother-in-law but thinking of what the brute was doing to her sister.

"Now Maud," said Hortense, steadying herself from the shock and a pleasure she had never known, "do you realize what an opportunity this is?"

"I don't follow you."

"I went over to greet him when I arrived and he then led me to the stable and had his way with me over my protests."

"Oh my, did he really take you?"

"I could do nothing, he is such a strong man, and I was not prepared to fight him even though it was a new experience," she said, hoping that sounded convincing.

"I didn't realize he could be so cruel to me, taking you. But I don't know, killing him is such a risk. What would happen if we were caught?"

"We must dispose of him and look, he is literally digging his own grave. I have always wondered how we would dispose of the body after we killed him, but he is doing the work for us. We will choose a day the maid is off, there is no gardener and afterwards, all we have to do is fill in the trench after the arsenic has worked."

"Arsenic? What then?"

"If anyone were to ask for him, you can simply say he is visiting a relative, if he has one."

"He has a younger brother who is a butcher in Carlisle, about as far away in England as one could get from here and they are rarely in contact."

"You see, it is quite a simple matter. You can tell the Vicar's wife later on about his having to tend to his mother or some such story and that you want to stop the lease. Then you move to London with me, or to some other part of the country, and no one will be any wiser."

But as a poet once reminded the world –

'The best laid schemes o' mice an' men
Gang aft a-gley.'

Aye, and yor wummun too, as Robbie would have said.

The Smythes and the Gargerys were among early buyers from the British Isles of chateaux or villas in the Alpes-Maritimes as opposed to those buying or building near the sea at Antibes on the Cote d'Azur or in Monaco. They had been preceded by royalty such as the former Prince of Wales or very wealthy families, and a place to which painters from the new Impressionist school had begun to enjoy because of the quality of the light for many years.

The Smythe's chateau was in the cork forest north of Ramatuelle, convenient for the sea but in forty hectares, it offered all manner of activities that

Nature supported, particularly walking. The Gargery villa in Vence was now fully refurbished with gas lighting and running water with its three levels looking across wooded land to the sea.

The families met on several occasions, almost always at alfresco lunches and alternating their visits. The Gargerys used the time to read widely, while their children played in the pool for swimming which was becoming a necessary part of a foreign home in the sun. Malcolm determined to read the Communist writers, Marx and Engels, but also works about the working class such as *Les Miserables* and an obscure novel by Emile Zola called *Germinal.* He also tried to get to grips with protagonists in the Dreyfus Affair but found it baffling. Clara on the other hand was immersed in English novels, Thackeray, Trollope and others which made her feel comfortable as they described an almost familiar world. What she had read of Dickens was beyond her ken.

As they walked through the forests, picking cork from the tree-trunks and playing with it in their hands, conversations between Malcolm and Clarence often veered to automobiles and their future

"We have seen such magnificent inventions this last century that the idea of having a machine rather than a horse on which to travel is certainly not outrageous. Indeed, one can imagine a future with automobiles. After all we have locomotives taking us everywhere, virtually unknown even when the Queen came to the throne."

"I worry about the interim, Clarence. Locomotives have their own tracks and only intersect where they cross a thoroughfare, but what would those thoroughfares be like with horse-drawn vehicles and automobiles traveling at the same time?"

"I am told they can be very noisy and dangerous so will certainly frighten the horses."

"The more I consider this, Malcolm, the more I am sure of the need for separate routes, to keep horses and automobiles separate. In London, Regent Street might be reserved for horse traffic and Oxford Street for automobiles."

"That is very worthwhile our consideration as I am sure someone will build an automobile for transporting the public like the horse-drawn buses which are nowadays such a convenience for some."

When they returned, the others were sitting in the afternoon sun.

"What do automobiles feed on?" Asked Clara, "like horses they must have some sort of food."

"As I understand it, Malcolm, when engineers built the first stationary engine, they saw that steam was not the most effective fuel as it is with a loco-motive. I think the engine has what they call internal combustion."

"What's that?"

"Somehow, and don't ask me how, power is generated inside the engine where a kind of oil they call petrol explodes which turns a rod around which then turns the wheels."

"I think I see that. The rod could then turn wheels, from the power generated."

Such conversations often took place on lazy afternoons. When not walk-ing in the forests, the two men lay under a canopy to protect themselves from the sun. Customarily they sipped lemonade, immersed in the comfort of wooden chaise-longues covered with silk cushions, their books and drinks on low tables which also temporarily held their straw boaters.

At dinner on their last evening, Clarence laid out their journey. Carriages would take them to Cagnes-sur-Mer where they would board a train to Lyon and Paris but he did not know whether they would change the train at Marseille. After a night in Paris, they would travel by train to Stuttgart and take a car-riage to the factory of Daimler-Motoren-Gesellschaft at Untertürkheim, the company being known for its creation of the first internal combustion engine in a self-propelled automobile. Clarence had booked rooms for everyone at the Kaiser Wilhelm Hotel in the old city and everyone was excited by the thought of seeing such a machine.

The party arrived at the works in a carriage on Wednesday the 9th of September at precisely ten o'clock. Emblazoned along the factory wall on the outside was the name of the company. The building itself looked new, and indeed some parts of it seemed unfinished, but a young man came out to meet them.

"We have come from England," said Clarence, "to view the automobile you manufacture."

"Of course," said the young man in perfect English, "I am Gustav Daimler, Herr Benz has heard from our London embassy about your planned visit. Please come."

The young man led them into a small hallway with offices on either side and then into a large office where Mr. Benz was working on papers.

"Guten Morgen, ich spreche kein Englisch, also wird Wilheim hier Ihnen helfen. Es ist mir eine Freude, Sie kennenzulernen und ich hoffe, Sie werden eines meiner Automobile kaufen."

Clarence looked at Malcolm and Clara looked at Emma and Emma looked at Clarence and Malcolm looked at Clara, none of them understanding a word.

With a smile, Gustav said, "Mr. Benz welcomes you and wishes me to guide you, and he hopes that you will buy one of his automobiles," at which there were smiles and a shaking of hands.

"What a fine looking gentleman," whispered Clara to Emma, "such distinction."

"Indeed. What a gracious fellow."

"Please to come with me," said Gustav, "let me first show you our most recent product and then we can see where the automobiles are made if you wish, though it is rather noisy."

"Tell me," said Malcolm, "did you not have a fire recently?"

"Yes, that was in our Cannstatt works but we had planned to move to this larger building so the production of our automobiles was not delayed."

At the end of the hallway was a glass door which led to a large room with glass windows and there in the middle was the new automobile.

"This is our four seater tourer," said Gustav, pointing to this magnificent machine, painted in red, quite different from any automobile they had ever seen.

"Can we touch it?"

"Of course, and please to allow the children to get in it, at which George and Andrew and the younger Smythe girls clambered in with George in the driver's seat, playing with the steering wheel."

"Fascinating," said Clara, "We would have to learn how to operate it, rather different from a horse."

"Yes, we recommend a period of discovery to understand where the levers are."

An hour later after hearing about the process of manufacturing, Clarence asked Gustav what was the cost of such a machine.

"I should first tell you that we have orders stretching into late 1905, over two years. A deposit of five thousand marks will put you on our list. I do not know what the price will be then, but I do not think it will be less than twenty thousand pounds sterling. These machines are the work of craftsmen and production takes time too, I am afraid. Of course, as production develops, we may be able to deliver it to you earlier."

"Deliver it? Would we not come and fetch it?"

"Oh no, we will arrange for transport which, of course, would be an additional cost."

Wilhelm then took the party to a small restaurant on the factory premises, used by Carl Benz and the senior management. It was clear to both these potential buyers that while this was a modern wonder, the expense was daunting. Only Clara wanted to put down a deposit, thinking that such a beautiful object would grace the street outside her Down Street house to be admired by everyone, and she would not care if it was never driven.

XI

Elizabeth and Charlotte were well settled in Boston by September, although Mary-Lou's health gave cause for concern, experiencing constant shortness of breath and her doctor was not encouraging, merely thinking that she was suffering from old age. Elizabeth was thus sufficiently concerned to talk with a doctor at the City Hospital, an institution now over a hundred years old. He suggested that shortness of breath indicated a heart condition for which there was no real treatment, though he advised exercise and what he called a sensible diet.

Those comments upset Elizabeth, especially as her mother did not seem to be improving.

"Mother, I want you to take a walk in the fresh air with me each day to try and improve the condition of your heart."

"Oh honey," she replied, using an American expression Elizabeth detested, "my heart will last just as long as it was intended to last. I've had a good life, you know, though I hope not to die for several years yet. In any case we have the Drew cousins coming to visit this month."

"Remind me, who are they again?"

"My aunt Mildred's children. As far as I know there is a Charles Drew who will be about my age and he had two sons and a daughter, Cedric, Gary and Florence. I doubt whether they will come, but they would be your cousins of some sort."

"How about your father's relatives?"

"The Beauregards? I don't know. The Drews may well know. What do you propose to do, Elizabeth? You've been here a couple of months. My only friends are ladies older than me. All the Count's friends disappeared when he died, not that I liked any of them, either flirts or bores, or both."

"I just want to stay here with you for a while, Mother. We have lost so much of our lives together, haven't we? Charlotte and I are enjoying Boston. It's a pretty place and we like taking walks and seeing the sights, and occasionally going on the river. We take the little train up to Cambridge and walk around Harvard College, partly because I want Charlotte to think of a university."

"I think you need to marry again, as I did. Are you really going to spend your life as a widow? You are still a young woman."

"I know, Mother, I know. Although I was once wary of any entanglement because of my memories of Timothy, but I do have what you from the South would call a new beau. He is coming to visit quite soon, and I will tell you all about him then. He is Simon Brandram."

"What an odd name, but I am sure he is as handsome as a peacock," a comment that Elizabeth let slide.

For Elizabeth, the visit of the Drew cousins was a complete disaster. Charles Drew came with daughter Florence and one of the sons, Gary. It took a great deal to shock Mary-Lou but she was more than angry after they left.

"I knew there was a reason I have not kept up with them. They are all noisy boors, able to talk about nothing but themselves. Florence walked around this house, criticizing everything. My mother's lovely desk was just an old plantation relic, the decoration in the dining room was out-of-date, and she had the temerity to ask Charlotte whether she liked staying with an old person. Really!"

"I agree, Grandma, I have never met people so uncouth. That man Gary treated me as though I was with an orphan or a dullard."

"Charles treated me as though I was available," said Elizabeth, "so I told him I had never been so insulted in my life."

"I am glad they are gone. But, my dears, why not take a train down to Charleston South Carolina, it will be so beautiful in the Fall. I have an old address for Eunice Beauregard, a cousin. Stay in the best hotel and stay for a few days, anyway, maybe find a relation or two.

"I'd like to do that before Simon arrives, certainly."

The visit to Charleston proved a shattering experience. The Francis Marion Hotel was very comfortable, named after some hero or other as Elizabeth told her daughter with a sniff. Their efforts to find any member of the Beauregard family were to no avail. Enquiries produced different types of information, that Eunice was buried in Chesterfield county, that the main family moved to Louisiana, that one Dickenson Beauregard was in prison for murder in Jamaica, and so on, but not a Beauregard in sight.

Three days of the search passed and Elizabeth and Charlotte gave up the search for family and decided to take a day's drive into the country. The hotel provided a splendid picnic and hired them a comfortable carriage, with a coachman dressed in a hotel livery. Once out of Charleston, they headed for Maryville, a little town which the hotel concierge said was a pretty place by the river.

"What is your name, driver?" asked Elizabeth as they set off.

"I'se Samuel, Samuel Beauregard, ma'am," said he.

"I beg your pardon," cried Elizabeth, "I have been in Charleston for three days searching for my elderly mother's relations, and their surname was Beauregard."

"Oh there's no white folks of that name around here anymore. No, I suppose me and my sister, we's the only one left here, apart from my kiddies, of course."

"We must be related, then," said Elizabeth cautiously.

"I don't rightly know, but my granddaddy and grandma were slaves on the Beauregard plantation, though that's all broken up since the war and my own mamma used to tell me we had this French name because my grandma was old man Beauregard's favorite."

"But Samuel," said Charlotte, "we must be cousins or something."

"No, ma'am, just let things be. I suppose we might be cousins," and he laughed, "but there ain't nothing to be done about it."

The summer sun was hot, even tropical, but the gentle speed of the carriage ensured a coolish breeze. As they approached Maryville there appeared to be what Charlotte later described as a ruckus in the center of town. Samuel stopped the carriage.

"We's go no further," said Samuel, "Just you wait here and have your picnic if you like but I am going for a long walk. Folks like me don't need to be around this," at which he dismounted and hurried back along the track in the direction of Charleston.

"Let us wait and see what this crowd is about, though perhaps we should get down and follow Samuel; I've no idea why he has gone away for a walk," said Elizabeth.

Coming toward them was a sight neither of them would ever forget. They could just make out a crowd of perhaps a hundred men following a horse dragging along the ground what appeared to be the body of a man.

'Death to the nigger, death to the rapist, kill him, kill him, kill him' were among the shouts and screams of this mob of madmen. The man was black, his assailants white. It took Elizabeth and Charlotte a few minutes to realize what was happening.

A couple of hundred yards away from them was an old willow oak. Two men took a few minutes to throw a rope over a branch and the two women watched in horror as they could just make out a noose at the end of the rope. Then the man was released from the horse, his hands were tied behind his back, but he was hardly able to stand as one of his legs was obviously broken, but two men stood him up increasing the poor man's pain, at which he was punched and pummeled by several of the men, blood dripped from his eyes and nose, and he was screaming in pain.

"Cut 'em off, cut'em off," was a shout from the mob.

The man who seemed to be in charge screamed various oaths attempting to describe the black man's sin which, as far as Elizabeth could make out, was smiling at a white woman and with each accusation, he beat the main with his club.

The noose was put around his neck. Three men tugged on the rope so that he was suspended in mid-air. A stake was driven into the ground and the end of the rope tied to it, but then the weight of the man was too great and he fell to ground, screaming again as he recovered some consciousness from the release of the noose as he fell. With more shouts and screams from the crowd, he was hauled up once again.

"Hold the rope till he's a goner," the man in charge called out. So for the next ten minutes or so, the crowd danced around the tree where the man was hanging, whooping and wailing and shouting out blasphemies and profanities, until, at last, he was obviously dead, at which the crowd became a jostling and excited mass returning to Maryville, leaving the body hanging silently, twisting with the natural winding of the rope.

Elizabeth and Charlotte held each tight throughout, unable to sustain a look, appalled at the savagery and numbed by the experience. Samuel had obviously understood what would be happening and he was a good mile away from the scene when the ghastly performance was over. Both women in the carriage were weeping, feeling soiled by the experience of watching a lynching. Then long soft chants could be heard as men and woman came to recover the body, singing and weeping. Men took the body down and carried it back towards the north side of town, skirting the town center.

Elizabeth was now in floods of tears as she watched the terrible distress of the man's family and his friends. By this time, Samuel had returned.

"What do you wish me to do, Ma'am?"

"Let us return to Charleston immediately. Samuel, I can well understand why you did not stay."

"No Ma'am, these lynchings is terrible happenings and I don't hold with no barbarity. Black folks is treated like that regular. I saw one start when I was a little-bitty kid. My mamma worked as a hauler and carrier for a store in a village near the old Beauregard Plantation and I would sit out front. There was this young white girl, and she smiled and said hallo to a black man walking in the street. Then men from the salon across the street ran over and grabbed him. I ran back to my mamma at the back but my daddy said she should've known better. Those men have a blood lust and want to terrify black folks into submission, a wicked sin against the Lord."

After an impossible night's sleep as this grim memory haunted them, Elizabeth decided that their visit to the South was over and both women promptly returned to Boston on the train. Tired and in considerable distress at what they had witnessed, they walked into the house to greet Mary-Lou.

"What on earth is the matter with you two?" said Mary-Lou emerging from the drawing-room, "Tell me all about your visit over dinner, but go up and wash and change first."

That done, Mary-Lou wanted to know every detail.

"The only Beauregard we could find happened to be the driver of the carriage we hired to take us to Maryville."

"To Maryville?" Asked Mary-Lou now visibly alarmed.

"Samuel was a very polite man of middle age, I suppose, and he had been told that his grandma had given birth to two of what he said was Old Man Beauregard's children."

"Oh my, that was my daddy, the old fool. My mamma always thought he was using his slaves like that so he must have insisted his bastard children took his name."

"That was an interesting conversation, Mamma, but he refused any mutual recognition that we were somehow his cousins."

"I should think so too. That would be impossible."

"I don't see why," said Charlotte. "He was a perfectly decent man and I will go back and seek out my black cousins there when I am older."

"You do that," said Mary-Lou with the utmost condescension, "but, just remember, those black men are not to be trusted by a white woman."

"We saw that in the most terrible incident. Outside Maryville we watched a man being lynched."

"What?" exclaimed the old lady, horrified; "How on earth did that happen?"

"As we were approaching the town, this crowd of men came out with a horse dragging a man's body."

"I don't want to hear any more," said Mary-Lou, "What did your driver do?"

"He walked away from the carriage for a good mile and returned after it was all over."

"I will hear no more about it. I have been the cause of one to my eternal regret."

"How?" cried Elizabeth and Charlotte together, appalled by this confession.

"My dears, I have never told anyone this, not even your father, Elizabeth. It is all so long ago. I was a young girl of sixteen, being brought up as a Southern lady, and I used to take walks around the plantation and I'd chat with the slaves as they went about their business and I even knew their names.

"One morning I had gone into town with my mother. She went into a store and I stayed outside fanning myself against the heat under my parasol. One of the young men from the Plantation was carrying some goods for my father along the street on his way back. He was passing me and I said, 'Aren't you going to talk to me, Jonathan?' and he stopped and smiled, and said, "I'd better not, missy," and tried to walk on.

"So why is that important?" Asked Charlotte in a voice weary from travel, obviously wanting to be excused so that she could go to bed.

"Ah, my child, he was seen talking to me by some ugly white trash across the street, drinking in the saloon. Poor man, in a trice he was manhandled and within half an hour he was hanging from a tree just outside the town. Just awful how men could do that to a slave. My mamma came out of the store and asked me what he had done and I told her I had started to talk to him as I knew him from the Plantation. All she said," said Mary-Lou now in tears, was 'what a silly thing to do, my child, now they'll have lynched him, and your father will be annoyed his property has been lost.'"

"Oh mother," said Elizabeth, getting up to put her arms around her, "how terrible for you."

"Grandma, was there a little black boy watching you?"

"Oh, I don't know, why?

"Because Samuel told about his mamma working in a store and his watching a white girl say hallo to a man who was taken off and lynched."

"Oh my, now I do remember, as I gave him a penny, but the lynching was why I was sent to London right then with my mamma at age sixteen and married to your father within six months."

Elizabeth went to bed not knowing how to cope with this family legacy, but the following day a letter arrived from London to say that Simon expected to be in Boston by November 1st and would come to the Brimner Street address.

The responsibilities of His Majesty's judges include travel to Assize courts in county towns across the country for serious cases, murder and all types of felonies as local crimes demanded.

For the Autumn Law Term, Sir Hamish MacDonald was to be the Judge in the Assize Court at the county town of Maidstone in Kent. A large house was provided for him with a cook and a maid for his two-three month stay. Lady MacDonald would accompany him and Theophilus Mandrake his clerk would stay at a hostelry in the center of the City.

Hamish looked at the docket of cases two days before he was due to leave his Chiswick home, one of which, due in November, read:

Rex v. Eggleton and Wigglesworth. Murder of Charles Eggleton of Numquam House, All Hallows.

Hamish could not remember where he had heard that house name, so he called Mary into his study.

"Mary, does Numquam House mean anything to you?"

"Of course, my dear, that was Estella's house, and she left it to Nellie. Victoria and Albert lived there, but then she married Vicar John Eustace and they moved into the Vicarage together. Why do you ask?"

"I have a case coming up on the docket in Maidstone where two women are accused of murdering a man with that address."

"Goodness me. I'd be sure they would have put tenants in the house, so presumably it is about them."

"I have a couple of burglaries, another murder, and two with bodily harm to deal with before that case comes up, so we will find out in November."

Mr. Justice MacDonald strode into the Assize Courtroom in Maidstone, at exactly ten o'clock on the morning of November 3, 1903. The indictment had been issued in September and both sisters had been remanded in custody by the magistrate in Rochester but one of the sisters, Hortense Wigglesworth, was in Switzerland when her sister was arrested. She returned home in mid-October unaware of the situation but was quickly apprehended.

Hamish was fascinated with the connection to Numquam but saw no reason to recuse himself. He thought he had been there only once during Estella's life, and neither he nor his wife had any connection with the accused. Sir Septimus Goldflake Q.C., who had appeared before Hamish many times, was the prosecuting counsel and a jury was sworn in without difficulty. The clerk read the charges of murder in the first degree to the two women in the dock and both pleaded 'Not Guilty" so the trial began.

"M'lud, "said Sir Septimus, "the charges of murder in the first degree are the most serious in English Law. These two sisters, Maud Eggleton and Hortense Wigglesworth are charged with the murder of Mr. Eggleston's husband Charles, that between August 15th and August 30th they poisoned him with arsenic and buried him in the garden of the Eggleton residence known as Numquam House in the parish of All Hallows in this county.

"The discovery of the body was the result of a police investigation occasioned by the brother of the deceased, Arthur Eggleton, who will give evidence in due course. He had decided to come from Carlisle to visit his brother in his new home as he had a letter from him indicating that he had taken up gardening as a hobby, and the description of the garden at Numquam was sufficient to entice him to come down from Cumberland.

"On his arrival the maid, one April Shower, did as she had been instructed by the accused and told him that the deceased had gone to see his brother in Carlisle. When told by the visitor that he was in fact the Carlisle brother the maid was confused and called Mrs. Eggleton, now in the dock, who had not previously met her husband's brother for reasons that need not trouble the Court. She was not welcoming so he left hurriedly to return to Carlisle thinking that he and his brother's paths must have crossed. He expected to find Charles there, but his wife reported to her husband that his brother had not been seen.

"Arthur Eggleton immediately assumed that his brother Charles was missing and sent a letter to the police in Rochester and to Mrs. Eggleton. The police went to Numquam House to interview Mrs. Eggleton and her sister, Miss Hortense Wigglesworth, the self-styled Marylebone Medium, who was then staying with her. She is in the dock with her sister.

"Let me add that this lady, Hortense Wigglesworth, is indeed a medium of note for those who inhabit what I will call spiritualist circles."

"Should we anticipate the spirit of the deceased in evidence, then?" asked Hamish, which causes ripples of amusement in the Court and the Gallery but elicited an angry snort from the accused.

"The two ladies were interviewed separately, a matter which will interest your Lordship given your earlier animadversions on this practice by police, and they found highly contradictory stories from the accused. In particular the attitude of Mrs. Eggleton began to arouse their suspicions as the jury will hear from the police.

"A decision was made with the Chief Constable's consent to get a warrant to search the premises. When that happened, neither sister was in the house so the police broke in. Nothing of special interest was found in the house, but a can of arsenic which had clearly been in recent use was found in the garden shed and is Exhibit A. While searching the grounds, Police Constable Painter noticed an area of ground large enough to contain a human body where there had been recent digging. Detective Mallet ordered that it be investigated and there followed an exhumation of the body of Charles Eggleton in the state that Nature originally intended. The pathologist reported the presence of arsenic in the body.

"I will now proceed to call witnesses if your Lordship pleases."

"Call Arthur Eggleton," said the clerk, at which a stout man of medium build appeared dressed like an undertaker appeared but once he indicated that he was a butcher, the imagination of all in the court saw him in a straw boater and the distinctive blue striped apron of his trade. He swore the oath and Sir Septimus said:

"Mr. Eggleton, why did you make this long visit to your brother?"

"We were both involved in a dispute with our cousin over a legacy from our great-aunt."

"Tell the court what happened when you arrived at Numquam."

"It was as you said. The maid told me Charles had gone to Carlisle. I briefly met Mrs. Eggleton whom I had never seen before and she was not welcoming. So I went back home and as he had not been there, I assumed he was missing and wrote to Mrs. Eggleton and the police."

"Thank you. That will be all."

The barrister appearing for the sisters was a florid man, fat, very red-faced, one Magnus Pottleberry and after an enquiry from the judge indicated that he did not wish to question the witness.

After the detective had explained to the court how he came to be working on Mr. Eggleton's disappearance, Sir Septimus asked,

"How would you describe the response of the women in the dock when you met with them?"

"Mrs. Eggleton seemed to me frightened and very nervous, though at the time I assumed this was because her husband was missing. Miss Wigglesworth was quite different. She was very rude to me, calling me an 'interfering busybody,' although she said this so quietly and with such grace that I almost missed its import."

"I see, but did you ask what they thought about Mr. Eggleton's disappearance?"

"Yes, and Miss Wigglesworth immediately said, 'and a good thing too, we are better off without him,' although I was not aware she lived at Numquam House and that response triggered in my mind that there might be more to his disappearance than simply that of a missing person, such as a malfeasance of some kind."

"I will call Constable Painter directly, m'lud, but tell the Court what happened when you arrested them later."

"Mrs. Eggleton broke down, fainting on her settee. When Miss Wigglesworth was arrested later on her return from abroad, she screamed profanities and tried to assault me. She also said, 'he deserved what he got.'"

"Thank you. You may step down. Call Constable Painter."

"Constable, tell the Court about the discovery of the grave."

"Well sir," said Palmer in a Kentish accent, "we was told to search the grounds for anything that might seem suspicious, and I saw this piece of ground which looked for all the world like it was a grave in a churchyard. Now I knew there was no gardener and as it was freshly dug, so it seemed to me someone must have dug it, so I told Mr. Mallet."

"He told me to ask the ladies about it, and they both said that Mr. Eggleton had been gardening and wanted to plant willows there but hadn't had time. When I told Mr. Mallet what they said, he told me to dig there, and that's when I found the body."

There followed a further response from Detective Mallet about the finding of the arsenic can, and a doctor who witnessed that arsenic poisoning was the cause of death and the case against the two sisters was closed.

After lunch the Court called on Mr. Magnus Pottleberry to speak for the defense. Hamish was mildly surprised when he called Mrs. Eggleton into the box, as that would invite cross-examination by Sir Septimus.

"Tell me, Mrs. Eggleton, how were relations with our husband?"

142

Shaking like a leaf, she replied: "Not good, sir."

"Please explain."

"I am too ashamed. In recent months he had become very cruel, beating me, pushing me down the stairs, not letting me have any money of my own, I don't know what had got into him, and he had his way with my sister recently and with the maid."

"So, you harbored strong feelings of hate towards him?"

"Oh yes, I hated him alright," she said, her voice becoming clearer.

"So much so you wanted to kill him."

"No, that was Hortense's idea," at which the Court went silent.

"What do you mean?"

"She arrived one day to stay with me but she walked over to my husband digging in the garden. He led her into the stables, she told me later, and he had his way with her without her consent. Later she said why not kill him, and she went on about doing it and I didn't know what to say."

"So did you agree to murdering him?

"No, yes, I don't know."

"Was it you who acquired the arsenic?"

"No, Charles had it in the shed and when Hortense stayed with me for a while, I didn't know she was poisoning him, though I thought she was being more attentive to him than usual."

"But she told you what she was doing?"

"Yes."

"And what did you say?

"I was frightened about what might happen if we were found out, so I asked her to stop and she said it was too late. My husband seemed to have no sense of smell, but I could smell it on him."

"Once your husband died, did you assist with burying the body in the trench?"

"Yes, he had been digging this trench to plant willows, he had become very keen on gardening, you see."

"Explain to the Court how you did this."

"He died suddenly at dinner, falling off his chair. We took off all his clothes and dragged him to the kitchen door where we got a barrow from the shed and together we lifted him into it. Hortense is stronger than me and she wheeled the barrow and she tipped into the trench. I got a spade and helped with the dirt."

"What did you feel about doing this?"

"I was very sad and wished we had not done it."

"You say "we' had not done it, but you had nothing to do with giving your husband arsenic, am I right? Is it not clear, Mrs. Eggleton, that your sister went ahead with killing your husband against your will?"

"Well, yes and no. I suppose I protested a bit and wished we hadn't done it, but what could I do? I thought when she told me she had started with the arsenic, I would tell Charles he was being poisoned but, then I thought he'd kill me."

"Thank you, Mrs. Eggleton."

Sir Septimus indicated that he would cross-examine after Miss Wigglesworth's testimony.

Listening to the wife's evidence, Hamish realized this was a much more complicated legal situation than expected. Was Mrs. Eggleton trapped into going along with the murder? However, Miss Wigglesworth would provide an answer.

"Miss Wigglesworth," said Pottleberry, "you have heard your sister's account of the death of her husband. Have you anything to add?"

"Yes I do. That was a pack of lies," she said in her quiet mellifluous voice at which Maud collapsed in tears back in the dock.

"Let me ask you a few questions, then," said a startled Pottleberry, "to see where your accounts differ from your sister's."

"First on the origins of the decision to kill Mr. Eggleton."

"Her idea completely. Do you think I would trade my status as a renowned medium for killing a tawdry butcher?"

"And the administration of the arsenic?"

"I watched as she carefully prepared the portions in the kitchen to flavor his drink. I told her she should not be doing this."

"Were you shocked then when Mr. Eggleton died?"

"Indeed, he keeled over just before dinner as if he had been struck by lightning and I told her, 'Maud,' I said, 'that's that then. You've done it.'"

"Did you assist her in burying the body?"

"Of course, that was the least I could do. She didn't have the strength to lift him on her own."

"Finally, your sister said that the deceased had had his way with you, is that correct?"

"Yes, and it pleased me greatly as we were planning a future together when my sister wrecked it all."

An exasperated Pottleberry sat down with a thump as Miss Wigglesworth had upended everything she had told him in their private meetings which left him in a quandary about his legal obligations, but Sir Septimus was quickly on his feet.

"Mrs. Wigglesworth, I am told you are a medium, what exactly is that?"

"I am the medium through which living souls communicate with dead souls for whom they have a special interest in having such communion."

"So if I came to you and wanted to, say, chat with my grandmother, you would act as the medium for our conversation."

"In principle, yes."

"How do you achieve this?"

"Not on my own, of course, Cooperation is needed by the living and the dead."

"What sort of cooperation?"

"As a medium I can go into a trance which connects me to the spirit world."

"What is a trance? Could I go into one?"

"You might, I suppose, but it is heightened state of consciousness which allows me to act as a medium through which spirits come to connect to living souls."

"Tell me about the connection. Might you go into a trance now and ask Charles Eggleton who murdered him?"

"No, I don't think his spirit would be available."

"How do you know that? Come now, Miss Wigglesworth, is this not all just hocus-pocus? Don't you just put on this act for which people pay money and you fake a trance and an assistant behind the screens makes the appropriate noises?"

"I resent that accusation, sir."

"Your difficulty is, I fear, that your assistant is here and if need be I will call her to tell the Court of your deception on pain of perjury."

"I protest. Help me, Mr. Pottleberry," but answer came there none.

"You see, Miss Wigglesworth, if you are capable of pursuing a career in an activity which is clearly a means of robbing people of their money, are you not capable of deceit about your sister?"

"No, sir, it is as I had said. It was her idea and she did it."

"Why are you trying to shift the responsibility to her? It is perfectly clear that you assisted her at least in burying Mr. Eggleton's body as she is manifestly not strong enough to have done it by herself. Moreover, if you saw her mixing arsenic into Mr. Eggleton's drink and if you were so innocent as you proclaim why did you not inform the police?"

"I didn't think to do that, as she was my sister."

"Precisely, but now faced with the hangman's noose, you are prepared to betray her?"

"No sir, well, I did help her with the body and I did watch her give him the poison."

"My difficulty, Miss Wigglesworth is this. Your sister seems a gentlewoman in what was obviously not a good marriage. Here are you whose character is very strong indeed if you are able to carry out the deceptions involved in your trances; obviously a woman, whatever your appearance or indeed, your voice whose capacity for deception extends far outside the darkened rooms inhabited by manufactured ghosts. You see, Miss Wigglesworth, character can be important to the gentleman of the jury when the evidence is incomplete."

Under this questioning, the lady broke down and Mr. Pottleberry asked the judge if they could meet in chambers.

"This is a tidy mess, Pottleberry," said Hamish as they sat in the judge's room behind the court.

"It is certainly that, m'lud, and I am sure counsel will agree. I would like to be able to forego the responsibility of defending Miss Wigglesworth as her evidence in Court runs completely counter to my discussions with her a week or so ago, which to all intents and purposes she admitted the guilt and my eventual line of defense would have been on the dreadful character of the victim, not least in forcing himself on her."

"Might this mean, m'lud," said Sir Septimus, "that the Crown could call Mr. Pottleberry to give evidence?"

"Perhaps," said Hamish, "but presumably this woman realized that she would hang and struck out in all directions, specifically incriminating her sister. Let us suppose that you continue as her counsel. Would you then cross-examine the Crown witnesses?"

"No, their evidence is uncontestable."

"In that case, let us proceed to the summing-up, beginning with Sir Septimus obviously. My apprehension of what has been said so far is more on the levels of intent of each woman and I hope you will both address that."

Back in Court, Sir Septimus had cleared his head about the responsibility of each and concluded his summing-up thus.

"Gentlemen of the jury, it is important that you consider the precise behavior of each of these two women. What might be your conclusion for one would not be one for the other. Mrs. Eggleton was clear and frank about her husband's assaults and her remorse: She had been drawn into this evil by her sister but accepted that she was too weak to stop it and acknowledged her husband's behavior to her as a motive for her. Miss Wigglesworth on the other hand suggested that she knew nothing about the arsenic and indeed put the responsibility firmly on Mrs. Eggleton. You must decide where the balance of responsibility lies for the murder, yet what is abundantly clear, whatever the balance of responsibility, both these women committed murder."

Mr. Pottleberry for the defendants was indeed in more than a quandary. He decided the appropriate course was to be as brief as possible, citing examples of Mr. Eggleton's bad behavior which led to the sister's hatred and decisions to murder. He dare not mention just how contradictory Miss Wigglesworth's was from his discussion, so he concluded with an appeal for mercy for both sisters.

Hamish summed up the next day, focusing on just how much the jury believed the testimony of the women in the dock, but also concluded with comments about intent and responsibility and the importance of keeping the two women distinct in their deliberations. The jury returned within an hour, finding both women guilty but with an appeal for mercy for Mrs. Eggleton.

Theophilus appeared almost immediately with the black cap and Hamish sentenced both women to be hung, but he referred the case of Mrs. Eggleton to the Home Secretary for a decision about clemency. It was denied and both women went to the gallows in Holloway Prison at 8 a.m. on Tuesday, November 14, 1903. The Eggleton possessions at Numquam House were impounded and sold at auction, although Arthur Eggleton was allowed to take jewelry, watches and other small items.

For Victoria and John the whole affair was a set of successive thunderbolts. First the arrest of the sisters then the police warrant to search Numquam House and garden. Then the village was awash with gossip that the police were searching for stolen gold of great value, but when they were seen with a police hearse, the word was that the Marylebone Medium had brought about the death of the man in a séance. The newspapers carried the details of the trial in great detail and every scrap and morsel of the evidence was discussed in detail in The Rose and Crown, for nothing had ever been so important in All

Hallows since the arrival of the first convict hull in the estuary and the escape of two convicts many years ago.

On the morning of the execution, Victoria and John sat silently over breakfast, both having difficulty to comprehend that the two women they had known as their tenants, though not intimately, were now dead at the hands of the State. After a while John said quietly that he should have paid more attention to his parishioner and helped her although, as Victoria told him, it was difficult to see how for, as she said, Charles Eggleton was a very nasty man and any pastoral intervention would have had that to deal with.

1904

XII

Clara was thrilled to be home, even though the villa in Provence had proved a wonderful resting-place and the children had loved it. Her Down Street house was immaculate when the family returned as Matilda and Abdul, with help from the kitchen maids, continued to ensure the house was clean and delightful, a task that in the filth of London was both necessary and difficult - spick and span as Malcolm called it. Autumn had come and gone and she was deliriously happy; she would lay on her bed in the morning with her children rolling around, playing with her hair or lying comfortably on her breast so that she had this luminous and permanent smile of contentment.

In particular, she often considered how fortunate she was with her servants; Abdul short of stature but strong in spirit and character and Matilda, a pretty fair-haired young thing whose loyalty and quality was tested after Timothy's death. They kept the Gargery household running.

One day in early January, she came downstairs after a rest in her bedroom to find Matilda and Abdul standing at the bottom of the stairs waiting for her.

"What can I do for you two? Is there something the matter?"

"Can we speak with you privately?" said Matilda which surprised Clara.

"Come in, come in, both of you," leading them into the study, "now what is it? A problem with Cook?"

"No, Ma'am," said Matilda quietly, "Abdul and I want to get married."

"Married?" shrieked Clara, "Married? Are you sure?"

"Yes, Ma'am," said Abdul, "but we would be very, very sad if you did not want us to serve you afterwards because we are married."

"Now, let me talk with my husband and we will speak with you both later."

"Thank you, Ma'am, thank you," and they left.

Clara was thunderstruck, though quite why she should be so upset baffled her. She was still sitting in her chair an hour or so later when Malcolm came in after a visit to Liberal Party headquarters.

"What on earth is the matter, darling?" and he hurried over and put his arms around her.

"It's nothing."

"Nothing, you seem much out of sorts."

"Abdul and Matilda want to marry."

"What?" cried Malcolm, "Say that again."

"Abdul and Matilda want to marry."

"Goodness gracious me," he said flopping down into a chair. "We can't stop them, of course, and it would be a great misfortune to dismiss them. Have they thought about the difference in their race, let alone their religion?"

"I do not want to dismiss them. They are both loyal and efficient and they cause us no trouble, rather the opposite. They are also very nice people, but would it be sensible to have them in our house?"

"Of course Clara. They have come to like each other presumably because this is a house where they feel comfortable in themselves and with each other."

"I have worried for some time that their status is ambiguous. If they are to stay, I think we should make him our butler and she our housekeeper."

"Now, don't jump the gun, Clara, we need to have a serious talk with them about their differences."

"Let us think about it overnight and meet them together in the morning."

This was a very delicate situation for the Gargerys in terms of conventions. They both liked even admired the couple, and without saying it to each other, thought they would make a fine marriage. After all they had been with them in Port Elizabeth, so it was not as if the pair had not had time to get to know each other. They probably knew each other better than either Malcolm or Clara knew either of them. To avoid being served by them that evening, Malcolm and Clara walked along Piccadilly to dine at the Ritz, carefully avoiding several men clearing horse manure from the road.

By the following morning, the subject was exhausted and it was time to meet them, so they asked Matilda to bring Abdul into the drawing room.

"Let me begin by saying that my husband and I have no objection in principle to your marriage," at which the couple looked at each other smiling broadly.

"However," said Malcolm, "we want to know whether you have confronted the obstacles which I am sure you know lie in your path. To begin with, do either of you have family, relatives of friends of significance who would be intensely opposed to your marrying?"

"This is not a problem for me," said Abdul "as I do not plan return to my home country and my mother and my family would be most concerned about the differences in religion."

"And you, Matilda?"

"I don't think my father would care and my brother certainly wouldn't. My mum died when I was eight."

"Now to religion. Abdul, you are a Muslim, I assume, and what about you, Matilda?"

"I think I was christened, but apart from a short time at Sunday School when they wanted me out of the house, I don't really believe anything."

"This is important for your future, Matilda. Have you spoken to Abdul about religion?"

"Yes, Mrs. Gargery, she has," said Abdul, "and I intend to become a Christian."

"That is wonderful, Abdul, so you would be married in a church here."

"That's what we thought," said Matilda. "Neither of us are especially religious, but we thought we should definitely share one or the other, and we decided he'd be a Christian."

"Now," said Clara, "religion is one thing, but race is quite another. I can see that you love each other very much but the world may not be ready to accommodate a couple from different races."

"I don't see Abdul as of a different race," said Matilda, "I see him as my husband."

"That is such a lovely thing to say," said Clara.

"What do you think about this, Malcolm?" Asked Clara.

"Mrs. Gargery and I have discussed this carefully," he replied looking carefully at them both, "and I am delighted by what you have said. We decided that, if your responses to our concerns were as we hoped, we would offer you a new status in our household. Abdul would become our butler and Matilda, you would become our housekeeper, so between you, you will take on the responsibilities of our households and with commensurate wages."

"Does that mean we can stay on as a married couple here?"

"Yes, of course," said Clara, "and we will review the upstairs accommodation so that you have a bedroom and a sitting-room. We will also give you your wedding reception here as a gift."

At this, Abdul put his arm around Matilda and wept quietly into her shoulder saying,

"Thank you, Mrs., Gargery. Thank you, Mr. Gargery. This is the best day of my life."

"There will be much to learn for both of you as the position of butler means not only the management of staff below stairs, but knowledge of wines and food. For you, Matilda, you will take over all my responsibilities for the cleanliness, management of the staff and each room in the house, and especially the laundry, for with our five children, that is a significant responsibility."

"Pardon me, Ma'am but I must say something. You've been so kind to us both but we also want our marriage to be as happy and loving as yours."

"My dear Matilda, thank you," said Clara and as the couple left the drawing room, she said:

"Malcolm, what will we do when she has children?"

"Oh, goodness, let's cross that bridge later."

Elizabeth and Charlotte were spending the Fall, as Americans call Autumn, with several excursions from Boston and the month with Simon was exhilarating too. They were amazed by the wonderful colors of the trees as they turned to yellows and ochres, blazing reds and crimsons, a displace quite unlike Autumn in Hyde Park. Charlotte had never experienced men and women of races other than her own, unlike her mother whose international experiences in Paris, Athens and Washington had brought her into contact with a variety of people, especially as her husband had been a diplomat.

Simon came to stay for November but rarely conversed with Mary-Lou and never on family matters. Elizabeth was sympathetic to her daughter's new puzzles about race and it was in conversations with Mary-Lou that Charlotte began to understand them, and on an evening in late November, she began.

"Grandma, you told us about the lynching but when you were growing up, did you have many slaves on the plantation?"

"I suppose there was about seventy, though I never knew the precise number. We had a bailiff whom I disliked intensely, not that I had much to do with him, but I knew he was cruel to the slaves."

"How did you know that?"

"I sensed it at the time. You see my daddy had fathered four or five children by two of the negro women, and two of the girls, Mary and Martha came to the house to play with me when I was young, before I became a woman if you know what I mean and it was very important to me as I was an only child. One day they stopped coming and my mamma told me I would not see them again as they had been sold out of the county as my daddy thought I was too fond of them."

"How terrible for you."

"Well, I was growing up but I thought such things were part of life. I began to look at boys and I was taken to parties at nearby plantations I suppose from the age of nine to thirteen or fourteen, but I didn't like the white boys there. They were either loud and vulgar or they were so meek and mild."

"What did you think then about the white boys and the black slaves?"

"Everyone thought that the slaves were inferior by their nature but that always seemed to me to silly as I had grown up with Mary and Martha and they were my friends such I never thought of them as white or black until they were sent away."

"They were your father's children."

"Yes and Mary looked so like her mother, also a Mary. Now she was the prettiest woman on the whole plantation, which was why my Daddy bedded her, I suppose. She came to work as a house servant and she remained in the house. My mamma was very angry, but she could do nothing, but I suppose they did not have marital relations once my mother realized what was going on as I am the only child."

"My great-grandfather sounds like an awful man."

"I suppose so, but then you know, when you grow up with a pattern of life, you just accept it especially when you don't meet other people. I never truly accepted the idea that the negro was inferior. I thought Mary, my daddy's woman, was very beautiful, I thought Jonathan was very handsome, and he wasn't the only one, and then there was Mary and Martha. Of course any question of marriage outside my race was impossible, but romance, well that seemed just possible to a young woman."

"Do you think your daddy loved Mary?"

"Good gracious no. He just wanted this beauty for his own desires, and he came to see Mary and Martha his own children as his property."

"So you were sixteen when Jonathan was lynched ... "

"Please don't remind me," said Mary-Lou, beginning to weep, "that was the worst day of my life by far. I was foolish, but I simply could not help being nice to him and saying, 'good morning' and smiling, and that dreadful white trash seized him and killed him, simply for their pleasure."

"What did your daddy say?"

"I don't think you will believe this. Life is so different now. I can see him now, his face livid with anger, 'do you realize how valuable that nigger was, Mary-Lou?' And I said 'no,' and he said, 'he was worth well over three or four thousand dollars of labor,' and I was so upset by that, though I knew slaves were bought and sold. He packed me off to London the very next week, then, not because I might suffer socially, or because people would talk about me as a nigger-lover, but as a punishment for me destroying his property."

"How could he do that? How terrible. That was before the war, wasn't it?"

"Yes, the year before. He lost the plantation, of course, but my mother was a Drew, a Yankee, so they fled up north."

Elizabeth and Simon had listened to this conversation without intervening, exchanging glances of shock and bewilderment.. She knew only a little of her mother's story and was dumbfounded as she revealed it, aghast that her own grandfather could be such an evil man, without conscience, without compassion, buying and selling other people as if they were just chattels. However, Elizabeth was thrilled that Charlotte and her mother had had such an open conversation and she wondered what it would have been like if her mother had been as reflective and sympathetic when she was younger with a daughter. However, the revelation made up her mind to return to England promptly.

The following afternoon Mary-Lou took Charlotte shopping for Christmas in Tremont Street just before Simon was to return to England. Alone in the house, Simon and Elizabeth fell into each other's arms and hurried up to her bedroom. These were the most important three hours in their lives together. They were dazzled by their passion for each other and they determined to marry, or at least live together defying convention if Simon was unable to clear up his problems by the time she got home. Two days later it was time for him to leave.

Immediately after he departed, Elizabeth said, "Mother, I think we must consider returning to England soon."

"Oh my, well, you must do what you think. I can't claim anything from you after my neglect of you, but it has been a delight for me to get you know you both, and I like your beau very much. He will be good for you. I wish your boys could have been here too. But you should not return until the Spring. The Atlantic in winter is not a place to enjoy a sea journey."

"You are right about that, of course, so I will book passages for March. It is a shorter journey from Boston than New York, though the ships may not be as grand."

"I'm not well, my dear, and should I die, this house is yours. I am so glad to have had this time with you. In some ways, it completes my life."

Two mornings later Mary-Lou did not appear for breakfast and her maid came running into the dining-room crying "I think she's dead," at which Elizabeth rushed up to her mother's bedroom, but the maid had panicked and Mary-Lou was simply in a deep slumber. Elizabeth sat on the bed watching her and wept for almost an hour, an hour full of regret, tinged with anger that she had finally come to see that her mother's selfishness all those years ago were the result of such a perverse childhood, and how much more sympathetic to her she could have been had she known the whole story and, for that matter, that her mother had such a good heart and soul beneath that exterior.

In mid-December Simon Brandram disembarked at Southampton from the SS Carpathia, a Cunard Liner, and took the train to Waterloo, traveling on by the new underground train toward his Essex house. As it was clear that Margaret wanted an end to the marriage too he needed to discuss with her briefly the possibility of an arrangement whereby he would engage a woman and have a fictitious relationship in a hotel which would provide evidence of his adultery, thereby advancing the case for her to divorce him. His colleague Adam Masterson had reiterated that mutual consent was not grounds for a court's judgment on a divorce.

"Are you well after your transatlantic trip?"

"Thank you, Margaret, I have had a splendid time visiting cities on the East Coast. How about you?"

"As we are being frank with each other, Simon, I have been spending time with a widower of my age whom I met at a café in Selfridges, and while I am not yet certain, I think I would live with him, married or not, to get away from this terrible loneliness I have been suffering."

"I too have met a widow, and like you, I think she and I will pursue a stronger relationship."

An independent observer would see that Simon and Margaret were both dissembling and neither was being frank, but their marriage was so completely broken that neither wanted to share their probable futures with each other. Both of them disguised the fact that they were profoundly in love with these new 'friends' but both felt that, were they to confess to love, the other might be upset, even jealous, notwithstanding the gradual and careful move to a legal separation, and neither had any desire to hurt the other. Nor would the observer be surprised that they were both very curious to discover the identity of the new 'friend.'

"I have decided that I will definitely make an arrangement whereby I fictitiously spend a night in a hotel with someone which will provide grounds for you to sue for adultery, Margaret. Privately Adam Masterson will draw up a financial settlement, but for that to be equitable, he will need to know the overall financial circumstance of a putative partner, don't you think?"

"That is no difficulty. The person in question is much wealthier than you."

"Then I will have Adam review our assets and my income. I will be happy for you to have the house and for Jude to continue to use it as his home, if that is what you would wish. I would transfer the title to you as it is in my name."

"I would like the house, but I will be able to decide whether I need support from you when our case comes to court as by then my own situation will be resolved. I must thank you for shouldering the responsibility of providing the grounds for our divorce. I am convinced that our future happiness rests in that happening."

"My own thoughts exactly. I would like soon for us to have lunch with Jude and explain our agreement to divorce."

"Allow me to make the arrangements, Simon. I assume you will not be returning to our home in Essex."

"No, I have taken lodgings in central London."

"Simon, I do have many happy memories of our marriage."

"As do I, Margaret, and we have a splendid son to bear witness to that."

❧ ❧ ❧

Clarence sent a message to Malcolm just before the New Year saying that the member for the West Medway constituency had died suddenly and that there seemed to be no obvious successor, so he invited Malcolm to his home in Kensington Gore to discuss the matter.

"Malcolm, dear fellow, how good to see you, and the greetings of the season."

"Thank you for asking me and I am intrigued by your message."

"Indeed, old David Westham collapsed after a large Christmas dinner I am told, heart they said, didn't know the fellow well, but that creates a by-election. Now I happen to know there is no obvious candidate there and I thought you might enter the lists. I know it is not an industrial area, indeed the opposite in the marshes of northern Kent but it could be very good practice to go before a selection committee."

"That is intriguing, but I have wanted to ask you a rather different question first. We went to South Africa as you know and that put off the question on my eye, that is, when I should get a glass eye. Now I am quite used to my patch, but Clara and I were wondering whether I might find it easier in politics were I to have a glass eye rather than a patch."

Clarence smiled graciously, though he was tempted to laugh out loud.

"The eye patch does convey the likelihood of heroism in your background, you know. I suspect most people would look at a glass eye, wonder how you got it, but be too polite to ask. On balance I would say the patch has the political advantage. But I am delighted that you are thinking about the political life so carefully, and I am sure Clara will be helpful, just by appearing at bazaars or other celebrations. Our system of elections, unlike monarchies, allow one to put one's best foot forward and invite the people to elect you their tribune," at which they both smiled.

"I suggest you write to the Party Chairman in the constituency," he said, ruffling some papers, "and, ah, here he is, a Major Sidney Brockleton, and this is his address."

"How should I construct such a letter?"

"It's a very long time since I wrote one, but I suggest you start with a statement proclaiming your interest as a Liberal candidate followed by a paragraph describing yourself and your family, especially your lady wife, and then simply list the topics of the day that are of interest to you. Make sure you read the local papers first to see what matters will be of interest to the committee."

"That sounds straightforward."

"My guess is that you will be invited, but there may have emerged a local favorite, even the Chairman himself, depending on what his interests are. I am afraid I do not know these people."

"What will I do if they ask me to be their candidate?"

"Malcolm my friend, the best is the enemy of the good. This is a Liberal constituency and you would be an MP. You can create a public profile and I would guess that you could be asked to stand for another sure bet in the industrial area you want, not least because you will have spoken publicly about such matters. Politics, as they say, is the art of the possible not the ideal."

On his return home, he described those possibilities to Clara and she was very excited.

"My dearest, Clarence is absolutely right. Getting into the House will be a platform and, in any event, you might develop an interest in hops or apples whatever it is they grow down there. So write your letter, my dear, and be forthright. You may as well be hung for a sheep as a lamb."

Four days later, a letter arrived from Major Brockleton, stating that he would put Malcolm's letter before his committee and that he was confident of Malcolm being invited. He added a personal note asking if Malcolm knew a Captain Alec McPherson of the Gordon Highlanders whom he had met in India some years ago.

To this letter, Malcolm replied thanking the Major for his enquiry and he wrote that he knew Alec, as his sister was the best friend of his own sister, Mrs. Hannah Hesketh.

"Good heavens," he said to Clara, "I had almost forgotten Alec's existence. When we see them I must ask Hannah if she knows anything about him, I vaguely remember his being married."

"Is he the man with the tea plantation?"

"That's right, but this gives me a leg up with Brockleton at least."

"How interesting. Am I talking to the next MP for East Medway?"

"It is West Medway, darling. Important not to confuse them."

On December 16th Malcolm and Clara travelled to Chatham and the local Party office.

"Won't this constituency include that nice couple we met at the MacDonalds, you know the Vicar who is a Eustace like me."

"Of course, how foolish of me. We must try to see them when we are here, perhaps stay another night?"

"Let's see how the meeting goes."

"They may be able to assist us, you know."

It soon became obvious, however, that the Committee's thoughts were elsewhere. Any interest in Malcolm as the candidate seemed to him perfunctory. The members were polite but offered no responses when he spoke about education or any other subject. However, a young member of the Committee, a Mr. Harberry asked about his experience of the Boer War, so Malcolm explained, hoping to rescue his candidacy with his experience as an officer.

"I was stationed in Port Elizabeth for a few short years, sending reports to the War office about any suspicious movements through my Brigadier, though it was a safe position since the Boers had gained access to the sea through Delagado Bay. Then I was engaged with Miss Hobhouse ... '

"Oh that traitor," said a Mr. Wheelwright with a snort.

"Opinions may differ on her work," replied Malcolm, "but the conditions she reported on from her earlier experience were confirmed by the Fawcett Commission which, believe me, had no love for her."

"Anyone who takes the side of the enemy is a traitor," said Wheelwright.

"That is of course true and as a former major in the Gordon Highlanders, I am second to none in supporting your view. However, Miss Hobhouse was pointing out not merely that civilian women and children were dying of disease in some awful conditions, but that it was the responsibility of the British Government to attend to their distress."

"But they were helping their men."

"From within the camps? There is no evidence of that, although the Army did put women and children into camps who came from the towns where they suspected they were helping the enemy."

"That was unfortunate, but then many British soldiers died of disease and hunger."

"Mr. Wheelwright, I would just say that the conduct of the war is a very complex subject indeed, but I think the major distinction about our war with the Boers, as opposed to any war since Cromwell, is that citizens were being used as weapons and treated as such. It may very well be future wars will indeed include the slaughter or imprisonment of innocent civilians. I would hope not."

Major Brockleton then intervened, staying another Wheelwright intervention with his hand, "this is a fascinating subject, but the war is concluded and we must look to the future. Very satisfactory, Mr. Gargery. We will let you know about your candidacy, but before we part, I wonder if Mrs. Gargery has anything to say."

Clara had not been expecting this, but she launched into a description of her husband which made him blush and she ended with a challenge:

"Your constituency will miss a great opportunity if you do not select my husband. He is destined for greatness in the political world and there will be many a constituency who, once they met him and recognize his qualities, will not be dilatory in appointing him as their candidate."

"Thank you for coming, Mr. and Mrs. Gargery," said Brockleton.

"I am glad that is over, Clara," as they walked to their carriage, "shall we try and see the Eustace family this afternoon?"

"I suppose the experience was good for you, but we know, don't we, that they already have someone else in mind."

After a light lunch at the hotel, Malcolm and Clara drew up at the Vicarage in All Hallows as John was coming down the path.

"My goodness, here is my Eustace cousin," he said with a gay laugh, "come in, come in, I was planning to see a parishioner but that can wait. I know Victoria will be thrilled to see you both as we don't get many visitors here."

Effusive greetings followed and as they sat in the Vicarage drawing-room, Malcolm explained why they were in Kent.

"My dear fellow," said, John, "of course you will be our candidate as we have elected Liberals for years, it is a safe seat in my view."

"No I fear the Committee has set its sights elsewhere."

"But there is deep respect here for members of His Majesty's forces, I suppose it comes from being near Chatham where the Navy is."

"Victoria," said Clara, "one advantage of Malcolm's election, unlikely though that is, would be that we would find a house down here when Parliament in not in session, though, of course, we will be in France at our villa in the summer."

"Really?" said Victoria, "While you seem to doubt that Malcolm will get the offer, I don't know whether it would be suitable, but Numquam House where I lived with Albert is vacant."

"Of course," cried Malcolm, "that was Estella's house, wasn't it where her mother was murdered and the man was killed in the drawing-room."

"Oh my," said Clara, "and wasn't that where your nephews were killed by the tree?"

"All quite correct," said Victoria, "but there has been another murder since," and she went on to tell the whole ghastly story about the Eggletons, the Marylebone Medium Miss Wigglesworth, and how it was Hamish who sentenced them to hang for the murder of Mrs. Eggleton's husband.

"Well, well, but there is a long way to go," said Malcolm. "Even if I were offered the seat, I do have to be sure I want it. But if everything fell into place, it would make sense for us to use Numquam as our constituency residence and, if I recall it right, it will enable us to host some political dinners but we will need to see it is large enough for Abdul and Matilda."

"Who are they?"

"Matilda has been my maid for several years and Abdul is the Malay servant who came back with us from Africa. To our guarded delight, they are getting married and we have given them the title of butler and housekeeper."

"A mixed marriage?" said John, "what of their religion?"

"He is a Muslim but will become a Christian."

"We will see them in church then?"

"Please, please all of you, this jumping the gun makes me nervous that I will not be selected."

1904

XIII

Christmas had passed off without incident, though Simon stayed alone in his lodgings meeting his son Jude on three occasions after the New Year, after which he returned to his work.

"You are decided then?" Asked Adam Masterson.

"Yes, it is my intention to create evidence so that Margaret could sue for a divorce on the grounds of adultery, and you will presumably ask Margaret for her solicitor's name. You have her address of course. She will have the house, and I do not think that she needs continuing support from me, but I suggest a quarter of my assets would be appropriate."

"That sounds generous if her new man is wealthy, but we will see. Now we need to get on with the evidence. Let me call in Robert."

Robert came in immediately and Adam said:

"Mr. Brandram intends to provide evidence so that his wife can sue for adultery. The separation is quite amicable, I should add."

"I am so sorry, Mr. Brandram, but knowing you as I have done for these many years here at Courtisone and Jaggers, I am sure that you are an innocent party."

"Not a matter of innocence, Robert, just a breakdown."

"Right. When I was a very junior clerk to Mr. Wemmick, he introduced me to his habit of developing lists of men and women who might be used for various purposes to further the interests of any client of Mr. Jaggers. I have continued the practice and we were able to assist Mrs. Llewellyn in that unseemly business with a married man. I keep a list of women who would be available to reside in a hotel for the purposes required for a payment of course."

"Thank you, Robert."

"I will make arrangements with a small Brighton hotel we have used in two other cases and we reward the hotel owner when he provides the evidence. It remains to fix the date: when would be suitable?"

"Any day, though perhaps a Friday would be easiest, and the sooner we get this going the better."

"Right," said Robert, "I will arrange for a Mary Phillips to greet you at Brighton Station this coming Friday, February 12th meeting the 9.15 am from Victoria. She is a thirty-year old woman and will be carrying a yellow handbag and a matching hat, so she should be distinctive enough. You will then take a cab to the Rose Hotel, a quiet unassuming establishment, you will sign in as Mr. and Mrs. Smith. You will be shown to a room together, but you will also be given a key to the adjoining room, accessed by an inner door, so that your relationship with Miss Phillips is completely perfunctory."

"That sounds quite straightforward."

"We will then alert Mrs. Brandram's solicitors anonymously and they will no doubt take it from there."

Simon was very nervous about this arrangement as might be expected, but he had to keep its purpose firmly in his mind. He traveled down to Brighton as planned and immediately glimpsed a woman with a yellow hat standing near the platform exit. He had a vague sense he recognized her, but was so bound up in the exercise, he simply nodded to her and they walked out of the station, got into a cab and went to the Rose Hotel. Sitting in the cab, they did not look at each other. Finally, just before noon, they were shown into a room together and Simon was very pleased to notice the adjoining door.

"Hallo, Mr. Brandram," said Mary, walking into the room in front of him, turning round and taking off her hat, "don't you remember me?"

"Why should I?" said Simon looking out of the window at the hotel yard.

"No, I suppose you wouldn't, would you."

Simon turned to look at the woman whom he immediately saw as quite attractive and he exclaimed, "My God, you're Ethel."

"That's right. When Mr. Gillingham told me it was you this time, I thought of telling him to find someone else, but then I thought it would be fun to see you again, as I always thought you was very handsome indeed, when I worked in your house."

Once Simon realized who this was, the memories of those hideous days came flooding back, seeing his daughter's body, the trial of that devil Charlesby, and the disappearance of this very woman, the maid Ethel, whom the police had looked for as they were sure she had some part in Frederica's assignment with her murderer.

"Oh my God, Ethel. Please, please tell me everything about you and Frederica. I must know now that I have met you. We were never able to explain how she came to be with that villain."

"Oh no, I can't do that now can I, Mr. Brandram? It would upset you too much, but, I tell you what, it's a couple of months now since I had a man, so if you'd come to bed with me, I'll tell you everything. After all, that is what we are supposed to do here, ain't it? I used to dream of you stealing up to my bedroom when I was working in your house. You see, if you don't bed me now, I could say nothing happened to her lawyers, couldn't I? Then you wouldn't get your divorce from your silly wife."

Simon was disoriented, especially as she began to disrobe, looking at him seductively, and that disturbed him as he had been celibate since his afternoon of passion with Elizabeth in Boston.

"That's not possible."

"Oh come on now, its Simon isn't it? I remember. I was dusting in your bedroom one day and heard you coming so I popped into Mrs. B's big wardrobe to hide. You was humming to yourself, and you was changing your clothes, and oh my, when you was in the altogether I took off my knickers but had to stop myself from jumping out of my hiding place and stripping off completely. Christ, I could have done with you then just as I could do with you now. How about it? I'm something of an expert, you know, and here's my young body for you for free."

Simon braced himself and tried to think like the lawyer he was.

"Ethel, I must go for a walk now and will return later after I have considered your proposals. At the moment, I can simply call our liaison off and find some other woman to attend a hotel with, were I not anxious to pursue my divorce."

"Oh I wouldn't do that, Mr. Brandram. When I tell them lawyers, I might tell them all sorts of stories about the nasty things you did to me and how you promised to keep me, couldn't I? But, you know, I want you to do the nasty things to me anyway and I wouldn't tell. Come on, Mr. Brandram, let's have some fun. You'll love it."

Simon hastened out of the room, shocked at his lust for her body, but he needed help from this vindictive woman who seemed to have trapped him. As he went down the stairs, he knew that if he bedded her he could never rely on her not being a continuing trouble so the thought of it rapidly changed from desire to disgust. After a short walk he passed a post office but then returned to it quickly to send an urgent wire to Robert telling him to come to Brighton immediately and that he would wait for him at the station.

He sat in the station waiting room watching the arrival of several London trains with increasing concern but then he breathed an immense sigh of relief at six o'clock when Robert and Adam got off the train.

"What on earth is the matter?" Asked Robert.

"Come with me, and I will tell you everything," said Simon as they got into a cab and made their way to the Rose Hotel. Robert was soon very angry that one of his reliable women should act so disgracefully and, moreover, not reveal her real name. Adam was his lawyerly self, privately regarding the whole arrangement as deplorable, though his anger was directed at the law, rather than at Simon.

Four hours after he had left Ethel in the room, the three men went up the stairs to the room. Simon went in first, the other two staying outside but listening to hear what happened.

"Oh my god," Simon exclaimed loudly, "Ethel, please put some clothes on."

"I've made myself ready for you, though you've been such a long time out there thinking, I wasn't sure you'd be back, but here you are. Take me or else," at which Robert and Adam both came into the room.

"Oh my gawd, what are they doing here?"

"You have deceived me mightily, Mary Phillips,' said Robert, "and I don't take kindly to being deceived. Please dress immediately, and we will await you downstairs in the hotel lounge," at which the three men left the room.

After half an hour in which Simon told them what he knew about his murdered daughter and this woman, Robert decided to see why Ethel had not come down. He returned to the lounge to tell the others that she had disappeared.

"Now," said Simon, "will you please arrange a different assignation for me soon?"

Letters between Simon and Elizabeth passed regularly and Simon explained the whole saga of the Ethel incident which also fostered her eagerness to return home, but March it was to be. Simon and Margaret had met Jude for lunch at her home in mid-January to tell of their separation and the young man indicated a complete lack of interest with an off-hand sense that his parents would be better off without each other. Simon left that lunch as soon as he dared.

At the end of January Clarence had a note from the Daimler-Benz firm to say that a motor-car would not be available for another year at least. He was both excited but relieved with the thought of delaying the expense of the automobile. His participation in discussion about Malcolm's political fortunes was continuing at an unending pace with the Gargerys. Pip and Harriet were also involved, neither of whom could not imagine a scenario in which Malcolm would be rejected.

"Even if I were to become the candidate, Clara," said Malcolm one lunchtime, "that would not stop me from accepting an industrial community's nomination if one came up."

"You should put that out of your head," said Clara, "you are a mere thirty-six years old with a good thirty years ahead of you. Who knows what might happen? If you get West Medway don't think about somewhere else. You don't them want to spend the next two years before the General Election searching for some other berth."

"It is of course true that if I become a candidate there, it will be hard to lose the General Election, given its tradition of electing a Liberal, but also because the Tories are running out of steam having governed far too long."

Continued discussion was interrupted by Abdul bringing in a telegram for Malcolm. He snatched it from him, tore it open and his face dropped. The message said that Michael Longhampton, presently Liberal MP for East London Whitechapel was to be nominated as the Liberal candidate for the West Medway constituency. Malcolm was not surprised, though disappointed, but it was Clara who saw immediately the advantage in the rejection.

"Look, darling, think of it like this. You have had the experience of a presentation, you know what is involved. All you need now is Clarence's influence to get the open seat in East London Whitechapel as that Longhampton is going to East Medway."

"Of course! Let me look this up and he hurried into the library and came back, hurriedly opening Booth's London Poverty Maps. Ah, Whitechapel as a constituency goes east of the Tower of London into Stepney as well. If I can get this, we don't need another home as we live on the west side of the city in Mayfair."

"That would be a bonus," said Pip who had been silent, awaiting Malcolm's response to rejection.

"I must go," said Malcolm and within the hour was being welcomed by Robert at Old Square.

"Good afternoon, Mr. Gargery. I'm afraid Sir Clarence is in court for at least another hour. Would you like to talk with other lawyers?"

It occurred to Malcolm that Aaron would be knowledgeable about the East End.

"Is Mr. Levy in?"

"Yes indeed, let me show you upstairs."

"Malcolm, how good to see you. We don't know each other well, apart from Board meetings. What can I do for you?"

"I expect you have heard that I am seeking a constituency in the Liberal cause. I have recently failed to get the nomination for the by-election in West Medway, but the selected candidate is the MP for East London Whitechapel, a sprawling constituency east of the Tower, designed as such, I am sure, because there will be fewer eligible voters per square mile than there are say, in Chelsea."

"I think I can surmise what you are after."

"Oh dear, is it so obvious?"

"I suspect I am the only Jew that you know, am I right?"

"That is true, but it is not for neglect or prejudice, I think."

"Let me tell you what I understand about the East End. As you may know, my family goes back into English society after Cromwell allowed Jews to live here. I suppose I am part of a cultivated elite, and while most of us still maintain our religious ways, we have been influenced by English religions, appropriately I think. The East End Jew, however, is very different."

"How so?"

"For the past thirty years and especially in the last twenty, Jews have left Eastern Europe in droves, Russia, Poland, even Hungary. They come from shtetls, these small towns in the Pale of Settlement where they have been persecuted and their people and families have been killed, simply for being Jews."

"I have read very little about it, but what a travesty."

"Yet, as I hear about it from my rabbi and others who help them, their very poverty encourages them to regard us wealthier Jews with distaste. They also come from different countries, let alone the shtetls, so there is some cultural in-fighting. They were rarely farmers as their ownership of property was so limited, so those that work follow trades like tailoring but also gold and silversmithing. Living conditions are bad."

"So are there likely to be many men who can vote in that community. Of course, the franchise is limited to men over 21 who own property or 'paid rates', and any man who receives poor relief would be disqualified."

"I would guess that only a very few of them can vote, even if they understood it," said Aaron. Another problem is language of course. Most of them will speak Yiddish, but also Russian, Polish, Serbo-Croat wherever they came from. Yet, they will be very ambitious to improve themselves and they will do their best for their children."

"I will use Booth's maps to get a full picture of how wealth is distributed in Whitechapel."

"Invaluable, aren't they, those maps? Almost any client I get who is obviously not of gentle birth and who lives in London, I find myself looking up his or her residence both to discover the quality of the neighborhood precisely, but also what Booth's researchers determined was the wealth of the neighborhood, even the street."

"I hear Clarence arriving, so you will want to talk with him, I am sure."

"Indeed and may I talk with you again? I wonder whether the Jaggers Trust might do some work in Whitechapel."

"That is an interesting idea."

Robert knocked on the door to say that Sir Clarence would be glad to meet Malcolm so he shook hands with Aaron and left. Clarence was in very jovial mood having won a case before a jury which he had expected to lose.

"Now Malcolm, you lost West Medway, but Michael Longhampton's move makes Whitechapel a real possibility. I know him quite well as we find ourselves sitting on the benches together quite often during debates and we usually have similar reactions to the Conservative Front Bench. I am in the House tomorrow and I will speak with him."

The funeral had taken place at a small cemetery outside Boston near Cambridge on the last day of February and Mary-Lou's body was laid above that of her Romanian Count. Elizabeth decided not to tell the Drews as there was no true connection with her mother or herself. Only Mrs. Peggy-Sue Clandestine from number 32 attended. However, she was a widow from an

Illinois farming family and Elizabeth could not bear to hear her tale of woe so after the introduction she turned hastily to Richard Lodge, Mary-Lou's lawyer.

Elizabeth had informed him immediately of her death and she now took him to one side to hear that she was the sole heiress, apart from gifts of one thousand dollars to each of Elizabeth's children. He briefly mentioned she had some property in Texas and some worthwhile investments. He intimated that they might need to meet later but that he wanted her to know that she could immediately regard herself as the owner of Brimner Street, probate notwithstanding. Elizabeth managed to digest all this information but then she left the cemetery to walk along the Charles River with Charlotte for a while. The following day they spent some time sorting through Mary-Lou's possessions.

"Well, we cannot say that she did not give us a sign, Charlotte. I need now feel no guilt about leaving her and we will return to London as we planned. I don't think we need to keep any of her clothes, so would you please call the maid and tell her to empty all these cupboards and dispense them to whom she wishes."

"I will, Mamma, but only the cupboards for the moment?"

"Yes, and, oh they are closets to Americans, remember that."

"I will look through the chests directly, and then at her jewelry."

"I expect there will be some objects to keep there," said Charlotte, "she told me once that Grandpa Fitzroy had given her that gold and diamond bracelet she always wore."

"Really?" Said Elizabeth, "I didn't know that. Oh dear, here is a letter from her, dated only a month ago." While Charlotte rummaged around in the second dresser, Elizabeth sat down in a chair to read the letter, realizing that her mother's death was not a matter of continuing grief for her.

The letter was a long rambling missive, an *apologia pro sua vita*, thought Elizabeth, a nice Latin phrase she had seen on the cover of a book by an English cardinal in a Boston bookstore recently which she was not tempted to buy.

"There's nothing new here, Charlotte," she said running her eyes quickly down the page.

"Wait, she says that when her father was a young man he bought two thousand acres north of Corsicana in Texas as a speculation, and here, listen to this:

'This is a lot of land, honey, and I guess he totally forgot about it and he probably thought it was worth as much when he died as it was when he bought it. Why he didn't go there to get away from the war, I'll never know, but then there was nothing there except scrub, was there? Anyway, my dear, I saw in the papers a few years ago that prospectors had found oil in that township, so you should check it out.'"

"Charlotte, are you listening?"

"Yes, mother?"

"This means your grandmother has left me two thousand acres of land in Texas where they have found oil."

"We don't need oil, though, do we?"

"The automobile runs on it, well, not oil as such but liquid derived from it."

"So the land might be very valuable?"

"Indeed. She has also left me this house, several thousand dollars in cash, her jewelry and this huge parcel of land miles from anywhere. What on earth shall we do, Charlotte?"

"You don't need the money from the house, do you? Why not have an agent lease it?"

"That seems quite straightforward, but, fiddlesticks, what about this land?"

"We should find a lawyer or a businessman who can tell us. Certainly there is little point in visiting it, is there, if it just a piece of land?"

"No, my child, and I think New York may be the best place to find the right person. Perhaps the Meyers would know. We saw Daniel Meyer and his wife Sarah for lunch when we were in New York, and they were quite civil. Let us go to New York tomorrow for a few days. I will write to Daniel now and I will ask him to leave a message at the Algonquin where we will stay."

Two days later, Daniel arrived at their hotel for lunch. He was a handsome man in his late twenties, tall and distinguished, and Elizabeth remembered a letter from his mother saying he had fallen in love with a women older than he by a couple of years and although she was of a middle class Jewish family, she thought she was most unsuitable.

"How is your wife, Sarah, is it?"

"She is well. She spends her time doing charity work for poor Jewish immigrants so, in fact, our paths cross much less than I expected. We have no children, though not for want of trying."

"I hope things improve, Daniel, but I need your advice. My mother died ten days ago in Boston and her lawyer tells me I inherit everything. In a letter she left for me, my mother mentioned that I was now the owner of two thousand acres in Texas, and she added that it was close if not part of a place called Corsicana where a large oil field has been discovered."

"Goodness me, what an inheritance. I know nothing of the oil business but the royalties from such land would be very considerable or you could sell it. I can get in touch with an oil broker here in the city on your behalf, and I am sure that will be the best way to decide what to do."

"Thank you so much. I will, of course, reimburse you for your services. I really want to go home but we must return to Boston first and decide what to do with my mother's house."

When they parted, Elizabeth and Charlotte turned their thoughts to going home to London.

Meanwhile Tom and Hannah had one constant topic of discussion alongside the politics; how to bring up their children. Hector Thomas was now nine years old and Louise Katherine was four. The day was over and Tom was sitting on the edge of their bed, detaching his leg and propping it near a crutch on his special nightstand, then rolling himself over so that he could sit up and read. He now had very strong arms so it was not difficult for him to lift his weight. Hannah was watching him, book in hand. Once he was settled, she said:

"My memories of my mother have become slight in terms of how I was treated."

"That was because your parents' commitment to the Mission overrode consideration for children."

"I suppose so. I have been starting from scratch, if I think about it."

"We both have, and perhaps all parents do. For me as an only child, I was the apple of my parents' eyes and their attention to me was as close as could be, even though my father was a soldier and away from home frequently. But when he returned, he behaved just as he had before, and oh my goodness, I loved them so."

"I suppose I am more inclined to be soft-hearted whereas you are more sensitive to matters of discipline."

"It's a fine balance, Hannah. We both hold that children are rational creatures and understand common sense if it fostered in them, so that we both address a childish misdemeanor with a phrase like 'what did you think you were doing?'"

"I agree. We do, and I think the idea is not so much to cultivate a reflective turn of mind, though it does that, but always to have them imitating or echoing what we do as parents."

"That certainly comes first, but we do want them to think for themselves later on."

"Of course."

"I do try to say, 'watch me' or 'did you see what I did then?' I have had to leave Hector once or twice as he was being quite odious and I know I would have flown off the handle," and they laughed.

"People of our class often have nannies, of course, but that is just a way of discarding your responsibilities. It's a hard business, methinks, having children," she continued. "I feel so possessive of them, perhaps because I had such difficulty bringing them into the world. I read Rousseau for reasons I now have forgotten but his central idea that parents should keep out of their children's way always seemed to me extravagant, but we both dislike intensely the idea of sending their children to a school for boarders, do we not?"

"Absolutely, darling, fortunately I did not have a boarding school in my youthful experience so I am disinclined to inflict in it on my son, though it seems the conventional thing for people of our class to do. I want to bring up Louise as a thoroughly modern woman, independent and self-confident, certainly not like some of young women whose thoughts extend little beyond marriage. Of course," he said turning to kiss her, "I really mean I want her to be a replica of you, darling."

"Thank you, my dear. In some ways, yes, but in other ways no, I don't want her going into medicine just because that is my interest. Would it not be lovely if she could become a lawyer, for instance?"

"Oh my goodness, might that be possible in our lifetime? You know, I was of a conservative bent when I was a soldier, but as I have said too often, once I reflected on killing men, fathers, husbands and so on, and then the experience of the Clumber Plantation in Ireland and more recently that brief glimpse of the Welsh coalfield, I have become quite progressive, even radical. The State must be impartial between capital and labor. It must help the poor if we are not to suffer the kind of disorder in France in 1789 and 1870."

"That is wonderful, darling," she said, closing her book and settling down to sleep, "my sense is that in politics we need to try to get past the class barrier. Yet with the rise of this Labour Party, it is going to be difficult to bring working men into the Liberal Party."

"If we were to win the next election, I believe such men will flock to us because we will address these issues. As far as that is concerned, Clarence has been promising to introduce me to his local committee and I hope they invite both of us to meet them."

"Did I tell you that the Three Musketeers are planning a major campaign for both our parliamentary candidates?"

"And who the blazes are they?" said Tom, with a startled look as he turned to her.

"Clara, Emma and myself. We had in mind Elizabeth as D'Artagnan but she has skedaddled to America."

"The one thing Elizabeth would never do is skedaddle, if I have her right."

"I know and it is somewhat upsetting. Anyway, we plan to work together for you both and Dumas' characters came immediately to mind. That Elizabeth really is an example of fortitude, Tom, quite apart from her exceptional beauty. To be told first that your husband has committed suicide and to handle all the terrible emotions that would accompany that, and then to be told that he was, in fact murdered must have required immense strength of character. It has been on my mind from time to time: Does the Government really have to right to deceive so brazenly? Why could they not tell her the truth from the outset?"

"To protect themselves, of course. It is the same thing with a political party, and I think I will find such problems very difficult if I become an MP. In the Egerton case, the Government could brook no dissent and must cover its own weaknesses and failures, but that extends to political life in general. One must toe the party line, though where there are national considerations, like an Entente Cordiale with France, it will be country before party."

"Yet your career as a soldier has surely taught you to do just that, has it not?"

"Not the same thing. The objective was always quite clear in terms of the strategic target. Tactics were then developed, but there was always space for individual initiative in combat as the situations are so fluid. But, as I said earlier, the more I learn about the human predicament in this country and in the Empire too, the more radical I become. I could seriously see myself joining the Labour Party at some point in the future. When you've seen the ugly side of warfare, you realize one thing: That the men around you have as much human worth as yourself."

"I am sure you will find your place within the Liberal Party."

"Those words express exactly my multiple dilemmas. I do not want to be pigeon-holed with a party system. You know the expressions – Hesketh is tough on Ireland, soft on pensions, and so on. I know that is somewhat foolish as I have to develop positions on matters of great moment. I suppose I dislike the very idea of 'party' as a community to which one is bound hand and foot, so I may well become something of a maverick."

"You will think through issues in great depth if I know you. You will give criticism and be open to it. You will find the balance between clinging to your own opinions and taking part in a sensible solution. You will be popular because you have bottom, as they say. You will be respected, even feared because your mind is like a razor. You are also a man of principle. Oh, and I love you. I am the luckiest Gargery alive!"

"Time to sleep if you love me," said Tom. They kissed and slept in each other's arms.

XIV

S imon was beside himself with excitement as he stood looking at the liner that had docked at Southampton in the early morning of April 3rd, 1904. He scanned the railings of the ship but could not see Elizabeth or Charlotte, but then the gangways were put down and there they were, the first passengers off the boat, followed by a porter.

"Mother made me stand for hours so we could be first off the boat," said Charlotte as Simon enveloped Elizabeth in his arms, "not that I minded, it was a very rough crossing as Grandmother said it might be."

Breaking free, Simon put his arms around Charlotte to which she responded with some fervor, and they walked on either side of him towards the London train.

"We can wait for the main luggage to be delivered to us," said Elizabeth, waving the porter to follow them to the platform. Once settled in the compartment, Simon gave the porter a sovereign and sat down next to Elizabeth.

"Well?" She said.

"Will you marry me?" He said, at which Charlotte broke into tears and jumped across to hug her mother saying, "Say yes, say yes, please."

"My goodness, that's sudden. Of course I will," she said smiling, as he pulled a small box from his pocket. She was brimming with pleasure and delight as he pushed the ring down her finger, a solitaire diamond.

"Gee, that is beautiful," said Charlotte, using an Americanism she had picked up. Simon and Elizabeth got up and embraced each other but the train started with a lurch and they fell back together into the seat, laughing with joy.

"All is clear then?"

"All is clear and I will tell you the full story later."

"When will you get married? Can I be a bridesmaid?"

"Of course you can, but we cannot have a church wedding as Simon has been divorced from his wife."

"No, and we are not attached to a church anyway, but we will have a wonderful celebration."

They chatted as the train hurtled through Hampshire and were soon at Elizabeth's home in Eaton Square. Charlotte rushed off to her bedroom in the excitement of being home and Elizabeth led Simon into the music room where they embraced each properly.

"Goodness me, we have such a lot to talk about, darling. Our wedding, how we organize our finances, the organization of this house and my furniture such as it is."

"Those matters are of such importance but matter little in terms of what I have to tell you, Simon."

"Really, what could possibly be more important?"

"I am with child."

Simon sat down on a chair with a thump.

"How bloody marvelous," he cried, then promptly getting up to cover his wife's face with kisses while murmuring, "how wonderful," "what a surprise", "are you sure, really sure?" "Will you be alright at your age," indeed such an unending volley of endearments mixed with surprise and caution that she could not stop laughing.

"Listen to me, darling. We know precisely, don't we, the day of the conception when my mother took Charlotte shopping, so we can expect our baby in June. Now it is a huge surprise to me that I did not bleed in either November or December and have not since, I must now see my doctor here in London to confirm it. Of course I have taken care to conceal it by wearing looser clothes but touch my stomach. I thought Charlotte might notice, but she hasn't."

"Oh my goodness me! Oh my darling! Oh my goodness!" he exclaimed as his hand traversed the small lump.

"I clearly do not need to ask if you are thrilled," she said smiling. "Of course I thought when I missed my monthly event that I was starting the change in life for women and I was mildly puzzled as to why that had not started. But the third month I was starting to feel different, but I decided to tell no one as I wanted you to be the first to know."

"Thrilled? I cannot imagine anything more beautiful, anything more lovely in the universe. But now we really do need to talk. I did not know it was possible for you to conceive a child at fifty-two years old. But what on earth will people think? I mean, first I am divorced which to some is still unacceptable, and you will be pregnant on our wedding day."

"Let us think about this. I am sure my children will be thrilled, and my guess is that your Jude will also not be bound by conventions. I'd be sure the romantic Harriet will be delighted as much by the breach in custom as being pleased for us, and I expect her Joseph may be influenced by some of the radicals in Cambridge."

"Pip will be shocked but Harriet may tame his attitude given their past."

"Yet, darling I really don't know what the Smythes or the lawyers or Hamish and Mary will think. Put that to one side for the moment and let us enjoy ourselves."

"I am sure we need to protect you with immense care for the remaining months."

"I have always found child-bearing reasonably difficult but not horrid, so I anticipate giving birth without difficulty. I need to rest now after the journey, so let us go to bed."

They lay for a couple of hours, sleeping, fondling each other, with Simon constantly running his hands over her belly, neither of them concerned at their dramatic breach of social convention.

"This is my suggestion, darling," he said. "We invite all our friends to a party here soon, but we get married quietly that morning, perhaps with Jude and Charlotte only as witnesses. Then we celebrate your return with them, our marriage and our baby so that everything is then open and understood by everyone. I will also then put a notice in The Times announcing our marriage for the following day. What do you think?"

But answer came there none, as she was fast asleep.

Lady Emma Smythe sat in her drawing room in contemplation one April morning after her husband had left for the House of Commons. She was anticipating Clara calling mid-morning and was delighted when she appeared with two of her boys, George and Andrew, who were promptly invited to the nursery, long since out of use, but replete with toys and games which Emma's children had long outgrown.

"Beautiful boys, aren't they?" Said Emma, "alike but not alike with different fathers."

"Yes, they are lovely, though I say it myself."

"I am relieved that we are almost at the point of having no responsibility for my children," said Emma.

"I confess to a lack of diligence in finding out about my friends' children as I have been so wrapped in bearing and caring for my own. Remind me about them."

"Young Clarence has left Cambridge with a degree in Law and is now gadding about Europe before taking examinations for the English Bar."

"Was his undergraduate career unblemished?"

"Why do you ask?" She said laughing, "he did get into one or two scrapes we heard about, and I expect there were more, but nothing beyond high spirits, as with your Oliver at Eton. No forlorn maidens abandoned, fortunately."

"Will he join Courtisone and Jaggers?"

"I certainly hope so: lawyering is such a profitable occupation."

"How about Sophia? You presented her at Court, I know."

"She has inherited my looks and is now in her early twenties, but unmarried, the result of a romance which exploded when her suitor chose to pursue another young woman with a title, a huge dowry, but as plain as a pikestaff. The experience left Sophia cautious and plenty of time for her painting, and she goes to Kensington daily for tuition at the School of Art."

"And Alexandra your second daughter?"

"She gave us much concern and she hated the rituals of coming out after watching the brouhaha over Sophia, but she chose to find a place at Cambridge University. Clarence was delighted at not having to shoulder the colossal expense which a father incurs when his daughters, and he had three, are presented at Court. I was pleased too, and I think conversations in the League had alerted me to my daughters becoming independent and not be slaves to worries about marriage."

"I share that view now. One or two of the women I have met with experience of a university seem so much more content as well as knowledgeable and forthright. I wish I had had that experience."

"We are quite worried about Elizabeth, our youngest. She is almost nineteen and like Alexandra refuses to be presented at Court, but she is not interested in a university either. As a young child, she was passionate about animals,

Rufus especially. I was taken aback when I found her one day in South Africa, lying in Rufus' bed with his paws and her arms entwined! He is a big brute, but since then he always seeks her out, lying at her feet. She says she wants to work with animals and I don't think that means farming."

"Goodness me, that is a surprise," said Clara, "I have not heard of such an infatuation."

"Clarence's family has an estate in Sussex and there are two farms, one of which rears cattle and horses, so we suggested she might like to visit and she was thrilled. One of Clarence's distant cousins is the gentleman farmer, I forget his name, no Richard Smythe, that's right, Richard and she leaves next week."

"That would have been unthinkable a generation ago, wouldn't it?"

"Indeed. If she really enjoys the country life, I hope Richard will introduce her to men who share her passions, not merely his horses and other livestock."

"That goodness I don't have to think about all that for a few years."

"That reminds me. We must have a meeting of the League. So much is going on these days. Since we were in Stuttgart last September, Clarence is determined to buy a motor-car which frightens the life out of me, though I suppose I will get used to it."

"True for Malcolm too. He drops these hints constantly about the Stuttgart visit, though spending that amount of money on an automobile is unconscionable. I told him we must wait until something less expensive becomes available. He was terribly excited the other day to read that a couple of men, names of Rolls and Royce as I recall, who were joining up to produce an automobile. He spends too much of his time garnering every little snippets about the machines, and I am sure he would like to invest in a company making them, as he foresees the end of horses as transport in cities."

"If it works properly, it would be an immense help in transporting the family. I love our carriages and the horses for that matter but bouncing around in a carriage on a long trip is not designed to soothe the nerves: not that I expect the automobile to be that much better."

"That must also be the question of the surfaces on the road, I suppose."

"Yet, I know not. Boys will be boys, I suppose: Back to the League, my dear. We joined Millicent Fawcett's group but I do not see much progress on voting for women."

"As every newspaper says the movement is obviously in the doldrums," said Clara. "I expect that somewhere there is a group, one of the Pankhurst family in the lead, starting to think militantly about the issue."

"Have we had any news of Elizabeth and Charlotte?"

"I had a letter three months ago saying that they had met with her mother and were enjoying America and expected to return this month. It seems as though this was a reconciliation between mother and daughter."

"Elizabeth certainly regretted their breach, at least in later years."

A maid entered with the lunchtime post and Emma was intrigued by a large envelope.

"Good gracious, it is from Elizabeth. She is back and is holding an afternoon party next week. She says she has just returned home, three months earlier than she had at first intended and she would love to meet everyone. Quite informal, but how exciting. I am sure there will be an invitation in Down Street too."

"It will be very interesting to see her again. I wonder whether she met anyone in America. It is so contrary to my own experience that she is still unmarried so long after Timothy's death."

"Gentlemen, gentlemen," said Clarence, addressing the April meeting of his constituency party committee: "It has been my privilege to serve as your Member of Parliament for many years and I must now turn my attention to my law practice if I am to retire comfortably," at which there was general laughter.

"I have talked to Mr. Brownlow, our esteemed Chair, about my plans for several months but now is the time to tell you that my intention is firm, even though I will serve until the end of this parliamentary term. But we Liberals must be well prepared to fight this ghastly Tory government when the election comes, certainly now within two years. Some of you will think 'not before time' and others will say 'he is irreplaceable'" at which there was general laughter and cheers from the twenty or so men in the small room at the party offices which, it hardly needs to be said, was filled with smoke from the pipes and cigars which most men were enjoying.

"However, while announcing my departure, I want to introduce a man who will prove a credit to this constituency, the Party and the country when you have invited him to be your next Member of Parliament. I have talked with most of you about Tom Hesketh, formerly a major in the Gordon Highlanders in India where he lost a leg, and a Scot by birth but we should not hold that against him. Let me first introduce Mrs. Hesketh, who is a doctor, and her husband Tom Hesketh. Tom, why don't you say a few words?"

"I am honored to be here and when you have heard me, you may wish to look for another candidate."

Cries around the room included, "of course not" and 'why would we do that?' and other such indications that his selection was a foregone conclusion.

"Thank you, gentlemen, thank you, but a thing is not settled until it is formal. However, let me tell you briefly where I stand. First and foremost my Scottish upbringing and my military experience has led me to an uncompromising belief in the equality of men and the importance of moral rules in every walk of life. I have spent time in India on the North-West Frontier and I know too well that a country should never treat the young men who fight for it as fodder for the enemy's cannons. Our empire demands soldiers, but every one of them has a mother, sometimes a wife and children too. Whatever our views about our war with the Boers, far too many men died unnecessarily."

The room felt deadly quiet, as he went on.

"We must bring about Home Rule for Ireland. An Empire as large as ours will not suffer from such a move and our mutual hostility must turn into kinship. A Liberal Government must also do more for the laboring poor, even though this constituency is comprised of families and commercial concerns which are not troubled by that social weakness. I recently visited the Welsh coal mining districts and found the conditions there appalling when one considers that our home fires are lit by coal, our locomotives run on it, and our steamships are powered by it. We owe them our care."

At this there was general applause.

"Then, of course, there is an elephant sitting here in our midst: Votes for women, but also of course, votes for men, many of whom are still ineligible with the property qualification. My sense is that we need to make a distinction as we grapple with the franchise issue. We know what is morally right, namely that every citizen of a polity should, as in Ancient Athens, have the right to vote. The problem is political: How do we bring that about?

"My own sense of the future is that fifty years from now, people will look back on our deliberations on these matters as archaic and they will wonder why so much heat and not much light was generated in our national discourse. I confess not to being sure about how to achieve the final goal, but I do know that 'one man, one vote' and women too, is the goal," at which most men in the room applauded. Hannah smiled grimly.

"But of course that goal does not mean much if we ignore education. Our present system is a muddle. We must live up to two sentiments expressed about education in recent decades. The great Education Act of 1870 was promulgated by the Liberal minister, Mr. W. E. Forster and his comment was 'we must now educate our masters,' and even Dizzy said that what a parent wants for his own children, a nation must want for all its children.

"The tide of Liberal progress is unstoppable, my friends, and we must lead it."

The applause was enthusiastic and might have been called thunderous in a larger environment. The Chairman rose as Tom sat down and asked Mrs. Hesketh if she would like to contribute.

"Gentlemen, it is most kind of you to invite me, and you will not be surprised that my support for my dear husband is unbridled. He did not mention, so I will, that he has endured not merely the loss of a leg as a result of combat, but the dire struggles of fitting and using his prosthetic leg. He is a man of determination, gentlemen and I anticipate making the strongest contribution to his election."

"That concludes the presentation," said Brownlow. "I move that we invite Mr. Thomas Hesketh to be the Parliamentary Candidate for North London following in the footsteps of Sir Clarence Smythe," and the motion was carried *nem com.*

Clarence congratulated both Tom and Hannah.

"That was a splendid address, Tom. Clear, forthright, and in a logical order. You have won hearts and minds here. This is a conservative area, that is, people are wary of anything but gradual change. You could be the MP here for many years."

"Not without your continuing help and guidance, Clarence."

"We agreed the other night we needed to talk about our finances," said Elizabeth as the carriage carried them toward Caxton Hall for their wedding - on St. George's Day as it happened. Jude had stayed in the house overnight and had utterly changed from the rather surly young man who heard the news of his parents' divorce into a young man strongly supportive of his father, not least as his best man. Charlotte was a blushing bridesmaid, delirious with happiness for her mother, both supporters following in a different carriage.

"I have some money, Elizabeth, but not a fortune, but need money worry us?"

187

"Not at all, but I had some news in Boston that I was keeping as a surprise."

"Goodness me, another surprise?"

"Yes, and it shocked me too. My grandfather apparently bought two thousand acres of scrub land in Texas many years ago and my mother inherited it and has left it to me."

"Should we build a house there?"

"No, darling, prospectors have discovered oil on it and a New York firm wrote to say I can expect some forty thousand dollars annually at a minimum in royalties, and that could rise to six figures."

"Now I know why I fell in love with you," he said laughing, "but seriously, what a windfall."

"Now we need never worry about money. I was so impressed by the Trust and Angharad Llewellyn's generosity that perhaps we should have our own little Trust to help young musicians."

"A splendid idea, so typical of you."

"So you agree then," she said, turning to kiss him gently on the mouth, "oh, goodness me, you have brought me such happiness that I would gladly give you everything I have."

"As your lawyer," he said laughing, "I can tell you that you do not have to do that any longer."

The ceremony was soon over and Mr. and Mrs. Simon Brandram returned to the bride's home in Eaton Square to await the arrival of their evening guests. Simon insisted that Elizabeth spend the afternoon in bed, for he had heard enough of older women being very distressed at unexpected pregnancies. Meantime Charlotte was surprised that Jude asked her to walk with him to the Tate Gallery by the Thames which opened in 1897 but which both of them had yet to visit.

None of the guests were aware of this liaison let alone their marriage, but earlier worry about the attitudes of their friends had evaporated with the delight that their love for each other had brought them. Nevertheless, both were still prepared for some kind of a furore.

The first couple to arrive were Mary and Hamish whom Elizabeth admired so much, Mary for her courage and loyalty and Hamish for his compassion as a judge. Mary herself was mildly taken aback to see that Simon Brandram and his son Jude had already arrived, but she could not find the right question to ask about their presence or about Margaret's absence. She greeted Elizabeth very warmly wondering vaguely why she had put on so much weight, but immediately thought that must be due to American eating habits, while Elizabeth trembled with anticipation at Mary's coming reaction to her marriage and her baby.

Speculations were shared quietly among the women who were arriving, but the room was very soon full of the guests, the Smythes, the Gargerys, the Heskeths, the Levys and the Mastersons, and their older children too. Waiters scurried around offering champagne before Simon called for a toast to Elizabeth and there followed cries of 'Welcome Home.'

"Thank you, thank you," said Elizabeth, "Charlotte and I are very glad to be home, tinged slightly by sadness as my elderly mother passed away just three weeks before our return. I was able to get to know her properly and to understand the variety of problems she had faced. I was very grateful indeed for the experience."

Around the room there were murmurs of sympathy.

For a moment she seems lost for words and Harriet suddenly had this vision of her as the shy young pianist she had met with her aunt Charlotte all those years ago. However, Elizabeth pulled herself together quickly and said:

"I have an announcement to make and I invite you to share my joy, and I hope that you won't find what I have to say too dreadfully unconventional. For those who think we have gone too far, please understand us," at which remark one could hear a pin drop.

"My darling Simon and I were married this morning," at which the room erupted in astonished cries, followed by shouts of congratulation. Clara and Harriet rushed across the room and covered Elizabeth in their embraces, while Malcolm and Tom assaulted Simon with the vehemence of their congratulations. Mary flopped into a chair flabbergasted, partly confused by the realization that Simon and Margaret must be divorced.

As the delighted reaction to this news died down, Elizabeth continued, "but wait, everyone, I am sure my second announcement will meet with even more profound disapproval in most quarters of society but for us, it is a matter of unalloyed delight. We are expecting a child in June."

In such a polite company of Edwardian families, there was now a stunned silence, except for Henry and Oliver, Elizabeth's own sons who bounced out of their chairs and rushed over to applaud their mother, throwing their arms around her in tears of joy and burying their heads in her breasts, laughing and crying with excitement.

Elsewhere there was consternation and silence.

Emma Smythe looked at Clarence and he looked at her, both in shock, as if to ask each other whether they had heard what had just been said:

"One moment," said Clarence almost as if he were in the House addressing the Prime Minister, "what did you say Elizabeth? I caught the sentence about your marriage, but then what?"

"I am with child," said Elizabeth meekly.

"Oh my ears and whiskers!" Exclaimed Clarence, which broke the tension as everyone remembered Rabbit's phrase in Alice in Wonderland, although Emma moved very close to her husband, holding his hand as if she needed protection from a looming catastrophe. Pip put his head in his hands and Harriet promptly whispered to him quietly so that when he looked up at Simon and Margaret, he seemed to be saying to himself, sotto voce, there but for the grace of God, was I. Nevertheless while he could not help but be appalled, Harriet had to bite her tongue as she wanted to scream with delight at such romantic love.

The young lawyers were with their wives and Adam Masterson told them quietly about Simon's divorce procedure.

Then Mary got up and with a crackle in her voice, said:

"This is an enormous surprise, I must confess. We love you both dearly, but I am not sure what to think. We must assume, must we not Simon that your previous marriage was ended?"

"That is so. How can I say this politely? I will say simply that we did not anticipate the end of my former marriage," a remark that quelled doubts in his audience as to whether this married pair were adulterers. Many of the young people at the party looked askance at each other, being carefully brought up on the sins of affairs outside marriage and the even more unseemly event of a woman being pregnant on her wedding day.

Silence was then broken as guests digested the news, comments rumbling among the tables, and Simon and Elizabeth held hands watching their friends to see what else might be said. Their marriage had obviously pleased their friends, but it was the bombshell of her pregnancy, blowing a hole in convention as it did, that had everyone else struggling to come to terms with the news.

It was left to Hamish to break into the muffled conversation and in his calm and steady penetrating voice with its Scottish lilt, he said:

"My dear friends, what could be more joyful than the expectation of a child? I hesitate to make the comparison but let us remind ourselves why we Christians celebrate Christmas. To be sure, there is nothing as special in human life as that a new person will enter it, especially one conceived in love. While Elizabeth and Simon have manifestly acted outside the boundaries of our normal social conventions, we can hardly tell them they were mistaken and that they should put it right according to our conventions. What's done is done, and I speculate that Elizabeth's being with child was not a possibility within their wildest imaginations."

"You are certainly correct there," said Simon, "while we are thrilled and delighted, especially at our age and as we are both parents of grown children, we cannot say that we expected Elizabeth to be able to bear a child."

"To every rule," Hamish continued, "there is an exception. Let us suppose that instead of celebrating a marriage and the coming of a child today, we were celebrating the marriage today, and the coming of a child in three months. If this latter were to be the case, we would have no doubts, no sense of a wrong, no accusations, simply sheer joy. This is a simple matter of timing, nothing else. Let us share in their joy."

"Of course, Hamish, my learned friend," said Clarence, "you are perfectly right, but," he said turning to his own children and wagging his finger, "don't you dare think you can emulate Simon and Elizabeth," at which there were peals of laughter, "or your mother and I will be deeply upset. These two have the privilege of age."

The mood in the room changed quite abruptly after these two senior men, known for their moral probity, had given everyone permission to welcome the news, so to speak. Thus Simon and Elizabeth's breach of social convention began to be well received by their friends, as they were such lovely people, and that was reflected in the conversations of their friends.

Mary whispered to Clara that she thought that marriage to Margaret was doomed anyway after the daughter was murdered. Malcolm and Tom agreed that a marriage to Margaret was not a state either of them would have enjoyed. The smile on Harriet's face was like the face of the sun, a smile that would have encompassed the Grand Canyon which, sadly, the visitors to America had been unable to see. The Smythes kissed each other, Clarence so pleased for his colleague, and Emma suddenly grasping that her great friend would need her strong support, put her arms around Elizabeth in a tight embrace, whispering that she would always be there to help.

"You see, Pip," said Harriet grabbing his arm, "what tremendous happiness can occur from attractions which are not bounded by convention. Do you remember?"

"Of course and goodness gracious, we are such romantics; I must say this looks a marriage made in heaven. He's a damn lucky fellow. She is such a beauty."

"Did he go to America, Pip? Her child is obviously due within a few months, if I am any judge, so it must have been conceived there. I must ask her, and about her mother," and Harriet walked over to Elizabeth and Emma, at which Pip turned to talk to the Mastersons and the Levys, whom he did not know well, but it soon became apparent that the lawyers were talking law.

"I understood that divorce was not possible without an Act of Parliament," said Pip as the conversation turned to Simon's freedom.

"No longer," Adam replied, "and the changes keep me in business. Nowadays divorce is dealt with by the courts, but mutual consent is not seen by the judges as justification which was the case between Simon and his wife. In fact it is really only adultery that moves them."

"So how was this divorce achieved then?"

"There are really two aspects to it. The first is that one of the parties must be willing to be caught in an adulterous state. The second is that lawyers like myself seek to keep the proceedings out of the public eye as far as possible, though of course formal court proceedings are announced in the Gazette, which few people read."

"Fascinating. In case I should ever need one," said Pip laughing, "do tell me about this procedure as I gather we do not have the practice in Islam where I am told the man just has to say, 'I divorce you' three times for it to be so."

"No indeed," said Adam laughing. "But, and this is in the strictest confidence. We know most of the divorce court judges well and we can, as we did in this case, ask his Lordship to expedite the proceedings so that they do not excite the interest of any passing journalist. Sir Michael Hartington in this case simply listened to the hotel manager, as presented by Mrs. Brandram's lawyers, asked for further comment, said that he had seen the property settlement and the case was proven, and the decree nisi was ordered within ten minutes. Quite a triumph and a blessing for Simon."

"I share the excitement," said Emma to Clara and Harriet on the other side of the room, "though I was horrified at first, but I think we do have to worry about society for surely it is up to people like us to set a good example, otherwise divorce might become commonplace and marriage itself be under assault as an institution."

"Good Heavens, perish the thought," Clara replied. "It should be difficult enough to get a divorce that most people stick at their marriage, and I strongly agree about our responsibility to set an example; but here are Simon and Elizabeth."

"We must congratulate you both," said Clara, "for the last few months this beautiful romance has been going on and none of us has heard the slightest whisper."

"I agree; it was so convenient that Charlotte and I were in America."

"Yes, and that Margaret and I both recognized that our marriage was simply dead, and then that Adam did such sterling work on my behalf."

"But do tell us," said Harriet, "how did it start?"

"Simple, really: We were seated next to each other at lunch after a Board meeting. We did not know each other, except that we knew each other's names, and, how to explain it, it was a miracle. I saw this handsome young man next to me. We looked at each other and saw in that look all kinds of possibilities."

"And the baby?

"Ah," said Simon, "we had been rigorous about keeping our distance, but I was in Boston with Elizabeth for a month after my divorce. Her mother took Charlotte shopping and so we were together for several hours … "

"And the dam broke," said Elizabeth.

"Have you not been apprehensive about pregnancy at your age?" Asked Clara. "I am curious as I hope to continue to have children at your age."

"Oh my dear Clara, we are well aware how complicated it might be, but we are being very careful. I must say it was a total surprise to me especially as I was getting older and the changes happening to many of my friends were not happening to me. Now, to be frank, I am cautiously confident."

"Well, we are all so excited and thrilled for you. After all the trials and tribulations of your lives, you deserve happiness and peace."

At a table in a corner of the room sat Simon Garthwaite and Aaron Levy, the juniors in the Courtisone and Jaggers with their wives. Notwithstanding the professional conversations, all four were in a state of shock that they should be closely acquainted with people who so readily had broken with what was proper in society such that it was a source of some bewilderment for them.

"Wealthy people always do what they want," said Simon.

"The heavens have not fallen," said Aaron.

"We have not looked outside to see," said Judith, his wife smiling.

Mrs. Simon Garthwaite had been stunned into silence, as if she was witnessing a tragedy unfolding before her eyes, but then said:

"I suppose we will have to witness more of this sort of thing as women throw off their shackles. Of course, the very poor pay no attention to these kinds of social conventions, the rich have the wealth to ignore them, so it is poor old us, the struggling middle classes who feel obliged to sustain the moral codes."

" Really, my dear, is our marriage just a struggle then?"

"Don't be silly, Simon," and the four of them laughed heartily.

XV

O n the first of August 1904 Frederick Timothy Jude Brandram arrived in
a large bed attended by doctors and midwives at St Thomas Hospital
where his mother had been confined for most of July on advice that a woman
of her age should take no risks. Infant Freddy, as he was instantly called, appeared with a shock of blond hair and his mother's blue eyes, as if he had been
shot from a cannon to his mother's great relief and his father's delight. That he
was called Frederick was a tribute to Simon's father, but also to Frederica, his
murdered step-sister. His safe arrival was a further cause for joy among his much
older brothers and sisters.

Elizabeth had borne her pregnancy with grace, suffering the need to rest
for much of the day. Doctors at St. Thomas Hospital had kept a close eye on
her, and Simon and her children were constant in ministering to her. The day
after Freddy's birth, she said,

"I feel immensely proud to have come through this, Simon."

"The doctors were cautiously confident and quietly amazed that you were
so comfortable, and they seem to think it is a record. Sometimes I think it is a
divine blessing on our marriage, but then I shake myself and regard it as a gift
of Nature. I cannot tell you how proud I am. I look in our bedroom mirror
and tell myself of my good fortune, not merely to love you, but to share a child
with you. How clever you are, my darling, and goodness me, you look more
beautiful than ever."

Throughout the summer, Simon and Elizabeth found great delight in
their growing child. Their house was constantly full of their friends, their children and their friends, such that by Christmas, Freddy was a very contented
baby. At the chambers in Old Square, Aaron Levy and Simon Garthwaite
were not as friendly as heretofore, rarely smiling when they met Simon, and

seemed anxious to avoid conversation, still disturbed presumably by the fact that he had broken an important social code with impunity. Simon did not share this cold shoulder with Elizabeth to avoid anything that might upset here equilibrium.

"We must think about our ages and the future," said Elizabeth one night as they were going to sleep. "I will be seventy before Freddy comes of age."

Birth and death, however, are the inevitable predicament of the human race and every living creature.

For at the other end of the world in social terms but in a simultaneous time frame, a pit with two shafts was being sunk throughout the summer of 1904 in the tiny village of Ynysddu, near Caerphilly and close to Newport, the third city of Wales after Cardiff and Swansea. The dangers involved in sinking a pit included the weakness of shale or dirt over the coal seam, the possibility of water trapped in the rock being released in the process of excavating and building walls or wooden props to enable access to the seams. On the 13th of August a wall burst open with the pressure of both weak shale and water and the sinkers, as men were called who initiated a pit, were covered in bricks resulting in the death of seven of them and serious injury to nine others.

Angharad Llewellyn read the newspapers and immediately took her carriage down to Cardiff, calling at her bank to collect two hundred guineas, then the train to Newport and then hired a carriage to take her up to Ynysddu and up to the mine. There she found the pit manager, Gwylym Owens.

"What can I do for you, madam, we are quite busy you know?

"I am Angharad Llewellyn and I want to speak with the families of the bereaved."

"Now wait, I know you, you were Dai Llewellyn's wife, am I right?"

"Did you know Dai?"

"I worked under him when he was at the Trehafod pit, wonderful man. So what brings you here?"

"I want to help the families in this disaster."

"Well there are sixteen in all, seven dead, nine badly injured. They were sinkers mainly, as we have two shafts on the go but we are trying to sort out the disaster down there and recover the bodies. The injured are already in a hospital in Newport. If you want to help, go to that fella over there, Dai Evans, we call him Dai the Committee as he's on every bloody committee you can think of, union or management. He was injured years ago and he can't go down anymore, so he's a helper."

"Thank you, Gwylym."

"The wives are going to the chapel in half an hour, so you'll see them there: no funerals as the bodies have yet to be recovered but we know who they are. Hwyl fawr (Goodbye)."

Half an hour later, Angharad went into the Bethesda Chapel where women were moaning in their distress awaiting Pastor Gruffyd. She sat at the back waiting. He arrived as if brought in by a storm cloud and spoke in a high-pitched tenor voice.

"This is a terrible moment in your lives, but my friends, your loved ones are safe in the arms of the Lord, basking in his glory, looking down on you in your sorrow, and begging you not to mourn. Blessed are they that mourn for they shall be comforted, so now I have given you comfort, you may cease your mourning," which made Angharad feel quite sick that such gibberish was being handed out to women who did not know how they would provide for their children.

"What will we do, sir, when we have no money? How will we feed our children?"

"The Lord will provide, I am sure. Come to Chapel on Sunday as there will be a collection for you."

"Pastor," Angharad called out, "I am a visitor, may I speak to these women?"

Surprised by this elegantly dressed woman who was also clearly Welsh, he said:

"We are not presently in an act of worship, so please do."

"Which of you is bereaved?" Seven women put up their hands all of whom were in the front row.

"I want a list of your names and addresses, and Pastor, would you mind writing them down in my pocketbook," she said with authority.

Reaching in her handbag, she gave him her pocketbook and then pulled out from her bag little packets which each contained ten guineas, those small bright coins in solid gold, which most of the women had never seen before. Shrieks of delight and relief resounded through the Chapel as each woman opened her packet and astonished cries of glee rang around the chapel as Angharad repeated the process for the wives of the seriously injured.

"Now look, ladies," she said as the excitement died down, "my Trust will see you right. I expect you'll want to spend some of this on funerals and that's as should be here in Wales. The Pastor's writing down your names and addresses, so the Trust will give you a pound or more each week, depending on how many children you have. My husband was a pit manager and he used to tell me something of the distress women, wives and mothers suffer when there's an accident."

Completing the recording of names, the Pastor spoke:

"Did I not tell you that the Lord will provide? He has in the person of Mrs. Angharad Llewellyn."

"Don't blame the Lord, Pastor, it was my first husband, an Australian sheep farmer, who was the wealthy one."

The women left the chapel, relieved and excited, regaining their confidence, knowing they would not now be the object of pity, even perhaps of envy. Each woman knew that with this money in their purses, they could put something by for the future, though ruefully acknowledging that their the sons would follow their fathers underground, and their daughters would marry such men, and that accidents would continue to be the threat hanging over their lives. Such was the life of miners and their families.

"Pastor," said Angharad after they had left, "I need someone in this village to help with the distribution of future money, and I wonder if you would help? I am not a religious person, look you, so I am relying on your honesty to distribute this money weekly without fear or favor to the women on your list. I would be very angry were you to use this money in any other way than that for which it was intended and on the days I will stipulate."

"I would never do that, Mrs. Llewellyn and I would be pleased to support you in our generosity."

"Then, I will give you twenty guineas for such uses in your Chapel as you think sensible."

"I am quite overwhelmed myself. I have children too, so this will be a gift of such munificence as will help us all through the coming months."

"I was thinking more of the needs of your Chapel, but I suppose that includes the Pastor's upkeep. Good afternoon."

She shook hands with him and left to go back down the valley in a carriage to Newport and then took the train to Cardiff. She stepped down from the train, stumbled and a gentleman caught her as she fell. She rested in a waiting room and resumed her journey home an hour later.

Hannah had received a letter from her old friend Jeane McPherson in which she regretted not writing for six months but she had been busier than anticipated with her photography business. She was also saddened that her courtship with an officer of the Black Watch had come to nothing.

Tom came into the room as she finished reading the letter.

"Darling, I don't think you ever met Alec McPherson, Jeane's brother, did you?"

"No, I don't recall him; he was the tea planter fellow, wasn't he?"

"That's right. It appears from her letter that he is coming to Scotland with his wife and children for keeps and that they will not return. Apparently he has never got used to Darjeeling, it being a place of frequent earthquakes, and he and his wife Cecily want some respite back here in Scotland to take stock."

"But I thought she was born in India?"

"I thought so too, so there must be something other than earthquakes to bring them home."

"We will see. I must say that I would never, ever want to live in an area where there are earthquakes. The very idea of the ground moving under my feet and furniture falling about a room frightens me to death. Terra firma for me, and the firmer the terra the better."

"Goodness gracious me, I agree wholeheartedly," she said laughing at his little joke. "In the last five years or so, Japan suffered with an earthquake that killed more than twenty-thousand people as I recall. I wondered how they manage to mount a rescue operation, what doctors were able to do, and how long it takes to clear it all up."

"There was also one in India too, as I wondered at the time how the Army dealt with it. It was in Assam and killed fifteen hundred souls.

"Alec's a charming man, Tom, and I have told you how he decided to join the Gordons when Malcolm announced his intentions."

"You have. When do they arrive?"

"In two weeks, I believe. Did you remember that he courted me but wrote from India to say his affections had moved elsewhere."

"I do, but were you disappointed?"

"Initially, I think, but then I met this wonderful man Tom Hesketh and my life changed," at which they embraced each other, she stroking his beard and whiskers, he putting his hand round her neck, their quiet mutual passion for each other being the bedrock of their lives.

"So what is this former courtier like?"

"He is very charming, impetuous to a fault, and delightful company, very Scottish too. I cannot imagine what his wife Cecily is like. Nor do I understand quite why he should surrender tea-planting; perhaps another impetuous move."

"I am fascinated to see them. By the sound of it, I may have no difficulty in liking them."

"Apparently they want to stay in London when they arrive."

"Do they have children?"

"Two, I believe, but I do not know their ages though I think one is a son."

Hannah invited Jeane to London in anticipation of the McPherson's arrival and indeed a wire arrived from Southampton to say they were on their way planning to stay for a week at Greens Hotel in Kensington, a small new establishment which gave the two women some idea of how well placed these McPhersons were financially.

The two old friends had spent two days telling each other all their news and Jeane wanted Hannah to come with her to meet her brother and his family, notwithstanding their earlier relationship. Jeane was in awe of Hannah's time in Ireland and wished that she could have come across the Irish Sea to photograph the estate and the cottages, as well as the Irish scenery. Hannah told her that was still possible as the Trust continued to manage the estate.

However, they sat together nervously in the foyer of Greens hotel after lunch and shortly they heard a cab outside, and Alec came in alone and ran to his sister, enveloping her in his arms saying,

"I have missed you so, wee Jeannie," and he burst into tears. He put his arms around Hannah, saying how good it was to meet again.

"Now I must fetch my family from the carriage," he said, and minutes later a boy and a girl came into the hotel and walked slowly up to them to shake hands.

"I'm Henry McPherson," said the boy.

"I'm Abigail McPherson," said the girl.

The two friends responded in kind as Alec came back into the hotel, supporting his wife, saying, "this is my wife, Cecily."

She was clearly a very sick woman.

"Cecily has a very bad case of what doctors call Parkinson's Disease, apparently named after an early nineteenth century doctor who first identified it."

"Great Heavens," said Jeane, "I have never heard of it."

"I have come across it," said Hannah, "and I am so sorry. But introduce us anyway."

"Cecily darling, this is my sister Jeane and her friend Hannah."

In a slurred slightly slurred voice, a constant trembling of her limbs and with obvious physical difficulty, she raised her hand as if to shake hands, but then her hand fell away, but she smiled wanly and said:

"How wonderful to meet you both. Alec has often talked about you. Forgive me, I seem to be losing everything about my body everything except my mind."

"I am so sorry you are ill," said Jeane, "but perhaps we can find a doctor in London who can help you."

"How wonderful that would be and that is our earnest hope," said Alec, "but we must sign into the hotel and find our rooms so that Cecily can rest. The children and I would like to have lunch with you both if you can wait while Cecily is settled. It has been a long hard journey."

Jeane and Hannah moved to a small room off the foyer.

"Do you know anything about this disease?"

"Very little is known about its pathology, Jeane, though there are several doctors in the last century who have contributed to our understanding of it."

"How is it caused?"

"No one knows, but I heard tell recently of a brilliant young man at Edinburgh, one Samuel Kinnier Wilson, and he has just moved to the National Hospital in Queen Square, specializing in nervous diseases which I suppose this is."

"But how brave they are, especially Alec."

A while later, Alec and his two children came down the stairs and they all went to lunch in the dining room of the hotel.

"I will tell you briefly for the moment about Cecily as I don't want to rehearse everything that has happened in the past five years. It upsets Henry and Abigail, does it not, my dears? Anyway, Cecily started to find difficulty walking and began to shake slightly and she had always played a large part in the running of the two plantations, especially after her eccentric father died and she inherited his property.

"As things got worse, I needed to spend more time caring for her, so I became very concerned that I could not run the plantation properly and that we needed to come home to find better medical support than we could possibly find anywhere in India. Henry and Abigail were at a small private Anglo-Indian school in Darjeeling but we all agreed, didn't we darlings, that we would come hope and try to find help for our dear Mamma. So here we are."

"That was a wonderful decision and I assume you sold the plantation?"

"Not at first. I originally put local managers in charge, men who have been working with me and know the ropes as Cecily's disease progressed. But then we decided to sell both plantations which was a great financial success."

"Now you are here, I assume you will live in Scotland."

"Yes. What happened to our house when the parents passed on?"

"You know me," said Jeane, "a thrifty Scot. I leased it for the income as I started a photography business."

"Oh yes, I was forgetting that."

"You can live in our old home with your wife and children. It was too big for me."

"That's excellent. We will stay in London into the New Year to see doctors, but then go to Edinburgh. That will be wonderful, won't it darlings?" The children nodded their assent.

"Aunt Jeane," said Abigail, "is it very cold in Scotland?"

"I am sure you will take time to adjust but I am sure it is much cooler than Darjeeling."

"How about school, Father?"

"We will look out my old school and I know there was a sister school for girls, but let's see what we can do for Mamma first. Tell me, Hannah, how are you?"

"I am married to my dear Tom Hesketh."

"Was he a Gordon?"

"That's right: He lost a leg and Malcolm lost an eye and they came home together and became firm friends, though they had not met before."

"Oh," he said with delight, "so Malcolm is still around? I long to renew our acquaintance."

"Yes, you know he married his Clara, and they came back from an assignment in South Africa, must be two years ago now. Malcolm and Tom both now are candidates for Parliament."

"How excellent is that. We must meet everyone."

"Now," said Hannah, "how old are you, Henry and Abigail?"

"I am eight," said Henry, "and my sister is seven."

"We must find some children among our friends for you to meet. I know Andrew Egerton, Clara's son by her first husband Tom is more than ten but I don't know how much."

Discussion continued for a further hour before Alec said:

"I must now go and attend to Cecily as she will be awake."

"We must go too," said Jeane, "but I am staying with Hannah and Tom so you must contact us every day and do bring Cecily. I am sure it is better for her to see the world than be stuck in a sick room. The sights and sounds of others will please her, I know."

"That is one of the saddest conditions I have ever witnessed," said Hannah as they rode to Chiswick.

"Indeed, I am pleased that Alec seems to be so devoted to her. As you know, he was a bit of a rake when young."

"We will see what happens. The children are delightful, are they not, but the change from Darjeeling will be a shock, though maybe the schools won't be that different."

"I am sure they will enjoy a splendid Christmas."

Angharad was soon in the public eye in Wales. Her donations to miners were constantly reported in the Cardiff Times and the Western Mail and she was interviewed by a correspondent for the Mail. Such generosity had caught the eye of Welsh MPs, Keir Hardie, the MP for Merthyr Tydfil and David Lloyd George, the MP for Caernarvon Boroughs. Both men had emphasized the importance of the mining industry and the problems of mine safety in their political speeches.

She was invited to address a meeting of Welsh MPs in November. At the age of sixty-four, she was still an attractive woman and age had not yet undermined her looks or her vivacity. She was still slightly nervous about talking to such distinguished men and women, but, on the other hand, she had found that her wealth gave her enormous freedom, so she could say what she liked.

She arrived late to the meeting at the Angel Hotel but the men were very curious to see who was this woman who had become a leading philanthropist in South Wales. After a short introduction, she began:

"I was the daughter of a farmer in Cowbridge many years ago and a young Australian sheep farmer came looking for a bride. I was sixteen, swept off my feet and before I knew it I'd had four children and my husband had amassed considerable riches in sheep and sugar in Queensland. He turned out to be a right bastard, if you'll pardon my French," at which there was loud and prolonged laughter.

After it died down, she said, "But you don't want to know about my first marriage, however he and his farm friends got into a fight with the aboriginal folk and he was so badly wounded in his brain it took months for him to die. I returned to England with three of my children and with advice from my London lawyers, settled in Radyr. I married Dai Llewellyn, a pit manager who was a million miles from my first husband. But I learnt a lot from Dai about the conditions for miners.

"He died, a few years ago now, and I went back to my London lawyer, but he had become a judge so I was advised by other lawyers in the practice. That firm had been much involved with the Jaggers Trust for the Relief and Education of the Poor and we have set up a Llewellyn Trust which I chair and my directors are from the Jaggers Trust. I sit on their Board too. I am trying to help miners and miners family. So let me be frank:

"I am going to continue helping miners and I may well give some funds to the Union for their charitable purposes. I'd like to see the owners show more charity, too, but that dreadful strike and lockout in recent years damaged everyone." More applause.

"Though a farmer's daughter from Cowbridge will be told to keep silent, I have a prediction this morning that the mining industry may well be completely wrecked by the next strike which will come if the owners do not manage the industry fairly." Louder applause.

"I heard a man say recently that those pieces of a nation's life which are vital to a nation's survival should be under government control. I wondered about that. The navy and the army are vital, why not coal? Coal is the lifeblood of industry, of our ships and much more.

Anyway, Noswaith dda and diolch yn fawr." (Good evening and thank you.)

The MPs were impressed: As the meeting broke up and drifted into groups, Kier Hardie approached her and said she should be in the Labour Party to which she replied that she had joined every party to see what was going on in each. However, none were more impressed than Mr. David Lloyd George.

"Mrs. Llewellyn, my dear," he said catching her hand and stroking it gently, "you are a woman after my own heart. Your words were like magic to me, and what a beautiful woman you are. Call me David."

"Now then, David, I know a little bit about your reputation with women."

"Thank goodness, then you know that I am a lover of women of some experience, and I suspect that you have been a widow for too long and missed the delights of a man around the house and in your bed."

"Your deep Welsh charm almost convinces me, David. You are such a handsome man with your startling eyes and your golden mane, and were I younger, I might well be tempted. "

"You are as old as you feel, my dear," he said," but why don't we have dinner as I would like to take up your challenge to government when we are in power?"

"Where will you take me?"

"In my hotel room if you don't live nearby."

"Don't be naughty, David, I meant for dinner."

"Oh dinner, well, the dining room here is quite acceptable with the desert in my room, perhaps?"

Angharad realized that she was merely a diversion for this famous politician, well known to be a philanderer, as Malcolm and Tom had discovered in Rye. This talk of hotel rooms reminded her of her childish attempt to seduce Hamish all those years ago. This man was much younger than her, though that would have its advantages. As they walked to the dining-room, she wondered whether she was ready.

The dining-room at the Angel Hotel in Cardiff was far from a private place. David was constantly approached by men of rank and station in Cardiff, businessmen, local politicians and what have you. One man, an obvious friend of his, smirked at Angharad while talking to the famous man and least two young women kissed him on the cheek while he was still seated. One beautiful young woman approached him with her older husband in tow and kissed him and then turned to Angharad as she was leaving and as her husband was talking to Lloyd George.

"You two have a good time," she said with a smile, and then bending down, whispered in Angharad's ear, "he's extraordinary, I have never seen anything like it," which left her puzzled at first, but then the meaning was clear and she giggled, knowing she was open to his advances, her curiosity quickly obliterating any reservations.

Every constituency party in the country needed to be sure of its candidate for what was assumed to become a battle royal in the next election. Balfour was proving an unpopular Prime Minister and none was more serious at finding a replacement for their MP than the constituency of East London Whitechapel.

Clarence had persuaded Longhampton to support Malcolm, but he made excuses for the date the Committee would choose its candidate

Malcolm was the third candidate interviewed on a long November evening, and the Committee was of a similar social composition, primarily tradesmen who had lived most of their lives in the East End of London. Clara decided she would dress up to the nines in a striking chiffron dress with a hat bedecked with flowers and a smile that would have launched a thousand barges on the Thames had she but wandered down to the river.

It is a truth often to be observed that grown men of toil when presented with a woman of overpowering beauty lose their bearings, and such was the case here, for no such woman had ever graced this Whitechapel trading establishment or indeed was ever to be seen in its streets. Thus, while they asked this new candidate their questions, it was if their powers of listening had been completely curtailed as their eyes were fixed on this transcendent beauty sitting not feet away and who smiled at each of them as her husband spoke. The chairman of the Committee, Albion Snipperton, a grocer with two shops and considerable means, found his voice cracking as he tried to sum up the meeting after each member had asked their planned questions.

Malcolm was so well prepared to answer hostile questions that he experienced a mild disappointment when Snipperton announced, without taking a vote of his committee, that the Committee would welcome Mr. Gargery as their candidate at which each of the five members clapped so vigorously that the noise disturbed a member's dog who, until that moment, was lying quietly under the table, but then let loose a shrill bark or two before returning to his slumbers.

Each member came up to congratulate Malcolm and then turned to Clara who had not been invited to offer support to her husband but found herself surrounded by eager admirers, though the smell of the grocer, the fishmonger and the brewer on the committee forced her to summon up all she had to prevent her fainting from the odors wafting around her. Fortunately Malcolm rescued her with some remarks about the need to see their children before they were put down to sleep.

As they left, the Chairman said he would be writing a formal note of invitation and shook hands with both of them and Malcolm expressed his most grateful thanks for such an enjoyable evening.

"Darling," he said as they climbed into the coach. "I think it is you who should be the candidate not me."

"I must confess to being rather surprised at their attentiveness to me, but once it began I decided to make no attempt to deflect it, rather to use it in your favor."

"That is all very well, but it means you will have to be with me continuously."

"Do you think that would trouble me?" she said laughing.

1905

XVI

Since her meeting with the MPs, news of this Welsh philanthropist had circulated among the great and the good in South Wales and even across the Bristol Channel so that she found herself invited to what she saw as posh occasions such as Mayoral dinners, often held in the New Year. However, it was at a civic celebration for the patron saint of Wales Dewi Sant (Saint David) on March 1st, with leeks and daffodils much in evidence, that she met a man she thought was a possible husband. Many of the men she encountered were either married or too old or, in one or two cases, prone to the same antics as the MP for Cardigan Boroughs with whom she had spent an engaging few hours with the clear understanding that this was an ephemeral engagement, however much she enjoyed it and however much it whetted her appetite.

Sir Cyril Hunterspoon was a former mayor of Bristol. His wife had died recently and Angharad was placed next to him for dinner at one of these civic occasion in Swansea. He was tall, grey-haired of course and clean-shaven, an unusual feature of men in the early twentieth century. He had blue-grey eyes and what Angharad told herself was a lovely smile.

"How d'ye do, Mrs. Llewellyn, I must say I am mightily impressed with your philanthropic work for the miners."

"Thank you, Sir Cyril, I am a woman of good fortune and I am pleased to able to try to help families in distress."

"I understand you have founded your own Trust for these purposes. What is the endowment?"

"A hundred and fifty thousand at the moment, but I expect to add another hundred thousand shortly."

"Goodness gracious, what munificence."

"Not really. My first husband got in early on sheep farming in northern Australia and, how do they say it in America, he made a packet."

"What an odd expression."

"But then he was killed in an argument with the native peoples enduring a terrible head wound and a coma such that he died six months later. So I sold up and came back to Wales."

"I am lost in admiration. I have had similar good fortune, with a bequest from a distant uncle who was a gold prospector in the Yukon, and that arrived when I was a mere forty years old, so my wife and I lived a very comfortable life."

"May I ask," said Angharad, "was her passing painful?"

"No indeed. It was a complete surprise. She walked toward the dinner table one evening and fell down before she could reach it. She was dead. Heart failure, so the doctors said."

"What a shock that must have been."

"Yes, but oddly I had an inkling that she was ill. She complained of pains and breathing difficulties, not a good sign."

"How have you coped, Sir Cyril?"

"Please, call me Cyril. Badly, but not if I am honest because I mourn for her. I should not say this, but I think her heart was her problem for some time and she had become very aggressive and truculent, indeed difficult to live with. I loved her, of course, but I tell myself that her time had come and that I should not grieve over her."

"How interesting. That was true of my first husband. I thought good riddance as he was so cruel to me. My Dai was different, but then I have never been one to look back, always forward. You were from Bristol, am I right?"

"Indeed, a fine city of which I rose to be Mayor."

"Is that where you were born?"

"Oh, no further south in the Mendip Hills. My father was a small farmer and I left there to seek my fortune elsewhere."

"I am a farm girl too, from Cowbridge."

"Angharad, I wonder if we might spend more time together. We share a great deal personally, background I mean, but I would like to get to know you better.

"Me too, Cyril."

"I recently bought a country house overlooking the sea on the Gower Peninsula and we intended to retire there. Would you be my guest for a few days and we can get to know each other better?"

"Now that we are done with St. David, that would be delightful. I will take a carriage on Monday from Radyr, quite a long journey so I will start early."

On the 6th of March Angharad arrived at Caswell House, a lonely spot in those days, the house overlooking Caswell Bay.

"My driver had difficulty finding the house," said Angharad after Cyril and she had exchanged greetings.

"It needs work, I'm afraid. Too many draughts, facing the sea, but it is comfortable and I have great plans for it."

The time passed amicably, and neither of them was anxious to commit to anything more than friendship. Angharad thought to herself that marrying this man might be a very good way to live out her life. He was charming and not aging, but vigorous and in good health as they walked along the beach and clambered over rocks, enjoying the sight and sounds of the sea.

Newspapers were brought from Bishopston each day, but they were always a day late as the hamlet of Caswell was somewhat remote.

"There's been an explosion at a pit in Clydach," he said as he spread out the newspaper over breakfast."

"Oh my goodness, when?"

"Friday evening as the shifts were changing, so the loss of life was limited to thirty-three men."

"I must leave immediately and go to help."

"Shall I come?"

"Do you want to?"

"Not really. I am sad for the men and their families, but I am not bound up with the mining communities as you are."

"I understand that, but I must go. Cyril, this has been a charming few days and I hope you feel as I do that we must continue to build our relationship."

"Angharad, nothing would give me greater pleasure. You are such a fine woman and I think we might spend many happy years together."

"Let us not rush this, Cyril. I am certainly of a mind to pursue our friendship and see where it leads. For the moment, let us enjoy each other's company."

"Excellent, my dear. Now you go off and comfort your miners and I will be in touch with you in Radyr in a week or so.

She thus spent a week spent in Clydach which she visited each day from her Radyr house, helping out families. Angharad then sent a wire to her new friend Cyril Hunterspoon in Caswell, asking if she could visit. An immediate reply of welcome had her packing and ordering a carriage to carry her the forty odd miles from Radyr which meant at least a half day's travel, depending on the surfaces, especially if rain had influenced the safety of the roads, not unusual in Wales in early April.

She had a fortunate journey and Cyril greeted her very warmly to which she responded.

"What was it like after the explosion?"

"Thirty-three dead and more injured. It could have been much worse, of course, but seventy-seven children are now without fathers. I was able to bring some comfort by relieving the widows of impending financial disaster, but I have to find way to make conditions better so that these accidents don't happen as often."

"I know little about it, but I can imagine nothing worse than confronting the dangers underground."

"Oh and seventy-eight horses were also killed."

"Horses? In a mine?"

"How else do you think the coal and the slag can get from the coal-face to the lifts?"

"It had never occurred to me, I must say."

"I am going to make a list of the dangers of mining when I get time. It's not just explosions, but the effect of the dust on the men and much else."

"I expect there will be questions in Parliament; we must look out for them in the newspapers "

As they had done before, they spent four days talking and enjoying the countryside and the beach and Angharad and Cyril, separately began to think that this might be a long-term partnership.

Angharad was preparing her return to Radyr one morning when a carriage drew up and two men got out. She went downstairs where Cyril was waiting until the men approached the door.

"Good morning, Sir Cyril. I am Detective Strangwell and this is Constable Wright from the Bristol Police, and we wish to escort you back to the station in Bristol.'

"Good God, Cyril, what is this about?"

"I don't know, my dear. What am I to be questioned about?"

"We were alerted by one of the finance clerks in the Mayor's office many months ago and we want to question you on matters related to missing City funds over a long period, indeed throughout your Mayoralty. We will need you to answer very specific questions about expenditure from your office and under your direction which we suspect may lead to charges of embezzlement. But that is for the future. At this juncture, we wish to take you back to Bristol so we will go the train in Swansea and get to Bristol quite promptly."

Angharad had sat down in a chair in the hall of the house while Strangwell spoke, completely stunned. Then Cyril said:

"My dear, please stay here as long as you wish. This is all a terrible misunderstanding, of course, but I do have to go with these gentlemen to explain what seems to be the difficulty. I am sure I will be back within a week."

"No, I'll go to Radyr tomorrow and perhaps when you have completed your visit to Bristol, you can call on me in Radyr."

"I certainly will. Now I must change before these gentlemen escort me to the City."

Cyril was about to go upstairs to change, when Strangwell said,

"Before you go upstairs, Sir Cyril, we have a warrant to search your house, especially your study, so please remain here with Constable Wright. Your wife is not involved."

"She is not my wife and I have nothing to hide," he replied, and with as much grace as he could muster promptly hastened to his bedroom, after showing the police to his study.

As a young woman, Angharad would have been shrieking in protest at the arrest of a friend, but now, as an older woman, she was outwardly calm, but inwardly confused, though not terrified. If Cyril was a criminal, so be it. She hardly knew the man, but police don't usually travel a hundred miles to arrest a man without solid evidence, she thought.

"Cyril, I think you may need a lawyer whatever the outcome to assist you with explanations," she said when he came down the stairs.

"I'd rather not use my Bristol lawyer, I think."

"I know some very distinguished lawyers in London. Should I contact them? I am to go to London shortly in any case."

"That would be most helpful."

It was an hour before Strangwell appeared from the study.

"Wright, come and collect these two boxes."

Strangewell wished Angharad good day and escorted Cyril to the carriage which then went down the short drive and into the lane on its way to Bristol.

Angharad went to her own bedroom to pack, but it was too late in the day to travel to Radyr so she sat for an hour or so gazing at the sea, before the maid called her in for dinner.

Ah well, mumbled Angharad to herself, down the drain goes another relationship, "the bloody idiot," she said out loud as she walked into the small dining-room, "how can people be so stupid?"

"Pardon, ma'am," said the maid, "I am sorry, I didn't understand."

"It was just me making noises. Sir Cyril will be away for a while. Please keep the house in order till he returns. I assume he has paid you your wages up to date."

"No, Ma'am, we haven't been paid for six months."

"Right," she said concealing her anger, "we will deal with this tomorrow before I leave. Thank you, Janet," and the maid departed leaving Angharad sipping her soup as anger built up inside her.

"The bastard," she said to herself, "he was just after my money and a bleeding crook to boot. All that nonsense about an inheritance from some gold prospector. What a liar."

Ever the philanthropist, the following morning Angharad called the two staff to the drawing room, gave them six months wages and said they needed new jobs as she thought Sir Cyril would not return any time soon. She left Caswell in a raging temper, cursing men and their stupid ways with a mix of profanity and blasphemy but deciding to go to London promptly to ask Clarence if the firm would offer Sir Cyril representation, not that she cared one way or the other, but she always tried to keep her word.

The McPherson family had gradually recovered from their arduous journey from Darjeeling but Cecily in particular was exhausted. She was somewhat recovered from a lunch party at the Gargerys and a week later was able to join in the conversation at Clara's informal lunch while experiencing some tremors, but she clearly enjoyed meeting people, especially the Heskeths. After the lunch Henry and Abigail were escorted upstairs by Andrew, Clara's eldest child and to judge by the excited voices wafting down the stairs, that was a success.

After lingering at the dining table for a while, Clara and Hannah escorted Cecily into the drawing-room, leaving Alec, Tom and Malcolm to talk.

"It was immensely hard work taking over the first plantation. The tea bushes were in disarray after years of neglect and the bungalow and the outbuildings equally distressed, but Cecily and I brought it round with her father's help. After three years it began to have the income it promised."

"As far as I recall," said Tom, "there are now many plantations in or near Darjeeling."

"Indeed," said Alec, "Darjeeling tea has this distinctive taste, it is said, because the soil is rich in specific nutrients, such as potash and phosphorous. The bushes are grown on hills so that the water does not collect around the roots."

"But you needed many laborers, didn't you?"

"After Cecily's father died and inherited that plantation, we were fortunate to have women who had worked there for years, and they were happy for their daughters to follow on as pickers."

"No men, then, in the harvest?"

"Usually members of a family have worked there for generations, but picking the leaves requires delicacy, as it requires plucking two leaves and a bud at a time. Pruning is done by the men and that gives the plant young shoots which are easier for the women to pick. Then we sell the crop to factors who turn it into the barrels for transport around the world."

"I have been fascinated by the number of tea shops opening in London," said Tom. "Interesting that ladies now have what is called afternoon tea as if it were an occasion like dinner not a mere drink."

"Yes, in India that is called tiffin. Over the centuries, Tom, it first became a drink for the upper classes but then with the amounts being produced, it has become a staple for the laboring classes. I am told that this is healthy in that it is a stimulant cheaper than beer, and it requires boiling water to make it which some say prevents disease."

"It is certainly in high demand."

"Now Alec," said Malcolm, "I used to know you well enough to be direct. Did you enjoy this engagement with tea-planting?"

"I remember urging you to take up with the lovely Clara when we were commissioned, so I suppose that counts, as sufficiently intimate as friendships go. Frankly I came to wake up every day wishing I was somewhere else. I was brought up in Edinburgh where any number of delights were available just by taking a half-hour walk or a carriage ride. You are both city-lovers, you will find it difficult to imagine what it is like to be virtually without social life."

"But surely, there were other owners to know."

"Of course, but very limited and most of them eccentric in one way or another. After a year of immense and brutal activity day in day out getting the second plantation into shape, I began to feel trapped. I did not have any male friends."

"And female friends?" said Malcolm laughing at which Alec blushed and said, "Of course not, marooned up there in the hills. Cecily had been used to being able to travel perhaps once a year to other parts of India, Simla, Delhi, though she did contribute to management of her father's plantation, but such opportunities for travel for both of us were few and far between."

"So Cecily's illness gave you the opportunity to return home to Scotland."

"Yes, but I had talked to her about selling long before her illness, probably three years after we started. Of course, poor dear, she was horrified, never having been outside India, but her opposition gradually weakened as she became ill. The children were thrilled with the idea of coming to this magic place called Scotland."

"Do you have any specific plans other than returning there?

"Not really. We have sold up and are comfortable in our investments and financial matters, but we do not have wealth enough for us to be entirely without other income. That is partly because I am locking up capital for my children. I might talk with Jeane about her photographic business. I have a hunch that this is becoming an increasing part of family life, I mean that people want pictorial records of people and places, events and occasions."

"How interesting," said Tom, "I had not thought about purchasing one of those cameras but it would be delightful to have pictures of my children growing up, other than the studio portraits."

In the drawing room, the conversation initially covered much of the same territory.

"We do hope you will get good treatment when you see Wilson, Cecily," said Clara.

"Thank you," she replied with some hesitation, "I am sure I will get better treatment here than in Delhi, though with other illnesses we had no complaints of Indian doctors. For my two confinements, my ayah was a wonderful help and very knowledgeable too."

"You lived there all your life, am I right?" Asked Hannah.

"Yes indeed, and in an odd sort of way, I think my illness forestalled the complete breakdown of my marriage," a remark which alarmed the others.

"Good gracious me, that sounds frightful."

"As I am quite likely to die well before my time I no longer feel any of the constraints of secrecy; rather I have not had the opportunity to speak with ladies of my class with any intimacy, so I am trying it out on you both," and they all laughed.

"Thank you for taking us into your confidence," said Hannah.

"After two or three years of immense hard work of setting our plantation to rights, I saw that Alec is too much of a social character to enjoy sitting on his veranda smoking cheroots and watching sunsets. We had bitter arguments because he was bored with tea-planting, urging me to come back to Scotland which I strongly resisted as I had no experience of what life in Scotland would be like, apart from a few school years in England."

"Knowing Alec well," said Hannah, "that does not surprise me. Everyone he knew was surprised by his fervor about tea-planting, apart from my cousin Duncan Urchadan who was angry for months after he resigned his commission."

"Even in the early days, I encouraged him to take short vacations on his own in Delhi or Simla, as I wanted him to see that he could have a more balanced life when the plantations were running well, but that became a source of tension too as I sensed he was meeting another woman."

"So that increased the difficulty in your marriage?"

"Oh yes indeed. He never admitted it, which exacerbated the matter, so I really do not know whether it was true and I was above searching his desk. Oh God, please forgive these tremors and shakings. I just cannot control them."

"Please, please go on," said Hannah.

"Before I was married, I never understood how or why women let their husbands get away with it. When I was married, I sympathized with them."

"But Cecily, if you didn't know whether it was true and he would not admit it, why was it such a problem for your marriage?"

"Jealousy and intuition."

"Ah," said Clara, "that will do it. Suspicion would gnaw away at you, day by day, especially in his absence when your imagination feeds you images of his debauchery."

"Exactly," said Cecily. "The first two or three times he was away, he came back and genuinely seemed pleased to have returned, but then after one such visit, his mind seemed to be somewhere else and his affection for me stilted, not genuine. When challenged he seemed completely shocked that I could think such a thing, so I let it pass, though it rankled."

"How long did this go on?"

"Until I started with this Parkinson's disease, four years ago. He has never been away since, but has been so devoted to me, it is almost unbearable. I feel guilty that I even thought he would be unfaithful and then even more guilty about developing this disease as it has so spoilt his life. He cares for me deeply, he is so kind, so tender, so helpful. I am ashamed."

"Now look here, Cecily," said Clara. "I have never been in a position to doubt either of my husbands, but I firmly believe that a woman's intuition about such matters is invariably correct. For you, life has changed so dramatically with your illness, but you need feel no guilt about your suspicions, even if in fact they were misplaced, which I doubt."

"I agree wholeheartedly," said Hannah.

"Now," said Clara, "I have had a chair with wheels delivered for your use, so I will call the gentlemen and we will go for a walk in the Park."

After her disappointment with Cyril, Angharad hastened back to London in early July as she had promised to ask her lawyer friends if they would appear for him. In her first class carriage as the train was stopped at Swindon for the engine to take on water and some passengers, it dawned on her that finding a husband in London would only be possible if she could become attached to some social set or other which would require leasing a house in the smart part of the capital, say Kensington or Chelsea. Desirable husbands in Cardiff were as difficult to find as streets paved with gold. She remembered that Clarence told her they lived in Kensington Gore, so she would ask his advice.

It had been a dry summer and people in London seemed dressed for fine weather with plenty of parasols and brightly colored clothing. She was put down at Old Square and as usual Robert was delighted to see her.

"How wonderful to see you again, Mrs. Llewellyn. If I may say so, you look very well."

"I am always ready to be complimented, Robert, especially from such a kind man."

"Thank you, thank you. Sir Hamish is in court, but Sir Clarence has just returned though he does have a client coming to see him later. I am sure he can meet you for a half hour."

Robert shepherded Angharad through to Clarence's office and he was also delighted to see her. He found her quite extraordinary as he had never really thought that a farm girl from some distant part of Wales or other could transform herself into this elegant, charming woman of principle.

"My dear Angharad, what brings you here?"

"Two matters, Clarence, though first I should say I met Mr. Keir Hardie."

"Did you now? We have been trying to extend our pact with the Labour Party."

"I dare not tell you about my meeting with Mr. Lloyd George."

"If he is within a mile, I lock up my daughters," and they both laughed heartily.

"Clarence, I wish to move to London as the group I know in Wales whom I might befriend are limited in various ways. To be honest I would like to marry again as I do get very lonely, especially when I appear on my own at some charitable occasion or other."

"That seems very sensible, but did you have anywhere in mind?"

"I thought I could lease a small house somewhere in Kensington or Chelsea."

"Excellent, now Robert might be best placed to help with that, and I am sure Emma and I can introduce you to various social groups where you might meet someone."

"That would be exciting, but I have another matter, somewhat connected to the first."

"In the last four months, I became very friendly with a former Mayor of Bristol, Sir Cyril Hunterspoon, a widower with a home in the Gower Peninsula overlooking the sea. I stayed there on several occasions, no funny business, if you know what I mean. Obviously he knew about my wealth as we met at a charitable occasion, but last week when I was there, police arrived all the way from Bristol with a search warrant and took him into custody for enquiries about embezzlement."

"Goodness me, has he been charged?"

"I don't know, but it would be odd for the police to travel all the way to Caswell if they were not very certain of their ground."

"You are right, of course."

"Anyway, I told him I would consult with my London lawyers and see whether they might work with him."

"It would not be me, that is certain. I suppose Masterson might help. I know the others are busy but we must ask Robert as he manages us all," and he called out for Robert.

"Tell me, Robert, do we have anyone who might work with a distinguished public servant charged with embezzlement?"

"Oh dear, I don't think so. As you know, the briefs are coming in like shoals of fish and we can only manage about a quarter of them. You see, Mrs. Llewellyn, Courtisone and Jaggers has become one of the most sought-after practices in London, so I am very careful about accepting briefs. I try to mix pro bono work for the poor with the high fees that we can charge the rich. It is a way of helping the lawyers with their consciences," which elicited a guffaw from Clarence.

"Do we know whether he has been charged?"

"No."

"Where is he?"

"In Bristol."

"Oh," said Robert sagely, "my advice to you, sir, is that we leave this man alone. It seems to me very unlikely indeed that a charge of embezzlement by a public servant would be a weak case. Fraud cases as you know are only brought by police when they are very solid indeed. More than that, we do not really know whether the man concerned would have the wherewithal to pay us for our services as, if he is found guilty, he is likely to face at least a prison sentence and a hefty fine plus costs which will be extensive and probably bankrupt him if he has had to rely on embezzlements. But, may I ask, is the person concerned a friend or acquaintance of Mrs. Llewellyn?"

"A former friend, no longer an acquaintance."

"Your reply enables me to imagine the circumstances in which you have been placed. If I may speak freely, I suspect that you are in danger of succumbing to a misguided loyalty and that you should leave him to stew in his own juice."

At this, Clarence laughed heartily and Angharad smiled.

"You see, Angharad," said Clarence, "our esteemed senior clerk can deliver exactly the kind of advice that a lawyer would deliver, but with a far more vigorous expression," and they all laughed again.

"Well, I must say, when the police arrived with a search warrant and took away boxes from his study as well as him in person, I said some very profane things out loud after they left as I had not realized he was after my money. In fact, I need to know this, Clarence, am I now legally entitled to control my own property if I marry?"

"You are indeed, but Mr. Llewellyn never exercised that right, did he?"

"No, fortunately, not that he would have gambled it away or anything, he was the sweetest and gentlest of men."

"To your first matter," said Clarence, "Robert, you are to help this good lady find herself a suitable property in Kensington or Chelsea, but you do not need me to help in that regard."

"Let us go to my office, Mrs. Llewellyn and we can discuss the matter further."

"Can you find me a husband at the same time?"

XVII

Angharad and Robert decided that she should buy, rather than lease a property as she had the capital and property always increased in value, whereas rent was, well, rent. She planned to come to the office on July 12th early and they would view areas of Kensington and Chelsea. However, glancing at the papers after she finished her breakfast at Claridge's she saw that there had been a major explosion in a mine at Wattstown in the Rhondda Valley. It seemed as though over a hundred men had died, so she sent a message to Robert cancelling her visit and prepared to go to South Wales.

In the late afternoon, her carriage brought her to the pit head where it seemed that everybody in the Valley was waiting, grim-faced, some weeping, children crying, a scene of such distress that Angharad herself began to weep, the crowd so large that as she looked down at it, it seemed to swirl like water in a bucket. She had collected two hundred sovereigns from Coutts her banker before she left and brought them with her. Although some thought this was not the best way to help stricken families, she believed it was the quickest way to help.

She noticed a man taking notes on the edge of the crowd so getting down from her carriage, she walked down the slope and hurried over to him.

"Excuse me, are you a reporter?"

"Yes, Ma'am. Good God, you must be that rich woman, Mrs. Llewellyn."

"I am."

"I'm from the Rhondda Sentinel and my editor wants a long article by tomorrow."

"What happened? Do we know?"

"To be honest, no figures yet, but it is disgusting so soon after the accident at Clydach, but then you know all about that."

"I do, terrible it was, tell me what happened here."

"There was an explosion in the nine-foot seam, as I've been told. The story is that the manager was at fault."

"Oh my god, what was his name?

"Meredith, I think."

"I met him once or twice when my husband was alive."

"He was killed, I'm afraid. They say he decided to blast through a barrier of coal to drain water into a sinking pit. He should have brought the water up the shaft, they tell me, but you know, money rules, and it was too expensive. For my part, there should be much more attention to safety procedures in the mines."

"My Dai went out of his way to make sure his miners were safe."

"I wasn't there, of course, when the explosion happened, but I was told it happened about noon. Debris shot out of the pit's mouth and there was this thunderous rumble from underground, and of course it could be heard and felt the length of the valley up past Ferndale and down through Porth."

"I can see that they are bringing up bodies now and taking them over there to a mortuary."

"That's the old blacksmith's shop."

"Let's go over there see what is happening. What's your name, by the way?"

"Owen Griffiths, Ma'am, but call me Owen."

"Call me Angharad too."

"I have never seen anything like this," said Angharad as they approached, "I am going to have to steel myself if I am going to help here."

"Please keep back, lady," said a policeman as they approached a cordon around the shop. "You don't want to see those bodies. I was inside for half an hour and I had to be replaced."

"Why is that?" Asked Angharad.

"The wives can't identify the bodies as they are so smashed about. We have to bring out possessions or scraps of clothing to show to the wives. It is gut-wrenching, I tell you. I brought out a red handkerchief and four women claimed it. Things like that make it much worse than it is if that's possible. Far too many of the dead are boys, and there are several horses dead too, though those are still in the pit."

"I must talk to the wives," said Angharad leaving Owen at this mortuary. She had felt a strange kind of strength after viewing the bodies, albeit from a distance, and felt a sense of elation about her mission. There were large groups of weeping women, mourning together the loss of their husbands and sons.

A woman broke from a group in great distress, falling on the ground weeping and Angharad said:

"Can I help you?"

"Oh God, oh God, why does He allow this?"

"It is so awful, a form of Hell, I think, but who are you?"

"I'm Mrs. Rees, my two Dais, my father and my eldest son were down there and now they are lying battered to pieces over there."

"I am so sorry, let me give you something to tide you over you over till your compensation comes through."

"Oh, thank you, ma'am," said Mrs. Rees, slipping the five sovereigns into the pocket of her apron. "My daughter died of the meningitis last year, and now losing these two, I don't know what will happen to me. It's not just me now, there's my neighbors, the Halletts and the Berrymans, and more I expect, they've lost their husbands and sons too. I must go home to my babies," and she scuttled away.

The rest of the day Angharad spent time watching bodies being brought up, wives screaming when they were a scrap of clothing, or some other object that might lead to identification, but there were still three bodies so badly crushed that little identification was possible and three distraught women, not allowed to the bodies, but trying to think of some way they could take their husband home. Over the course of the day, she had given away well the two hundred sovereigns.

The newspaper man hung around the pit talking with the rescuers and trying to put together the story. As the crowd of watchers had largely dispersed, he said to Angharad:

"Why do you do this, Mrs. Llewellyn?"

"I told you to call me Angharad but look at it this way. If you were rich and you saw men and women having this terrible hellish human experience, would you not want to help?

"I suppose so, but of course it has never crossed my mind as I am just a poor reporter."

"Well," said Angharad, "I hope you do justice to this horror."

"I will try."

"But as you are poor and I still have ten sovereigns in my purse that I have not been able to give away, I want you to have five."

"Thank you, thank you, my wife will be in ecstasy."

"Good. I left my carriage a half mile away, and I am sure my driver will have been sleeping all day, so I must wake him up and get down the Valley to my home in Radyr before dark.

"What do you make of this war in the Far East, Tom?" Asked Pip as the family gathered for lunch on another balmy day in August. Indeed the weather was so good and summer was at its height that Harriet had a table laid in the garden.

"It is shattering from the viewpoint of foreign policy, for we know so little about the politics of Japan, but that maybe just me parading my ignorance. Whereas Turkey has been the sick man of Europe, it could be that the description might fit Russia well after that humiliating defeat. I gather the American President is trying to get both sides to a treaty which shows how worried they are."

"Why would they worry?"

"Because both Russia and Japan are in fact quite close to them geographically, at the Alaska end of the continent."

"It is more than that," said Malcolm. "I was speaking to the party members in Whitechapel the night before last and I suggested that a weakness in Russia might encourage the Kaiser to create some mischief. I spent two days in the British Museum looking at translations of Russian and Japanese newspapers and I was struck by the fact that those two countries including ourselves have begun to design battleships with much more powerful guns. The British ship is to be called HMS Dreadnought, the name betraying its intent."

"Exactly," said Tom, "and the Germans will not be far behind, so that we will in this decade find ourselves in a race to see who can built the biggest and most powerful ships. All the elements of a competition are in place."

"Well," said Harriet, "God save us from any European war, but then as the Kaiser is both a bit stupid and related to the King, I don't see him firing the first shot. Enough of foreign policy, both of you, tell us about your constituencies."

"Malcolm and I talk about almost nothing else, even in bed," Clara said with a chortle.

"That's because we both find it so fascinating," said Malcolm. "First I must say how well informed and articulate the ordinary man is about domestic matters. I explained in detail Liberal policy to my committee on a national insurance idea and immediately there was intense discussion about the unemployed, how widows would be compensated, what sort of pension would it lead to and would it have a means test."

"My experience was exactly the same," added Tom, "except that the discussion began with the iniquities of the 1902 Education Act and the need for comprehensive reform and expansion of public education immediately we take office. Work has begun on planning that bill."

"That is so exciting for you both," said Pip, "but it proves that the franchise should be extended to all men ...

"And women," added Hannah.

"And that was another topic of intense debate between the gradualists and the all-inners."

"Who are they?" said Pip.

"The all-inners, my own phrase, men who think all women should have the vote now, men who want to go the whole hog on the matter of votes for women, and men, I should add. At any rate that is what they are now calling them in my constituency party after I labelled them as such. I am temperamentally an all-inner, but then I suspect that is true of all of us because the women we know are of such high intelligence that a gradual process seems ridiculous."

"So," Tom continued, "I asked the gradualists whether their wives should have the vote and there was almost uproar."

"Why?"

"They started talking about their wives and the knowledge of politics. Some of the phrases which stuck in my mind were "she don't know a vote from a hole in the ground," and "your wife would soon tell you how to vote," and "my Bess knows more than the ruddy Queen," and so on, such that the conversation became more like a drunken discussion in a pub than a sober committee meeting. Such a contrast to their careful thought earlier."

"Was anything resolved? Did anyone change their mind?" Asked Harriet.

"Oh, I doubt it, but there was one fellow, Alfred Roman, who said his wife was out of his control on the matter and that she was supporting the Pankhurst women, one of whom wants to become more militant on the suffrage."

"I am beginning to feel like that myself," said Harriet, "but I am now too old to engage in their activities. I am fed up to the back teeth with listening to all the specious nonsense that circulates about women and the vote."

"I agree," said Hannah. "I am going to align myself with Christabel Pankhurst and join the Women's Social and Political Union."

"Who is she?" asked Pip.

"Oh, Father, did you not see that she was arrested for disrupting a Party meeting with her friend, Annie Kenny?"

"What were they doing?"

"Shouting out demands for the suffrage. She was fined but refused to pay, so went to prison."

"Women will get nowhere if they break the law."

"Tell me, Father, why should they have to wait until men wake up to this massive injustice?"

"My dear, when God made the world ... "

"And on the fourth day He ruled that women should not have the vote," interrupted Hannah which made everyone laugh.

"No, I am serious, my child."

"Please do not patronize me, Father, I am thirty years old. Just get used to the fact that all women will have the vote in my lifetime," at which Pip fell silent, feeling his age.

At that moment, Mary was shown into the room, anticipating a cup of tea and a natter with her friend Harriet, but she was delighted to find the Gargerys together.

"I was coming to Harriet with a suggestion, but I can express it to everyone. Hamish has decided, in consultation with his colleagues on the Bench, that it is not out of order to have a dinner party for his friends and at the same time invite acquaintances who are politicians. What say you all?"

"Mary," said Clara, "I was about to consider the possibilities with the other Musketeers, but I am considering a monthly occasion of that kind until what I assume will be an election in the six months. On the other hand, it would be a grand idea to start with a bang, an illustrious occasion."

"Hamish thought that we should invite conservative politicians as well."

"Oh dear no: how can we be outspoken if the enemy is present?" Asked Hannah, "although I would like to give the Tories, any Tories, a piece of my mind."

"But is it not a weakness in our polity," said Pip, "if we cannot reason together?"

"The common weakness in politics as I am experiencing it," said Malcolm, "is the conflict of interest between the individual and the common good. That sounds terribly grand, but reasoning depends on the individual's starting point. Common ground is difficult to find."

"How right that is, my future parliamentary colleague," said Tom. "If I were to predict a political future for this country, I would say that when we are in government, which will surely happen, we will have a serious constitutional fight with the House of Lords. If ever there were a conservative institution, that is it."

"I had not thought of that," said Clara, "but of course progressive ideas from the Liberals may indeed meet the stone wall of the aristocracy with their inherited notions of their right to rule."

"If the Lords shoot down an extension of the franchise which is highly likely, as Tom suggests, that will make other matters quite insignificant."

"In that case, let Hamish and I to be sure to invite a couple of them to our party. We don't want those who are dyed-in-the-wool, of course, but conservatives who might be described as on the fence about such issues."

"The wisdom of that," said Harriet, "lies in the need to know one's enemy."

"What frightens me is this," said Pip, "the miners have shown that they are prepared to strike and the mine owners may well be prepared to use police to get their way and miners will resist. Desperate men will take desperate measure and we could face serious civil disturbances."

"Very wise, Father," said Malcolm who was nevertheless impressed by Pip's seriousness, although he thought the comment far-fetched.

"Goodness me," exclaimed Clara, "this is getting even more exciting than I imagined."

"Indeed," said Pip lightening the mood, as my father used to say: 'What larks, eh, Pip?'"

"Odd isn't it," said Malcolm, "though we use that expression from time to time, no one here knew him except you, who was his only child."

"He was a wonderful man, wasn't he?" said Harriet, "salt of the earth. While Pip and I were together when he was alive, our relationship was such that I could not meet him."

"He would certainly have been astonished by our new plan. Clara and I are to acquire an automobile."

"Goodness me," said Pip, "how exciting."

"We thought touring our constituency in a car, as they are being called, would not only be a very convenient form of transport, but would make a good impression."

"It is difficult to know," said Hannah, "whether the poor in your constituency will regard a car as evidence of your wealth and despise you, or evidence of your progressive character and admire it."

"A little of each, I suspect, but we went to the Olympia Exhibition and saw a Mercedes which we have ordered from Cannstatt Mercédès, but it is in stock so we can take possession of it next week. It is quite different from the one we saw in Stuttgart."

"What color is it," said Hannah excitedly, "is it comfortable?"

"We took a very short drive," said Clara, "and it was delightful. Now Malcolm has to learn how to propel it."

"How frightfully exciting," cried Harriet, "so modern, so progressive! But where will you house it?"

"In the stables at the rear of our house, I suppose, as we will have little need of the horses, though I will continue to ride in Hyde Park. We must find a groom for the car, too, though I am not sure that groom is the appropriate word for someone looking after an automobile."

At the end of June, Victoria had been surprised to receive a letter from Clara Gargery inviting the family to stay with them in France for two weeks in July. Clara used to be worried about Victoria as she had been through such tribulations with the suicide of her first husband and more recently the scandal of the murder at Numquam. The Eustaces were not directly related, but, thought Clara, a Eustace is a Eustace and while her father might not be related to Victoria's husband John Eustace, she was sure they could become friends.

Three weeks in the south of France was the most pleasurable experience for the Eustace family who returned to All Hallows each with their own glow of satisfaction at such a wonderful vacation. Philip had been a quiet young man since the dreadful experience of causing a death, but he came completely out of his shell on vacation from his final year at Oxford, proving to be witty, thoughtful and caring in playing with the Gargery's older children. Beatrice was now a school-teacher and she proved a tower of strength too in looking after the three younger Gargerys when they went down to the sea, and Nellie

Eustace became absorbed by the tropical plants in the garden which were quite outside her ken as she had just started her studies in biology at the university in London.

The adults became fast friends too, and when they left, Clara told them that they must come every year. However, the day after the family's return in late July, the Reverend John Eustace was surprised to receive a message of invitation to the Lord Bishop of Rochester's palace for eleven o'clock on Friday July 13th.

The Right Reverend Edward Talbot, Lord Bishop of Rochester was typical of Victorian bishops in terms of his aristocratic background and his marriage, but John knew that he and his wife had founded a college for women in Oxford when he was Warden of an Oxford College. That suggested to John that he was a man of liberal leanings, even though he had not risked asking the Bishop for permission for Pip to celebrate his wedding, but that was just a way of forestalling the possibility of a negative answer when he explained it to Victoria.

The butler showed him into the Bishop's library in the historic building which was as grand as he expected. The Bishop was sitting in a comfortable armchair near a blazing fire, dressed in gaiters as a prince of the church should be, and he invited John to take a seat opposite him. John had some difficulty in holding himself together before such ecclesiastical majesty.

"How do you find the All Hallows parish, John?"

"Quite delightful, my Lord, especially since my marriage, as my wife is an outstanding help and succor in the work of the parish."

"I have had many favorable reports of you from the Archdeacon. I must tell you in complete confidence first that I am about to be translated to the see of Southwark which my wife and I will enjoy as the diocese extends over various mixed class areas south of the Thames, so God's work there present special challenges, rather different from bucolic Rochester.

"I want to bring clergy I know and respect into Southwark. There is a vacancy at St. Chrysostom in Bermondsey which has a strong middle class and is a thriving church. I would like you to consider accepting this somewhat prestigious living and come to work with me. I choose this parish for you as it is near Southwark. I have had long discussions with the Dean, or the Provost as he is called in Southwark and I am confident that he shares my ambitions. What say you?"

"My Lord, I will do God's work wherever I am needed."

"John, I know of your earlier tragedy, and I am pleased for your sake that you have now found happiness in a marriage. You probably do not know that before the tragedy that engulfed you and your move to All Hallows afterwards, you were being noticed as someone who could go far in the Church. Why not take your wife, it's Victoria, isn't it, to view the church and the vicarage, but you must let me know within a week as my consecration at Southwark is next month and I will be formally resigning here next week? If you accept, I will make the offer formal as soon as I am in harness in Southwark."

"I cannot tell you, my Lord, how grateful I am for this opportunity. It presents me with a magnificent challenge which, I must confess, is limited in a country parish and, while we must see Bermondsey first, I doubt very much that I will refuse your formal offer when it comes."

"Thank you, John. I look forward to working closely with you."

The driver of the carriage taking John back to All Hallows was surprised by the expressions of elation coming from behind him. Moreover, when they arrived at the Vicarage in All Hallows, the Vicar leapt down from the carriage and rushed into the house.

"Victoria, Victoria, Victoria," he shouted.

"What's the matter?" she replied, hastening down the stairs, "what did he say?"

Slightly breathless, John said, "he is to become Bishop of Southwark and he is offering me a splendid living, St. Chrysostom in Bermondsey. If we like it, he will make me a formal offer after his consecration next month."

"Wait, where exactly is Southwark and Bermondsey?"

"Southwark is a huge diocese just across the Thames from the city of London, and Bermondsey is but a stone's throw from the Cathedral, and parts of the parish must be on the River itself. I expect there are docks within the parish too."

"So we are to live in the dirt and grime of South London?"

"No, it is south of the river. Before we start thinking of reasons one way or other, let us go there next week and see the church and the vicarage."

"I am not averse to this move, John, as I am not especially wedded to All Hallows. Let us take the children too when we visit."

"Indeed we will, but not the first time, I think."

John and Victoria took the train from Rochester to London Bridge and stepped into a world they knew little of. They took a cab enquiring of the driver where he would accompany them for a few hours as they wished to tour the parish: First to the Vicarage in Thurland Road, a large rambling house built at the beginning of the previous century, more than enough for their needs, but as yet they had no right to enter, so walked along the road the short distance to the church.

"This could accommodate two of our All Hallows Churches," said Victoria.

"Look at that huge painting above the high altar and the galleries. What a fine pulpit."

"Oh my dear, this could be your church. I am not quite sure what class of people attend, but it does not look to me like a church for the poor."

"We must see what the parish is like."

The carriage took them first up to the river to see the city on the other side with the Christopher Wren's Monument and St. Paul's Cathedral towering over the city.

"What magnificent erections," said Victoria, "how do they construct buildings that high?"

"With scaffolding, my dear, based on the architect's plans and designs."

"We will be able to take a short walk and look at them every day."

"It looks to me as though the area near the river and the docks houses the poor, for where the church is located, there seem to be quite substantial houses."

"Well, we will have the river, but do you think we will hear the railway noises from the house."

"Well, it runs just two hundred yards to the south of the Vicarage, but there are no stations nearby, so the noise will be continuous and I am sure we will get used to it."

The driver then took them through streets to the east of the church and there indeed were more substantial houses, ladies walking in the streets with their children, clearly different from the poor areas near the docks where children clustered in groups – and rags.

By evening, the driver recommended the George Inn as a welcoming hostelry to stay for the night and after they were settled, they came down for supper to a room with a few travelers, though the trade had declined as the railway extended into Kent.

"Why does this Inn have a gallery like that?"

"I don't know, Victoria, but perhaps when it was built around Shakespeare's time, there were plays acted here and people could watch from the gallery. But tell me, my dear, are you excited by the idea of this move?"

"John, it is really your decision. It is a way for you to resume you career in the Church, cut off by the sad tragedy of your wife's death. I am in favor of it for that reason. But I am anxious too. I will have to manage a larger household and we will do more entertaining and we will be invited to many a social occasion. That means new dresses, new hats and so on, although we are near enough to London shops. For the children, I think they will enjoy life here."

"It will be a new experience for them, won't it, after the quiet country life."

"There will be many opportunities for them to have friends, of course, and in fact we will be much nearer to both the Gargerys, the Heskeths, and the MacDonalds which will be an excitement."

"Did you once tell me you had lived in London?"

"Yes, when I was a young woman, my mother arranged with Estella Pirrip for me to come to London and become a lady, as they envisaged it, and I lived for a while in her magnificent home near St. James Park."

"Good, I thought so. Life in London will not be all that strange for you."

They set off again the following morning on their exploration of the parish.

"Oh my, look at these large houses," he said as they rode along Jamaica Road, then down Salisbury Street and Janeway Street,

"Why is it called Jamaica Road?"

"I expect one of these merchants had property in Jamaica. dear."

"With slaves, then?"

"Probably, but we can discover more about that when we are here. There will be much for us to learn together, Victoria."

They traversed the whole parish and went into the church again where an elderly woman was polishing a silver chalice, a pattern and several large silver candlesticks.

"Good morning," said John, "I am John Eustace and this is my wife Victoria."

"I'se Flossie Nugent and I comes here regular to clean the silver."

"It looks wonderful, very sparkling."

"Well the old vicar said we must keep it polished as a tribute to the Lord."

"I am sure he was right."

"Begging your pardon, sir, are you the new Vicar?"

"Not yet, but my wife and I may get the opportunity soon."

"Lor bless us, you'll need a firm 'and 'ere, sir. There's all sorts going on, as far as I can see."

"Oh dear why?"

"First it's the bells. We have ten of 'em all made from Napoleon's cannons, so they say. But there's this Jewish merchant up Salisbury who's complaining about the noise they make. Then the man who plays the organ wants it repaired, I don't know, what goings-on, eh? Then there's the choirmaster and I hope the rumors about him and the choirboys ain't true."

"All useful information, Flossie, and I hope we will meet again."

An hour later, as they sat comfortably in the first class carriage of the train on the way home, John said "What do you think, my dear?"

"It is such a splendid promotion for you, John. While the church clearly attracts the well-to-do, there will be plenty of opportunity for work with the poor if we judge the parish right."

"One attractive feature for me is that I will be able to enhance the intellectual content of my sermons as well-to-do people will understand me. I can set out dilemmas and difficulties rather than just sending out orders about going to church and what to believe."

"I do have one question. Is it like All Hallows where you have the freehold of the Church and Vicarage but if you were to die, I would have to leave very promptly?"

"Yes, usually within two months. Are you thinking about Numquam?"

"Indeed. I thought we should sell it but let us keep it. We can decide whether to lease it, but given the recent experience, I am not sure."

Edward St. John Peregrine Matravers Talbot was consecrated as Bishop and the following week came a letter expressing his wish to appoint The Reverend John Eustace to be Vicar of the Parish of St. James, Bermondsey.

A quite new world was opening for the Eustaces.

"A letter arrived for you earlier, my dear, and it has Clara's Down Street address on it."

John opened it carefully with a paper knife. In a scrawling script Matilda was enquiring whether Abdul and she could meet with him, in Kent if need be. Mrs. Gargery suggested it.

He showed it to Victoria asking what on earth that could be about.

XVIII

Elizabeth developed a regular morning ritual after Simon left for his chambers. She would stand in front of the cheval mirror in her bedroom, holding Freddy in her arms, gazing at herself. Not that she was vain, but the sheer wonder of her child was a possession to be savored to its limits. She knew of the antagonisms many people of her class would feel at Freddy's conception, but even when she tried looking at him as others might see him, her whole being swelled with such emotion that tears frequently came to her eyes. She cherished Hamish's comment that he was a grand wee fellow, and as a result, Simon took to calling Freddy his grand wee fellow when he laid him on his lap. To no one's surprise, she often took Freddy to see her friends, particularly Harriet.

"My dear, Pip and I were talking about you the other day," said Harriet when Elizabeth and Freddy called, "such courage to bear a child at your age. Mind you, looking at this beautiful child, it is more than worth it."

"He has transformed our lives, it is quite miraculous, but you know, if we had thought it was possible, we would have baulked at the very idea of a baby."

"You were quite a disgrace not to tell anyone of what you were up to, but I think it is quite enchanting that you have this remarkable gift. How has Charlotte responded and how was she in America?"

"She dotes on Freddy, of course. As for America, she much enjoyed meeting her strange grandmother and of course we had that frightful experience which has left its mark on both of us. The visit has improved her, not a doubt, in the sense that she is now certainly an adult. We were always close and I took the opportunity to explain something about my past with Albert. After all, she is now my age when I began that relationship."

"Since Frederica's murder if I had a daughter I have wondered whether I could ever tell her about my past. Pip has told Joseph about us, I am sure."

"Simon still grieves for his daughter, you know, but he has fallen hook, line and sinker for Charlotte which is quite delightful, and she is as delighted as he. He told me that Margaret admitted the mistake of encouraging Frederica's independence with men when she was far too young, which merely illustrates what a weak woman she was. There is some kind of secret about the maid Ethel which Simon won't tell me, but he still feels guilt at not noticing what was happening with his daughter, too busy establishing himself at Courtisone and Jaggers, as he puts it; but, oh my goodness, he does fret about Charlotte quite unnecessarily."

"I am sure Charlotte would never be as foolish and reckless as that young woman, Elizabeth. I don't know what mothers do these days, but have you talked with Charlotte about men?"

"As far as I know, she has yet to meet any young man who interests her, not least because she has become quite involved in studying matters of race. It is quite obvious where her sentiments lie in that respect from her conversations. When Oliver asked her casually if she thought there was anything of substance in this eugenics theory, she got very angry; indeed I have never seen her so furious."

"Oh my, that is fascinating. At her age I was wallowing in literature."

"And I was spending my days at the piano, but no, I see no reason to talk with her until a man appears."

"Thinking back, you know, I have begun to see myself as a fraud."

"Good heavens, why?"

"I find myself displeased with my own life in one respect. I love Pip dearly, always have and always will. Yet when we met I talked gaily with him about free love on the basis of a couple of brief earlier experiences, but once I met Pip, it was emotionally quite out of the question to be intimate with another man. For my own satisfaction, I thought up an argument about it being a matter of integrity not to take a lover when I was with him. That was a shield to ward off the interested, that man Friedrich in particular. Of course, when I decided much later after Pip and Susanna disappeared to Africa that I wanted a child before it was too late, I made sure the father was not someone I might be in contact with. I was not really a free lover at all, just a fraud."

"H'mm. How thoughtful. Tell me, would you in your free love philosophy have drawn a distinction been men who were married and those who were not?"

"In general, Elizabeth, a man who cheats on his wife would obviously not have found it difficult to cheat on a lover. Yet had I decided to take a male lover, he would not have been attached to someone else formally or informally."

"Then there's the age-old problem, I suppose. In matters of personal relationships in my view, nothing can ever be hidden. Something will happen, an inadvertent smile at the wrong time, a maid listening at the door and gossip spreading, a neighbor turning up at a place the lovers thought themselves to be invisible, and so on and so on. I suspect that is why the French by and large are quite open about affairs."

"Come, come: What about Simon and you then? You were successfully hiding your affair."

"Oh dear, yes, in our case we did not form any kind of commitment until it was clear Simon and his wife were to divorce."

"That must have been a difficult business."

"My dear, I have told Simon I want to hear nothing of it, just the outcome."

"How sensible."

"Do not tell anyone else," she continued in a more contemplative mood, "but there is a very small part of me, that wants Charlotte to be like me at her age, taking a lover, as I did."

"Let me think about that calmly," said Harriet: "Here we are, two women who have flaunted convention in our younger years by enjoying intimate relations with men outside marriage. I assume you are not saying that you should urge her to find a lover."

"Goodness gracious me, no."

"I read last year that story of Thomas Hardy's, Tess of the Somethings, and wept most of the way through it, this poor blameless child as I saw it, so badly misused."

"One should insist that one's daughters read it, as Charlotte has, and I'm afraid she thought the poor girl was very foolish and she made no critical comment about the seducer."

"Really? A surprising point of view for a woman."

"That's what I mean about her being an adult. She cannot stand people, women in particular, who do not take care of themselves. I am sure I should soon introduce her to some eligible young men."

"Here's a thought. Why don't we bring our children together, Joseph and Charlotte? At least that would give them both experience. I'm fairly sure Joseph meets no women in Cambridge."

"A splendid idea, Harriet. One hopes, of course, that whatever she decides to do does not end in tears."

"I wonder what my daughter-in-law Hannah would say to all this," said Harriet who had got up from her chair and walked to the window where she saw Hannah arriving without her children, which was unusual, "but she is too much of a Presbyterian to enjoy such a conversation, so need not draw her into it."

Hannah was shown into the drawing-room and introduced to Elizabeth and Freddy whom she had met only briefly.

"No children today, Hannah?"

"They are both deep into nursery projects, so I slipped out leaving their nanny in charge. Tom is at some party meeting or other, so I thought I would pass the time of day with you, if I may."

"You know Elizabeth, of course?"

"I know of your husband's tragic death, and offer my congratulations on your marriage, though I fear my religious principles do not allow me to extend my congratulations on this beautiful baby here. No I don't mean that, I mean simply that I regard intimate love as something within marriage not outside it."

"Thank you for the clarification and I quite understand. I was interested in your work in Ireland which Harriet told me about. Now I hear a slight Scottish lilt in your voice, I remember how Timothy and I always had plans to visit Scotland, but somehow we never managed it."

"Oh, you must go. The Lowlands are more like the English countryside, though different of course: and there's Hadrian's Wall, but Edinburgh is a fine city you know, and Glasgow is not far behind, though it has become more industrial. This is not to mention the majestic beauty of the Highlands."

"That sounds most enticing. I will persuade Simon to take a vacation there soon, and perhaps Harriet will come with us, and Pip too?"

When Elizabeth came home, Charlotte was working at a simple Beethoven sonata on the piano and her mother sat down beside her, helping her understand the music and how to interpret it. After that conversation with Harriet, she decided to take the bull by the horns.

"First, my dear, Harriet and I think it would be good for us to meet with you and Joseph, her son, for lunch or afternoon tea."

"That would be very pleasant. I know little about him, but I would like to acquaint myself with men."

"I think so, too, and this is a good moment to talk with you seriously about me, darling. Let me say just some things about life which have become so clear to me in recent years: The greatest gift you have, Charlotte, is your independence of mind, body and spirit. However, as I found out early in my life, full intimacy with a man gives great pleasures, though it must never be lightly given, and only to someone you think you love. I do not believe that that there is only one man in the world for a woman, though I do believe that a man and a woman are lucky, as I was with your father, if you come to feel you were made for each other."

"I think I am quite conventional in these matters, perhaps because I have yet to fall in love, but I would not rush into intimacy before I married, indeed I would not contemplate it."

"Well," Elizabeth replied, determined to conceal her surprise at this reply, "two matters are important in getting to know a man. The first is to care for yourself, ensuring that you do not spoil your future in any way, especially in the most unlikely circumstance that you would find yourself with a child. The second is to care for the man, by that, I mean to respect him even if that respect is not love. Yet, never, ever be used. The plain fact is this," she continued, "in the early time that I was with Albert, life was bliss, but then he went his own way and eventually betrayed me, so let my experience be a warning, but not an obstacle. He used me."

Elizabeth then took Charlotte by her hand and led her out into the garden at Eaton Square.

"Thank you Mamma, I am very cautious indeed, especially since I had a long talk with Simon about Frederica. He was so wise and helpful. Yet I also have two older brothers, so I hope I would be able to manage any complications with a man."

"Yes, you handle those two with great panache," and she smiled.

"I would like to meet Joseph, from what I know he is a solid type. I cannot do that on my own and, thank goodness, I have not had to deal with that awful business of coming out."

"Had your father been alive, he might have insisted you come out, but I would have tried to thwart his plans," and they both laughed. "At least meeting Joseph is a start. He's a scholarly fellow too, I am told, and I am sure he'd be interested in your studying matters of race."

Neither of them knew at that point that Harriet had walked up the street and confided in Mary, telling her of the plan to bring Joseph and Charlotte together.

One singular social feature of Victorian and Edwardian England was the dinner party, an occasion in which romance sometimes bloomed or wilted, gossip was exchanged, family troubles were revealed, and where politicians and their wives plotted and schemed. Delicious.

The status of a hostess in Edwardian England depended in part on class and status. Aristocrats such as Hanah de Rothschild, married to the former Prime Minister Lord Rosebery with a home like a palace, was at the top of the social tree. The richest of the duchesses such as Westminster or Bedford even Scottish duchesses like Buccleuch were equally distinguished, and each could solidify their status by their association with royalty.

The only possible claimant to true aristocratic status among this group of friends was the former Elizabeth Egerton, now Mrs. Simon Brandram. Her maiden name was Fitzroy, the name originally given to the bastard son of a king. Yet the Fitzroy family needed no extravagant display of wealth or status, indeed successive family patriarchs had regularly rejected any elevation to the peerage partly because they despised the House of Hanover, those damn Germans with their uncouth ways, but also because they were of a thrifty and careful ilk. Yet one of Elizabeth's uncles was a shooting chum of the Prince of Wales. For the most part rather than being denizens of Victorian society the Fitzroy men gravitated to public service much like Elizabeth's father who had been a diplomat.

It was also a peculiarity of British aristocrats that they regularly called each other by their titles or surnames, taking their cue from Queen Victoria who liked to talk about herself to others as the Queen, or Trollope's Pallisers who so clearly manifested the practice, calling each other Duke and Duchess. All and sundry at the right social level addressed the Duke of Wellington as Duke, not Arthur. Political titles were similar: no one would have thought of calling a Prime Minister anything but Prime Minister, unless they were very personal friends, with the exception of Lord Salisbury whom all his peers and friends appear to have called Bob.

The MacDonald dinner party, however, was planned to support Malcolm and Tom with their political aspirations, not to burnish their status with aristocratic and titled guests. Nevertheless Mary and Hamish spent some time deciding who to invite, though the date was fixed – Thursday, September 29th.

"The Gargery families, Pip and Harriet, Malcolm and Clara, Tom and Hannah, the newly-weds Simon and Elizabeth and our senior politician and his lady, Clarence and Emma. Angharad should certainly come," said Mary, starting to construct an invitation list.

"I'd like to get to know Augustine Birrell," said Hamish. "He's a very distinguished lawyer and an MP. He changed constituencies in 1900, poor man, and then was defeated in 1900. He'd be in a Liberal Cabinet."

"I know of him, Hamish. He published a Handbook for Liberals a year or so ago, and I promptly sent copies to Malcolm and Tom. So Birrell and his wife too. I suppose we should ask Winston Churchill, though I am not sure he is even 30, younger than Malcolm and Tom, but clearly a rising star. I wish Emily Hobhouse was back in London, but she is in South Africa and, in any case, is apparently unwell."

"H'mm, but I am sure Churchill detests her."

"Then he's a fool. With us, that will be sixteen, six couples with Angharad and Churchill," Mary concluded.

"I would like us to present a very splendid dinner."

"Do you mean five or seven courses, Hamish?"

"Five plus desert, as we had at the Lord Chancellor's last year. Oysters to start, then soup, fish next, followed by the entrée, followed by a roast of beef and appropriate vegetables, then asparagus to clear the palate and a salad with game. We could ignore the salad and have desert."

"Wine with each course, I suppose?"

"Indeed."

"Then you must go down to the cellar and choose it. We will have cook get more staff to act as butler and waiter or perhaps we could borrow Abdul. The important achievement will be to have Birrell and Churchill, my dear, established Liberal figures to foster their support for Tom and Malcolm, and of course with Clarence backing them as well."

"Certainly."

"What would you say to our inviting Harriet to bring Joseph and Elizabeth to bring Charlotte? I'd like a couple of young people to hear politicians make fools of themselves."

"No objection, my dear, they will be a silent adornment, but do seat them together or they be embarrassed by noisy politicians."

It had been six months since the McPhersons returned from India. Before they left London for Scotland, Cecily attended Mr. Wilson and Sir William Gowers, the leading medical figures in work on Parkinson's disease, but although they seemed to understand the nature of the disease and its trajectory, they offered no real hope of a cure. Jeane had rapidly made the accommodation for Alec and Cecily's use in the McPherson home in Edinburgh, his elderly parents now dead. Her photographic business was growing and Alec took a strong interest in it, but it was Cecily's decline that occupied most of their time in the family home.

Death came more quickly than expected that September. Alec found her one afternoon, her face now calm, as death had brought her relief from this crippling infliction. Her countenance seemed restored to its former beauty, and he wept and lay next to the corpse for an hour before he felt ready to tell his children. It was the worst of Scottish weather in early September when the sodden cortege with its black horses made its way slowly through the granite streets to a small cemetery on the outskirts of the city. Cecily would have been thirty-eight years old in November.

Alec particularly valued the presence of the Gargerys among the small group that travelled north for the funeral, though, if truth be told, it was a relief for both Malcolm and Tom to get away from the grind of constituency appearances. Many believed an election would be called before the end of the year, but there had been a lull in the early Autumn in the activities of campaigners. Pip and Harriet decided to come north too, though they scarcely knew Cecily but Alec had been a friend of Malcolm's in his military days and if weather permitted, they would then tour the Highlands, a trip they had talked about several times in the past.

The reception at Alec's house passed off with all its usual patterns: Short tributes, small cakes, plenty of whisky and a few tears, the children Hugh and Alexandra trying to be brave at the loss of their mother and wondering why people could appear so jolly as if a wake were some kind of party. After breakfast the following day Alec and Malcolm were having a conversation in the small library.

"She wanted to be buried under a jacaranda tree in the Plantation, Malcolm," said Alec wistfully.

"You didn't want to take her back there, though, did you?"

"Good Lord no, but of course she was born there, it was her real home. It has been a hard and cruel time for the children and me watching this slow deterioration. I feel as though I am being punished in some way."

"Why on earth should you feel that? She had this disease and nothing you could have done could have stopped that."

"Aye, I know, but I still feel guilty about it."

"Again, I really do not know why you should feel such guilt, Alec."

"I am going to confide in you because I will go mad if I don't have someone share my secret."

"Oh dear, what on earth is this about?"

"I had a lover in Simla whom I used to visit whenever I took a break from the plantation. In fact our relationship began before I was married and continued after she was married too."

"Goodness me, there must have been a very special attraction."

"We might have been excited to marry, though we never discussed it as the difference in our stations made it quite out of the question."

"I am fascinated, go on."

"You must swear never to tell this to anyone, not even Clara."

"I will try, I promise."

"She is now the Maharini of Pratish."

"The wife of a Maharajah?" Cried Malcolm, leaping out of his chair.

"Be quiet, man, be quiet."

At that moment, Clara came into the room asking what the noise was about.

"I was just telling Malcolm about the elephants my father-in-law kept, Clara, and about how I had to handle them after he died and one of then pulled me up by his trunk and sat me on his back and I swear I could hear the other elephant laughing."

"What did you do?"

"I sat there for about ten minutes while the elephants chortled between themselves and my elephant then got down on his front knees which enabled me to slide off to the ground. Then I took his trunk and blew into it which, my father-in-law said, was like kissing the animal."

Meantime, Hannah and Tom had returned from their walk with the children and joined the others in the Library.

"What are your plans now, Alec. You are still a young man, a mere thirty-five is it?" said Hannah.

"I intend to leave a life of leisure for a while, ensuring that the children settle here properly and cope with Cecily's passing. I am going to help Jeane with her business, but apart from that I have no plans."

"Why not travel?" Asked Malcolm, breaking into conversation with him.

"Of course I am unfamiliar with Europe and its many treasures, even Asia Minor and the Levant, but I could not possibly do that without a companion."

"You know," said Clara, "why don't we all meet next summer at our house in Provence and visit those Roman places like Arles and Nimes, even Avignon and maybe venture into Spain."

"Goodness me, do you have a house in the south of France?" Asked Alec. "I am beyond excitement at the possibility."

"I am sure the Smythes will be at their chateau at the same time too," said Clara.

"Who are they?"

"Great friends actually, he is an MP and a lawyer and they have this big rambling place nearby."

"How wonderful, a summer house party in France. My children will love it."

"All the children that want to come can, though it is usually the youngsters."

"Indeed," said Malcolm as Tom came into the room, "but we politicians have to return to London this afternoon."

"I have an early meeting tomorrow," said Tom, "so are the older Gargerys coming to the train as well or heading north? I know Hannah is staying on with the children for a while, is that not right, darling?

"Yes, darling."

Malcolm shook Alec warmly by the hand, and said:

"Whatever your fate, it is excellent to see you again back home and I hope those lovely children of yours can cope. We'll see you in France then, but before that I expect."

"We will be thrilled to come."

Angharad travelled from Cardiff on the train and was very excited as she had been invited by Mary to a large political dinner party on behalf of Tom Hesketh and Malcolm Gargery, both of whom had become candidates for the Liberal Party. Yet Angharad was muddled about politics, thinking that her sympathies would be with the Labour Party for she thought Kier Hardie the nicest of men, yet her friendly indeed over-friendly relationship with David Lloyd George made her think more of the Liberal Party. She would probably support the Liberal cause.

Mary's customary worries about the dinner were enhanced by being very much on her guard about Winston Churchill. In 1904 his parliamentary behavior had made him a constant topic of the newspapers, especially as in the summer he crossed the aisle from being a Tory and became a Liberal, a sensational move which those on the Tory side viewed either as a tragedy because of his talent or good riddance because of his ambition. Mr. Birrell at least would provide a calmer political presence.

"I am getting too old for this kind of palaver," she told Hamish.

"No, my dear, you are a social expert after so much practice."

The party assembled in very good order.

"I must congratulate you, Churchill, though it is some time since your speech about money as the Mammon which dominates our lives," said Hamish as the soup was served.

"Thank you, Sir Hamish, Now that I have crossed the floor I feel much more comfortable confronting the various evils and legacies of the present administration which I am sure it will soon be consigned to the outer limits of the galaxy."

"It is a singular achievement for you, Lady MacDonald," said Mr. Birrell, "to have lured our friend to our midst. Although he is still a young whipper-snapper we all expect his ascent to be like that of a meteor in Parliamentary circles."

"Now then, now then, Augustine," said Churchill, "but thank you. I must confess to ambition as my major vice, made of sterner stuff, I hope."

"As long as you do not overreach, like your father," said Clarence playing the older statesman.

"I won't discuss him any longer in any but the most private of circumstances."

"Ambition takes a great deal of courage, Mr. Churchill, although you need friends, I am sure," said Mary.

"Ah, Lady MacDonald, the wise man will tell you that if you want a friend in politics, keep a dog, though I prefer a pig myself. You know where you are with a pig," at which there was laughter around the table.

"I am so glad you are now with us, Churchill," said Malcolm. "I said to myself after that meeting at General Blood's in Delhi that I would follow you, and now here we are, but had you stayed a Tory, I am afraid that would have been difficult."

"Thank you, Gargery. Those were fine times in India, mostly playing polo."

"Incidentally Mr. Birrell," said Tom, "I must congratulate you on your most helpful book."

"What book is this?" said Clara.

"I put together a book with a clumsy title, but its subtitle reveals it as *A Handbook for the Use of Liberals*. For reasons that are impossible for any rational man to understand," he said with a smile, "my constituents at the last election indicated that they had enough of my services and sent me packing. That gave me time to put the book together, but I do have a constituency for whenever the next election comes. When do we expect it, Churchill?"

"I'm not a gambling man, but it could be as early as next month. Though I don't know my man well, my Tory friends of whom there are almost none tell me Arthur Balfour is tired out. Of course, he's been done in by Chamberlain's peregrinations around tariffs. That man just want to line his own pockets, I believe."

"If Balfour goes, Tom and I must gird up our loins for the battle."

"This administration is weary, Mr. Gargery, and the surprising thing about politics is that for many people, especially those in high office, an election defeat often comes as a relief," said Birrell. "The dust has accumulated and the cleaners are needed to freshen up the place. That will be we Liberals, I am convinced."

Both Harriet and Elizabeth were delighted both to be asked to attend this illustrious gathering and even more interested that Mary should invite them with their respective children. As they were quickly seated shortly after they arrived, there was no opportunity to talk. So dinner and conversation proceeded.

"Let us hope so," said Tom rather grandly, finishing off his entrée and carefully wiping his mouth with his napkin, "for those of you who are unaware, in this book Mr. Birrell has set out all the matters under headings which the present administration has handled, with quotations from their luminaries and detail of the Bills that Liberals have put forward as contributions to their solution. It is a book which a neophyte candidate like myself and Malcolm find invaluable."

Angharad had been sitting quietly throughout the dinner, almost but not quite overwhelmed by the conversations among people she had only read about in the papers. She thought Mr. Birrell was charming, if a bit ugly, and that Churchill man was interesting enough but obviously quite a killer in his own way. She noted the two young people who both looked as if they would not say boo to a political goose especially the ganders around the table.

"Is there anything about Wales in your book, Mr. Birrell?" She asked across the table.

"Indeed, Ma'am. Religious equality, temperance, land, these are the major issues of which I wrote and this Government has violated some of the deepest convictions of the Welsh people."

"Well, it is true that we are in the midst of a religious revival and that is a Nonconformist affair, but I am especially interested in the plight of the miners. I am told that House of Lords blocked safety regulations..."

"As they will block all Liberal measures in the future, I am sure," said Churchill.

"To be honest..."

"We would expect no less," said Churchill, interrupting in a jocular way and smiling around the table for approval.

"Please don't interrupt, Mr. Churchill, or someone might accuse you of bad manners," said Angharad tartly, at which Joseph almost died of shock.

"I beg your pardon, Madam," Churchill replied.

"I am very fortunate to have become a wealthy woman through no effort of my own and I am devoting portions of it to supporting miners' families in their distress. You see, I cannot understand why coal is not regarded as the lifeblood of the nation and why those who bring it up from the ground are not given due respect."

"Mining," said Churchill, "is indeed a hazardous occupation, but the owners surely know that they must treat their people with respect or their businesses would collapse."

"I thought your argument about capital," said Hamish, "was precisely to point out how such owners think only of money and disregard the welfare of their laborers."

"I admire the miners, but not when they strike, as they did in recent memory."

"I can see you need a lesson, Mr. Churchill; you need to get down to the Welsh Valleys and see the conditions under which that different race of people live." At hearing the word race Charlotte sat up in her chair like a jack-in-a-box but soon relaxed when her mother smiled at her from her end of the table with a plea for silence in her eyes.

"Mrs. Llewellyn, I read about the conditions of poverty in York and I am beset with alarm about our army in South Africa when so many men were turned away as undernourished. That must be corrected. I suppose it is the very idea of a strike that offends me, something that has only occurred with the growth of these trades unions, surely an abomination we have to suffer."

She was sitting at the table next to Simon who whispered,

"I must congratulate, Mrs. Llewellyn, in my eyes you have just made a fool of that Churchill man."

"The problem is, Mr. Brandram, that English people regard the Welsh as an appendage, or like a child to be put in a corner and forgotten about."

"Almost like the black people in America?"

"I suppose so, certainly miners are treated badly, but they are not property, are they, don't people buy and sell negroes over there?" Charlotte was now very intrigued to hear this conversation, bending her ears to catch the conversation.

"They do, but I sometimes think about men tied to a job as becoming part of the machine producing something."

"How interesting, I have never thought of it like that: It sort of makes them less human doesn't it?"

"It does indeed, Mrs. Llewellyn."

Such were the political arguments round the table until the ladies withdrew and the men continued the discussions about the coming election. At the dinner table, both Joseph and Charlotte had listened with interest to the fascinating conversations, each very much aware of their neighbor, exchanging smiles from time to time, especially when asparagus was served, a vegetable neither of them could easily stomach. Charlotte imagined such after-dinner occasions to be dull and boring, focused on gossip or trivia, but she was surprised that her mother started a serious conversation.

"Talking of treatment of those beneath us," said Elizabeth once the women were served coffee, "my daughter and I once witnessed a lynching."

"What?" cried Emma, as the other women stopped at her remark and began to listen.

When she finished the description, a high horse came galloping out of its stable with Angharad in the saddle to redirect the conversation.

"I am sorry to harp on this," said Angharad, still steaming inside at this terrible man Churchill, such a know-all, typical of upper-class men. "Of course killing like that is terrible, but treating the miners badly is not killing them directly, but then mine owners should often be blamed for deaths as conditions are so poor. But in general it is the way people can treat others badly in so many ways that shocks me."

Conversation then proceeded on mining matters until the men finished their port and cigars and came in, most of them proceeding to the table for coffee.

As the party was breaking up, Joseph asked Charlotte if they might meet privately. She looked at him carefully and replied:

"We were supposed to meet with our mothers, I believe, but I'd love to, perhaps you would call at my home in Eaton Square tomorrow and we can go for a walk?"

They walked out of the MacDonald's home together, talking easily about the conversations they had heard, as their mothers joined them.

"An excellent evening, Mamma," said Joseph, "and, Mrs. Brandram, I am so delighted to have met Charlotte."

Elizabeth gave Harriet a splendid smile as they all said good night, leaving the politicians still arguing.

"It has been a wonderful evening, and we politicians must prepare for battle," said Birrell, "Clarence, are you planning to be on the campaign trail for these two aspirants."

"Most certainly, but CB wants me in his inner circle plotting the next government if I understand him."

"Who is CB?" asked Angharad.

"Sir Henry Campbell-Bannerman, the leader of our Party."

"Tell me, am I allowed to give you politicians money to support your campaign?"

"Yes indeed, Mrs. Llewellyn, we would be most grateful. Such money goes to our staff and our costs, not, I must confirm into our private pockets," said Churchill.

"Then I will make donations to each of you, impressed as I am with your vigor and enthusiasm and I will expect you to pay attention to issues in Wales if you are in government."

"Nothing will give us greater pleasure," said Mr. Birrell, "I have the sense that a Liberal Administration will be one for this new century."

Later Hamish and Mary sat in their drawing-room, reviewing its success.

"It will be quite strange to have a Liberal Government after this long period of Tory control, though we should not assume that will come."

"It seems to me inevitable," said Mary, "but as I read the newspapers there are so many complicated problems for them."

"Let us count," said Hamish: "The Irish problem is not settled, the trades unions are a challenge, there's the education mess to sort out after that dreadful Act of 1902. Then there's the matter of pensions and taxation in general. I also anticipate a crisis with the House of Lords for the stick-in-the-muds there will hamper most Liberal legislation."

"Surely they will see sense and not go against the express will of the people."

"I wish that were true, but these aristocrats are unlike ordinary people. They will fight to keep their power and their wealth."

"I was fascinated," said Mary, "by Clarence being in CB's circle. As he is leaving the Commons, I would not be surprised if he were given a peerage."

"Well deserved too, an exceptional man of great integrity. Isn't it strange, Mary? I was hired when there was only Jaggers and Old Pip, and it was not clear whether the practice could survive as Jaggers was losing his faculties. Then the merger with Courtisone, the hiring of Clarence, the move the Old Square, additional lawyers, then my elevation and now we are one of the most respected practices in London."

"It is such an achievement, isn't it, when you rattle that growth off in a sentence. Jaggers and Wemmick would be astonished."

"By the way, was this your intuition that a Pirrip-Egerton romance might be a possibility?" he said as he rose from his chair

She gave him an enigmatic smile, as he took her by her right hand raised her from the seat, put his arms around her and kissed her warmly.

"Clever woman, and I would have been nowhere but for your love and counsel."

"Oh nonsense, you are an exceptional man, even for a Scot," and they laughed gently and went upstairs to bed.

XIX

"Here we are, my friend, about to engage in the most serious battle of our lifetimes."

"I don't see it quite like that, Tom. I think we are aspiring to be do our particular patriotic duty by serving our constituents in Parliament. I am always suspicious of military metaphors in politics, except of course for the fun we had in Battle that time."

"That is so, but before we get finally into the fray I would like to spend some time trying to understand where we might be in a few years' time and what it is about the Labour Party that seems to be so attractive."

"We might consult Birrell or Churchill, I suppose, but they will now be far too busy although we did meet them at the MacDonalds a couple of months ago. Let us take Clarence to lunch and try to get him in a philosophical mood. He is an extremely intelligent man and I am sure he has thought deeply about politics, but I do so long for Balfour to resign."

Two mornings later after a flurry of messages had been exchanged, the aspirants arrived at the offices of the retiring Member of Parliament and Robert showed them in. Various jokes were exchanged as it was November 5th, Guy Fawkes Day.

"'I am sure you two will blow up Parliament with your rhetoric," said Clarence.

"As things stand we may have to blow up the recalcitrant House of Lords," Tom replied, "though not, of course if you ever get a peerage and are in the Chamber."

"I wish sometimes I had had more experience with explosives when I was in India."

"More trouble than they're worth," said Tom and with that Malcolm said:

"Many, many thanks for seeing us, Clarence, and we would very much like for you to paint a canvas of politics, broad and far-reaching, beyond the challenges of the coming election."

"It is interesting that you should ask because I am considering penning a book on just this subject. When there is a dissolution of Parliament, I will be free as a bird, or would be, were it not for the briefs that Robert sends to me daily and I suspect CB will find me something to do."

"I am surprised," said Malcolm, "at the rise of the Labour Party and it will be interesting to see how many seats they get. I gather we have some arrangements in constituencies we are not likely to win that will have just one opponent to fight the Tory."

"Indeed but that gives me cause for concern. If these Labour people win over fifty seats we will no longer be the party in sole occupancy of the left wing of politics. We will be fighting future elections on two fronts."

"I have toyed with the idea of becoming a Labour candidate, Clarence, but I don't see how I could every get a constituency."

"You see! If an intelligent fellow like my friend Tom here can even consider that, think of the thousands of voters who might feel likewise, armed as they will be with a desire to shake up politics."

"Don't dream of doing that, Tom. It would be a fool's errand." said Malcolm, "but Clarence, I am very curious about Chamberlain?"

"He's a stiff-necked Unitarian and once he got the tariffs idea he stuck with it and wrecked his own party as Free Trade has been at the core of agreed imperial policy for decades. Protectionism and Tariffs indeed: are we really so afraid of the industries of other countries? Frankly, I was stunned by him, returning from South Africa with this gospel of tariffs surrounding the country's economy like a wall, through which only our imperial countries could be allowed a hole! Outrageous, but it did destroy the Tories who are now split more than ever.

"But let me paint a broader picture. The Conservatives in general, and Balfour in particular, regard governing as a leisure pursuit. There will come a time sooner or later when there will be a constitutional crisis over the House of Lords for, if we do get a Liberal government as everyone expects, we are going to have real difficulty in getting legislation of any kind accepted, except the budget of course, though they might challenge that, especially if it taxes their wealth.

"Since we emerged from the shadow of the Whigs, we Liberals have been solidly for peace and progress, though we like our wars to be fought by other nations or, at any rate, not near home. We are for a human view of Empire, more missionary Pip Gargery than pioneer Cecil Rhodes. Incidentally a German friend wrote to me the other day saying that one of the foremost theological scholars had given up his university posts and gone to darkest Africa as a missionary. Schweitzer, I think he said his name was."

"What of the Conservatives then?"

"A broken reed, I believe, though who knows what the future will bring. Their in-fighting was always nastier than ours but Chamberlain has unleashed a dog-fight and it is difficult to see who or what will emerge."

"If Balfour resigns, will he serve out his Parliamentary term?"

"He probably will and he is a tired man who may not run again, but if he does, he might well be defeated. I think the King will invite CB to form a government and he will immediately ask for a dissolution which means a January election. When that comes I will be prepared to help, but I must share something with you in the greatest confidence which may or may not actually emerge, but you referred to it earlier, Tom. The Prime Minister has told me he wants more Liberals in the Lords and I may find myself there in January perhaps with a minor Cabinet post."

"Congratulations," said Tom, "and thank you indeed for these perspectives."

"Hear, hear," said Malcolm, "we hope Emma and you will come and dine with us soon, though I think Clara is imagining a Christmas to end all Christmases."

"Good for her: Another celebration always cheers the heart as one gets older."

Malcolm came hastily to their bedroom one morning in early December and the children hearing his excitement came running from the nursery, ignoring their nanny.

"Clara, Clara, Balfour has resigned!"

"Goodness me, what does that mean?"

"I think he has miscalculated. The King must ask CB to form a government and my guess is that he will call an election immediately."

"Then we must get ready. It can't be before Christmas, can it?"

"Oh no, I would expect Henry to kiss hands and then tell the King he wants a dissolution promptly, so we would expect it to begin sometime in January."

"Come here, children," said Clara from beneath her satin sheets, as four children clambered on to the bed and nestled around her in various positions.

"Now we are going to have a very exciting Christmas as your father will be running for Parliament."

"Is it a race then?" asked Andrew.

"No silly," said George, "it's a competition."

"Well, a race is a competition."

"Now then," said Malcolm, "you are both right. There are two of us wanting to become the MP, and some of the men cast a vote as to which man they want to represent them in Parliament. But we won't know until next year when the voting begins."

"I hope you win, Father," said George.

"Me too," cried the others as their nanny appeared and left with them, leaving Malcolm and Clara somewhat nervous that now, after three years, the time for the political test had come.

The Hesketh household was similarly excited.

"This was Clarence's seat, Hannah, and as he is working so hard for me, I think I have a real chance. Of course, favorites do lose, you know."

"Put the possibility of losing quite out of your head, Tom. I was dreaming last night of you standing outside Downing Street waving to the crowds as the Prime Minister. For some odd reason, you still had your real leg and you showed it to the crowd."

"Showed it to the crowd?" Asked Tom.

"And you were making some very silly remarks about 'getting a leg up' and 'putting your best foot forward' and I woke up feeling covered with embarrassment."

"Oh my dear, I am so sorry to have made a fool of myself in your dreams. I didn't tell you this as I thought you'd be angry, but at one of the hustings recently a man in the crowd, obviously a Conservative, shouted out "Show us your leg, you're a fake hero." I did not quite what to do, so I told him to come up to the platform and touch it. He refused of course and the crowd cheered me."

"What did you say then?"

"I said I'd take it off and show him, at which the crowd shouted even more, and it was a foolish thing to say as I realized then that someone might have said 'go on then," and I would have lost the initiative, so I switched into telling the tale of how I lost it, in great detail, which I never wanted to do on the hustings."

"How nasty can men get! I am so sorry, Tom, how awful for you."

"Not really. Did you know Malcolm had the same experience with his eye? He refused to remove his eye-patch, so he told the tale of how he lost it and some men in the crowd jeered until a man stepped forward and shouted: 'I was there,' and it turned out to be his corporal, I think he said Lawson was his name, so Malcolm called him to the platform and shook hands heartily with him and told the crowd what a brave soldier Lawson was in a courageous and patriotic platoon of the Gordon Highlanders that he had commanded, and Lawson stepped off the platform saying what a great officer Malcolm was and how everyone must vote for him."

"What a coincidence, talk about turning the possibility of defeat into a magnificent victory," cried Hannah, "and how wonderful for Malcolm to get such a tribute. I'd judge anyone there who was uncertain about who to vote for would have been decided to go for Malcolm."

"Both of us have had this problem all along. I know that Malcolm has not had a glass eye fitted because Clarence told him he might evoke more sympathy with an eye-patch as it would obviously have been acquired in the service of the Queen. With a glass eye, all kinds of speculations would occur."

"But neither of you have used your infirmities as a vote-catcher, have you?"

"No; except in these two incidents which no doubt gained us more support. We talked about the problem a long time ago when we decided to run. We want men to vote for our policies and our government, not because we lost a leg or an eye on some foreign field or other."

"Now look, Tom. Men are voting for a person, not a party hack. Your personality, who you are matters to the man voting. They don't necessarily want a hero, but they do want a man of character and integrity, as well as experience. A change has begun, some time ago now. Aristocrats at the beginning of the previous century owned the seats in the Commons one way or another."

"That is true. As the franchise has expanded candidates are now not just in the pockets of the wealthy, but genuinely independent. I would not be surprised if I were to be faced with a challenge in the years to come and have to assert my independence, for as a member of the House, I will not have an allegiance to some well-born aristocrat, but to the people who elected me."

"That's all very well, but you are not just an individual soul, but the member of a party with obligations to it."

"Of course, but as that fellow Churchill has shown, there are limits, though I very much doubt whether I would ever cross the aisle and become a Tory. I might have joined the Labour Party, however."

"We must get you elected first. You must expect, dear Tom, not to have anything like Clarence's majority. He has been their MP for years, as you know."

"I hope to get a larger majority than he. I am confident of that."

"Good gracious, with such confidence you will move mountains, but your interest is in foreign policy, and that means Empire these days."

"It does, but European politics is turbulent with the instability in Russia and the dominance of the Japanese military in that war. The Tsar's prestige is badly damaged for now, if not for good."

"I forgot to mention, darling, I had a card this morning from Victoria Eustace to say that John has been appointed Vicar of St. Chrysostom's in Bermondsey, so I am sure we will see more of them. Perhaps we should hear him preach at some point in the future."

Joseph was living at his parents' house in Chiswick after the end of the Cambridge term in early December and at breakfast conversation was always subdued as everyone read the papers.

"Mother, I have been invited to go with a group of young Fellows of Colleges for a vacation in Zermatt in the New Year,"

"Just for a vacation?"

"No, we intend to read all the historical Shakespeare plays together."

"How thrilling and are you seeing Charlotte today?"

"Yes indeed, we will go for a longer walk this morning, probably in Richmond Park."

Since his undergraduate days in Cambridge, Harriet thought he had grown into a somewhat austere young scholar, tall but not gangly, with a sad expression on his face which one could discern beneath his whiskers. Yet when he laughed or smiled, his face lit up and he seemed a different person.

Perhaps his serious demeanor came from his occupation. Of course she also wondered whether he had friends and the knowledge of the Zermatt trip eased her worry.

"I must be gone," said Pip,

"It is such a blessing for you to be so occupied," said Harriet.

"I love Christmas," he replied, "today with other friends and volunteers we are gathering together gifts and food for our church's mission to the poor in South London, Southwark or Lambeth. Philanthropic on a small scale, not like the work of the Trust," and he kissed his wife as he said goodbye.

Later, Joseph called into his mother's bedroom to say goodbye. She was not in the least disappointed that he wanted to stay in London to see Charlotte regularly after their August meeting at the MacDonalds. Indeed, he brought Charlotte with him to the house two or three times and they were obviously getting great delight and satisfaction in each other's company. She even saw that he was holding her hand as they came through the front door recently, which warmed her heart.

Charlotte was at the door when he arrived and welcomed him into the house, taking him by the hand.

"Joseph, it occurred to me that you have not seen Mother's portrait," and she showed him into the dining-room. Elizabeth heard the invitation as she came down the stairs with Freddy and followed them into the room, curious to hear his response. He had never been in this splendid dining room as on other occasions they usually had tea in the drawing-room.

"Oh my goodness, what a brilliant and charming portrait," then turning to look at her with sparkling eyes, he said, "forgive me, Mrs. Egerton but it is one of the finest portraits I have ever seen, quite sumptuous, quite wonderful."

"Are you a connoisseur of portraiture then?" Replied Elizabeth with an innocuous smile.

"Any college hall in Cambridge is littered with portraits of glowering divines and some great men from the mists of time, so, yes, I see plenty of portraits. But yours is quite breathtaking. Most of the portraits I see are forgettable, although I did see a Holbein in Oxford once, but this is of a quite different genre."

"Thank you, Joseph, for those compliments, I am delighted with it too."

"Sargent started it before my father's death and completed it afterwards and my brothers and I were so pleased as it is also a tribute to my father as she looks as she did when he was alive."

"Quite marvelous," he said, looking more closely at the canvas.

Freddy was becoming restless in Elizabeth's arms and Joseph turned to admire him, saying:

"I know nothing at all about babies, I'm afraid, as my life is spent in libraries," said Joseph, his face now alive with a broad grin, "but Charlotte has said there is really something quite remarkable about Freddy."

"Ah," said Charlotte, "I did not tell you exactly, but it is exceedingly rare for an older woman like my mother to give birth."

"I see," said Joseph, a little perplexed as the mysteries of womanhood were still beyond him.

A short while later they took the carriage to Richmond Park, those gorgeous acres of land originally intended as a royal deer park. Both were wrapped up against the December chill and as usual conversation was serious and interesting. Indeed they had walked in town or along the river almost every day since their first meeting, conversing on every topic under the sun, religion, their histories, Pip's health and so on. She had been to Cambridge on two occasions too.

"Odd really," said Joseph as they got out of the carriage, "Malcolm is such a brave man to throw his hat in the ring. Do you think I should help him in an election?

"I am sure he would value anyone's support. When I was in Cambridge for the day earlier this week there was some interesting talk of an invitation for some of us to go to a university in California for three months so tell me, what was the best and the worst of your experience?"

With the gathering warmth and friendship surrounding them both, Charlotte spent several minutes recalling in detail that being with her mother and grandmother was the best, but that witnessing the lynching was the worst.

"What a dreadful experience that was. You must write down your account," said Joseph.

"Why?"

"Forgive me, Charlotte, I am a historian and I believe we should all record any unusual experience in a form that those who come after us can read it. You must write it all down while it is fresh in your memory so that your children and grandchildren can read it."

"That is excellent advice coming from a scholar of history."

"I suppose so, but I am thinking more about family and keeping records for future generations. You probably know my father is a French painter whom

I have never met and I feel I want to know him, not for any particular emotional reason, but because his blood is in my veins and I ought to know him."

"Do you really want to do this or is it a passing fad?"

"I am intensely curious, though my mother probably does not really want me to explore my origins, and we have not talked about it for a year or so."

"I think you should seek him out. In my family we find huge delight in the doings of our forebears. For instance, my great-aunt after whom I am named was married to a mad Norfolk Vicar and the legends about him are such fun, though I am sure it did not feel like that to my aunt. Who knows what you might discover about your lineage?"

"That is true and so encouraging and you have helped me to make up my mind, I will go sometime to seek him out, perhaps on my way back from Switzerland."

They dismounted from the carriage and began their walk, hand in hand. Charlotte was discovering that under this shy exterior was a most attractive young man and now that he had revealed his paternity she could see the French countenance in him, quite apart from his telling her of something so intimate, but he continued:

"I am a confused man, Charlotte, here am I locked in this ivory tower with only men for company. There is still considerable hostility to a don being married. I await being elected a Fellow on my college which would give me lifetime privileges, but I feel as though I am looking down a narrowing tunnel with colleagues who are mostly terrible bores. All that apart," he said quietly, "I must confess that I am sure after these months that I love you."

He turned to her, and carefully, gently, and seriously kissed her on the lips for the first time, the warmth of their kiss so different to their faces, cool in the December air.

"Let me tell you this, Joseph Gargery," grasping his hand tightly, "I love you too, and you are not to condemn yourself to some crusty old bachelor domain. You could get a lectureship in London."

"Far too much to think about. Frankly, a Fellowship is no longer my ambition. Meeting you has made me imagine a different life. I don't know what to think of the situation in Cambridge, it is so much wedded to the past. Of course, there are women's colleges now and I have lectured with women in attendance."

"I do not see why men and women should not study together and I am sure many of the young women come to gaze at your beauty, dear Joseph."

261

"Stuff and nonsense," he said laughing as he kissed her with more fervor.

"Seriously," she said as they cut short their walk as the weather was getting colder, "Were I a student, I would be more intrigued by race, I mean, the different races of the earth, how it has come to be like it is, for presumably God did not create a number of different Adams and Eves, each with different color skin."

"Presumably," said Joseph, "Adam and Eve would have been Jewish anyway," chortling quietly to himself in a donnish sort of way.

"No, be serious, Joseph. As you know, I believe there is a God, but I do not believe the Creation story, wonderful though it is. So we have to look to science for origins as Mr. Darwin indicates, and it really is a great puzzle as to how different races often have different physiognomies, if that is the right word. We know from literature and history of how people far away, in China for instance, look so different from those in Africa and so on. How did it get like that?"

"I suppose that is a historical question, though we lack evidence. But always in history if we think we have isolated a difference, we look for similarities as well. Presumably every human as a human being has a heart, liver lungs, arms, heads and so on which, if we think about it, makes the difference in skin or appearance less important, except that the difference is palpable. And of course, human beings conceive offspring in the same way."

"Ah, talking of offspring, can I assume that you would like to have children?"

"Of course, but one thing that has struck me about us both, and I think about us most of my waking days, is that we are rather prim and proper, even conventional."

"What do you mean?"

"I think that you would agree that neither of us would dream of following our mothers in their relationships with men."

"Good heavens, no. I could never become your lover if we were not married."

"That thrills me so. How extraordinary and satisfying it is because I did not know what you might think about us in that respect. I see loving you as close to a form of worship. What I mean by that is that when I think about us and the possibility of our marriage, I think of the physical experience with something like awe."

"How marvelous that we are in tune on that matter. I look at my mother, Joseph, and I love her more than I can say, and Freddy is a miracle, a completely wonderful miracle, created out of the deepest love you could imagine. I know quite well that there are masses of people who treat intimacy as merely a bodily function, and while I am only mildly religious, I do think of marriage as somehow endowed with holiness."

"I agree, but I do struggle with that, for I am a man not conceived in love, I think, but in a profound jealousy."

"Good gracious me, what do you mean?"

"I have not explored this with my mother in a single conversation, but putting the pieces together, as historians do, she decided on my father because she hated Pip going to Africa with Susanna because she loved him so. I'd surmise that she thought of asking Pip to be my father, so to speak, though I'd be somebody else in that event."

"Is that not intriguing, the thought that if one had a different physical father or mother, one would be a different person?"

"Of course one would be a different person, so one cannot really fathom how 'me' becomes some other 'me.'"

"We are decided then, are we not, Joseph, that as our love deepens and marriage becomes a possibility, we will not become lovers."

"To be sure, but please think about what we might do if I get this America opportunity, won't you?"

"Yes, I will. Thinking about your mother. I think it wasn't jealously but she just wanted to have a child, a being whom she could see as her own."

After such an afternoon, Joseph returned home and sat with his mother in the drawing-room.

"Well?"

"I want to meet my father."

"Oh my dear, are you sure? Did Charlotte convince you?"

"Yes in part. She is such a gracious and lovely person, isn't she?

"Much like her mother."

"I thought I would stop in Paris on the way home from Zermatt. I just want to see who he is. I may never want to see him again, and vice versa, but I also think I should meet him. Who knows? He may regret taking no interest."

"I will write to Aristide immediately if I can find his address as it is not for me to stand in your way, darling. Indeed I hope you will find that you want to see more of him. Brush up your French, as he speaks no English."

Elizabeth called on Harriet just before Christmas.

"Charlotte has confided in me that she is getting very fond indeed of Joseph. He is very kind, quiet and manifestly in love with her. He is being very helpful indeed with her fascination with race, and she has visited him in Cambridge at least once."

"That was my impression too."

"Charlotte is quite fascinated to find a man who is serious but gentle and playful.

"Goodness me, but how lovely that my Joseph is finding romance. She will become a great beauty like you."

"Romance? Joseph?" said Pip as he entered the room.

"Yes, He has been meeting Charlotte regularly."

"That is wonderful.

Shortly after Elizabeth departed, Harriet's head was buzzing like a hive, so she troubled Pip who was sitting with a book on his knee, his mouth open, sleeping soundly.

"Wake up, darling,"

"Goodness me, was I asleep?" he said as he gathered himself together.

"Are you not thrilled that Joseph has formed this strong attachment with Charlotte? I am ecstatic. But he wants to meet his father."

"I see no harm in that, indeed I think it will be good for him. We have met Charlotte of course and as an Egerton she is utterly appropriate for our son."

"I have been talking with Elizabeth about them and it appears to be very promising indeed."

"I should also say that I am also very relieved. I hoped that his lack of women friends might convey that he was, you know..."

"Please do not say it, Pip. We disagree so profoundly about men loving each other, but, on the other hand it is a relief not because it would be tragic for Joseph, but because if it were the case it would come between us since you are so strongly against sodomy."

"No, my dear, were it the case, I would do my level best to support him. Fortunately it isn't."

1906

XX

Neither Tom nor Malcolm need to have been worried. Between the 15th January and mid-February when the election was completed, their party won over 400 seats, reducing the number of Conservative to a mere 129 MPs, so that Sir Henry Campbell-Bannerman as Prime Minister led a party with a majority of 358. As usual Clara held a party in late February to celebrate the election which eclipsed even the parties held before Christmas in its magnificence and in the number of politicians who came if only for a little while, Lloyd George, Churchill and Birrell among them.

The size of the victory let loose many a post-mortem on the party now in opposition and Liberals gathered everywhere to talk, especially in the bar at the House of Commons, including those not yet sworn in as MPs.

"We need to think carefully," Birrell said apprehensively, "why was there this huge collapse in their vote? I know the party is split over Chamberlain and tariffs. I know any long-term administration can be exhausted and people want a change. None of us, even David here, promised detailed reform proposals. Obviously the Trade Unions were opposed though their members' votes will have gone to the Labour Party with its fifty odd seats."

"My sense from discussions with people in Manchester is that there is a millennial urge for progress and we Liberals represent that."

"That's all very well, Winston," said Malcolm with some hesitation in contributing to a conversation with such august figures, "but we must put some meat on the bones, education, pensions, reform of the mines and so on. I also worry that if we do not do this, and I saw signs of this in Whitechapel we are suddenly going to find ourselves engulfed by Labour."

"More to the point," said Tom, "we will need to think carefully about our foreign policy, not merely rejecting the Tories' disastrous importation of Chinese labor to South Africa, but what to do about Europe."

"I hope CB gets me into the Colonial Office," said Churchill. "There is such a challenge in the administration of our Empire."

"I am concerned about Europe," said Tom. "Our dreadnought battleship is about to be launched and will outpace and outgun anything the Germans could produce, but we need absolute control of the seas and I am in favor of building ten more dreadnoughts, battleships that make any enemy flinch at their appearance."

"Now, look you," said LG, "we must quickly institute those reforms you talked about, Gargery, but now we have the tools of office, we have to build our electoral support in depth. Consider this. Let us extend the franchise first, and we will certainly have to decide where we are as a party in terms of women voting."

"David, you must leave that alone. We will never get such a bill through the Lords, you know."

"I know, I know, Winston, but it must happen sometime. I am also very concerned about the success of these trades unions, especially in South Wales."

At that point, Clarence came to join the conversation and it was Churchill who asked him, as he had been asked many times before, how he felt about relinquishing a seat in the Commons.

"I have very mixed feelings, but I saw CB today at this request. He wants me to accept a position in the Lords."

"What a splendid idea, it will be a hereditary title so your eldest son will inherit and your daughters will be Honorables, if they are not already honorable," said Churchill, please at his pun.

"Good Lord, he is not making me a duke, merely a baron. Still Emma and I half expected it after the election results, so we have been busy finding a title."

"And which city, town, or hamlet have you selected?"

"Now, Winston, you know I have to have dealings with College of Arms first, but I promise not to become Lord Woodstock. We have looked in Sussex near my family home but that is all I am prepared to say."

Leaving the conversation and signaling to Malcolm to come with him, Clarence held him by the arm into the foyer, saying," Malcolm, I have news that I hope will delight you."

"What's that?"

"I have ordered a Rolls-Royce."

"Oh my goodness, tell me about it. It's frightfully expensive."

"Indeed, Emma took some convincing, and I told her it was an investment which mollified her but when we went to see it, she was all for it. It is a Silver Ghost, six cylinders in the engine, and we talked with Charles Rolls in his Fulham showroom. He is an admirable fellow and he talked warmly of his partnership with Henry Royce. He is especially pleased with the Palladian front of the motor-car where the radiator to cool the engine is placed, and it has a badge of two Rs linked together, quite unlike the tri-star of your Mercedes. I think both Rolls and Royce are engineers though Rolls is now more interested in developing and selling the cars."

"That will be your prize possession I am sure, fitting for your new status as a peer of the realm."

"Yes, I do intend to drive it myself, not hire a chauffeur as people do. I will need to employ a groom for the motor, of course, well, I call the job a groom as I am not sure what to call it, now we're moving quickly way from horses as forms of transport."

"But Rolls told me of various matters which are of interest. He wants to produce the best car in the world. He knows it will always be expensive, but he anticipates selling to governments here and abroad, to monarchs and very rich people."

"So you will be in excellent company."

"Yes indeed, though I am more of an enthusiast for the mode of transport than for the status. I now think I'll be someone who will start racing motor-cars as I have done with horses, much to Emma's distress. However, Rolls had word from an American enthusiast that a man called Henry Ford is trying to build a vehicle which will be as inexpensive as possible and appeal to the ordinary man."

"That's an excellent idea and full of promise I would say, but typically American."

"Yes, I suppose it is, but someone will start something of the same here in Britain, I'd be bound. But you know, this fellow Rolls is a dreamer. You know the Americans manage to fly an aeroplane with an engine three years ago. He is fascinated by the question of whether he could put a Rolls-Royce engine in a flying-machine."

"But surely, those engines are very heavy."

"I know, I said so, but he is undaunted. Marvelous chap, really."

"So when do you expect to get your motor-car?"

"They said nine months or so, December, but there's many a slip."

After dinner on a February weekend evening Joseph and Charlotte sat quietly hand in hand on a wall outside the Eaton Square house. It was six months since the dinner party and they had gradually but easily become strongly committed to each other, chattering away about their family Christmases and about his visit to his father. He had stayed longer in Paris than he intended and rushed back to Cambridge to teach, so only now had he time to tell her about two serious developments in his life.

"What is he like, darling Joseph? Is he as handsome as you?"

"He is in fact quite short, but with a splendid smile and great charm. He told me he decided too quickly not to have anything to do with me after their affair under pressure from my mother because she had told him she just wanted a child, not a friendship. He is now married to a woman Sophie whom I met and they have four children, the last of whom, Gerard, has a physical disorder of some kind and is confined to a chair."

"Oh my, that must have been a lot to digest as it is your new family."

"It was all so interesting. We had two long conversations over coffee at a small bistro in Les Invalides, though my French was as limited as his English. He had moderate success as a painter but now teaches Art at a private studio, which, he says, is really only a supplement to his wife's wealth. Apparently she comes from a landed family in Brittany and they fell in love when she was in Paris as a young woman wanting to become a painter as her mother was related to Beth Morisot."

"And his family?"

"Genteel, as I understood, but with some financial catastrophe in the past involving his father, a banker from Lorraine but I could not understand what happened."

"Was he Jewish then?"

"Oh no, I don't think so."

"Do you plan to see him regularly?"

"I would, but I have now received a formal invitation from Stanford University, California to be in residence for three months." He continued to grip her left hand with his and put his right arm around holding her close.

"Remember I asked you about America? This new university have now asked me and a dozen others from Oxford and Cambridge to help them think about their university's future for three months, beginning in April. It is very well paid, travel and everything including residence. I have discovered that I can get leave from my college. I would love to go, but not without you."

"I am uncertain about that, my sweetheart. I don't know whether there are social or religious obstacles to our living together there, that is, without being married, and it would be a temptation, dearest Joseph, but it is only three months," she said, taking his head in her hands, and looking into his eyes, "I do not want to anticipate our marriage by our becoming lovers, much as I desire it, and I want you to go for your own sake."

"I am so very pleased to hear you say that, my darling, and I will go. I confess I am firmly, totally and excessively in love with you. Let me be conventional, Charlotte," and he got down from the wall and knelt on the pavement holding her hand while she sat demurely on the stone wall.

"Charlotte Egerton, will you marry me? I would like to buy you a ring and for us to become engaged to be married before I go. I love you so desperately that I need to know I can return to you, lonely as I will be the other side of the world, irrespective of how long the time is before we marry."

"My darling Joseph, I do want to marry you. I love you dearly, and the answer to your delightful question is of course yes, with all my heart."

They both stood up and facing each other, and with the kind of kiss that speaks not of desire, but of commitment.

"Three months will give me time to prepare myself as your wife, emotionally of course, but in all sorts of other ways. I am going to have to decide how much I want to purse my study of race, whether I can do that here in London, to think about where we might live and much else. The fact is that I think it will help us if you go to California on your own. It is a mere three months, and you can concentrate on your work there and it will be over before we know it."

He gathered her more closely to him and they kissed with some abandon.

"You are right, darling Charlotte. If we were there together, I would be distracted, thinking all the time about you through what will be endless meetings, what you are doing, what we should do this or that evening."

"But its almost Valentine's Day and you have to be there soon, so we must now plan an Atlantic crossing and a continental train for you as you must be there in six weeks.

"And now we must tell our parents," she said.

"Together or separately?"

"Together but not immediately. Formally, I am not yet twenty-one, so you must ask my mother's permission, but can we leave that till tomorrow. "

"You know, I am quite astonished that you love me, a musty old scholar of twenty-seven."

"My dreams are much more down to earth, Joseph. You are such a lovely person in every way and my dreams are almost entirely filled with the intimacy which we have yet to experience. I want all of you, not just your body. Let us marry when you return."

"Excellent, excellent, but give me a month after I get back to prepare myself."

They kissed gently again for some time, wrapping their hands around each other's heads and neck, then he walked out of the square to call a cab to go home.

The following lunchtime they visited Elizabeth first and were surprised to find Simon at home.

"Mother, Simon, Joseph has something to ask you, and I will leave the room while he does."

"That is somewhat forward my dear, but a welcome to you, Joseph Gargery," she replied holding Freddy over her shoulder.

"Mr. and Mrs. Brandram, I am not sure of the etiquette here, so I will ask both of you for permission to marry your daughter Charlotte."

With a broad smile, Elizabeth said, "I am not sure of the etiquette either, are you Simon?"

"I think the reply should be entirely yours."

"So, you want to marry my daughter Charlotte. I am delighted and the answer is, of course," and she called Charlotte back into the room.

"Well, thank you, thank you, a thousand thank-yous," as Charlotte came back and kissed her mother and Simon and then Joseph.

"You know I am a young don at Cambridge. I have been asked to go to California for three months to a university only twenty years old. They are inviting a small group of European scholars for them to judge what faculties they wish to establish, and I am one. I cannot but accept, out of curiosity and adventure mainly, not from any particular opportunity to work with specific scholars."

"And, Mother," said Charlotte, "we have decided, Joseph should go on his own and indeed he must be there by April 1st."

"No time to lose then," said Simon.

"That was excellent," said Joseph as they left for a walk. "My goodness, your mother is such a beautiful and powerful woman, and I was delighted by Simon's stance to us."

"You should hear her on the piano, she could have had a career as a concert pianist."

They finally arrived at Cheyne Row after returning from their walk and a celebratory lunch with Simon and Elizabeth, with Freddy lying asleep in a cot next to his mother who simply could not bear for him not to be with her.

"Joseph, darling," said Harriet as she led them into the drawing room, "and welcome again Charlotte. How delightful. First, are you lovers yet?"

There was at first an embarrassed silence for Joseph had not experienced just how outspoken his mother could be in matters of love.

"Well, come on, are you now lovers?"

"Mother, that is such a personal question and the answer is simply – no. We have just been to visit Mrs. Brandram and she has given her permission for Charlotte and I to be married."

"How wonderful, I detected that you might have been celebrating. My warmest congratulations to you both," and she took Charlotte in her arms and kissed her saying "welcome, my dear daughter."

"I have told you about my invitation to go to California, and we have decided I should go alone."

"So you are not asking my permission, are you?"

"No, but we do want your advice and blessing."

"I see. We had better bring Pip into this conversation," and she walked to the door and called her husband from his study.

"Oh how delightful to see you, Joseph. And you are?" He said turning to Charlotte.

"I am Charlotte Egerton, Elizabeth's daughter."

"Oh Pip, you are getting far too old, you have often met Charlotte."

"Of course, of course, and I can see the likeness you out mother now, as beautiful as her mother, don't you think, Harriet?"

"I do, but they have been telling me of their plans. Joseph has been invited to spend three months at an American university and they have just become engaged to be married."

"America? Surely that is a dangerous place, is it not?

"That is to be discovered. The University is in California."

"But that is the other side, thousands of miles away and full of earthquakes, as I have been told. I'd be very careful about committing yourself to putting yourself on such a dangerous path."

"Pip my dear. Do you remember a young man who had returned from a distant war with a wounded leg who, within three years, found himself in a harsh industrial neighborhood full of capitalist gangsters and cowboys, let alone the starving poor, with a lover whom he met on a coach?"

Pip laughed heartily at Harriet reminding him of his youth, though she was finding it tiresome that she had to remind him each time it mattered. "Of course, Joseph must go where his spirits take him," he said, "and engaged, do you say? Well, well. Congratulations."

"Yes," said Joseph, "but sadly Charlotte will not come with me."

"When will you leave?"

"I have to be at Stanford University by April 1: A week or more sea journey to New York, then at least two weeks we are allowing for Joseph to get to California, so I must book passages directly."

"Let me know, my dearest son, if we can help."

"I will talk with you about those needs later."

Elizabeth was very excited about the marriage of her daughter and was looking forward to spending the next three months planning a wedding. While Joseph was shopping with his mother, she called Charlotte from her room, saying:

"I have a surprise for you. I have invited almost everyone we know to come for a going-away party this evening. I had a reply from Philip Pirrip to say his country cousins were in town for a few days and he asked to bring them, so I agreed."

The evening party was an exquisite celebration. Henry Egerton led a toast to Joseph in a philosophical mode.

"I want to be quite serious for the moment. We have entered the century full of hope for progress. Indeed we young men and women are living in something of a paradise. We are healthy and wealthy. Our country is not at war. We have a vast Empire. We can travel to exotic places, like California. Sometimes it seems like paradise." he said, at which there was much laughter.

"Now I know that being committed to progress means being ready to meet challenges which events bring to us. But we British are, I believe, uniquely equipped for that. But we must beware of one danger which my dear sister Charlotte is all too aware. It is that of racial superiority, and with it of treating other races as if they were not human beings which I regard as a terrible danger in an Empire.

"Personally I was immensely pleased to learn how the Gargerys, Malcolm and Clara have welcomed the marriage of their butler and their housekeeper, Abdul and Matilda, although we all know and some of us feel, the anxiety of a mixed marriage. I am a young lawyer working in a famous practice, the most senior of whom is a High Court judge whose express commitments to justice above all makes me proud for justice must be the right of all human beings. There is a lesson from your destination country, Joseph. They have spoken and written rhetorically of justice and liberty but have denied them to their negro population.

"I have wandered around a bit now: I have spoken of paradise but remember that the Angel from the Garden of Eden is watching us, so we must not sully it with war or hatred.

"Joseph, we wish you godspeed, and we will a party for your return, but we are also here to congratulate you on your engagement to my beloved sister. I can think of no other man to whom I would have liked to see her betrothed. Let us raise our glasses for a toast," at which there were many a 'Joseph and Charlotte' spoken; Oliver led a verse of 'For they are jolly good fellows' at which Charlotte wept on Joseph's shoulder, Beatrice Smythe hugged Henry for a fine speech, Jude put his arm round Beth Pirrip, and Philip surprised himself by kissing Alexandra Smythe warmly.

Elizabeth had watched these young people with a mix of delight and dread. As the cheers died down, she turned away to go to her bedroom hoping wistfully that in time to come, she would never have to say that Henry's was the paradise the bottom fell out of.

Once Joseph had departed, Charlotte had only a postcard from Southampton of the RMS Cedric, but she did anticipate a letter from New York when the ship docked. It contained everything she needed to know, ideas for their future, continuous protestations of love, descriptions of her beauty especially in comparison to his own self. She had been composing a letter to send to California which was reciprocal to that one she had received. She expected there to be a rhythm established for their correspondence, but that changed early in April.

First she received a wire from him indicating that he was quite safe. The relief was tremendous as the newspapers that morning had contained early details of a horrific earthquake that had struck San Francisco. The city was burning, the damage was colossal and the conditions for any kind of recovery frightening. Later letters were much less alarming. He described the fascinating work he was doing, and his ruminations on the scandal of the murder in March 1905 of the wife of the founder, Jane Stanford, from strychnine poisoning at a villa in Hawaii. Yet that was a small part of the correspondence describing his longing and devotion. But one mutual commitment shone through this correspondence. Not just that they were in love, but that they urgently wanted to be married as soon as possible on his return.

Meanwhile Angharad had come to a momentous decision. She decided to take a reconciliation holiday in June at a village near Saltash in Cornwall, where her daughter Gwyneth's husband Richard Smiles ran a prosperous hotel along the south coast of the county. She booked into the hotel by letter which Richard showed to his wife, and her response was profane if not blasphemous. This couple had two children Ezekiel and Angharad, both of whom were boarding at schools in Devon, an indication that this was a prosperous middle class family.

It was not a happy visit, even after decades of distance.

Matters came to a head on the afternoon Angharad was leaving for London on the last day of June.

"What is the matter with you, Gwyneth? Here we are trying to let bygones be bygones and you seemed determined never to forgive and forget. Whatever is it?"

"Alright, I'll tell you. You gave me a Trust, didn't you, like you did the others. Now I see you parading your wealth in the newspapers as some kind of do-gooder with your fancy ways and fancy ideas. Oh yes, I read about you and I thought this is my mother and that's my money she spending on those miners."

"Oh dear, you are a greedy woman, aren't you? Like your father, to be honest."

"Yes, and you left him to die in Australia, didn't you? He was always a loving father to me."

"Good God, child, he was a filthy brute who beat me up and got what he deserved from the Abbos."

"I bet you deserved it."

"You devil! How could you be so cruel? I have left you and your children more than you deserve in my will, but I can see I need to change it immediately I get back from London."

And so on, for an hour or two after lunch they sat in the garden in the sunshine, both steaming with anger.

Angharad's train was due to leave Plymouth at five o'clock in the evening, planned so that she would be in Claridge's by ten o'clock when she'd be ready for bed. On the way from the village, however, a wheel on the carriage was troublesome, and while it did not give way, the driver said he could not go further. As a result, Angharad eventually arrived at the station half an hour after her train had left and the next train was a boat train from the Ferry due to leave at eight o'clock, but that too was delayed as the boat arrived late from France. She had to wait some time for this late train, as she was not going back to her son-in-law's hotel.

As she sat in the ladies' waiting room on the station, she tried to forget the vicious altercation with her daughter. Now all she wanted was to get to London and tomorrow decide on a Kensington house or flat which Robert was finding for her. Well after midnight, she found herself sitting opposite a man of about her age in the dining car where a short meal was being served.

"Gee, I like the speed of these English trains. I'm Elmer Schultz from the good old state of Pennsylvania, and to whom do I have the pleasure of speaking?"

"Oh," said Angharad who, although as garrulous as anyone in general, observed the British habit of keeping oneself to oneself on a train or a carriage journey, "I am Angharad Llewellyn."

"You English have the cutest of names," he replied, "but have you been long on the Continong, Miss Angharad?"

"No, I missed my train earlier. I have been with my daughter near Plymouth."

"That's swell. I have two daughters. They are married now, but my dear wife passed away in 1900 and I decided to give myself a treat. I'm going to London, then to Paris and then to Berlin where my dear old grandma came from when she was just a little-bitty baby. Now that must have been before the

War, but they were with a bunch of settlers in Pennsylvania from that great land of Germany."

"I was in Australia when I was a young woman," and she was about to go further when the speed of the train bounced them both in their seats, the soup spilled over the bowls in the supporting saucers, and Angharad exclaimed, "to be honest, I've never been this fast in a train, have you?"

"No, and my soup spilled over the bowl, as did yours. Still I suppose we all want to get there as early as we can after arriving late," he said with a guffaw.

"We will get there before we left at this speed," said Angharad laughing, and Elmer let out a roar of laughter such that other boat passengers looked around.

"This good lady said at this speed we'll get there before we left," called Elmer to his American companions."

"This speed is beginning to frighten me," said Angharad, "why are we going so fast?"

She never got an answer.

As the speeding train turned the steep curve near Salisbury Station in the early morning of July 1ˢᵗ it left the tracks and ploughed into a milk train going in the opposite direction. One moment, Angharad and Elmer were seated comfortably, if slightly alarmed; then they were suddenly hurled from their seats on to the roof of the carriage amidst the appalling noise of wood metal, and human bodies, plates, soup and waiters being tossed around, then smashed through glass windows, their bodies finally coming to rest beside a half dozen milk churns spilling their contents on to the track. Pinned to her head was Angharad's hat.

Both were dead, as were twenty-six other travelers. The wreckage of the trains was spread over a couple of acres, bodies so gruesomely destroyed that rescuers turned away and retched before summoning the courage to wrap them in bags and take them to the mortuary in Salisbury. Finding the bodies beneath the wreckage took all the following day.

XXI

"Did you see the news of that horrible train crash near Salisbury? There ought to be rules about speed, Malcolm. There will also need to be limits for motor-cars on the road."

"I find this business so distressing. Here we have these locomotives and carriages, wonderful inventions and yet they attract misuse and catastrophes of this kind."

The crash raised issues about the speed of all vehicles in the public mind.

"I did not imagine trains could go so fast," said Clarence as he looked at the newspapers the day after the crash. "Seventy miles an hour, good gracious, I would have thought they could fly at that speed."

"Now, Clarence, I have been meaning to talk with you about your new car," pleaded Emma. "Please do not speed, for my sake and the children's. If you were to hit anything, especially other people, you would be thrown out of the vehicle and God knows where you might land."

"Do not worry yourself, my dear, I have no immediate intention to race my pride and joy," he said contrary to his remark to Malcolm. "I am too old for that sort of thing."

"The papers are so full of that crash, I cannot bear to read it."

"Nor me, the gory details are too much, though one theory is that as the boat was late, American passengers had bribed the driver to get to London fast."

Similar discussions took place in Cheyne Row.

"Why did God allow us to invent the railways if they cause so much destruction?"

"Oh Pip, it is human error that is the problem, not the trains themselves."

"Those poor Americans: how will their families be informed? Imagine, you're sitting at breakfast in some street in Philadelphia and a message arrives saying that your father or mother has been slaughtered in a train crash far away."

"Yes, I cannot imagine it. Think of what you then have to do to bring your loved one back home."

"Look at this list of those killed. Several American names, obviously. Oh Pip, good heavens! Oh Pip, O goodness me, how terrible! One of the dead on this list is Mrs. Angharad Llewellyn. It can't be her, but it is such an unusual name. Could it be coincidence? I must call on Clarence."

"It can't be her, my dear, why would she be on a boat train from Plymouth? It can't be her, no, I am sure, it can't be her. That would be too terrible."

"Well, I do remember her once saying she had a daughter in Cornwall."

"Even so, we also know there are Welsh communities in America. It is a dreadful coincidence, I think."

"Nevertheless, I am going to call on Clarence."

Early the next morning Clarence, now Lord Wallbury, took the train as far as he could to a point where the London and South-Western Railway whose train it was, had provided coaches for the ride into Salisbury. After questioning a policeman on duty, he found the mortuary in the city.

"Can I help you, sir?" Said the overseer, "my name is Cyril Pewsey."

"Mr. Pewsey, I am Lord Wallbury, senior partner in Courtisone and Jaggers a law firm in London. I have a client, a Mrs. Angharad Llewellyn, and it has been drawn to my attention that one of the deceased in this terrible accident carries that name. Now it might be coincidence that an American lady of the same name was on that train, but I need to verify that my client is not one of the deceased."

"I understand, sir. In normal circumstances, you would have to be a member of the family, but you do need to make sure about your client as I am sure questions of legacies and wills and such would be involved if it were she," he said in a manner that was both official and obsequious. "Please take a seat and wait here for a few minutes while we display the woman's corpse identified, you might wish to know, by her name from an envelope in her handbag."

Ten minutes later, an orderly summoned Clarence to an inner room with white harsh walls and metal cupboards designed to hold bodies and a table on which was a white sheet was obviously covering a body. Mr. Pewsey came with him.

"Now, you must steel yourself, sir. The woman's face is not a pleasant sight. However, among the objects recovered is the handbag which you may inspect afterwards."

Clarence held his breath. He had only seen two corpses in his life, his father's, and at first he dare not view his mother's out of dread that he would collapse in tears at the sight of this brave loving woman who had worshipped him. Yet then he had to say goodbye, so he had looked at his mother's body, nothing like as awful as he expected, with her calm and soft expression even in death. His stiff upper lip had begun to quiver ever so slightly and he shook his head at the memory.

"Please remove the sheet."

Her face looked as though someone had hit her on the nose with a sledgehammer, but her hair was immediately recognizable as she had been wearing a hat, so he was told, which somehow in the turbulence of the crash had stayed on, presumably because of the pins.

"That is my client," he said, his voice breaking, "this is Mrs. Angharad Llewellyn of Radyr in the County of Glamorgan, "what on earth was she doing on that boat train?"

"There are no clues, sir, though boat trains usually carry only passengers from the Ferry. Here is the handbag, sir."

The bag had obviously been crushed.

"Where was this found?"

"My understanding is that the straps were wrapped around her left hand."

"May I open it?"

All the modern accoutrements of a fine lady's handbag were smashed to bits, including a small watch which had stopped at 1.57. Tucked inside an inner pocket was a small purse with some sovereigns and his calling card from Courtisone and Jaggers which he showed to the overseer.

"Look, Mr. Pewsey, she has even written my wife's name on the back with our home address."

"But you're Lord Wallbury, and this card says Sir Clarence Fotheringaye-Smythe. Why is that?"

"The King has seen fit to make me a peer of the realm and it is so recent an ennoblement that my clerk has not yet had the new cards printed. But if I may I would like to take charge of Mrs. Llewellyn's remains. She was a friend, not merely a client. I will pay you the costs of having the body moved discreetly to a City of London undertaker, Grapple and Grapple, and I will arrange for a funeral. Meantime I will obtain a magistrate's permission to go to her house and see if we can get in touch with her children. She told me her eldest son was a sheep-farmer in Australia, one had died of meningitis, but the daughter lived somewhere in England.

"I see no objection to that but the Salisbury Coroner must order the release of the body. The inquest is tomorrow."

"Who is the Coroner for this city?"

"Sir Archibald Clariton."

"Old Archie? Well, well, we were at Cambridge together. I'll call on him immediately and will then find a hotel and send my wife a wire."

"The Red Lion should suit your needs, my Lord."

Sir Archibald and Lady Clariton had a fine house in the close of Salisbury Cathedral, a city where he had built a very successful practice before accepting the role of Coroner at the urging of the Mayor. It was not expected that the job would weigh heavily on Sir Archibald's time but a rail crash of such enormity flung him willy-nilly into the limelight.

When his butler brought Clarence's card on a silver salver into the drawing room where he and his lady were enjoying a glass of sherry before dinner, Archie jumped out of the chair and strode into the hall.

"Clarence, old boy, this really is a surprise. What brings you to this beautiful city?"

"A distressing responsibility, I'm afraid."

"But, of course, I must congratulate you on your peerage. I assume this means a junior post in the new Ministry."

"I fear so, but I am here because a wealthy widowed client of mine was killed in this awful train crash which I only found out from a friend who had read the list of the dead in The Times. I have just come from identifying her remains, as I don't think anyone else could. From my conversations with her, she is estranged from her children. One maybe two are abroad and the whereabouts of the daughter is a mystery."

"How good of you to do this: it must put you out greatly," said Lady Clariton.

"It was the least I could do, Lady Clariton, but Archie, I wonder if you would favor me with permission to have her body transported to a city undertaker in London. My clerks will seek out her daughter and we hope to find her before her mother's funeral. You see, Mrs. Llewellyn was very wealthy after the death of her first husband, though she was the child of a Welsh farmer, but after her second husband died, she became a philanthropist of no mean record, supporting families where husbands had been killed in mining accidents. Indeed the Jaggers Trust and hers are linked through overlapping directors. She has many friends in London from our circle, but at the moment it would be appropriate for her to be buried in Wales, near her home, as I am sure the miners will want to give her a good sending off too."

"Of course, dear boy, of course. They've a reputation for singing and sentimentality," and he laughed quietly.

"Now Clarence," interjected Lady Clariton, "you shall have dinner with us quite shortly and I will be mortified if you do not stay the night here. Then Archie and you can while away the small hours swapping Cambridge gossip."

"That is so kind, Lady Clariton."

"Please call me Mildred."

"Might your butler arrange for me to send a wire to my wife?"

"Of course," and he called out: "Blossom!"

"Yes, sir," said the butler with the unusual name.

"Lord Wallbury wants to wire his wife. Please see to it, Blossom."

"Yes, sir. My Lord, if you will come into the Library, you can compose the wire there."

Since February and their election to the House of Commons, Tom and Malcolm had been discussing when they would make their maiden speeches. The Liberal platform had been put in the mouth of the King when he opened Parliament and debate on the King's Speech was always extensive. With the summer recess coming toward the end of June, they had to make up their minds on whether to attempt to catch the Speaker's eye. That was a difficulty, for the Speaker appropriately called each side of the aisle in turn and as the Liberals were so dominant and had so many new members like themselves, it could be difficult to get a parliamentary word in edgeways, so to speak.

That conversation was being renewed on the sad occasion of the funeral of Angharad Llewellyn. Gwyneth Smiles, her daughter, had been traced by Robert. They searched the house in Radyr and found addresses for Gareth in Australia and Gwyneth in Cornwall, and such a plethora of dresses, jewelry, hats and shoes that left Robert speechless. The furniture on the other hand was quite inexpensive, and there was a small portrait in oils of Dai Llewellyn which Robert admired.

Clarence gave Robert instructions to meet with the Manager of the Wattstown Pit where Angharad had been so generous after the disaster in 1905, so he went north in a cab from Radyr to Porth and then up the valley to Wattstown. Used to open country he found the heaps of slag from the mines on top of what must have been green hills so overpowering that he thought he was in a dark tunnel until the cab completed it journey up the hill.

"Mr. Meredith," said Robert, "I am Robert Gillingham, senior clerk at Courtisone and Jaggers in the city of London and I bring you bad news."

"Any news is better than another mining disaster, Mr. Gillingham."

"You will recall Mrs. Angharad Llewellyn who gave financial support to the families of the disaster."

"Of course! She did more bloody good than all the bloody governments put together. So what's the bad news?"

"I am afraid she was killed in the Salisbury train crash."

"Good God, bless my soul, and her such a splendid woman. Now that really is bad news."

"My firm of lawyers is in charge of her funeral. We have talked with her estranged daughter who, to be frank, seems not to care where she is buried."

"Good God, really? Now that's disgusting that is, quite shocking really, how could a daughter be like that whatever the problems between them?"

"I agree. But my partners wondered if we might conduct the funeral here in Wattstown or Porth and bury her in the cemetery at Radyr."

"Oh, no, there's no cemetery at Radyr, boyo, you'd have to go to Trealaw for that."

"Where's that?"

"Closer to Wattstown than Pontypridd. The boys would go there, but you'd need a chapel first."

"Alright. Do you think some of the miners might want to attend?"

"Want to attend? Robert, my friend, there was hundreds of thousands at the burials of the men who died, so I'm sure there'd be a crowd, and the boys would want to sing too. The 23rd Psalm is a favorite, and, of course Cwm Rhondda, then there's Myfanwy. You know that is about a lovely lady, so it would be a tribute. I attend the Independent Chapel at Cymmer, a bit of a walk to Wattstown and Trealaw too, but I can fix you up with Pastor Jones."

"What would be a good time for the miners to attend?"

"Any Saturday afternoon will see many of them free and better for them to be in chapel rather than the pub."

All the Courtisone and Jaggers partners, together with both Gargery families, the Heskeths the MacDonalds and the Brandrams took the train to Cardiff from the station at Paddington early on a Saturday in late June. Robert Gillingham and his wife came Edith too. Grapple and Grapple might be described as a fashionable undertaker in London, if fashionable is an appropriate word to describe an undertaker, but they had made all the arrangements with Evans and Sons in Cardiff. Evans senior had also spoken with Pastor Jones and a printed Order of Service was available in very large quantities.

Three carriages took the London party to the Rhondda Valleys from Pontypridd Station and as they made their way up the hill to Cymmer Chapel from Porth, the carriages had to slow down as what seemed like hundreds of men were making their way up the hill, although it was a full hour before the service at 3 o'clock.

"Good Heavens, what on earth? Are these men going to the funeral?"

"It looks like it, Clarence," said Elizabeth who was travelling with Lord and Lady Wallbury,

"I look forward to your remarks. Difficult to get right, I suspect," said Simon.

"I have, and Emma thinks they are satisfactory, don't you dear, and we have asked the Wattstown Pit Manager, one Meredith by name, to pay tribute too."

They finally got to the Chapel to be met by the Pastor who escorted them to the front seats where a couple were already seated, and from her looks it was an easy matter even for Clarence to determine that this was Angharad's daughter. Suitable introductions were made, after which Gwyneth said:

"I am most grateful to you, Lord Wallbury, for all this and I am so moved by the number of men who want to attend."

"It is good to meet you, and if I may I wanted to let you know that you will receive a substantial legacy from your mother in the form of stocks and bonds. My Senior Clerk Robert Gillingham knows your address and we will be in touch."

"Oh, thank you, Lord Wallbury. I am afraid my mother and I parted on the worst of terms and it was my fault."

"Your mother was the most extraordinary woman and these men are here to pay her tribute."

Angharad's body was lying in an oak coffin covered with flowers in the chapel which was set out quite differently from the traditions of the Church of England with the pulpit not an altar as the centerpiece.

Before the service proper, the Welsh national anthem *Hen Wlad fy Nhadau* was sung with typical gusto, followed by prayers which Harriet thought far too long as they were *ex tempore* in the Nonconformist tradition. Crowds of men outside the chapel who could not be accommodated took up the singing too, the volume being such that men and women in the main street in Porth two miles away lent their voices to the anthem, for this was Wales, the land of song.

Then Mr. Meredith spoke:

"My friends, we pay tribute today to the work of this remarkable Welsh woman, Angharad, whose bounty warmed the hearts of all of us, especially our brothers and sisters and their families who have suffered from the disasters that bedevil us in our proud work of removing black gold from the land of our fathers."

He continued for a while, extolling her philanthropy but also making it clear that even as pit manager, the owners could do more to relieve some of the conditions under which miners work, which had made him a man popular with his men.

"H'mm," said Simon to Elizabeth in a whisper, "I suppose he has to try to make such peaceful noises to calm the miners' spirit," at which Mary looked along the row with a disapproving look.

Pastor Jones then called Lord Wallbury to say a few words. Clarence got up and stood in front of the pulpit, and his experience in Commons and in courts enabled him to pitch his voice so that all in the Chapel could hear:

"First, I should thank Pastor Jones for allowing all of us to celebrate the life of Angharad Llewellyn, and we are glad to see her daughter Gwyneth here. I suppose that few of you know her history but it embodies the strength of character of a young Welsh woman which we see, do we not, in the wives of those who die in the pits and who struggle to regain their footing after a tragedy, a cause to which Angharad was devoted.

"I have consulted the records in my offices and it all began when a young Australian came to London looking for his father. The lawyers could not help as his father was dead and the young man then went to South Wales in search of a bride and found Angharad, daughter of David Jones, a farmer in Cowbridge. With this husband Ezekiel Unworthy she travelled back to his extensive sheep farm in Queensland where she bore his children. Sadly Ezekiel died after being wounded in a fight with Australian natives, leaving Angharad not merely with children, but a fortune as the growth in the demand for wool worldwide had grown exponentially and his sheep farm had become so valuable.

"But she was still a young woman, not yet thirty-five, and Sir Hamish MacDonald, then a young lawyer helped Angharad gain control of her funds. She developed a long relationship with Llandaff Cathedral as she lived in Radyr where she married Dai Llewellyn, a pit manager whom many of you may have known and they had twenty happy years together before his death several years ago.

"After his death, she came to see our law firm again explaining how she wanted to help mining families. We are responsible for the Jaggers Trust for the Relief and Education of the Poor and together we set up the Llewellyn Trust of which she was chair, and the two Trusts have overlapping membership.

"You can all bear witness to the bounty which Angharad showered on those in great need. In her will, she has left a substantial amount of money for the establishment of a small village hospital at a location in this valley to be determined," at which there were murmurs of approval around the chapel.

"So my friends, let us give thanks for the life of Angharad Llewellyn, a proud Welsh lady of great love, immense fortitude and limitless generosity."

Cries of 'Amen' around the Chapel were the signal for Pastor Jones to say a blessing. Then the choir began to sing the haunting tale of Myfanwy, and it was as if the whole valley was filled with song and melody, especially with the final verse, which, though sung in Welsh was printed in both English and Welsh in the Order of Service so that the London Party could understand it:

> Myfanwy, may your life entirely be
> Beneath the midday sun's bright glow,
> And may a blushing rose of health
> Dance on your cheek a hundred years.
> I forget all your words of promise
> You made to someone, my pretty girl
> So give me your hand, my sweet Myfanwy,
> For no more but to say "farewell".

Then as was the Welsh custom, the men followed the cortege down into Porth and up the road to the Trealaw Cemetery which was flooded with miners all of whom doffed their caps as the coffin passed by in a black hearse led by two black horses with their plumes tossing around as they walked. As he walked Clarence made a mental note to acquire a stone. Gwyneth's husband came up to him and offered a bizarre explanation about the estrangement which Clarence indicated was really none of his business.

The London Party re-formed later in the center of Porth, the gateway to the Valleys, and sped down the road to Cardiff and the London train.

"What an extraordinary event that was, Hamish."

"Yes, the Welsh know how to do these things. You know, she really was remarkable, wasn't she? With that fortune many people would just have bought big houses, travelled and watched it blow away. What an extraordinary life."

"Did she not have any siblings?" Asked Mary.

"We tried to find them," Clarence replied, "but all Robert heard was that her brothers and sisters had all gone to Canada years ago when their parents died."

XXII

One very early morning in mid-October, Horatio was awakened in the Cottage to a voice at his door shouting:

"Fletcher, Fletcher, that house of yourn, she's a burning down. Fletcher, Fletcher … " as he opened the small bedroom window and shouted:

"What you'se talking about, Billy, what's to do?"

"I was passing along the lane by that big house, Numquam or summat and I sees smoke rising from the roof."

"Bets," he said., shaking his wife awake, "Numquam is on fire."

"Throw some water on it, Whaaaat? On my Gawd!"

"I'll get over there now. Billy," he shouted, "wait a mo'!" and he hurriedly threw his clothes and crashed down the stairs, waking every child in the house, rushing to the small stable to saddle his horse and, lighting an oil torch, with Billy following, he galloped along the track in the dark before sun rose, and then across fields. Quite soon he could see the smoke and flames billowing into the air and then flames starting to dominate the smoke. He tied up the horse on the gates to the house his father had made, so as not to frighten the animal and then ran past the old elm tree with Billy, stopping in amazement thirty or yards from the house. Watching the roof collapse, with the vast shower of sparks scattered all over the ruin, he realized that the stables were in danger.

"Come with me, Billy," and they ran around the side of the house to the stables which stood some twenty yards from the kitchen door. Sparks were flying in the wind over the stable and other small outbuildings.

"Them sparks going to fire that that stable, Harry," shouted Billy to the roar of the flames.

"Stay here, I'll get a ladder and a couple of shovels, Billy, and Harry broke open the stable doors and emerged quite quickly with a ladder and then returned, and then came back with a shovel and a witches' broom. Billy had set up the ladder and they both climbed up on to the roof which had a pitch just enabling them to walk on it carefully.

"Get the other end," shouted Harry, now realizing the sun was coming up and the wind blowing the sparks of timber was beginning to relent, but they moved around, Harry with the shovel, Billy with the broom, extinguishing any sparks that fell on the roof.

It took much longer than expected to guard the stable from the conflagration. Meantime, Bets had sent Arthur their eldest to the Bargemen and shortly men began to arrive to offer help.

It was far too late.

The final collapse was the old chimney, the brick and stone crashing through what was the dining room and kitchen with a tremendous roar. The walls stood without their windows, also blown out by the heat.

The men all sat down on the dew-covered grass of the lawn in silence.

"Good old house that were," said Josh. "I remember when I was a young man, I came to help your Ma and Pa, Harry, when your Ma was being attacked by that Whistler fella. Now that was a to-do."

"Yeah, they talked about that sometimes, 'cos they was still ashamed they'd killed a man."

"Now he was a mad dog, that Whistler, anyway the beak said it was justified."

"My Ma's best friend, that Mrs. Pirrip what everyone called Estella, she bought it. Do you know why, Josh?"

"I don't rightly know, no."

"It were like this, see," said Harry. "That Estella, she was adopted by a mad woman, her wot was called Miss Havisham who had her dress caught on fire in the old Brewery House where she lived. My Pa used to say that after she died from the fire, sometime later, that old Brewery House went up in a blaze too, and Estella then lived in the lodge till Mr. Pirrip, he that was the old Pip, found her and she bought this house."

"Now I remember, they took down the Brewery too, didn't they?"

"You know," said Hubble who had just arrived, "I don't suppose anyone will build here again, do you?"

"No," said Harry, "but thank you all for coming, we must just let the fire burn out and I must send a message to my sister who owns the ruin with me."

Late in the afternoon a postman arrived at the Vicarage in Bermondsey with a letter from Kent. Victoria and John were preparing for their dinner and were sitting in the small drawing-room. After the maid brought in the letter and handed it to her, she got up and took a paper knife from her small desk and slit it open.

"Numquam has burnt down," she said and began to weep.

"Never, I don't believe it," said John, suddenly realizing that somewhere in mind his ejaculatory 'never' was translation of Numquam and apologizing though Victoria did not understand what the apology was for.

"'Dear Sis,'" he writes, "'I was called early this morning by Billy who said the old house was on fire. I went over in the dark and together we managed to save the stables, but it is all gone. When you can come down her and we can think about it.'"

"I can't go until next week, I am afraid, dear, but you must go."

It was indeed a sorry sight for Victoria. She had loved the house though it brought back memories of that dreadful time with Albert, but also when her Mum Nellie had lived there after Estella bequeathed it to her. She stood with Harry looking at the ruins, shedding a tear from time to time, but then she looked over to where the old elm tree stood and she knew its wood would be still there, stacked behind the stable. They walked toward the orchard, passing the memorial to Molly, Estella's murdered mother, and Harry said, "what shall we do with that?"

"Nothing, I suppose. But I've been thinking for some time about Numquam on the way here. Why don't you take it over? There's enough land here for a large smallholding. You could have the kids start to work here, using the stables as the base, till the land, grow some vegetables, carrots, parsnip, cabbages, and fruit from the orchard and take it to market. Maybe too, the bricks in the ruin will be valuable for there's no clay here around."

"Oh I don't know about that, but it is true, there's only blacksmith work for me and we've got some bairns to start and they can take over. Doesn't the house also have that meadow at the back? That could be tilled and used. I'll talk that over with Bets, but you'll come and stay the night, won't you."

"I'd love to and we can talk about old times."

"The member for London North-East," cried the Speaker.

Tom rose to his feet, steadying himself on his leg and began his maiden speech. It was October 4[h], 1906. He was fortunate to be called but it was late in the afternoon and the House was not full of eager men trying to catch the Speaker's eye, though Birrell and Lloyd George were lounging on the Government Front Bench.

"Mr. Speaker, His Majesty's Government need to pay more attention to the naval needs of the Empire, begun recently with the commissioning of the Dreadnought battleship. The Japanese Navy has shown last year that it is a formidable force capable of giving the Tsar's navy a bloody nose, if not something worse, such that what was a formidable autocracy is now unstable.

"If we peer into the future, Mr. Speaker, I see the burgeoning of other empires, particularly Germany. The fact that the crowned heads of both empires are members of one family should not disguise the fact that families can have mad uncles and prodigal sons (Laughter).

"His Majesty's Government must not merely seek to stay ahead of others by a vessel or two, but the Empire is so dependent on control of the seas that we should strive to have as our resource double the amount of all Empire navies put together. That, Mr. Speaker, would mean the immediate commissioning of six new Dreadnoughts. To those who would cavil at the expense, I would ask 'can we afford not to?' (Mild applause from both sides of the House.)

"My second theme arises from a study of strategy and tactics used by American generals on both sides in their Civil War. Of great interest to me is the use of the machine gun, and at the Battle of Gettysburg in particular, the Southern Army was devastated by this weapon but that Army failed to respond to the weapon with new tactics, merely allowing men to traverse land and be mown down.

"The British army must be led by officers from the Field Marshal downward who will study battle plans and results in other wars to ensure that new weaponry demands changes in strategies. The Army cannot loose personnel to the extent that it did in South Africa, although I am aware that was complicated by disease. We do not have an inexhaustible supply of men and we must never think of British men as cannon fodder. (Applause)

"Mr. Speaker, to my Right Honorable friends on the Front Bench, I suggest that we arm ourselves with an even more powerful navy to meet the needs of the future not just of the moment, and that the Government order the Army, especially at its Sandhurst College to conduct a review of the effect of new weaponry on strategy and tactics." (Applause)

In the Gallery, Hannah was thrilled to see Tom perform with such elegance. Replies from the Government were non-committal on both ideas, one from a junior minister that enraged Tom, the argument being that the politicians should leave the details of soldiering to the experts. Malcolm hastened along the benches to congratulate Tom, but he was alone in offering support.

The debate on a bill to introduce a national pension scheme was under debate. Clara was in the Gallery most days waiting to see if Malcolm caught Speaker's eye. It was three weeks later that he was finally noted, and, as it was just after Prime Minister's questions, the House was reasonably full.

"Mr. Speaker, I hope you will allow me to draw a bow at a venture in my response to His Majesty's Speech, for I want to set out the primary obstacles to the implementation of so many of the policies the Government has laid out. First, we are all aware that the intransigence of the other place could lead to the Government being unable to fulfil the will of the people. I advise the Government to consider either abolition of that House, the restriction on what it may deal with, or the creation of enough peers to ensure the will of this House is respected (Some applause).

"Second, only thirty-five per cent of adults in the country have the franchise which makes a mockery of our claims to be a country where laws express the will of the people. The Government should immediately move to extend the franchise to all if we are not to expect increasing disorder, especially from women. Their movements have shown immense intelligence and fortitude which should encourage this House to bring them into the franchise rather than use the Law to inhibit them. (Applause and Boos.)

"Third, as a liberal Government with such a command in this House, we should move expeditiously to insist that commerce and industry create pay and working conditions appropriate to citizens of this realm. We must be radical, not gradualist. (Cries of No and Applause.)

"The danger is this. For the upper middle class in this country life is now so prosperous that it acts as a shield to protect them from the conditions of the working class. Members from the Labour Party in this House will recognize this social gulf as their constituents view it from the other side. The very existence of that Party is due to the failures of successive governments to treat those conditions with any seriousness, indeed, in some cases to set up obstacles to their amelioration. (Cheers from Government benches)

"I issue a warning to members of my own party. It is this. If we do not pay serious attention to the mandates that members of the Labour Party bring to this House, I predict that our own Party will disappear as a political force within a generation. (Prolonged boos.)"

Malcolm sat down and Lloyd George rose from the Front Bench to say:

"Mr. Speaker, first let me congratulate the member for East London Whitechapel on a forceful maiden speech. I have no doubt that whatever wisdom there is within the dross of his remarks will be taken seriously by the Party leadership. The difficulty for him is myopia, but then he has only one eye from which the view our situation," and he sat down to mild laughter, but the disgust at the personal remark drew thunderous boos from the Opposition Tory and Labour benches.

As they rode home, Clara expressed her total admiration for her husband and her own disgust at Lloyd George.

"Never will I have that man at my dinner table again unless he apologizes."

"A man with such a quick mind, my dear, can produce remarks from his head as if it were accidental. I will be surprised if I do not get a letter from him."

"You showed you were a prophet, my dear. You pointed out that within the sunny sky there is a gathering storm of some proportions."

Christabel Pankhurst and Annie Kenney had shouted at Churchill in a meeting in the summer of 1905 and demanded to know whether he would support votes for women. The strong arm of the law removed the two ladies, who subsequently went to prison for refusing to pay the fine imposed by a curmudgeonly magistrate. When Antonia had read of the meeting in Manchester in 1905, she was angry with herself that the League had gone dormant.

The quest for the vote for woman was still in the doldrums. Antonia had lost touch with Harriet primarily because she lacked the time with six children to bring up after her husband's death. She remembered that at their last meeting, the League had affiliated with National Union of Women's Suffrage Societies (NUWSS) and that must have encouraged some of the women to wash their hands of the League recently as they were no meetings. The Union had affiliated with the Independent Labour Party which might also have encouraged Liberal women in the League to lose interest. Meantime in 1903 Emmeline Pankhurst had started this breakaway group, the Women's Social and Political Union (WSPU) which was declaring a more militant policy, but care for her children triumphed over suffragism.

However, Antonia was finally stirred to action by Charles Hands an obnoxious journalist in a London newspaper, the Daily Mail, who in April 1906 had coined the word 'suffragette' to describe the women supporters of the suffrage movement. She realized with others that the description indicated just how powerful such a label of women in the movement might be but was further infuriated with a private Bill for women's suffrage that was 'talked out' in April 1906 and the pandemonium that ensued from the women in the Gallery. By June 1906 her mind was finally made up and she visited Harriet who was thrilled to see her long-lost friend.

"Where have you been? I have thought of calling once or twice, but then I realized that your children would be keeping you busy."

'They do, but I am getting increasingly frustrated by the failure to get the vote and I considering joining the WSPU and involving myself in militant action."

"Do be careful, Antonia. If you do that and get locked up, some nosey-parker might want to take your young children away."

"Is that the law?"

"I don't know but it is the sort of thing that women have to endure, isn't it?"

"Is there point in convening the League?" Asked Antonia, "or has everyone moved on?"

"My impressions of the others is that they continue their support but feel they need do nothing. The philanthropic impulse has died away since most of them are, one way or another linked to the Jaggers Trust. On the other hand, in recent years the whole issue has been pushed to the margins of politics as our political life has been so turbulent. It is the militants who are forcing the issue."

"None of the League members have been involved, have they, Harriet?"

"I don't think so, but there was that recent occasion when sixty women arrived at the Commons but the constables admitted only the well-dressed women not the thirty or so who were obviously of the working class. Apparently MPs then gathered. Mary Gawthorpe made a speech and the women stood around her but there was then a real brouhaha as she was arrested and ten of the women were charged with a breach of the peace.

"Goodness me, that is what militancy is about," said Antonia musingly.

"Yes, they refused to pay fines and were all sent to prison for two months, but such actions will merely bring in more financial support."

"Now Harriet, I would like to resuscitate the League and bring in the young women, the children who are of age, and I am sure you know some."

"Let me think, Emma Smythe has two, Elizabeth Brandram has one but she is to marry my son in October, I believe."

"How wonderful: We must talk about that later."

"Victoria Pirrip has two, and I'm sure I could think of more. Emma's husband is in the House of Lords so she may not come. I agree that we should bring in a younger generation. As usual we are bereft of women of a lower class. Of course now we have two MPs in our family, Hannah's husband Tom Hesketh and Malcolm Gargery, my step-son."

"That will be to our advantage, but will Hannah and Malcolm's wife come?"

"I am sure Clara would and Hannah too perhaps."

"Could I impose on you to call a meeting? I think we could meet soon, do you think?"

"It should be here. I am sure Clara would be delighted, but it might be too much to ask her as she is an MP's wife."

Harriet decided to host a meeting of the reborn League on a hot summer day in late July. It would have been impossible for such a meeting to have been held fifty years before this year, and it demonstrated how women's status had been changing and the turbulence to come. Moreover a new generation was on hand to continue the struggle. That all those invited were in attendance showed a consciousness which Marx might have admired but then called it false. Lady MacDonald brought along her daughter-in-law Emily, now into her early thirties but still childless. Victoria brought Beatrice and Nellie, and Emma was there with her three daughters, Sophia, Alexandra and Elizabeth who, while only sixteen, had developed strong views about the suffragettism. Elizabeth Brandram, Antonia Penoyre, Clara Gargery and her sister-in-law Hannah Hesketh came. Margaret Brandram used to be a member, but after her divorce and her subsequent marriage, she ceased to be on the attendance list.

After all were gathered in her drawing-room Harriet opened the proceedings with a brief history of the League which fascinated the many who had no inkling that it was so long established. Then she asked Antonia to start a discussion who said,

"I know that in the past there have been so many discussions about a multitude of matters pertaining to women, but this past year with the formation of the WSPU, the question is necessarily before us as to whether we should pursue the suffrage with the kind of militancy so recently shown in Parliament. We do not need to have a common view about this, though it would make our League cohere, but the pros and cons would be useful to think about."

The discussion that followed was vehement, testy and, if it had been a meeting of men, might well have led to fisticuffs.

"I am in a militant mood," said Beatrice Smythe, "though I doubt whether I would risk prison, because whenever I hear the matter discussed, I feel as though I am somehow second-rate, that men are making decisions about me, and it makes me very angry."

"My dear," said Mary, with a degree of condescension that was not quite rude, "we can manipulate men without hitting them on the head."

"And look where that has got us," said Antonia vehemently, her voice rising sharply. "Mill wrote about the franchise over fifty years ago and for all the words, words, words, we have achieved absolutely nothing. I feel a depth of anger I have never felt before when I read of how women were treated in the House of Commons recently. How dare they? How dare they?"

"Well, I agree with Mary," said Hannah. "An acquaintance from the hospital told me that she had said to her husband that women won't get the vote in my lifetime, and he replied, 'damn good thing, we don't need people like you voting.'"

"Did she hit him?" Asked Antonia.

"Good Lord no, he is the sort that would have hit her back."

"Odd, isn't," said Emma, "how men resort so easily to violence."

"But that is why we have to resort to militancy, Mother," said Sophia, "it seems as though it is the only language men understand, although I do think that the young men in our circle favor women voting, perhaps just to win our hearts," at which there was general laughter.

"What I want to know," said young Elizabeth, "is how far we are prepared to go. I mean, might we assassinate Campbell-Bannerman to make a point?"

"Oh no, we could not go that far."

"Why not?" Asked her sister Alexandra.

"I see the point my daughters are making," said Emma. "Once you start being militant and violent, and your opponents do not surrender, you have to up the stakes and find more militant methods, which of course was where Guy Fawkes found himself and his conspirators."

"Surely, even the most militant of us would not think of blowing up the House of Parliament," said Hannah, "but there is logic to militancy which could lead to that at its nadir."

Harriet had lunch prepared and the discussion continued. As with the women's movements in general, the goal of votes for all women was a unanimous goal: disagreement was profound on strategy and tactics. Nor was the split between the young and the older, but a matter of temperament. Some of the women felt they had too much to lose through militancy, exemplified by Elizabeth Brandram who put the case for non-militant activity well:

"I see the issue as a domestic dispute where the use of force is not to be countenanced. Up and down the land, husbands and wives will be arguing about this. All women and all men should of course have the franchise now in my view. We have come a long way in a century since the 1832 Reform Bill and I don't like upsetting apple-carts. We must continue the drip of sound argument with our adversaries rather than becoming militant."

"That would be ideal," said Antonia, "if men were open to reasoned debate, but when you read the egregious prejudices of men like that Churchill, it is only force that will make him think again, and believe you me, they will not hesitate to use force against us. If we have to become militant, I am going to train in ju-jitsu so I can throw a policeman over my shoulder," which created long and loud laughter.

They did not vote, but among the fifteen of them, it became clear that Antonia had a militant company of Beatrice, Alexandra and young Elizabeth, with Hannah and Emily, while Harriet, Mary, Margaret, Clara, Elizabeth and Sophia were the non-militants. Yet favoring militant action did not mean that the individuals were prepared to engage in militant acts though they would support those who would.

On a brilliant morning, Saturday October 20th, 1906, with that crisp feel in the air that so often marks the end of an English summer, Simon Brandram was waiting nervously for his step-daughter Charlotte on the steps outside the house in Eaton Square. She came down the staircase stunningly beautiful in her brilliant white wedding dress, accompanied by her mother Elizabeth carrying Freddy in her arms. Mother and daughter kissed each other, but without tears and the bride then walked down the steps to her step-father.

The bride had decided that they should walk along Eaton Square to St. Peter's Church and, although a quiet square off the beaten track, neighbors came out to watch. Waiting nervously in the church was her groom, Philip Joseph Gargery, supported by Oliver Egerton, the bride's brother, and the Reverend John Eustace was waiting at the church door for the bride. The Joseph Gargerys planned to live in London where the groom had acquired a position at the University, much to the delight of all his friends and family.

When it was all over and the captains and the kings had departed, Harriet listened as Pip sat in his chair in their drawing room puffing at his pipe, his morning dress somewhat rumpled after the wonderful celebrations at Simon and Elizabeth's house.

"I often think back to my dear father, Joe Gargery, a man whose whole temperament and outlook was one of generosity and fairness: Somehow being just was embedded in his blood and bones. While the idea of women voting would never have crossed his mind, I'd be sure if he had met this galaxy of brilliant women, yourself my dear, this beautiful bride today Charlotte and her mother Elizabeth, Emma, Mary, Antonia, Clara and all their daughters and granddaughters, he would have agreed.

"Tell me what he would have said," said Harriet who loved Pip's imitations of his father.

"Well, my dear old chap, I's awfull dull and I don't rightly know about such matters, but my Biddy, she's a sensible sort and she'd tell me how to vote. Yet you know, as I thinks about it, I never thought about why I couldn't vote, leave that to them that knows things. But if my Biddy's going to tell me how to vote, as she would, it'd be fair for her to have a vote too, wouldn't it? Then if everyone had a vote, we could make it a celebration, and that would be a lark, wouldn't it, Pip?"

Harriet chortled at her darling husband saying "well, at least we now do have a Joe Gargery to continue the name if not the blood-line."

"That would not have bothered my father, a pragmatic man if ever there was one."

END

CHARACTERS

Note: To emphasize that wives are not appendages of their husbands, every living married woman among the Principal and Secondary Characters has their own entry below, although this may seem like otiose repetition.

PRINCIPAL CHARACTERS

Pip (Philip) Gargery b. 1837.
    m 1.   Susanna (née Urchadan) Gargery 1865: d.1883.
            -       Lachlan Finlay Joseph (dec'd) 1867-1877.
            -       Malcolm Philip 1869.
            -       Hannah Emily 1873.
    m 2.   Harriet (née Middleham) 1893
            -       Joseph Gargery (father: Aristide Bruant) b. 1878.

Malcolm Philip Gargery b. 1869.
    m.   Clara Eugenia Eustace (née FitzCuthbert, widow of Sam Eustace) 1895.
            -       Andrew Edward Samuel b. 1895.
            -       Susanna Eleanor b. 1896.
            -       Charles Joseph Samuel, b. 1898.

Hannah Emily Gargery b. 1875.
    m.   Thomas Hesketh, 1895.
            -       Hector Thomas, 1896.
            -       Louise Katherine, 1900.

Harriet Gargery (née Middleham), b. 1838.
- Joseph Gargery (Father: Aristide Bruant).
m. Pip (Philip) Gargery, 1893.

Clara Eugenia Gargery (née FitzCuthbert.)
m   1) Samuel Eustace, b.   d. 1895
- Andrew Edward Samuel b. 1895.
- Susanna Eleanor b. 1896.
- Charles Joseph Samuel, b. 1898.
m. 2) Malcolm Philip Gargery, 1895.
-

Thomas Hesketh. b. 1862.
m. Hannah Emily Gargery,
- Hector Thomas, 1896.
- Louise Katherine, 1900.

Angharad Llewellyn (née Jones) b. 1836. d. 1906
m. Ezekiel Unworthy, 1854 d.
- Gareth, b. 1855
- Gwyneth, b. 1856

m. Dai Gwyn Llewellyn b. 1834, d.1899

Victoria Pirrip (nee Fletcher). b. 1858. m. Albert Pirrip, 1879. d.1900
- Beatrice, b. 1880.
- Philip (Pip) b. 1881.
- Ellen, (Nellie) b 1892.

Hamish MacDonald Q.C. (later Mr. Justice MacDonald) b. 1840.
m. Mary MacDonald (née Hamilton) b. 1838 m.1871.
- James Hamish b. 1872. m. Stella Gilmour 1897.
- Emily Mary, b. 1875.

Mary MacDonald (née Hamilton) b. 1838.
m. Hamish MacDonald, 1871.

- James Hamish b. 1872. m. Stella Gilmour 1897.
- Emily Mary, b. 1875.

Honora Brandram, b. 1842.
  m. Husband Frederick, b. 1830, d. 1885.
- Simon b. 1860 (father unknown)
- Jude, b. 1860, (twin to Simon,) d. 1879
- Jane Margaret, b. 1874

Simon Brandram (father unknown) b. 1862. m. 1875.
  m. 1) Margaret Culpepper b. 1863 (d. of Randolph and Eliza Culpepper)
- Frederica (b. 1877, murdered 1894)
- Jude b. 1879

    2) Elizabeth Egerton (née Fitzroy), b.1852. m. 1904
- Frederick Timothy Jude

Margaret Brandram (née Culpepper) b. 1863.
  m. Simon Brandram, 1875.
- Frederica (b. 1877, murdered 1894)
- Jude b. 1879

Horatio Joseph Fletcher b. 1856.
  m. Beth Horsfield, 1885.
- Arthur, b. 1886.
- Beth, b. 1888.
- Charlie b. 1890, d. 1900
- Dorothy (Dottie-do-da), b 1891.
- Ernest b. 1892 d. 1900.
- Frank b. 1893.
- Georgiana, b. 1897.
- Horatio, b. 1900.

Beth Horsfield b. 1867.
  m. Horatio Joseph Fletcher 1885.
- Arthur, b. 1886.
- Beth, b. 1888.

- Charlie b. 1890, d. 1900
- Dorothy (Dottie-do-da), b 1891.
- Ernest b. 1892 d. 1900.
- Frank b. 1893.
- Georgiana, b. 1897.
- Horatio, b. 1900.

Sir Clarence Fotheringaye-Smythe, Q.C., b. 1840, later Baron Wallbury of Wallbury.

m. The Hon. Emma Sophia Victoria b. 1842 (d. of Lord Eustace) m. 1878
- Clarence Arthur Fitzherbert b. 1879.
- Sophia Margaret Louise b. 1881.
- Alexandra Mary Charlotte b. 1885.
- Elizabeth Anne Henrietta b. 1889.

The Hon. Emma Fotheringaye-Smythe, b. 1842 (d. of Lord Eustace)

m. Clarence Fotheringaye-Smythe, 1878.
- Clarence Arthur Fitzherbert b. 1879
- Sophia Margaret Louise b. 1881
- Alexandra Mary Charlotte b. 1885
- Elizabeth Anne Henrietta b. 1889

Elizabeth Egerton (née Fitzroy), b.1852.

m. 1) Timothy Henry Tatton Egerton. b. 1851 d. 1896
- Henry Tatton, b. 1879
- Oliver Charles, b. 1882
- Charlotte Elizabeth b. 1885

2) Simon Brandram (father unknown) b. 1862. m. 1904.
- Frederick Timothy Jude, b 1904.

Antonia Letitia Penoyre (née Wheeler) b. 1866. m. 1877

m. Aubrey St. John, b. 1866, m. 1887 d. 1900
- Aubrey, b. 1888
- Rex, b. 1890.
- Charles, b. 1892.
- Margaret, b. 1893.

- Estella, b. 1894.
- Ellen, b 1895.

The Reverend John Eustace, widow, b. 1858
    m.   Victoria Fletcher

Mary-Lou, Countess Wassilko Serecki (nee Beauregard) b. 1837. d. 1904
    m.   1) The Honorable Henry Fitzroy. 1854
           -      Elizabeth b. 1852
    m.   2) Count Wassilko Serecki b. 1841. d. 1895

Gwyneth Smiles (née Unworthy) b. 1856
    m.   Richard Smiles, 1885.

SECONDARY CHARACTERS

Robert Gillingham. Senior Clerk Courtisone and Jaggers.

Aaron Levy b. 1841.
    m.   Alice Jane Steinhardt, 1886

Alice Jane Levy (née Steinhardt) b., 1844.
    m.   Aaron Levy, 1886

Adam Masterson b. 1847 m. Anne Bright 1869
           -      Henrietta , b. 1871.
           -      Arthur 1873.

Simon Harold Garthwaite. b.1858, m. Sarah Higginbotham, 1880

Jeane MacPherson, friend to Hannah b. 1876.

Alec MacPherson, b. 1869 formerly Gordon Highlanders
    m.   Cecily Horniman-Heath, 1895.
           -      Henry, b. 1896
           -      Abigail, b. 1897

Cecily MacPherson (nee Horniman-Heath) b. 1863.
          m.   Alec MacPherson. 1895, d. 1905
          -       Henry
          -       Abigail

Abdul Ibrahim, Malayan Servant. b. unknown
          m.   Matilda Smith, 1904

Matilda Smith, b. 1873
          m.   Abdul Ibrahim, 1904

Emily Hobhouse, b. 1860. Campaigner for Boer women in camps.

Ethel Brackley, (aka Mary Phillips) former servant to Brandrams, woman in Brighton Hotel.

James Hamish MacDonald b. 1872. m. Stella Gilmour 1897.

Emily Mary MacDonald, b. 1875.

MINOR CHARACTERS

West Medway Liberals
    Major Sidney Brockleton, Chair
    Committee Members Messrs. Thistle, Wheelwright, Harberry, and Clamber

East London Whitechapel Liberals
    Albion Snipperton, chair
    Harry Brownlow,
    Ernest Longhampton, MP

OTHER CHARACTERS IN CONTEXT

Case before Mr. Justice MacDonald
    Theophilus Mandrake, clerk to Judge MacDonald

The Murder at Numquam House

    Charles Eggleton, victim

    Maud Eggleston,

    Hortense Wigglesworth, the Marylebone Medium

    April Shower, maid

    Sir Septimus Goldflake, Prosecuting Counsel

    Magnus Pottelberry, Defense lawyer

    Detective Mallet

    Arthur Eggleton, Victim's brother

    Constable Painter

The Rye By-Election

Dr. Charles Hutchinson, Liberal Candidate

Matthew Johnson, Assistant

Sally, Waitress at the Mermaid

Edward Boyle, Conservative candidate

The Balderstone Killing

Detective Splinting

Simon Garthwaite, Lawyer, Courtisone and Jaggers

Lamberton Gooding, Rochester Coroner

Ambrose Combleton, Senior Tutor, King's School

Mrs. Balderstone, mother of Eric, the victim.

The Welsh Mining Community

Gareth Pugh, miner

Owen Williams, miner

Gwylym Owens, pit manager

Pastor Gryffydd, Trealaw

Pastor Jones

Mrs. Gareth Rees, miner's wife.

Egertons in America

Daniel Meyer, broker

Pinkerton's Agent.

Samuel Beauregard, Carriage Driver,
Richard Lodge, Mary-Lou's lawyer

The Salisbury Train Crash
Elmer Schultz, American visitor
Cyril Pewsey, Mortuary Overseer
Sir Archibald Clariton, Salisbury Coroner
Lady Mildred Clariton
Blossom, the Clariton's butler

Non-fiction characters
David Lloyd George, MP
Winston Churchill, MP
Augustine Birrell, MP.
Arthur James Balfour, MP
Sir William Gowers
Mr. Kinnier Wilson
David Thomas, South Wales Coal Owners Association
William Abraham (Mabon) MP. Miners' Union

www.ingramcontent.com/pod-product-compliance
Lightning Source LLC
Chambersburg PA
CBHW070916260626
47162CB00007B/2694